No Strings Attached

MORE HOT READS FROM SIMON PULSE

The Shore
Todd Strasser and Nola Thacker

Endless Summer
Jennifer Echols

Fifteenth Summer
Michelle Dalton

Sixteenth Summer
Michelle Dalton

Seventeenth Summer
Maureen Daly

WINTRY READS TO COOL DOWN

Bittersweet
Sarah Ockler

Winter's Kiss
Jennifer Echols and Catherine Hapka

No Strings Attached

Includes *CC (Cape Cod)* and *Partiers Preferred*

Randi Reisfeld

Simon Pulse

New York   London   Toronto   Sydney   New Delhi

Excerpts from *The Outsiders* © 1967 by S. E. Hinton. Used by permission of Penguin Group (USA) Inc.

SIMON PULSE

An imprint of Simon & Schuster Children's Publishing Division
1230 Avenue of the Americas, New York, NY 10020
This Simon Pulse paperback edition May 2013
CC (Cape Cod) copyright © 2005 by Randi Reisfeld
Partiers Preferred copyright © 2007 by Randi Reisfeld
All rights reserved, including the right of reproduction
in whole or in part in any form.
SIMON PULSE and colophon are registered trademarks of Simon & Schuster, Inc.
For information about special discounts for bulk purchases,
please contact Simon & Schuster Special Sales at 1-866-506-1949
or business@simonandschuster.com.
The Simon & Schuster Speakers Bureau can bring authors to your live event.
For more information or to book an event contact the
Simon & Schuster Speakers Bureau at 1-866-248-3049
or visit our website at www.simonspeakers.com.
Designed by Karina Granda
The text of this book was set in Adobe Caslon Pro.
Manufactured in the United States of America
2 4 6 8 10 9 7 5 3 1
Library of Congress Control Number 2012931626
ISBN 978-1-4424-5978-6
ISBN 978-1-4424-5979-3 (eBook)
These books were originally published individually by Simon Pulse.

Contents

CC (Cape Cod)

What Katie Did

"Darling, your ride is here," Katie's mom trilled. "Should I call for Carlos to help with the luggage?"

"I'm on it, Mother," Katie volleyed back in a light tone, calibrated to match her mom's. "Be right down." She had only to force her bulging suitcase closed, and wipe away that last bitter tear.

For someone so petite, she was strong: mentally and physically. Way stronger than she looked, and fierce when determined. Nothing sidelined Katie Charlesworth. Certainly not a trifle like a Tumi bag stuffed to triple its capacity. Least of all a telltale emotion.

Katie surveyed her bedroom. Had she overlooked anything? The light on her phone was blinking, indicating multiple new messages. She erased them without listening. For good measure, she loosened the phone jack, just enough to break the connection without looking unplugged. She double-deleted her e-mails, then changed her password. No one would ever guess her new one: Lilyhaterforever. With that, Katie closed the door and descended the stairs, "game face" on.

"Just one suitcase?" Vanessa Charlesworth asked. Her professionally plucked eyebrow did a practiced arch as Katie came into the living room to say good-bye. "Won't you be needing more clothes? For an entire summer on the Cape?"

Her mom's question didn't signal skepticism. In sixteen years (seventeen in August), Katie had never once given Vanessa a reason to doubt her. Not that Nessa would've noticed, anyway. The matriarch of their Boston brownstone floated through life on her happy bubble, never conceding it could burst. If only she knew the truth, thought Katie, fighting hard to sound normal over the lump in her throat. "Duh. I FedEx'd the rest of the luggage ahead." The lone truth in a sea of lies.

Vanessa raised a glass to her daughter—her morning toast was liquid. "That's your Charlesworth brain, always thinking."

The taxi driver leaned on the horn, not for the first time.

"Have the best summer *ever*, Mother, and kiss Dad good-bye for me." Katie stood on her tiptoes to plant a kiss on Vanessa's papery cheek. "Be careful to use lots of strong sunscreen. You'll need it on the cruise of the Greek Islands and the tour of Bali."

To which Vanessa parried, "I will, sweetie. And you: Do not forget to buy Lily's aunt Sylvia a serious gift—something for the house, I'd think. And don't wait until the last minute. It was very generous of Sylvia and Henry to let you and Lily live at their home for the entire summer."

Katie nodded. "Already handled, Mom. I know exactly how to thank such gracious people." If an ounce of sarcasm escaped, it went unnoticed.

Pleased, Vanessa hit the "play" button in her clichéd (unfortunately, alcohol-addled) brain: "Breeding will always win out, a trait you and Lily share. I would have thought"—a tiny *tsk-tsk* in her voice—"she'd pick you up in the Lincoln Towncar. Why the taxi?"

Surprised that it had taken her mother that long to ask, Katie trotted out the prefab fib. "Her dad sent the Lincoln for an airport run, her mom's got the Esplanade, and one of her brothers commandeered the Jeep. By the time I get to her house"—Katie was afraid she'd spit if she said Lily's name out loud—"I'm sure one of the cars will be back. Not to worry, Mother, we'll arrive on Cape Cod in style."

Katie and Vanessa's exchanges were like a badminton game, light and airy volleys, little puffballs of superficial information bopping from one to the other. All very polite. No slamming, spiking, or sweating. Nothing weighty or substantive crossed into the other's personal space. Anything out of

5

bounds stayed that way, was not retrieved. And no one ever argued the point.

Katie didn't see any reason to change the rules now.

The taxi driver, grizzled, grumpy, and BO-stinkified, made sure Katie knew she'd been charged for "all the waiting time."

Whatever, she thought, resisting the urge to hold her nose.

"Where to?" demanded the crabby cabby.

Katie gave him the address of the bus station. She shuddered. Not that she'd personally ever been there, but she imagined the Greyhound terminal a depressing, grimy place with dirty windows, sticky floors, and surly ticket agents (for some reason, she pictured them old and wrinkly, with stringy gray hair and bad teeth). As for the passengers? Desperate and ashamed that bus travel was their only option.

Today she was one of them.

She'd been to Cape Cod dozens of times—by plane, limo, or SUV. She hadn't even realized buses went there. As a kid, she'd spent summers in the tony town of Chatham, staying at posh resorts, or renting a mini-manse where her mother would entertain and her father, a Boston banker, would come up weekends.

Once Katie's friends were old enough to drive (or find someone with a license), her crowd would go for weekends, crashing at someone's parents' summer home. The girls, bikini waxed and pre-tanned, spent lazy days on the beach, barbecuing and (except for Katie, who abstained) downing prodigious amounts of alcohol. Some capped evenings off with a random and/or romantic hookup. It never "meant" anything. Always, there was loud music, raucous laughter, salty munchies, like-minded friends, and freeform fun. Oblivion. Lovely oblivion.

That was Katie, then. Past tense. (Future tense, if she could swing it.)

For now? The present was just plain tense.

"'Necessity is the mother of invention,'" Grandmother Charlesworth used to cliché.

Necessity had caused Katie to invent a mother of a plan back in May, when she discovered something Vanessa didn't even know yet: The plug was pulled on the family funds. The horrifying discovery had set Katie's plan in motion.

She needed to fake it, make everyone think this summer would be exactly like those old carefree Cape weekends, *three whole months worth!* Only this summer she'd be living in a luxury mansion with her best friend—without parental supervision!— shopping, sunning, and funning, sprinkled with large doses of worthy (read: wealthy) boytoys.

If nothing else, it would give her time and space to figure things out, and the chance to earn money of her own.

Her (ex) best friend Lily McCoy had rubbed mock tears from her eyes after Katie confided the real reason she needed to bolt Boston, fly under the radar, and what they'd be doing during those long, lazy summer days.

"Working?" Lily had sputtered, barely able to get the word out. The privileged daughter of State Senator Louis McCoy had been incredulous. "Kidding, right?"

"Kid*dies*," Katie corrected her. "We're going to be counselors at a day camp at the Luxor Resort. It'll be a goof!"

"And the punch line is?" Lily wondered aloud.

Katie laid out for her best friend what she'd privately dubbed "Plan A," for Awesome. As long as they were ensconced in Lily's aunt's deluxe five-bedroom mansion-with-pool, and showed up at trendy clubs at night, who'd be the wiser?

"But what about sleeping in?" Lily had asked, realizing daily drudgery eliminated noon wake-up calls.

"Weekends! We can sleep away Saturdays and Sundays." Katie tried to make it sound like that was a bonus.

"So let me get this straight," Lily said. "Monday through Friday, we'll babysit snotty brats for drudge wages, and then . . . weekends we'll sleep? Forgive me if I don't see the Awesomeness of your plan."

"Where's your sense of adventure?" Katie nudged her. "It'll be just like Paris and Nicole, only without reality TV cameras."

"Right," Lily had said skeptically. "And without being able to quit in midseason."

That's when Katie played the guilt card. "*You* can quit, if you want. It's not *your* entire life that's being yanked from under you like some cheap rug. You're not about to suffer. . . ." She paused for maxi-effect. "But you can be the hero, helping your bff in her hour of need."

Laying the guilt-trip had worked. Eventually, Lily agreed to go along with the plan, help Katie keep up appearances, and earn coin. "Remember," Katie cajoled, knowing she was about to hit on Lily's (Achilles') heel, "I got us *day* jobs—every night we'll totally go clubbing and meeting guys." Lily McCoy was all about flings. Both a speed *and* serial dater, Lily's violet eyes were always out for a new conquest.

Just for security, Katie added the capper: "I'd do it for *you.*"

She and Lily had long ago pledged allegiance to each other, and the fabu-lives they cultivated, deserved, and treasured—no matter what deep, dark secrets they had to keep and cover up for each other. So it'd been set. A done deal. With Lily's help, Katie could have the life she loved, while figuring out how to escape the one she'd be coming home to in September.

Until, just like that! Poof! It got undone. Plan A had died an instant and painful death when her now ex-best ex-friend Lily McCoy drove a stake through its vibrant little heart and pulled out.

Lily's weapon of choice? The backstab, the betrayal, the "Something Better Came Along, and too bad for you" bludgeon. And it was all for a *guy.*

Bluntly: She wasn't going with Katie to the Cape this summer. She wasn't going to be a counselor alongside Katie at Camp Luxor. And she wasn't going to be able to offer her aunt's luxury mansion, either. She was really sorry. (Right.) But for what it was worth, she, Lily McCoy, would totally keep Katie's secret. She'd make sure everyone believed Katie was summering on the Cape, kicking it with heirs, scions, and trust-fund trendoids, their usual crowd.

For anyone else, the betrayal (for that's exactly what it was) would have been a deadly blow.

But Katie Charlesworth wasn't, had never been, anyone else. No one's victim, she—along with the mission the plan had been formulated for—was very much alive and kicking butt. It needed adjusting, was all.

Not for nothing was Katie called "The Kick" at Trinity High. She was the trendsetting, A-getting, acolyte-acquiring leader of her class. Katie's accomplishments were the stuff of popularity legend: captain of the tennis team, anchor of the debate team, she played offense on varsity soccer, pioneered the yearly clothes-for-the-homeless drive, and edited the junior class yearbook. Fashion-forward, Katherine Lacey Charlesworth was an authentic Boston blue blood without, so the myth went, a care in the world.

She was also hot. Not in that willowy Uma Thurman scary way—more "petite Reese Witherspoon as Elle Woods" adorable. Small, but far from ana', Katie's athleticism gave her curves a muscular tone. Her fine, platinum hair and kelly green eyes were offset by freckles, and a toothsome smile. Katie projected confidence and accessibility, the can-do charisma kid. She was hard not to like but easy to envy (a few wannabes, like Taylor Ambrose and Kiki Vartan, pretended they didn't).

She did have a pretty (damn—Katie only cursed parenthetically) perfect life. She worked hard at it too. No way was she losing it now.

No matter her father's heinous life-changing screwup. No matter her mother's oblivion. No matter her once healthy bank accounts were now empty (which she wasn't supposed to know about). No matter Lily, the linchpin of her brilliant time-buying plan, had detonated the bomb too soon by backing out to stay in Boston with her latest tastycake. No matter Katie couldn't turn to any of her friends, or their parents' cushy Cape cribs—no one could ever know the truth—no matter, for the first time in her life, she'd have to go it alone.

Katie did what Katie does: She went to Plan B. Finding there was none, she created one. If it worked, the B would stand for Brilliant.

Technically, Katie wasn't old enough to get into a Cape Cod summer share house. But if she did, she would at least get to keep her job at the Luxor. Listing herself as eighteen, she went online and found the cheapest option still available. She'd bunk with strangers, stragglers like she who, for whatever reason, had waited until the last minute, when all the decent possibilities were long taken, and signed up for the last share house left. It was in downmarket (according to everyone, anyway) Hyannis, not Chatham. It had five bedrooms; Katie made the fifth housemate. A full share was $2,000, but she was able to split that in half by finding someone to share her room with.

Katie twisted her neck to look out the rear window of the taxi. Rows of stately brownstones off Boston's prominent Newberry Street stared back. Would the mailbox still say CHARLESWORTH when she returned? In the hot, smelly taxi, Katie shivered.

Harper Hears a
"Who Are You?"

Harper Jones plunked herself down on the rickety steps of the wood-shingled cottage at 345 Cranberry Lane. Placing her journal in her lap, she stuck her pen in her mouth and once again attempted to catch her thick, springy hair in a ponytail. The flimsy elastic holder was no match for the strong ocean wind, which insisted on blowing curly coils back in her face. For emphasis, it knocked her bike to the ground.

She'd been the first to arrive at the share house. The front door was locked—a credit card could've opened it—and a peek through the windows confirmed no one had moved in yet. She thought she might occupy her waiting time by writing, but her surroundings weren't exactly inspiring.

The clapboard house looked like the neglected barefoot child on the otherwise beachy-keen Cranberry Lane, less temporarily vacant as just plain abandoned. The front lawn was weedy and overgrown, a pile of local freebie newspapers lining the gravel driveway.

Yet Harper knew she was in the right place, this shabby shack she'd call refuge for the next three months. Katie Charlesworth's luggage—delivered just minutes ago, and for which she'd signed the FedEx slip—was proof of that. Five freakin' Vera Bradley suitcases jolted her into the realization that maybe—okay, probably—this hadn't been such a great idea. Too late now.

Harper would be rooming with Herself, the princess of the profligate and popular, queen of the quasi-wholesome and supremely superficial at Trinity High School. Why Katie had to resort to the desperate measure of posting a "want ad" for a roommate was a head-scratcher.

The first time they'd met—a week ago!—in the school library, Katie had scrunched her pert nose and tilted her head, genuinely curious: "So you really go here? And you've been here since sophomore year?"

Harper would've liked to pretend she didn't know Katie, either. But that'd be straining believability. At Trinity, Katie was known as "The Kick." Half the school claimed her as a close personal friend, the other half wished they could. Harper didn't fit into either group. To her, Katie wasn't a person so much as a symbol—of everything Harper detested. Like:

permanent perkiness, fashion slave, trust-fund Tinkerbell, teacher's pet, *and* valedictorian-bait. File under: "Good things come to those who need them least." On grades and test scores alone, Katie would probably be offered a free ride to college.

Spending the summer in Katie-twit-land was gonna blow.

But, Harper grudgingly admitted, it would blow less than a summer spent at home on Commonwealth Avenue, where she lived around the corner from the one person she could not bear, and was completely bound to run into.

Harper would not have survived bumping into Luke Clearwater. With or without his new girlfriend.

She shaded her eyes and surveyed. So this was Hyannis. Sounded like a shout-out to your rear end if you took a wrong turn at Pronunciation Junction. All she knew of HyANNis— not Hy-ANUS—was "Kennedy" and "compound." And that, only from some random TV sound bite. Harper didn't follow celebrities, political or showbiz, never read fan mags or tabloid rags. She just didn't care enough to bother.

And if Hyannis was where the rich and famous came to play? Harper thought they could've done better.

New York, city of her birth and temperament, was the real deal—her real home, too. Always would be, no matter that three years ago she was uprooted, savagely ripped from her turf, her friends, everything that counted.

All because her mom, an actress-slash-activist, had gotten

the part of "Susie Sunshine" on a Boston-based children's TV show. The steady gig translated into college tuition for Harper. Hence, the family—all two of them—had packed up and moved to "BAH-ston." Nothing good had happened since.

Certainly not her enrollment at the tootsy-snooty Trinity High School, a pricey private school for the talented and gifted. Except all you really needed to get in was money.

A fact that Harper's old lady refused to concede, insisting Trinity was the right place for her daughter. "You have a gift," Susan Allen kept reminding her. "It's time you accepted it."

Music. That was her gift, one she'd like to have returned.

Bored, Harper got up to stretch her legs. The house really was an eyesore, a pimple on an otherwise smooth ass of a beach town street. What royally pissed her off was the price! They were charging $10,000 for the summer! What kind of thieves, except those in the government, could get away with that kind of grand theft robbery?

Had to be its backyard. Every bit as ramshackle as the front, at least you got a fenced-in patio, two picnic tables, and a barbecue grill. Beyond was the beach. Walk out the gate, over the grassy dunes, and your toes were in the sand, the endless expanse of ocean big enough to swallow your troubles. Maybe.

The crunch of tires on the gravel driveway brought Harper back around front. A Volvo, boxy and staunch as a Republican, pulled up.

Out stepped J.Crew.

Or what Harper imagined the "real" Mr. Crew might look like: posture-perfect, square-jawed, sunglass-wearing, baseball-capped, decked out in polo shirt, faux-hunting khaki shorts, and Docksiders. In other words, straight-up and tight-assed.

"Ah, you beat me here," preppy-boy square-jaw said, taking off his shades and extending a large hand. "I'm Mitch Considine. Welcome."

Harper dusted off her cutoffs and introduced herself. Up close she noted crow's feet wrinkles around his eyes.

"I hope you haven't been waiting long. I was getting keys made." Mitch dangled a large ring jingling with keys. "Six—one apiece."

Harper nodded, unsure what she was supposed to say.

"So how'd you get here? Plane? Bus? Hitchhike?" Mitch asked genially, maneuvering one key off the ring and handing it to her.

Harper pointed to her racing bike, again prone on the ground.

"You biked from Boston?" He blinked, incredulously.

Harper stopped herself from laughing. There was not an ironic bone in J.Crew-clone's body. He got points for that. "Actually the bike's originally from New York, but I didn't bike from there, either. It moved with me to Boston a few years ago. Figured I might need it, so I took it on the ferry. I rode from the ferry here."

"Good deal." Mitch took the two steps to the door in one stride. "Try your key, make sure it works."

"Have you been inside?" Harper found herself anxious suddenly.

"Just long enough to dump my stuff," Mitch admitted.

Inside, the house was every bit as craptastic as it was out: musty, dusty, dank, and dark. Harper's eyes watered; Mitch sneezed. A foyer led into a room too small for the furniture squeezed in it: two sofas, a recliner, club chair, coffee tables, floor lamps, and TV sitting on the fireplace mantel.

"Behold the living room," Mitch announced. "The kitchen's that way"—he paused—"ah-choo!

"We've got three bedrooms on this floor, plus a bathroom," he continued. "Two more bedrooms and another bathroom are upstairs. There's a basement with a washer and dryer, room to park your bike. Ain't much, but it's all ours, all summer long."

"And it's beachfront property, so that's something," Harper added.

"Hey, we were lucky to get this at the last minute," Mitch agreed, removing the baseball cap and running his fingers through his short-cropped blond hair. "I didn't expect to be here this summer."

"Ditto."

Mitch mentioned other plans that had fallen through,

his scramble to secure this house *and* find enough people to share it with. "I'm going to go pick up some cleaning supplies," he said. "Just so you know, all house expenses are shared. I'll spend only what we need to get this place livable. No worries, I've done this before." He winked and put his cap back on.

Confident and competent, as befitting J.Crew, Harper thought.

"We'll go over the house rules later, after we're all settled in," Mitch added, heading out the door. "I'll just go bring in your luggage."

Rules? There were rules? Harper hadn't considered that—or much of anything else in her haste to leave Boston. When Luke broke up with her, she assumed she'd go to New York, where she had friends, support. But when she saw the posting on Trinity's website, something crystallized. Better to spend the summer where no one knew her, and no questions would follow her.

Maybe not talking about him would lead to not thinking about him.

Her ex-hippie mom was cool with the arrangement, since a job at a day camp came along with Katie's offer. And Harper promised weekly cell phone contact. The only thing Susan Allen had given her shit about was not taking her guitar.

Mitch hauled the luggage in, which took two trips. "I suggest," he panted, "you snag the room with the biggest closet."

"It's not mine," Harper quickly clarified, "the luggage."

Mitch was confused. "Oh, I figured you sent it ahead." He checked the label. "Katie Charlesworth. That's your friend, right? Well, anyway, I'll leave it here and the two of you can deal." He slipped another key off the ring to leave for Katie.

"Hey, Mitch," Harper called as he headed out, "thanks. That was cool of you to drag it all in."

Our Lady of the Designer Luggage arrived soon after. She was sweaty, and obviously tired, but chipper. "Ugh! What they charge for taxis here is a sin," Katie complained as she trudged up the front steps, hauling yet another obscenely bulging suitcase. "I had the driver drop me off a few blocks away, when the meter reached double digits. I totally hiked the rest of the way."

Was Harper supposed to empathize? If Katie had blown her allowance, wouldn't Mumsy and Popsie back on Beacon Hill just send more? For that matter, why did Katie even need to work this summer, let alone spend time in a shitpile like this?

Ms. "I'm-The-Kick" *was* disappointed in the dwelling.

Harper could tell by the almost-frown. "So," Katie said, "are we the first ones here?"

"Not exactly." Harper told her about Mitch and handed her the key.

Katie chuckled. "Sounds like we've got a House Witch already!"

"A what?"

"I was reading about share houses online. Apparently, someone has to be Large 'n' In Charge. That person gets to pay a smaller share of the rent. And ours is a *guy*, a Den Daddy. How sweet. Guys are much more maneuverable."

Harper was ready to retch—and bolt. She and Miss Know-It-All weren't going to last out the day, let alone the season. "You'll notice he schlepped all your stuff in," Harper dryly pointed out.

Katie surveyed. "Let's find the biggest bedroom."

It turned out to be one of the upstairs rooms. Its twin beds, covered in red, white, and blue nautically themed quilts, were set under Cape Cod–style dormered windows. A double closet faced the beds, perpendicular to a desk and swivel chair. Must be quite a comedown for Katie, Harper mused, again wondering how the privileged princess ended up here.

The girls hauled Harper's duffel and Katie's stuff up the stairs, sneezing, coughing, and sweating the entire time.

"Air! We need fresh air," Katie declared when they were

done. Harper flipped on the ceiling fan as Katie threw the room's two windows open.

That's when the hurricane hit.

Fierce and unrelenting, it arrived wrapped in a miniskirt and whirled right smack into the room, shrieking, "What the hell are you doing here? This is MY room. Get out."

Mandy's Got Big Ones
(Hello, Plans!)

"**What part of *get out* didn't you understand?**" In her five-inch-high spike sandals, Mandy Starr towered over the twerpy twosome, sizing them up as she stared them down. High school chickadees, she'd bet, who'd scored a parent-free zone for the summer. It had to be illegal for the training-bra set to be here—so they'd lied about their ages. A useful little factoid. No way were *they* getting the room she'd staked out—via Web photos—for herself.

The pale blonde in the designer flip-flops and hot pink tank top chirped, "I didn't know this room was reserved. There was no sign or anything."

Mandy shot her the bird. "How's this for a sign?"

The other one, the coffee-complexioned Birkenstock granola girl—"ethnically ambiguous," a phrase Mandy had once heard—struck a hands-on-hips "bring it" pose. "We got here first."

Mandy thrust her own shapely hip out. "Which counts for a pile of shit. Scram, before I expose the both of you as underage."

Score! The flash of real fear in blondie's eyes told Mandy her instincts were sharp as ever. This one had grit, though. Wiping her hands on her Mui Mui capris, she extended her arm for a handshake. "Listen, we're going to be housemates, and this is off to a really negative start. I'm Katie, this is Harper. And you are—?"

"Pissed off."

Princess Paleface accepted defeat, and backed off. "We'll find another room, no harm, no foul."

Mandy wasn't certain the one with the gray-blue peepers would go down so easily. What kind of a name was Harper, anyway? Upon further inspection, Mandy hazarded another guess about this pair. No way were they friends. The underage thing was only part of their deal. The rest? Runaways maybe?

The caramel-complexioned one looked like she was ready for a fight, but the conflict never came. She growled, grabbed a couple of suitcases, and stomped out. The ones Katie couldn't carry—where did she think she was, the freakin' Hilton?— Mandy kicked out into the hallway.

· · ·

Finally! She slammed the door and allowed herself a long, slow exhale. Mandy needed out of the too tight miniskirt and the pinchy sandals. She dropped backward onto one of the beds and decided to unpeel completely. Then, just for fun, she unpacked her black lace teddy, the expensive one, and slipped into it. The breeze from the ceiling fan tickled her bare skin. It felt good.

Mandy noted small cracks in the plaster, dust ribbons in the crevices, and made a mental note to tell Mitch to get with the Swiffer and make like Sally Housewife. That was his job, right? For that matter, the windows could use a good scrubbing, and the rug a thorough vacuuming.

Okay, so this dump wasn't Trump Palace. Straight up, to Mandy Starr, it might as well have been. She had a real good feeling about this place, like it was "Go," and she was about to roll the dice. She'd been ready for a long time.

The whole gig had come by chance. Some random girl had darted into Micky D's, ordered the low-carb sucker meal from her, and all of a sudden started squealing that she and Mandy used to know each other. "It's me, Bev—don't you remember?"

She blathered on. It was just to shut her up that Mandy took an unscheduled break (for which her cheap bastard boss would dock her, no doubt) to sit and listen to Beverly Considine, who used to live next door to her. Whatdya know, a few hundred blahdee, blah blah blahs later, one thing led to another—the other being this summer share thing that Bev's brother was organizing.

At first, Mandy had been all "what's in it for you?"—skeptical. Curiosity had led to her boss's computer, where she'd Googled "Hyannis." Possibilities popped up. Like resorts where showbiz types vacationed. Like marinas, where yachts delivered old-money types, and mansions, where politically connected bigwigs owned summer homes. Something else about Hyannis appealed to Mandy.

Kennedys. Talk about your money, status, and all that jazz. And weren't there a lot of them? *Star* magazine always had pictures of hale, hearty, fun-loving Kennedy hotties with coin and connections.

Thinking about the juicy months ahead energized her. She sprang off the bed, found a pop station on the radio, and began rearranging the room. Singing and shaking her booty along with "Hey Ya!" she dragged the nightstand away from the wall and pushed the twin beds together. That'd work. Mandy wasn't planning on too many nights alone in this room.

She unpacked the rest of her clothes. She'd only brought the barest of essentials, accent on the bare. The ratio of teddies to tops, cute undies to outerwear was 2 to 1. The one eyesore in her closet was the dumb-ass uniform that Duck Creek Catering had sent her in advance.

Not that Mandy was complaining. She'd been lucky to snare the job. The quick online search had brought up mainly day camp gigs. Right, like she wanted to wipe the asses of snot-nosed rich brats. There were "exciting opportunities" like the one she already had McDonald's, but she was tired of customers asking if she could—"heh, heh"—supersize it for them.

Just when she was about to tell Ms. Do-Gooder from the old days what she could do with her share house opening, up popped a position with some la-di-da caterer, whose clients ranged from the rich to the richer. Mandy was in no way qualified for the gig. She'd slipped her friend Theresa a fiver to invent a résumé and pose as a reference.

Ah, well, at least the uniform was black. She could say the top button had been torn off when she got it.

She was in the middle of creating a workspace for her makeup, accessories, and toiletries when her cell phone rang. She didn't recognize the number, and answered warily. "Hello?"

"Sarah?"

Oh. Her. "Wrong number—"

"Sarah, it's Bev. Don't hang up. I just want to see if you got to Hyannis okay, how the house is."

No one called her Sarah anymore. When would Beverly Considine get that memo?

"Can't hear you, bad cell reception," she lied. "I'll call you later." She turned the power off and headed down the short corridor to the tiny bathroom.

Mandy washed her face and checked the mirror. Despite her wan complexion and freckles, she looked older than her nineteen years, but damn, a whole lot better than the way she used to look. She'd take the "after" version over the "before" any day. It was good enough to net what she'd come for.

Barefoot, Mandy padded back to her room. Her hand was on the doorknob when she heard footsteps climbing the stairs. Male footsteps.

Mitch Considine, ever the good guy, lugging a very large, thin, rectangular box up the stairs.

"Mitchell! I wondered when the welcome wagon would come a-knocking."

At the sight of her in her black lace teddy, Mitch's jaw dropped. He nearly sent the package bouncing down the steps.

Mandy laughed. "You can put your eyes back in their sockets, mister. How 'bout a hug?"

He blushed and stammered, "I . . . hi . . . you look . . . wow."

"So I guess you majored in speech at that fancy Ivy League college, huh?" Mandy teased, pleased with his reaction to her. Not that ol' Mitch was any slouch in the looks department. He'd grown up hale and hunky, even if the word "prep" was tattooed on his forehead. If she hadn't known better, she might've put *him* on her hit list.

Mitch collected himself. "So, hey! Welcome. I'm glad this worked out. I came up to give you this." He motioned at the package.

She smiled. "My full-length mirror. Where I go, it goes.

Maybe you can help me hang it in my room?" She posed suggestively—in a way she suspected might cause a boob to pop out the top of the teddy.

Flustered, Mitch thrust the mirror toward her. "Sure, later maybe. So listen, we're barbecuing at six, then all sitting down for a house meeting."

"Whoop-de-fuckin' do." Mandy twirled her finger in the air. "Can't wait."

"C'mon, Sarah. Don't be snide," Mitch warned.

"Hello! Sarah doesn't live here anymore. There is no Sarah. Think you can remember that?" To punctuate her point, Mandy thrust her extremely shapely leg out and let it brush against his.

"Sorry," he mumbled, trying not to look. "Just . . . well, put some clothes on before you come down. Mandy."

"Not to worry, Mitch," she whispered, leaning in to trace her finger down his chest. "I'll play nice with the other children."

She stood the mirror against the wall and unpacked the rest of her stuff. Her CD player, the food scale she brought everywhere, and her most cherished possession: her Scrapbook of Dreams. She stood it up on the night table. It was full of photos she'd clipped from magazines and newspapers—pictures of her quarry, her future. In addition to the *Star* mag Kennedy candids were shots of famous actors, producers, and directors, people she idolized and had made it her business to meet, people who, Web research had shown, often "summered" on the Cape.

People like: all the wealthy politicians, and their kin. Like John Kerry, and those ketchup scion sons. And snap, crackle, pop-a-doodle-do, some guy who produces the TV franchise *Law & Order* was making a movie on Martha's Vineyard. That was so close, she could almost swim there. And now that she looked so rockin' in her bikini, maybe she would!

Mandy was dreamily paging through her scrapbook, tracing make-believe hearts over her favorite movie stars, when her door burst open with such force, it banged against the wall. What the—? The wind? But . . . no! Oh-my-gawd-jesus-mary-and-joseph—"Heeelp!" she screamed and leaped for high ground. A creature! A thing! Like a bat outta hell, it flew in and skittered across her floor! It looked like the deformed baby of a goose and an elongated rat: long neck, light fur, slimy and slinky and low to the ground. The feral, alien creature squealed and squeaked!

Mandy jumped up and down as if her bed were a trampoline, and screamed as if her last horror pic audition depended on it. She didn't stop even when a flabalanche-fat girl appeared in her doorway, calling for the creature.

Mandy was freaked. She didn't know which grossed her out more, the fat girl or her stinky—and definitely off-limits—rodent-pet.

Alefiya Explains It All

"It's a rat! Get it out of here!" The redhead with bodacious lung power went flying downstairs with only a flimsy bathrobe to cover her lace lingerie. What a drama queen, Alefiya thought with a chuckle.

Then, all through the barbecue that Mitch had so thoughtfully put together for their first night, Mandy had complained, whined, demanded, insisted relentlessly. "She brought a mutant rat with her! It invaded my room—it has germs. It stinks! Make her get rid of it, Mitch!"

Mitch tried to calm her down, but Mandy wasn't having it. She directed her ire at him, acting as if Alefiya wasn't even at the table with them.

"Clarence isn't a rat," Ali clarified, chowing down on the

potato salad. "He's a ferret. Actually, a black-footed ferret, which is almost extinct."

"Kill it then, and close the deal!" Mandy ramped up her carping. And her whining, adding several syllables to "Mi-I-I-I-itch!"

Alefiya, who told her housemates to call her Ali, did her best to explain: "I'm really sorry he frightened you." Mandy wouldn't even look at her. "He's just scared too. He hasn't settled in yet and—"

"Settle in? Settle IN? He's not settling anywhere!" Mandy banged her fist on the wooden picnic table. "He's a filthy rodent!"

"Not really," interjected Harper, the girl with the dimples, awesome black and blond curly hair, and skin darker than her own. "Ferrets were bred to kill rats. They're from the weasel family."

"Ha! I rest my case," declared Mandy, finally turning toward Alefiya, shooting her a look of pure revulsion.

Ali smiled and shrugged. If she got insulted every time someone looked askance at her, she'd be a millionaire by now. She wasn't stupid. She recognized knee-jerk prejudice when she saw it, but it didn't make her angry. At least, not in this case. Mandy, she calculated, was not a happy human being. No one who feels good about herself treats others like that. Maybe Ali would win her over, eventually, maybe not. No way would she play the hate game, or be bullied.

She doubted she'd get Mandy to accept Clarence as a

sweet, curious, and loving pet. So she offered, "I'll keep Clarence in my room, away from you—is that all right?"

"No—"

"Fine." Mitch raised his palm like a Stop sign.

"Not fine—!"

"For now," Mitch said through gritted teeth, glaring at Mandy. "After dinner, when we're all here, we'll take a vote. That's how it's going to work, with this . . . um . . . issue, and everything else. Now, who wants another hot dog or burger?"

Ali jumped up. "I do! I'll help you."

In spite of mean-spirited Mandy, Alefiya was crazy-happy. Flipping hamburgers, turning hot dogs, just being here! Already Harper was her favorite. And that Katie! You just wanted to be around her, she radiated light. Mitch had to have the sweetest soul. The house itself oozed with charm. She loved the oddly shaped rooms, the cozy living room, her own slope-ceilinged bedroom.

The front lawn needed work, and here in the backyard the profusion of wildflowers and weeds could be plucked and replanted. Alefiya envisioned a garden with hydrangeas, impatiens, and maybe she could cajole some roses to survive. For Harper, a vegetarian, she could definitely do a vegetable garden. The poor kid had only eaten salad and bread for dinner. She must be starving. "Do you like tomatoes and cucumbers?" she asked Harper. "Those'll come up fastest."

Harper looked confused, and when Ali explained her idea, she said, "That's really cool, but why would you want to do that? Isn't it a lot of work?"

"Sure, if it'll buy your ferret-vote," snarled Mandy, who'd overheard and misinterpreted.

Ali explained, "I'm all about gardening, growing things. I'm working for a landscaper this summer."

Katie came over and, noting Ali's gray and blue college T-shirt, asked, "Do you go to Tufts University?"

"Botany major," Ali confirmed. "At least, that's what I'm declaring. I have two more years to get my parents to accept that."

Mandy mumbled, "If you have two more years, better invest in a much larger T-shirt, since this one, probably triple extra-large, is straining."

Katie looked stricken, and Harper looked like she was about to whale on Mandy, but Ali laughed, making a mental revise: Mandy hated her not for being an Indian-American Hindu, but for being fat. She said, "You're probably right, but that's okay. I'm fine with the way I look. Maybe you'll learn to accept yourself as you are too."

Mandy glowered. "So you not only look like Buddha, you even spiel that Zen crap. How perfect." She turned on her heel and stomped into the house.

Harper balled her fist. "She's toxic! She needs a lesson in courtesy, and if you don't want to, I'll teach her."

"Not the best strategy," Katie countered coolly. "We should back off. If you give people like her enough rope, she'll hang herself, without our help."

"So we should tiptoe around her like we did this morning and let her pop a fresh can of venom at everyone in her path? No way!" Harper contested.

"You—we—have nothing to gain by confronting her," Katie asserted. "I'm not saying we should let her step all over us, but we haven't been here one full day. Let's see how it plays out. Besides, I bet Mitch will be able to deal with her."

Steaming, Harper turned to Ali. "What do you think? Let her hang herself, or do it for her?"

Alefiya said thoughtfully, "I think the bitch has self-esteem issues."

Mitch Makes the Rules— Like It or Not

Mitch intertwined his fingers and cracked his knuckles. Time for the formal meet and greet. Which he'd planned to dispense with over a casual barbecue. But Sarah's—ahem, *Mandy's*— tirade had pretty much canceled that, flat out. Besides, the entire group hadn't arrived. Joss Wanderman, the first to answer Mitch's ad, would obviously be last to show.

Mitch decided not to wait any longer. This was his third summer at a share house, and he knew the drill. He didn't mind being "rule boy." It was just like being the RA at his college dorm, a position he was well suited for. He liked managing, imposing order on chaos, being proactive, smoothing things out, and making the peace. He'd been doing it all his life!

He gathered them in the living room, planted himself on the club chair, and took stock. Katie shared a couch with Ali;

Harper, her feet tucked under her, had claimed the recliner (though she sat upright in it); Mandy sprawled out on the other couch.

These first days always felt like MTV's *The Real World*, except these housemates were not handpicked by some producer to live together. This bunch was as random as random gets. As in: Unlike most summer share houses, whose members mostly knew one another, these were the scraps—like the people at a party who don't know anyone else. You bring them together hoping their one thing in common will be enough to forge a bond.

It was his first summer as a "scrap" too. In the past, he'd gone in on some cool house with his frat buddies from Harvard. This season was to have been different—only not like this. Mitch had planned to spend it in luxury, at his girlfriend's house—that is, Leonora's parents' palatial spread in Chatham, and without them there. Just thinking of her made his heart race.

But at the last minute, Lee's folks changed plans: They were spending the summer in Chatham after all. No friends, male or female: That was the rule.

Which had sent Mitch scrambling, ending up with this bunch. It was always a crapshoot, though, he told himself. You never knew how things would play out. Often the best of friends came out of the summer bruised and battered, not talking to each other. Maybe the scraps would prove a better mix.

He glanced at Mandy, already stinking up the room with her toenail polish. And at Harper, fire in her eyes.

Or not.

He chose the cute blonde, Katie Charlesworth, to introduce herself first. She had real charisma. He had a good feeling about her. And no, *not* just because she was obviously well bred and wealthy. He respected Katie for splitting her rent with the clearly less well off Harper Jones. Mainly, Mitch hoped to start this meeting on an up note, and Katie's smile was dazzling.

Katie did not disappoint. "I've lived in Boston all my life and, starting on Monday, I'll be working as a day camp counselor at the Luxor Resort. I'm pretty normal, really. No allergies or bad habits—that I know of! And the only thing I'm addicted to is orange juice!"

"What school do you go to?" Ali asked.

"University of Pennsylvania," Katie answered without pause.

"Yeah, right. I'll just bet you do, Doogie Howser," Mandy cut in.

"Rule number one," Mitch said in an effort to nip the sniping in the bud. "If you have a problem with someone, come out and say it."

Mandy pouted. "She's a college student like I'm a—"

"Trash-mouthed ho?" challenged Harper, leaning forward in her chair.

Mitch quelled the sick feeling in his stomach, although what Mandy said did give him pause. Was it possible she was right about the very young-looking Katie? At this point, it didn't matter. Who cared if she was totally underage? This *had* to work out. End of story.

"What exactly *is* your problem?" Harper shot daggers at Mandy. "You wanted the biggest room, you chased us out, you got it. Score one for the tr—"

Mitch started to interrupt, but Harper let it go. Folding her arms defensively, she said, "I'm a New Yorker, I'm a vegetarian, a Democrat, and"—she paused to stare down Mandy—"I go to NYU."

Mandy rolled her eyes, and blithely went on with her pedicure.

"One more thing," Harper declared. "I'm allergic to the stench of nail polish."

"Tough," Mandy retorted. At Mitch's glare, however, she closed the bottle. "I'm done, anyway."

Alefiya—Ali—went next, energetically describing her summer landscaping job. What was it about her that bothered him? Mitch had no qualms about Katie—or Harper, for that matter. Mandy, he could handle. But this one? He wanted to like her. She was sweet, easygoing, good-natured. She'd been the first to offer help with dinner. Of course, on the flip side, she'd done such a messy job of it, he'd had to spend an extra half hour scraping the grill. A sign of general slovenliness? That could be problematic.

"Are you going to cook curry?" Mandy asked Ali, "'cause I can't stand the smell of that shit."

Mitch was poised to intervene, but Ali breezily laughed. "I can't stand it either. No worries."

Relaxed, Mitch mostly tuned out as Mandy presented—rather, invented—herself, listening only to be sure Harper didn't kill her.

His own well-rehearsed intro consisted of his roots in Boston, without naming neighborhoods; his current status as a senior at Harvard, without noting all the circumstances; and his summer gig teaching tennis at the Chelsea House in Chatham. He mentioned he'd be up early every morning for a daily run on the beach, if anyone cared to join him.

Mitch craned his neck to look out the front window. No one was approaching. He shrugged. "I wanted to go over the house rules with everyone, but it looks like Joss isn't going to make it. So, I'll just begin. Feel free to ask questions."

Unsurprisingly, Mandy had the first one. "How come you get to make the rules?"

He patiently explained *again* that he'd signed the lease, thereby securing the house, and had taken on the overall responsibility for it. In language Mandy understood, he said, "My ass is on the line here, that's why." Besides, he was the only one with share house experience.

He cleared his throat. "First, the obvious stuff. Drugs. It's your business, but it becomes everyone's problem if you do it in the house. So don't."

He purposely avoided looking in Harper's direction, figuring her—dangling earrings, peace sign, earth-girl—for a potential culprit, at least for weed. But she gave no sign of caring one way or the other. No one did.

So he went on. "Overnight guests. Again, your business. But too many people in the house invites chaos. We should set some limits—maybe one to a person, two or three per weekend?

This time, Harper snickered, staring at Mandy. "How many in the starting lineup of the Red Sox?"

Mandy took the bait. "At least I'll be having guests."

Harper stared at her stonily.

Mitch jumped in. "Anyway, rule number three: parties. Great fun, bad idea. No matter how much control you think you have, stuff gets trashed, the cops come; if there's drugs, we're all screwed. What it means, people, is we end up paying for restitution. And I don't know about you, but I can't afford it. Any problems with anything so far?"

Katie contributed, "I agree. I've done lots of weekends,

like at my friends' parents' homes. And it always becomes this mass event—somehow word gets out, and even though you might've invited, like, ten people, before you know it, one hundred are there. It gets to be a scene pretty quickly."

Mitch smiled at Katie. An ally. "Now, for the more mundane stuff. Food. You're responsible for buying your own, so label yours—it's really bad form to steal, or 'borrow,' someone else's."

He avoided sending a "this means you" message to Mandy.

"Now, money. There's a landline phone we can share, and even though you all have cell phones, we'll split the cost for local calls. Anyone calls out of the area, just keep track of it. I brought a laptop, which I can keep in the kitchen if you want. Wireless Internet, for whoever needs it. Anything any of us buys for the house is split six ways. I've already bought first aid stuff—you never know when you're gonna need 'em. I put everything in the downstairs bathroom. Also, the cleaning supplies—"

Mandy interjected, "Speaking of cleaning? You need to clean my room. The windows are filthy."

"Actually, Sare—Mandy," he corrected himself swiftly, "we're each responsible for our own room."

He'd raised her ire, though whether it was his answer or his near-slip of her real name, he couldn't be sure. He rushed on. "What your rooms look like is your own business, but the common areas, including this room, the bathrooms, and especially the kitchen, need to be kept clean. To keep it fair, we'll rotate those kinds of chores. The kitchen is the biggie. We don't want any kind of insect or rodent infestation."

"Speaking of!" Mandy swung her legs off the couch and sat up straight. "I say we get to the rodent issue now."

Alefiya blinked. "Clarence is a ferret."

Mandy's face twisted into a clenched fist. "No pets," she hissed.

Mitch sighed. "Usually, there *is* a no-pet understanding in share houses. But the truth is, I forgot to put that in the ad. . . ."

The look on the Indian girl's openly surprised face told him she was not going to volunteer to get rid of Clarence. "So, in fairness, I say we take a vote on whether the . . . ferret stays or not."

Without Joss, and Alefiya of course, the vote was split down the middle: Mitch had to side with Mandy on this one; Harper and Katie were a team. They compromised: Alefiya agreed to keep Clarence in her room—at all times.

"Until Joss gets here," Mandy had groused. "Then we'll take another vote."

Mitch remembered one more thing. "No duplicating of keys. Do not give anyone else the keys to the house. Zero tolerance."

"I don't like the rules," Mandy sniffed, miffed at having to live with a ferret.

Then *leave*, is what he normally would have said. But in view of the situation, he backed off. "Let's see what happens. If something really bothers you, we can put it to a vote."

"Oh, like we did tonight?" she groused again.

Which led to all of them talking at once—a chaotic overlapping of challenging one another, cajoling, squabbling, while Mitch pled for calm.

"What'd I miss?"

The screen door squeaked and, as if they'd rehearsed it, the five housemates turned toward it. Standing just inside the small foyer was a tall beanstalk of a guy with long, messy hair, ripped jeans, and a guitar slung over his shoulder.

Mitch found his voice first. "You must be Joss."

Katie Knows Joss—
But She Doesn't Know Why
(She Also Knows More About Harper Than She Should)

"Welcome, counselors, to the Kids Club at the Luxor. I hope you're all ready for a wonderful summer—I know I am!" Eleanor McGeary, clipboard in hand, was exactly as Katie remembered her: robust, raisin-skinned, outdoorsy, and cheerful. As a kid, Katie had been a camper here while her parents, guests at the resort, were attending to their own priorities: supposedly, socializing and business. Which Katie now knew to be alcohol and fraud.

Ellie McG, as everyone called her, had been head counselor at the time. Now she ran the entire program. She remembered Katie and was beyond thrilled to hire her as a counselor and give her the assignment requested: the nine- to eleven-year-old girls—a group Katie liked best because they required the least amount of attention. In her (whatever, limited, experience) tweeners were all about cliques, clothes, and smartphones—texting their friends at home—not traditional counselor-led camp activities. Leaving Katie more time at the Luxor to pursue her agenda: meeting hot, rich guys—paying guests and their friends.

"Katie! So terrific to see you." Ellie came up and gave Katie a hug after she'd detailed the responsibilities to the group. "You've grown up beautifully, just as I knew you would."

"And look at you!" Katie, on Charlesworth autopilot, returned the compliment. "You haven't aged a day."

Ellie chuckled and wagged a finger at Katie. "You always did know exactly what to say." And Katie heard her mom trilling, "Breeding will win out." Her stomach turned.

Ellie turned her attention to Harper. "And you must be Lily. Welcome!"

Quickly, Katie cut in. "Actually, Ellie—here's the thing. She . . . Lily . . . couldn't make it. This huge family emergency came up at the last minute. So my good friend Harper Jones will be filling in. If it's all right." Katie prayed it would be. It had to be.

Eleanor was taken aback. "Oh. I had no idea! I'm surprised no one mentioned it before today."

Katie could practically hear Harper's echo, "So am I!" Accompanied by a purposeful kick to her shin.

"It just happened over the weekend," Katie continued. "Lily's so devastated—she so wanted to be here this summer! Isn't it lucky that Harper's available? She's really great, and totally experienced. The kids will adore her."

"It's a little late," Eleanor pointed out. "Camp starts this afternoon and we don't even have an application, let alone any kind of background information—references, that sort of thing—on Harper, is it?"

It *was* late—exactly what Katie had been counting on. Too late for the camp to find someone else, making it easy for them to accept a substitute, Alt-Lily. Katie doubted Eleanor would quibble, let alone put the kibosh on it. She'd done her recon. Harper Jones had no skeletons in the closet, and, even better (and this was a dirty little secret she'd unearthed), Luxor Resort was sensitive to racial issues. They'd been accused of restricting golf memberships, and of profiling their staff. Putting the politically correct foot forward was important to them. Here was Harper, black, or least partly so. And here was a Charlesworth, vouching for her.

They'd hire her on the spot.

Harper hissed, "When exactly were you planning to tell me this? Before or after Camp 'Sucks-or' deemed me unfit to be a counselor?"

"No way they wouldn't take you," Katie assured her.

"Look, I'm sorry I didn't say anything before. I had my reasons. Please trust me, okay? Anyway, our campers are waiting. I'll explain later."

With that, she broke into a smile and a trot, toward the gaggle of tween girls hanging out on the resort's tree-lined front lawn. The campers looked just as Katie imagined they would. The younger girls were ponytailed, cheerful, and chatty; the older ones, designer-bedecked, bored, sulky. The group replicated their counselors: one cheerful, the other Very Not. Harper had apparently settled for glaring at Katie the rest of the afternoon. It got irritating when Katie would make a suggestion like, "How about we call our group the Olympians?" and Harper would counter, "Rebel Grrlz is hipper." Or when Katie decided they should go over their daily schedule first, only to have Harper chime in, "Screw that. Let's get some ice cream first—my treat!"

Harper Jones was an odd duck, all right, Katie thought, watching the Rebels dive into DoveBars and Godiva sundaes at the Luxor Java Café. No wonder Katie hadn't known her at school. Harper defined fringe. Even though she was pretty, she dressed like a hippie, all faded denim, leather-strap sandals. And was there no end to her "statement" T-shirts, like REPUBLICANS FOR VOLDEMORT or CLUB SANDWICHES, NOT SEALS?

Just like at school, she kept to herself here, too, preferring the beach and writing in her journal over anyone's company.

But all that was okay with Katie.

In the game of roommate roulette, she could have done much, much worse. What if Alefiya Sunjabi had been first to respond to Katie's ad? Katie had nothing against Ali personally— except for her relationship with cleanliness, which was casual at best. The girl was unkempt and unconcerned about what others thought of her. She left her smelly clothes draped over the sofas in the den, and Katie was constantly tossing her food remnants, also left all over the house, before they were covered in bugs.

Or Katie might've ended up sharing with someone like Mandy, whose itch to bitch, whine, and carp had not abated one iota. She strutted around half-dressed, like she was the queen sex bee of the house and everyone else, her wannabes. And the mouth on her! Truck driver talk (as Katie imagined it, since she personally had never met a truck driver) paled in comparison. Vanessa Charlesworth would've called Mandy low-class trailer trash. Richard Charlesworth would've just called her.

Why Mitch put up with Mandy was a mystery. Their den daddy was a find, a gem. Capable without being bossy, and unflappable, he handled Mandy firmly but fairly. Mitch had one more year at Harvard, where he was prelaw. Katie might have put him on her "to do" list—but the boy was taken (overtaken, you could say); he was a smitten kitten. Somehow, he managed to work "Leonora" into every conversation. Sweet.

Joss Wanderman was her big question mark. Because she

knew him. Only not by that name. Nor by any other moniker she could think of at the moment. But there was something *very* (as opposed to vaguely) familiar about the lean, lanky latecomer. She'd figure it out, sooner or later.

Katie was focused on the "now." Time was her enemy, and it was a-wastin'.

Settling the group under a shady tree, she dialed up a big-sister persona. "Because you guys are cool, Harper and I have decided not to force some lame schedule of activities on you. We're the Rebels not for nothing! We'll rebel against the same old boring routine. Let's find out what you actually like to do, and plan our week around that. Agreed?"

Her answer was the rousing applause from her campers—even the older ones—and, unsurprisingly, a fierce glare from Harper. Katie hadn't consulted her about anything. She'd just economized, co-opted the whole Rebel thing, taking it one step further.

Later, Katie would confide that letting the girls do what they pleased (within reason—Katie was no anarchist) made for contented campers. Which translated into satisfied parents and bigger tips for the counselors. Surely Harper (just look at her!) could use the extra cash.

As anticipated, the Rebels self-divided into athletes and artists. Katie claimed the former—the swimmers, tennis players, soccer girls, and novice sailors—happily handing over the artsy, musical, computer geekettes and drama princesses to Harper.

After promising to take them for weekly shopping jaunts, Katie wound up with some very pumped Rebels. Excellent! Now she was free to scour the boy-scape for candidates.

First stop: the Luxor swimming pool. A long, languid stretch of pristine chlorine, it was free-form, bracketed by a diving board and an excellent Jacuzzi. While her girls—Tiffany, Morgan, Jenna, Whitney, and Nicole—changed into their swimsuits, Katie donned her Hilfiger bikini and slipped into what Lily used to call her (f*** me) slides.

She wasn't out by the pool five minutes when she was approached. Awesome!

"Hi, I'm Mike, I've got the ten- to twelve-year-old boys." A pale, skinny guy wearing red Reebok swim trunks and a water-resistant watch motioned toward the diving board, where his group was waiting for their lesson. "Maybe our campers can get together for swim period?"

Translation: Maybe you and I can get together.

Katie shot him a friendly smile. "Thanks, but I don't think so. This is our first day, and we need to bond as a group. Maybe another day."

Translation: Not today, not this summer. Not you (no offense).

Just then, Katie caught sight of someone lounging on a chaise just outside the cabana. His legs were outstretched, a frosty glass was in hand, and an iPod rested in that flat space where his Boss boy-kini ended and his cobblestone abs began. Mmmm.

Quickly, Katie rustled up a cache of comfy chaise lounges for her campers. She expertly advised them on applying "lots of sunscreen, first, and always." While they were following directions, she sashayed over to Boss-boy. "Hey," she said innocently, bending over a little to catch his eye. "Would you happen to know where I can score some towels?"

On cue, he shot straight up and removed the earbuds. He had thick black curly hair and a killer smile.

Katie pointed in the vague direction of her group. "I need them for my . . . sisters, and their friends." Admitting lowly counselor status wasn't prudent.

He swiveled at the waist to point behind him to the towel cart. "Right there. They're big and bulky, though. If you need help carrying them, I wouldn't mind the distraction. I'm Brian, by the way."

Standing, Brian looked even better than lounging. He was perfectly proportioned, and Katie found the gentlemanly offer smooth. When he removed his sunglasses, a startling pair of blue eyes twinkled at her.

Oh, Katie needed help, all right.

By the end of day one, Brian Holloway, headed into his senior year at MIT, followed by employment in his family-owned

Holloway Fund Management Group, wasn't even Katie's only candidate. Nate Graham was in the game too. During her group's tennis lessons, she'd wandered over toward the marina with a wire basket to see if she could round up the errant balls the girls had shot over the fence.

Nate, blond, cute, and clever, if a bit on the short side—and just arrived via personal yacht—had offered to help. Extraordinarily friendly, he'd even escorted her back to the courts, and given her suddenly tongue-tied giggly girls a few tips.

Again, the warm feeling of having done the right thing, against the Lily-pullout odds, filled her. Katie was having an A-plus day.

Ooops. Points off for Harper. Make that an A-minus.

The entire way home in the Lincoln Towncar—a freebie Katie had wrangled from the Luxor's courtesy driver—her (up to now clueless) co-conspiritor had been in her face, demanding to know why Katie hadn't bothered informing her she'd be assuming Lily's cast-off job. Had Katie just assumed Harper was desperate enough to go along with any plan? Or was it Katie's superiority complex, figuring, like, who *wouldn't* be honored to hang with her all summer? After all, she was Katie-The-Kick, wasn't she? All this, and so much more, Harper had shouted at her as the courtesy car sped along the highway.

Had Harper given her the chance to get a word in, Katie could've told her it was none of the above. Throughout the harangue, Katie kept her cool, knowing that no matter how furious the girl was, no way would she back out of their arrangement. Harper would stay the entire summer, be her co-counselor, pay half of the rent, and not be too nosy.

Katie's confidence was more than instinct. Katie had something on Harper. It was an unexpected find, an ironic and—when you thought about it—sickening coincidence.

At her first chance, when Harper went for a bike ride, Katie read through the girl's private journal. (Getting into other people's private papers, diaries, documents, and files, was a Katie specialty. That kind of intel came in very handy.)

But the Harper exposé? Juicy.

That boy Harper was pining over? The one she couldn't bear to be away from, even for an hour? Her erstwhile soul mate, the only one she'd ever loved, who had dumped her so suddenly, so violently, she'd felt (as described in the journal Katie read) "slashed open from chest bone to my belly, cut open and filleted, watching all the pieces of me gush out."

This boy, the reason Harper had fled Boston?

He wasn't coming back.

Nor was Katie's own erstwhile bff.

Luke Clearwater was Lily McCoy's better offer.

Joss Knows Harper.
Only He Doesn't Know Why.

Joss Wanderman stretched out on the sofa, tossed his guitar across his belly, and took a long pull of Budweiser. He leaned back, savoring the suds and the moment. The first quiet one he'd had since arriving here last weekend.

That it was well past 4 a.m. did not guarantee peace. Not in this house of harridans, as he privately called it. The recriminations, sarcastic one-ups—even the laughing, bedspring-rattling, and moaning, not to mention those infernal ferret noises—knew no curfews.

The main reason Joss had taken the late shift bartending gig—okay, the second reason—was to keep hours that kept him away from his housemates. Housemates! Had he ever used that word? Yet, as he languidly ran his fingers over the six-string, he kinda dug the sound of it.

The idea of being in one place for a while was really what had appealed to him. He'd been on the road for the better part of the year, the past eight months a different city, different hotel every other day, or inside a tour bus. His lowly roadie status, even with a big-name rock act like Jimi Jones, meant he didn't get his own space. In hotels, he had a roommate. On the bus, up to six guys shared the two rows of triple bunks.

So when the tour ended and this came up, a three-month summer share gig, with a private room, he impulsively took it.

It was turning out that impulses were not his strong suit.

Since arriving last, he'd taken the only bedroom left. He didn't care that it was downstairs or that it lacked air-conditioning. Nor did the peeling wallpaper bother him, or even the fact that it didn't have its own bathroom. What bugged him were the paper-thin walls. And in the whole "one man's ceiling is another man's floor" category, his spanned both Alefiya's and Mandy's. The last thing Joss cared about was listening—and potentially being drawn in—to everyone else's drama.

Mitch had sought him out, the only other XY chromosome in the house. The do-good dude regaled Joss with his Big Plans for Life with Leonora: the well-heeled WASP who offered old-money stability; status; long, winding driveways leading to sprawling homes; luxury cars; leisure tennis and golf games; 2.3 children with names like Taylor and Tucker.

Joss had no quarrel with Mitch—the cat was cool. Besides, it was easy to tune out the soliloquies.

It was impossible to not know what was going on with the girls on the other side of his bedroom wall. Katie and Harper—jailbait, like so many groupies he'd seen. In his habit, Joss had renamed them: Smilin' Suzie Q and Angry Young Babe. How'd this deuce end up roommates, anyway?

SSQ, so clearly a pampered princess from the not-so-far-away land of the Boston blue bloods, was such a phony! She wanted everyone to think of her as radiant, cool, collected—like she wasn't repulsed by the shoddy share house and her random roommates.

It was the condescending tone she used with Mandy when "complimenting" one of her trashier outfits, or "supporting" Mandy's getting-into-showbiz goal. If SSQ believed she was hiding her "I'm so above all of you" attitude, she was mistaken. Joss saw the way her nose scrunched whenever she tossed one of Alefiya's half-eaten overripe plums or sweaty peaches left in the den; the disapproving eyes she cast on the carefree chick when she brought home a stray. Ali's strays often came with gifts—cannabis, for sure; maybe other substances—and stayed the night.

Just to fuck with SSQ, Joss was sure, AYB purposely got closer to Alefiya. He liked that about her.

Not that Joss took sides. It was his misfortune to be able to see things from both points of view. He could make all the private fun of Katie he wanted, but he felt her pain, man. He knew the effort it took to put on a carefree face, to pretend everything was peachy keen, all the time. Why she was here, in this pit stop, let alone sharing a bedroom, was a head-scratcher, but he hoisted his beer bottle in a silent salute. He wished Katie well.

Deciphering Harper wasn't so easy. When she wasn't messing with Katie, she was making herself scarce. She wasn't here for the company, and she sure wasn't here for a hookup. Girls gave off vibes—he could always tell what they wanted.

He didn't know where the fury and subversive behavior came from. Not that teenagers, and he was sure she was one, needed a reason to be pissed off. But there was something about her that intrigued him. "Something," as the Beatles famously said, "in the way she moves," attracted him, was *familiar* to him. Like the way she stuck her lower lip out when she was pondering something; the way her eyes flashed when arguing with Katie; the unexpected dimples on those rare occasions she smiled; and those coltish, bordering on ungainly, strides even when her chin was stuck out defiantly.

Who did that remind him of? Between the beer buzz and the quiet, he settled in to ponder. His reverie was rudely interrupted by the slam of the screen door. He bolted up, saw her before she saw him.

Took in the angry slash of her mouth, the flashing eyes

58

furiously blinking back the tears, and the deliberate stomping of her heels. Mandy. Their very own menace to society was headed toward the steps.

Soundlessly, Joss lowered himself, hoping the high back of the couch would conceal him. If he could have, he would've rolled under it, disappeared until the coast was clear. No luck.

It must've been out of the corner of her mascara-smudged eye that she'd seen a flash. He heard her pivot on her clicking heels, away from the steps. Toward the sofa. There was no escape.

Before he could decide whether to acknowledge her or pretend to be asleep, she was staring down at him. Then she was bending over the back of the couch, making sure he got a load of her cleavage popping out of her waitress uniform. What, did she think he'd never seen boobs before?

"Whatcha' doing up?" she said, righting herself.

Joss propped himself up on his elbows. "Just got in from work. Looks like you worked the late shift too?"

He didn't really want to know the tawdry details of why Mandy looked like a train wreck, but he couldn't ignore her.

She sniffed and ran her fingers through her thick red hair. "Yeah, the late shift. You could say that." She nodded at his beer. "Any more in the fridge?"

"It's labeled," he warned, knowing there were a few bottles left with Mitch's name on them.

"Cool," she said.

She flipped direction again, heading toward the kitchen. Now's the moment he could feign exhaustion, or simply slink away. He didn't. Not then, or during the ten minutes it took her to go upstairs and "freshen up" either.

When Mandy returned, she was barefoot and clad in a silky robe. She settled on the sofa. His sofa. She sat on the far end, to be sure, but crossed her legs so the robe would part, revealing shapely thighs. As if he didn't get the memo, she licked her lips suggestively after her first chug of beer.

Joss sighed. Could she be any more obvious? He hoped he wasn't, acknowledging that, sometimes, his body had a mind of its own.

"So Mitch says you're, like, a drifter," Mandy said after a while. "True?"

He considered, plucked a string on his guitar. "I've been traveling a lot lately." Joss had deliberately stayed away from discussions of his background. It wasn't hard to do. Most people were more interested in talking about themselves, if you asked. Of Mandy, he asked what had happened tonight, why she looked so upset when she got in.

She tried to sound casual, but her eyes darkened. "Let's just say the night was disappointing."

"You're working for some catering company, right? Is that cool?"

Now she brightened. "Duck Creek. It's very exclusive."

"Is it, now?" Joss feigned interest.

"They don't advertise, they only take recommendations. That means really stinking rich people," she confided. "You wouldn't believe the mansions these people live in—and, for some of them, they're only summer homes! And the decor!" Or, as Mandy pronounced it, "DAY-core." They have real antiques, and big paintings on the walls, and chandeliers. Like you see in movies, only real."

Joss chastised himself. For Mandy, this was real. And hadn't he said he wanted to break out of his gilded cage and meet real people? He coaxed, "So your job is to butler food around, pass the hors d'oeuvres?"

"Well, that's what I'm doing now. But I'm not really a waitress."

"You're working toward another career?" he guessed, working at keeping the jadedness out of his voice.

Mandy stared at him. All he saw were her lips. Joss felt his stomach do a flip-flop. When she got up to get more beers for the two of them, she passed in front of him, the hem of her robe lightly brushing his leg. Joss calculated Mitch's beer was all gone now. He opened it, anyway. Mandy was about to tell him something. Please don't let it be, "I want to be an actress/rock star/model. This job is temporary, until I get my big break."

"I'm going to be an actress-model. And I only took this job . . ."

Joss swallowed, his eyes downcast. She'd finished explaining, was waiting for a response. He knew exactly what he should say: "Listen, I know those people, Mandy, and trust me, they're not going to help you. No matter what they say, or promise, this is not the way to an acting career. To them, you're a dime a dozen, a girl they'll string along, pretend to be interested in. Until they get what they want. Then they'll toss you away, like garbage." Only what Joss heard himself say was, "That's"—he took another swig of beer—"interesting."

"You bet it is," Mandy said. "I've been working a long time for this opportunity. Getting myself in shape, and stuff. Now's my time."

"So what happened tonight? Did someone stiff you?"

Mandy found that funny. Of course, she'd had a few beers by then. "You could put it that way."

"What other way could you put it?"

She shrugged. "Miscommunication. I thought I was saying one thing. This producer—he's about to start a big movie—thought I was saying something else. His wife had another interpretation."

Okay, she'd given him the opening to gently tell her that she might want to rethink this—her plan could only lead to disaster. But all that came out was, "I'm sorry."

She nodded toward the guitar. "Are you a musician?"

"You could put it that way." This was verbal foreplay. He hated himself for doing it. So he tried to repair, by talking. "I've actually been on the road with this rock band—I'm not in it," he clarified at her real interest. "I do some fill-in licks, but mostly I'm a roadie. You know, carry the equipment, stuff like that."

"What rock band?"

"Jimi Jones."

Her eyes widened. "No shit! He's, like, a guitar legend. Would you play something for me?"

Joss's heart was thumping. "I don't want to wake anyone," he whispered hoarsely.

"So play quietly. I'll come closer." As she did, the ribbon tying her robe fell loose. And Joss couldn't refuse either of her requests.

And on the Weekend, We Play.
But Not Before We Do Our Chores.
And Try Not to Air
Too Much Dirty Laundry.

Mitch Feels Flush. This Is a Good Thing!

Mitch arose extra early on Saturday morning, feeling pumped, like Johnny Damon on a streak. He went over his mental to-do list during his run along the shoreline. He'd decreed today as the first official cleanup day: They'd been in the house just over a week, and it was time. To that end, he'd slipped copies of the who-does-what housework "wheel" under everyone's door last night.

Experience of summers past had taught him that a communal breakfast would be a nice touch. After his run, he drove into town to get a dozen bagels, cream cheese, lox, freshly baked Cinnabons, and flavored coffee. His treat.

In spite of a few first-week flare-ups, the share house seemed to be running smoothly. Issues were part of the game, what with half-a-dozen different personalities crammed into one small cottage. Mitch was sure they'd iron themselves out, given a few more days. Mr. Optimism, that's how he felt these days. And why not?

The tennis-playing patrons at Chelsea House in Chatham loved him. Already, week one, he'd snared a cache of new clients who'd signed up for the entire summer. Regulars guaranteed him a nice salary and, if he could keep his A-game going, hefty gratuities by summer's end.

The diamond ring he'd been secretly saving for would be his—Leonora's—ahead of schedule. They could be engaged by Labor Day.

Mitch had been bummed at the last-minute boot from Leonora's house, but now saw the upside. If the marriage proposal was to be a magical surprise, not living together was actually better. He kept his ever-expanding cash-stash in his room: An arrangement had already been secured with a jeweler to get a better-grade diamond if he paid in cash. This way, Leonora couldn't accidentally discover how much money he had spent and start asking questions.

So far, Mitch and Leonora had only seen each other once, briefly, in the week he'd been there, but they'd talked every night. Mitch had the tiniest sense that something was wrong, but Lee hadn't responded when he'd asked. Whatever. He'd find out tonight. They were having dinner at Le Jardin, and face-to-face she never could keep a secret from him.

Harper Sees Red. This Is Not a Good Thing.

It was the aroma of the hazelnut and vanilla coffee Mitch had brewed that brought Harper to the kitchen counter first. No one did bagels like New York, but she had to admit, chomping heartily into the pumpernickel raisin, this came close. And the coffee wasn't from evil corporate monster Starbucks! Mitch got kudos for that, and for supplying the breakfast treats.

Cheerily, his square face aglow, he asked, "So, how goes it at day camp?"

Harper inhaled her coffee . . . mmmm . . . and shrugged. "It'll be fine. The campers are spoiled brats, and Katie caters to their every materialistic whim. . . ." She paused. "You didn't go there as a kid, did you?"

Mitch laughed. "Hardly. Thank you for thinking that, though. Very flattering."

Harper cocked her head. "Why?"

Mitch was guileless. "Why am I flattered? To look like I could've spent my summers at the Luxor, as a rich guest? Who wouldn't be flattered?"

He wasn't being sarcastic. He really thought that was a good thing. So, he hadn't been a prep all his life. Although . . . Harper took in his polo shirt, collar turned up, and belted

Hilfiger shorts. He sure was one now. Mitch really did believe everyone aspires, or should, to the genteel life. Harper could've argued the point. But another sip of the glorious coffee, and the soft, still warm, inner-tube belly of the bagel, mellowed her. In spite of his superficial values, Mitch was a good guy.

"You're a freakin' buzzkill, Mitch, you know that?"

Harper spun around on her stool.

And there was Mandy, bedecked in one of her bawdy boudoir ensembles, waving a copy of the chore wheel in Mitch's face. "I'm not cleaning the stinking crapper."

Harper had to clamp her palm over her mouth to keep from laughing. Could there be two people more opposite than Mitch and Mandy? And yet, there was this in common: They said exactly what was on their minds.

Mitch rounded the counter and put an outstretched hand on Mandy's shoulder. "No choice. Everyone's gotta do them. It's not a big deal."

"Yeah it is—the upstairs bathroom stinks! From her I-don't-know-what, her curry smell!"

Harper nearly choked. Mandy had spoken her mind, all right. Her racist mind. Harper bolted off the kitchen stool. But Mitch was all over it. He tightened his grip on her shoulder. "I'll pretend you didn't say that. I'll get some deodorizing disinfectant. You can spray it first, and then do the cleaning."

"I don't care if you fill the fucking room with fucking

Renuzit," Mandy cursed. "That smell won't come out. And I'm not submitting myself to it. Besides," she sniffed, "it's bad enough I have to live in the same house with her."

Mitch growled, "You don't like her? You're an actress. *Act* like you do!"

"Good morning!" Alefiya sailed into the kitchen, her sunny voice matching her ear-to-ear grin. "Smells so good in here! What is it? Coffee? Oh, and Cinnabons, too! What's the occasion?"

Silence. Ali looked from face to face. "What's wrong? You guys are so grim. Did we lose our lease or something?"

Harper jumped in: "Mandy thinks it's beneath her to clean the bathroom. But that's how this week's wheel of misfortune spins."

Ali looked puzzled. "That's the problem? Our bathroom upstairs? Forget it. I'll do it."

Mitch eyed her warily. "You'll switch jobs with her this time, you mean?"

Helping herself to a Cinnabon, Ali answered, "I'll just do it every week. I don't care."

Harper began to boil. She wanted to shake some sense into Ali, to tell her what a cheap little racist Mandy was. And look at her. Mandy wasn't even grateful! She just planted herself at the table and began butchering her bagel, tearing out the bready (caloric, and best) part.

"Ummm . . . delicious!" Alefiya managed that with her mouth full as she plopped down in the chair next to Mandy—who pulled hers away ever so slightly.

Mitch scratched his head. "You were supposed to do yard work, Ali. Do you want to hold off on that today?"

Licking the gooey sugary topping from her fingers, she said, "No, that's okay. I have to do the vegetable garden, anyway, so I'll do it all at the same time. It's all good."

Harper forced herself to chill. "It is so cool of you to do that garden. I'll help if I can." The garden was for her benefit. Ali's bid to fill the fridge with organic, homegrown veggies. The girl was just genuinely good-hearted. Harper wished her housemate could be more discriminating.

Katie waltzed into the kitchen. She looked like she'd been at a tween slumber party, in her drawstring Juicy Couture sweat bottoms and glittery pink tank top. Only, flip it: This was not sunny-side-up Katie. This Katie nodded curtly and made for the fridge. Flinging open the door, she whined, "Oh, sugar! Where's the orange juice? I just bought half a gallon two days ago."

Oh, *sugar*? Harper guffawed, nearly sending coffee out her nostrils. Who talks like that?

"And good morning to you," Mitch said genially. "How 'bout a bagel?"

Katie frowned. "Sorry. This stuff looks appetizing, I just like to start my mornings with OJ. And I was positive I had plenty left. She directed her comment at Ali. "I happened to notice you having a glass yesterday. Any chance that might've been mine?"

Ali shrugged. "To be honest, I'm not sure."

Katie's jaw clenched, but she managed to sound reasonable. "If you'd finished someone else's juice, you don't think you'd notice?"

Ali threw her hands up, surrendering. "I could be guilty. Sorry."

Harper couldn't resist the urge to butt in. "How do you know *she* finished it? Maybe it was one of us."

Katie colored. "It wasn't you. You only drink organic. It wasn't Mandy, who's off sugar. Mitch has principles, and Joss sleeps through breakfast. If it wasn't Alefiya, it was one of her overnight guests."

Ali conceded. "Okay, sure, it was probably me. My bad. I didn't realize how much it meant to you."

"Well, now that you know," Katie said a tad too brightly, "kindly stick to your own stuff from now on."

"Oooh, see Katie being cross," Harper taunted. "See Katie being disapproving. Why is Katie really so cross?"

Katie scowled at Harper.

No one noticed Joss saunter in. Clad in shorts, wife-beater tank top, and sandals, he was a taller, buffer Ryan Atwood pouring himself coffee. Katie cut her eyes at him and sniffed,

"I'm just a little tired. I got in late from a date."

"Miss Popularity strikes again," said Harper. "Whatever. I've got a living room to dust and carpet fragments to vacuum. Toodles, y'all."

Katie Sees Joss Blush.

Katie wasn't hungry. Her throat was filled with bile. Swallowing it was all she could handle. She didn't know who got on her nerves more: Alefiya or Harper. Not that Mandy, or whatever her real name was, was any great shakes either. She could barely believe she was stuck in this hovel with *any* of them.

Joss leaned against the fridge. "You were at The Naked Oyster last night, right? With a dark-haired guy? At the corner table, facing the bar?"

This caught Katie by surprise. "You were there?"

"I work there," Joss said, "bartending."

"Oh, duh." Sweetly, Katie smacked her palm against her forehead. "I so knew that! I can't believe I didn't say hi."

"Well, you looked kinda busy. Pretty . . . involved."

Katie grinned. Since meeting Brian and Nate, she'd been out with each. They'd hit select bars in Hyannisport, plus (of course) the Cracked Claw in Chatham. She routinely ran into people who counted (translation: Trinity elite and friends), and, one juicy night, reminded a couple of Kennedy cousins that they'd partied together one weekend earlier in the year.

Brian had been big-time impressed. At Blend, the excellent new club in Provincetown, she'd spied her archrival, Taylor Ambrose, and her snippy sister Kiki—ha! As planned, she made sure to parade Brian in front of them.

Partly, she wanted word to get back to Lily that she was doing great without her (between air kisses and "Oh, my god, I love that dress!" convos, the subject of where she was living, or that she had a job, never came up). But mostly? Katie thrived on her life—did not want to think about the fact that she might not be enjoying this part of it for much longer.

Last night, Brian had taken her to The Naked Oyster in Hyannis. They'd washed down an entire seafood tower: clams, oysters, shrimp, lobster, and tuna sashimi—all Katie's favorites—with Stella Artois (for him), Perrier for her.

Twirling the straw in her drink, Katie'd toyed with confiding in him. Telling him the truth about her family, and asking for advice. And help. Maybe he'd have an idea, or simply excess cash he was willing to part with.

But Brian had wanted to go dancing. And at Fever, the nightclub of the moment, he'd run into a bunch of old frat buddies. Her moment was gone. By the time she got home at 3:15 a.m., she was too exhausted for a heart-to-heart; he was too inebriated to listen, anyway.

Joss smiled at her. "Glad you're having fun." As a joke, he asked, "We're all having fun, right?"

Mandy purred. A glance in her direction told Katie why. The tawdry tramp was flashing knowing eyes at *Joss*. Who blushed! They're sleeping together! Interesting. She would not have made that connection. As she headed back to room to change for "kitchen cleanup duty," she wondered again why Joss looked familiar.

Mandy Sees a New Friend.

Mandy rose to toss her leftovers into the already overflowing garbage. And, to move farther away from piggy Ali and closer to Joss. His unshaven morning face, long, tousled hair, and drooping jeans turned her on. A guy like Joss, while not exactly her prey, could serve several useful purposes—already had.

Mandy was here to make contacts, not friends. And who knew? Bartender boy had recently been inside an actual showbiz orbit. Friend of an aging rock star was better than no important friends at all. And though she hadn't approached it directly yet, Mandy believed she could prevail upon Joss to hook her up with Jimi Jones. Better yet, his agent.

Why should Joss do her any favors? Well, she'd already—and quite successfully, if she did say so herself—given him a taste of what she brought to the table. So to speak.

For all her nineteen years, Mandy was no naïf. You had to give something to get something—that's how it worked.

Especially in showbiz, it was all about who you knew. Or, in her case, who you could get to know quickly.

She'd worked a week's worth of swanky parties at Duck Creek Catering so far, and was, like, 0 for 6, netting no return on her slave-labor investment. Not that the mansions and resorts she'd gotten inside weren't something else! The clients were the disappointing part. Bunches of big ol' bores: corporate suits and their BOTOXed wives, or bankers, politicians, and stuffy New Englanders. Not a Kennedy or showbiz type in the bunch.

She'd had hopes for a Mr. Roger Durkin, at the Art Gallery party last week. He lived, he said, in California. His bank had insured the latest George Clooney movie. Mandy had popped another button on her top and started to tell him about her acting hopes, when Mrs. Insurance Guy rudely interrupted. So that was a bust. So to speak.

"He was so nice, so down to earth." Alefiya, talking to Joss, was describing the owner of a mansion her landscaping company was working for. "If my friend Jeremy hadn't told me, I never would have known he was such a big star. Meanwhile, he ordered a rock garden and waterfall, and a statue of a kid in the middle—guess what part of the anatomy the water's coming out of?"

Joss was laughing. "Man, that is lame. But there ya' go: Money doesn't buy taste. I'm surprised he's supervising it himself. Where's the million-dollar-a-year exterior designers?"

Mandy swung around. "You're working for a movie star?"

"He's from TV," Ali answered. "This guy who used to be on *Friends*? He's from Boston originally. He lives in L.A. now, but when he was growing up, he dreamed of a place on the Cape. So now that he's a millionaire, he built this estate. I think his mom lives in it, but the other day he came out to talk to us himself."

Mandy was hyperventilating. She could feel Mitch's disapproving look behind her back, as well as Joss's bemused one. She didn't care. "Really? Have you met any of his . . . like, other celebrities?"

Ali cocked her head. "I'm the worst person to ask. I hardly pay attention to TV, so I might not recognize anyone. But Jeremy and some of the others on our crew worked at a bunch of celebrity homes last year and got friendly with a lot of people in that business."

Joss added, "Looks like Cove Landscaping is Cape Cod A-list. Turns out they made their reputation working for the Kennedys. Get this: Ali had to audition for the job by designing a mock topiary garden—shaped shrubs, the whole thing. Pretty cool, huh?"

Mitch couldn't restrain himself. "Hmmm, maybe you should have thought about growing vegetable canapés instead of passing them, Mandy."

Mandy didn't hear him. She hadn't gotten beyond "TV star" and "Kennedys." No matter how much blubber girl and her pet rat revolted her, Mandy made a resolution: She was about to become Alefiya's new best friend.

Joss Grows Suspicious. With Good Reason.

"Knock, knock. Anyone home?"

Mitch jumped, and was halfway out the kitchen before anyone could react. They heard him bolt through the living room and fling open the front screen door. "Leonora? Sweetheart! What a surprise!"

Joss knew this would be a good moment to make himself scarce. Mitch never let an opportunity pass when he could squeeze in an anecdote about Leonora. What were the odds he wasn't going to trot her in here, display her like some kind of trophy? Kind of like his own father paraded whatever number wife or girlfriend he was with, whenever he had an audience. Joss had no stomach for it. But he'd only managed a stride toward the archway leading to the living room when Mitch returned, beaming like a klieg light.

"Hey, everyone, this is Leonora, my girlfriend."

The chick on his arm was a photocopy of every debutante Joss had ever seen. Tall, thin, pale, bleached-white teeth, every golden hair in place. He noted the diamond tennis bracelet, the pearl necklace and matching stud earrings, and the Ralph Lauren outfit. Uh-huh. This one was no poseur. Mitch had found himself the real old-money deal, but could he hope to keep up with her?

Leonora was seriously uncomfortable. Her body language— arms folded over her chest, pasted-on smile, pleading eyes—all shouted, "Get me out of here." She had not come to meet the housemates—that much, even Joss knew.

"Ah, the famous Leonora," Mandy said, dripping with phony interest and extending her hand, "we meet at last. Mitch talks about you all the time. And I'm not exaggerating when I say 'All. The. Time.'"

Leonora tossed her head slightly. "My sympathies. I can imagine how boring that must be."

"You said it, sister. Anyway, I'm Mandy, and this is my friend Ali." Joss shook his shaggy head. Mandy was a piece of work, all right. She'd done the fastest 180 he'd ever seen.

Ali advanced on Leonora and enveloped the startled girl in a bear hug, nearly crushing the bony thing. "I feel like we know you already! Mitch has the nicest things to say about you."

Leonora extracted herself quickly, smoothing out her blouse and stifling the look of alarm. She stuttered, "That's, uh . . . so sweet. Thanks."

"Would you like some coffee? Or bagels? There's a Cinnabon left too. Your boyfriend is the sweetest. He brought breakfast for all of us." Ali motioned toward the spread on the kitchen counter.

"That's lovely," Leonora said, "but I really can't stay. I just stopped by to talk to Mitch and—"

"This is Joss." Mitch acted as if he hadn't heard his girlfriend at all. "Because of him, I'm not totally surrounded by gorgeous women. You should thank him."

Leonora managed a tight little smile. That's when Joss knew for sure something Mitch didn't. Something was askew in lovey-dovey land. He felt a pang and hoped that whatever was wrong with Miss Debutante wouldn't result in hurting Mitch. He was proudly shuttling "Lee" into the living room, insisting she meet Harper and Katie.

Joss eyed the two girls left in the kitchen with him. Mandy was street-smart and, he'd bet, had the same instincts as he did about Leonora. Ali? Nah. He sighed. It was time to do something he'd never done in his entire life.

Clean a bathroom.

Harper's Reverie

Harper was psyched that she'd brought her bike, since Cape Cod was made for cyclists. Miles of paths, flat and hilly, laced the landscape, offering radically breathtaking scenery. She'd grown up on city streets, where the only nature was Central Park, if you didn't count the odd sprouts of weeds popping up between cracks in the sidewalk. Strange, but she found riding past the windswept sandy beaches and over grassy meadows a balm for her raw wounds.

She'd read somewhere that if you allow yourself to just empty your head, surrender to the grandeur of Mother Nature, your own problems seem smaller, your pain less intense.

Still waitin' to feel that way, she conceded.

Her aunt, twice widowed, believed in the opposite: that being frenetically busy, darting from one adventure to another, helped, "Because pain can't hit a moving target," she'd counseled.

Harper hunkered down and pedaled faster.

When she'd fled Boston for the summer, she hadn't been consciously thinking about anything beyond survival. 'Cause if she so much as glimpsed Luke, with or without his new squeeze, she would not be able to breathe. So she'd grabbed on to the first lifeboat she'd found: the Web posting that had led her here.

In a perverse way, Harper almost welcomed the bickering of the housemates, the carping of her campers; didn't even mind Katie as much as she made out. All the noise helped keep her mind off Luke. And where her mind went, maybe her heart would learn to follow.

Late Saturday afternoon, Harper was riding along one of her favorite daffodil-lined back roads into town. Her cell phone rang, and her stomach twisted. No way would it be Luke, she scolded herself. She had to stop hoping.

The caller ID read MOM.

Harper could swear her mother was a mind reader: Susan could see Harper and know what she was thinking, no matter how far apart they were.

"Where'd I catch you?" Susan asked. "On the beach somewhere?"

"Close. I'm biking into town to buy some stuff." Her list included orange juice, to make up for the half gallon that Ali had unintentionally taken from Katie. And the locksmith, so Mitch wouldn't find out that Ali had lost her keys—again.

Her mother wasn't big on small talk, anyway. Just a few minutes into the conversation, Susan launched into the real reason she'd called: Harper's heartbreak. "Keeping all that hurt bottled up inside won't help," said her mom, "and running away won't solve it."

Harper sighed. "So what will help, Mom? You're the expert."

Her mother didn't flinch. "Opening up, talking about how you feel. And time. Getting over him will take time."

How much time? Harper wanted to ask. How much time had it taken her mother to forgive her father, who'd said, "See ya" before Harper had been born?

When she'd first realized that all her friends had dads—even dads who didn't live with them—Harper had pleaded with her mom to get her one. For years, Susan had managed to change the subject artfully, to divert her attention, citing all the loving friends and relatives they did have.

Had her mother forgiven her father by that time?

Years later, when Harper was old enough to realize what any onlooker knew in an instant—that the sight of her with blond, blue-eyed Susan meant her father was likely African-American—she pushed harder to know the truth: "Who is he? Why can't I meet him?"

Reluctantly, Susan agreed to make contact. Days, weeks, then months went by—Harper had counted—with no reply, no news. Suspecting her mom hadn't made the call at all, Harper demanded to know her dad's identity.

When she was twelve, Susan told her his name.

Which only made Harper want to meet him more. He was famous! That made her important! And she, a street-smart New York kid, could do this without her mom's help. But Susan dissuaded her. "He was never a father to you," she'd said sadly. "I think of him as a sperm donor, that's all. I'm glad I got you out of it."

That's how she knew her mother, for all the time that had gone by, had never forgiven her father for walking out.

The following year, having bulked up on after-school specials and weepy TV movies, Harper had demanded, "Does he even know about me?"

Susan conceded that he did.

"Did he ever try to contact me?" Harper had probed, hoping maybe her father had wanted to but Susan had prevented him.

Susan had taken a deep breath. "Here's the thing, honey. At first, he tried to send money to help support you—which I'm sure his lawyer put him up to—but I refused it. I signed a waiver promising I'd never ask for anything, and never make it public. Because a scandal is exactly what he would've wanted—it would've given his bad-boy image some street cred. But I wasn't playing. I was no one's victim, and you were no one's pawn. You were mine."

Harper had learned all this just when her friends were beginning to date, just when boys at school had begun to notice her. It was a lucky crossroads. She, unlike so many of her teary, brokenhearted friends, knew from the jump not to trust boys, never to be vulnerable, never to open yourself up to that much hurt. She practiced what she believed.

Until Luke Clearwater came along.

"Guess what?" Harper said as she swung into the room she shared with Katie.

Her roommate was at the mirror—how new!—applying lip gloss. "Mmwhat?" Katie said while smushing her lips closed.

"You can float away on OJ. There's a ton in the fridge with your name."

Not taking her eyes off the mirror, Katie frowned. "You're not helping her by cleaning up her messes. Even I stopped tossing away the half-eaten, fly-ridden fruit. I put them in her room instead."

"How thoughtful," Harper deadpanned. "I'm sure she appreciates that."

"That's not the point. Alefiya's never going to learn to be responsible for herself unless something impacts her directly."

This amused Harper. "Speaking of learning, how long do you think it'll take our Rebel Grllz to figure out your game?"

Katie bristled. "Since you've got it down, wanna clue me in?"

"That you could care less about them. That you're using them for their proximity to rich guys—and access to their parents' wallets." Harper hopped onto her bed.

"Your point?" Katie shrugged, continuing to separate and lengthen her lashes with her NARS mascara.

"It's not right, it's not moral. The only thing you're teaching them is how to shop and be manipulative."

"Who died and made you Oprah? The campers love me, and I'm not hurting anyone, so what's your issue?"

Seriously, Harper gave herself a mental jab: What *was* her issue? What did she care what Queen Katie did? It was true the campers worshipped Katie-The-Kick, from her silky platinum tresses to her cutesy designer sundresses. Katie was teaching them exactly what they wanted to learn, what most girls who came into contact with Katie wanted to know: how to be her.

As opposed to Harper's group, who were learning how to create the perfect protest poster, memorizing the ode to Barbie by Nerissa Nields ("If she were mortal, she would be/six foot five and a hundred and three,") and learning classic songs like "War, What Is It Good For?" and John Lennon's "Revolution."

Back to Katie, she mused. Why did the pocket-size princess need the money so badly? And why was she flinging herself at these random rich guys to get it? Didn't she have enough of both at home? This was the girl who, to Harper's amusement-slash-horror, *had brought her own toilet paper to the share house!* Like the community rolls weren't good enough to wipe her pampered butt. Katie tore from her own zillion-ply stash!

Harper sighed. Katie was crowding her head. She wandered out to the kitchen for a snack, where, unsurprisingly, more bickering was going on. Mitch was royally pissed at Ali, who apparently had left some chicken out to defrost—and had forgotten about it until the odor had stunk up the room. In related piss-off-iness, he was also questioning the number of guests she'd brought into the house. "What did you even know about that guy who was here last night? He looked homeless."

Ali shrugged. "He needed a place to crash."

"But this isn't a crash pad," Mitch reminded her. "It's our home for the summer."

"Exactly," Joss had tossed in, though no one had asked him, "*our* home. Ali's one of us. She has rights too."

Mitch looked betrayed. He was about to say something, but never got the chance. An eardrum-piercing, roof-raising series of shrieks shook the house. Mandy. She'd been on the toilet, apparently, when Clarence the ferret pushed the door open with his nose and leaped into her bare lap. Now she was running to her room, screeching at the top of her lungs. Her capris were down around her ankles and, Harper envisioned, pee was running down her thigh.

It was time for a "moment of Zen."

Armed with her journal and a big bath towel, Harper headed out. The narrow ribbon of sand backing onto the share house could barely be called a beach. It was grassy, and full of weeds. Harper came here often, especially at times like now, at dusk, when she had it all to herself.

She could hear the splashes of birds ducking and fishing in the surf, the rhythm of the waves lapping onto the shore. If the night happened to be clear, she could write by moonlight. That wouldn't be the case tonight. The sky had been tinny all day, the air thick with humidity. It'd rain soon. The gloom matched her mood.

Her relationship with Luke Clearwater had started as a friendship. Two outsiders bonding over poetry, writing. They'd met at Barnes & Noble. She'd been sitting on the floor, blocking the narrow aisle with Maya Angelou's inspirational *And Still I Rise* spread on her knees. People stepped around her, or over her, mumbling annoyed *"excuse* me's." Luke had knelt down next to her, clutching a copy of *The Collected Poems of Langston Hughes*. And for the next hour, shoppers had to avoid stepping on both of them.

It was through the words, then, written by others, that Harper and Luke had scripted their own love story. It had all seemed so organic.

And simple. He *got* her. Understood her passions because he shared so many of them. He wasn't put off by her moods—as her mom constantly reminded her, she was either sulky or sarcastic, serious or angry. She trusted Luke with her ideas, her own poetry, her real self. He responded kindly and constructively, admitting that "My Brother" (a poem reflecting Harper's longing for a sibling) made him cry. He'd helped her with one called "Flat," wondering if the poem about spiritual death wouldn't be more powerful if she killed that middle verse.

Harper had taken a big breath, and a bigger chance, exposing her soul to him. It was her first time.

Harper helped Luke, too. He was a senior at Boston Latin High School and delivered pizza after school, but he had the soul of a writer. Unfortunately, he had trouble stitching his profound, but scattered thoughts into a cohesive story. She'd worked on that with him, forcing him to think through what he wanted to say. "If you can think it, you can write it," Harper counseled.

Dude, she'd done good by him. One short story got published in *The New Yorker* magazine; an essay got selected for NPR, National Public Radio. Not that any of the kids at school would've heard of it. But both the literary magazine and the radio station were big, big deals. With Harper's encouragement,

Luke had just sent a collection to a literary agency, hoping maybe some agent would sign him up.

Their relationship had its physical side. Harper loved the way Luke kissed her—soul kisses that could last for days, as he'd written. And she loved the way he touched her, slowly, lovingly, all over.

He was willing to wait, he'd said, for the rest. He was willing to wait, he'd said, for her to be ready.

Until the day he'd casually said, "See ya," and walked out of her life.

Stunned, paralyzed, Harper had begged to know why. It wasn't about sex, he'd assured her.

It was worse.

He'd found another muse. His *real* soul mate.

A raindrop, or maybe a tear, squiggled down her cheek, dripped onto her open journal, and pooled on the page, blurring an entire paragraph. Harper used the corner of her towel to blot it up, and dabbed her eye as well. Even alone, she did not want to cry over him. It was *not*, contrary to popular pop-psychology belief, cathartic. In spite of what she wanted, the tears kept coming. She closed her journal, and let them—and the rain, for it was drizzling now—have their way.

Sometime later, over her sniffles, she heard the squeak of the backyard fence open and close, followed by squishy foot-steps through the wet grass. Harper froze.

"I looked all over, but I couldn't find an umbrella in the house. Brought the next best thing."

Harper turned her head and squinted. Through her blobby-wet eyelashes she saw Joss, a Yankees cap shielding his head from the rain. He was offering her one with a SPRINGSTEEN logo. He was toting a bottle of wine and a paper bag.

He looked so ridiculous, this reedy-thin hippie longhair in his torn jeans, faded Rolling Stones T-shirt, and baseball cap coming to "rescue" her. She started to laugh through her tears.

"Was it something I said?" Joss knelt next to her in the wetly packed sand as she took the alt rain hat from him.

"Just a surreal moment." She was grateful, and stuffed as much as she could of her springy hair under the cap. "So what, you looked outside and saw me sitting in the rain?" Harper hoped that hadn't come out as an accusation.

"Pretty much, yeah. And from experience? Girls rarely enjoy getting their hair wet unless there's a swimming pool nearby."

"True dat," Harper conceded. She nodded at the wine bottle. "On your way out?"

"I managed to liberate some libations, a lively little Bordeaux, along with some hors d'ouevres, courtesy of The Naked Oyster. Thought you might want."

Suddenly, Harper was salivating. "Did you bring a corkscrew?"

He reached into his back pocket and pulled out a Swiss Army knife.

"A Boy Scout," Harper said, making room for him on her blanket. "Who'd a thunk?"

"Never made it past Cub Scouts. I'm not big on anything organized."

Harper peered into the paper bag. "All right! Real imitation cheese-food. And one hundred percent artificial Doritos. Perfect."

"Hey, the price was right." Joss freed the cork from the bottle.

Harper grinned and took the wine from his outstretched hand. She wasn't much of a drinker; a random beer pretty much summed up the extent of her experience. Time to widen her horizons. She closed her eyes, hoisted the bottle to her lips, took a swig, and nearly spit it out. "Vinegar, much?"

Joss laughed. "You should see your face." He handed her a cube of cheese. "Can't be that bad. We charge something like eight dollars a glass for this."

"Dude, your customers are getting robbed," she said, wiping her mouth and watery eyes on her sweatshirt sleeve. "But as long as it does its job, I'm all over it."

"Self-medicating?" Josh guessed.

"I'll let you know if it works." She handed it back to him.

"It will—temporarily, at least," he assured her.

90

"Temporary will do. For now."

"So, anyway," Joss said, "I'm thinking you came out here to be alone. I'll split. Unless you feel like talking. There's a strict code of bartender-client privilege. What goes in here"—he pointed to his ear—"stays in here. If not, they revoke my license."

Harper giggled. He was trying to be cute. But on the real, Joss must be privy to a whole mess of sagas. A summer's worth of lonely hearts confessionals. Boozy babes coming on to him, loser dudes confiding their frustration at "never getting any." Harper could hear it all now. She would trust him? Not so much. But she *was* curious. "You like bartending?"

"It's cool. Between the gig and the share house, I get to stay put for a few months."

Harper was about to ask what he did when he wasn't staying in one place, when the loud crash of smashing glass made them jump. It came from behind them—the house. And now Mitch yelling, Ali pleading, and Mandy bursting her vocal cords.

Joss leaped up. "Better see what happened. Be right back."

Harper thought about going with him, but what could she do? Alefiya's laissez-faire attitude was going to rile Mitch all summer.

Joss returned about ten minutes later. "It seems, in a gross violation of house rules, the ferret got free—and, as usual,

Mandy lost it. One freaked-out ferret, and one large table lamp. You do the math."

"Equals," she quipped, "one apoplectic Mitch, one pissed-off bitch, and one Hindu pitching excuses about how the Not-a-Rodent just got scared?"

"That's rich." Joss kept the rhyming beat. "Poetry and irony—comes naturally to you, does it?"

Harper squirmed. "And what part did Katie play in today's episode of our daily domestic drama?"

"Bailed. I saw her duck out the door just as I got there."

"Typical." Harper tsk-tsked. "The queen of control doesn't like when things get messy. Her game is strictly passive-aggressive."

"I thought you were her friend."

"Not even remotely," Harper confessed. "She goes to my high school, she posted a Web ad, and I answered. End of story."

"So you and Katie are two agendas passing in the night, huh? I'm guessing you didn't like her much back in high school," Joss speculated.

"I don't like her much now. She's a self-centered, materialistic, lying, manipulative opportunist. A conniving witch in Abercrombie clothing who brings her own designer toilet paper to a crappy share house."

"But tell us what you really think, Harper," Joss cracked, taking another swill of the wine.

"Oh, come on, tell me you like her," Harper challenged. "Word to the wise, if you do—you're not her type. She's all about the money, honey. Working slobs need not apply."

Joss paused, as if crafting his answer required careful thought. Finally, he said, "I don't really know Katie. But I know her type. She probably feels she has to pretend everything's groovy even when things totally suck. It's a hard ruse to keep up."

Harper mimed playing the violin.

Joss laughed. "Point taken."

"Katie can fend for herself; girlfriend has got it all under control. It's Alefiya I'm worried about. Granted, she's messy, spacey—and forgetful. But she's good people, compassionate, generous, just real." Harper looked to Joss for validation. She found it in his furrowed brow. "The others can't stand her— I'm worried they might drive her out, do something really hurtful."

"Housemates," Josh deadpanned. "Can't live with 'em. Can't set 'em on fire."

Harper broke into peels of laughter, slapped the sand. "Good one."

Joss started to bury the now drained wine bottle. "My money's on Mitch, for the one with the troubled road ahead."

"Why? He's probably the most together of us."

"That's what he thinks too—and that's the problem."

Harper looked at him quizzically. "Do you know something?"

"Just what I feel," Joss admitted. "T'ain't pretty."

Maybe it was the buzz of the wine, or that Joss actually worried about other people—including herself—sitting out in the rain. But for the first time, she took real note of him. "Where are you from?"

"Nowhere in particular."

"Everyone's from somewhere," she scoffed, hoping he'd say New York.

"Mostly, I travel."

"A real wanderer," Harper mused, "from place to place, bar to bar, supporting yourself as it comes?"

"Something like that." Joss pointed to her journal. "And you? Poet? Writer?"

"Something like that."

The rain, never more than a steady drizzle, had settled for full-out mist, from which moonbeams now poked. And Harper found herself opening up—just a crack—to Joss. She admitted to writing, and yes, poetry was her thing. Why? No concrete reason. There was something about the way he looked at her, and who it *didn't* remind her of. Luke had been full of passion. He'd been smitten by Harper, and wore it on his sleeve. Not Joss. Joss seemed genuinely curious. Interested.

She found she was too.

Monday,
Joss Plays a Hunch

The night Joss joined Harper on the beach was not the first time he'd spied her out there alone.

It was the first time he had an excuse to go to her, be alone with her, get to know her. He wasn't into her in a sexual way, he didn't think. It was more an itch he couldn't scratch: Something about her continued to intrigue him. It seemed important to figure it out.

For her part, the sarcastic and contrary roommate—the one he'd nicknamed Angry Young Babe—was grateful for his company. He still couldn't nail who she reminded him of, but sitting close to her, talking, joking, swilling some wine, he'd learned a lot.

Someone had broken her heart; she didn't need to come out and tell him. But she was grieving. Still, she'd been funny, and smart and creative. Instinct told him that she was musical. Poetry, yeah. Put it to music, you call it lyrics. He'd bet anything she played *something*. Piano, possibly; guitar, more likely.

Lying in bed that night, Joss suddenly had a hunch about Harper. He decided to follow up on it in his spare time.

Not that he had a lot. Mostly, he was working, or otherwise engaged. Late nights he was at the bar, and even later nights he found plenty of distractions. Or rather, they found him.

Women had always told him he was sexy. How many of his father's bimbettes had secretly come on to him? Joss had stopped counting long ago. With girls his own age, it was the same deal. All through prep school, he'd been the catch, the meat, the prime, grade-A hunk. The big "get."

It did nothing for him. It was like this macho joke his dad used to repeat: A sexy young starlet approaches a big-time Hollywood agent at a party. She says, "Come upstairs and I'll give you the best b.j. you've ever had." The agent replies, "Yeah, but what's in it for me?"

Joss could not conceive of being that cruel to anyone, but like so many charismatic guys, he got the joke. He'd walked out on that life. No one knew him here, and yet women were drawn to him just the same. They found him mysterious, intriguing. That was cool. There were no strings, expectations, or pretenses. Just fun flings, safe and anonymous.

The one he regretted was Mandy. "Never shit where you eat." Another of Father's Favorite Filthy Clichés. Meaning, getting involved with someone at work, or who lived nearby, was doomed to end in disaster.

Between him and Mandy it was like this: Nights she came home disappointed, frustrated, pissed off—pretty much her three main moods—she came knocking at his door. A booty call.

It had only been a few times, but Joss was ready to knock it off. The momentary pleasure—he'd always been a sucker for redheads—wasn't worth the potential complications. For one thing, it prevented him from bringing another girl to the house, should he want to. It'd be too weird. For another, secrets weren't likely to remain so for long. The walls were paper thin, Mandy's mouth anything but.

Mandy Starr—yeah, talk about made-up names—was crass, but she was also cagey. He'd already told her too much, especially the part about being a roadie with Jimi Jones. He wished he hadn't disclosed that. She was digging for backstory like a dog pawing for a bone, and if she came up with even a partial truth, his cover was shot. Very uncool.

Something else was happening to Joss, something heady and amazing. He'd found a spot, a cove on a beach in Wellfleet. Afternoons, or those predawn hours after work, he'd started going there, just him and the old acoustic, the cheapest of his collection. On that sandy beach, he didn't have to push, to struggle. Music came to him. And stayed! Tunes composed themselves in his head there, while he was pretending to listen to someone's sob story at the bar, while he was making small talk with some babe, even while he was asleep. He put them all down in his iPhone and at his first opportunity tried them out on guitar. Damn! This was his first real creative streak. What a rush!

Tuesday Night, Katie Goes Out— Er . . . Stays In—with Brian.

"Hell yeah, I'm taking the summer off," Brian Holloway was telling Katie. "I deserve it." Late afternoon, with camp officially over for the day, Katie joined Brian by the pool, a habit she'd fallen into, and he welcomed. She usually found him stretched out on a chaise lounge—the very same one he'd occupied when Katie'd first laid eyes on him and looking every bit as luscious—coolly sipping a margarita.

She hadn't had to prod much to get Brian to open up about himself. Upon graduation, he would go into the family business, starting as a junior executive in his dad's fund-management business. "So this is my break, The Summer of Brian," he said now, without irony. "Probably the last summer of my life I'll be able to do exactly what I want, with no obligations."

From her own padded lounge chair, Katie leaned over to run her fingers through his thick inky curls. "I don't believe you," she said in her flirtiest tone. "I bet your whole life you've done exactly as you wanted."

Brian grinned. "Busted. So I'm being lazy for a few months. I still think I deserve it."

Katie, though sweaty and tired from her long day—getting her group ready for a Camp Olympics, she'd been on the run all day from swim practice to tennis to track—playfully licked his earlobe. "Wanna know what I deserve?"

Brian looked at her hopefully.

"Dinner."

He laughed. "Are you kidding?" He checked his Tourneau watch, which Katie had calculated was worth at least $4,000. "It's not even six. Give me a break, I only got up a few hours ago. But I'll order you a drink—"

Katie shook her head. The idea of a frothy fruity alcoholic mix was so not what she craved right now. A steak was more like it.

Brian said soothingly, "You look tired. Come snuggle with me, I'll make room here, and you can sip my drink. I'll get the waiter to bring us some chips."

"I don't think so," Katie demurred. "I'm kinda sweaty."

Brian winked. "Oooh, I like that in a girl."

Katie rolled her eyes, knowing she looked adorable. "Really, Brian. I was out in the sun all day with the campers and didn't get a chance to shower. And I am ravenous."

He bolted straight up. "Ravenous, huh? Well, when you put it that way . . ."

"Not kidding. Really starving."

"Okay, how 'bout this, then? Come up to my suite and take a shower. Then, we'll go out to eat. Dinner for you, breakfast for me. How's that?"

Brian was so amazing, between that jet-black hair, startling blue eyes, soft lush pillow lips, it was hard for Katie to keep her eyes off him. He knew how to treat a girl too. He had an agenda? What guy didn't? Katie could deal.

She had her own agenda (sort of). Without Lily, the plan wasn't exactly formulated. She kept hoping an idea would come to her. In the meantime, parading around the Cape with Brian Holloway was most excellent. By now, he knew she worked as a counselor at the Luxor, but he totally bought she was doing it to fulfill this "social consciousness" thing for her mother's "organization."

Later, after she'd indeed showered, riffled through Brian's drawers, and wrapped herself in one of his shirts and boxer shorts, he did treat her to a huge steak and crispy French fries. Via room service.

"We can't go out," he'd argued, putting some Norah Jones on the in-room stereo, "unless you want to wear my clothes. Which you look delectable in, by the way."

Well, duh. Coyly, Katie put her hands on her tiny waist and replied, "I thought I'd be showering and changing at my place, then we'd go out."

Brian, of course, had other thoughts, other intentions— only some of which Katie was willing to give in to. Not that he wasn't an incredible kisser. Brian kissed with his eyes closed, his long lashes tickling her cheek. Wrapping her in his arms, he always started slowly, with tiny pecks, then gently opened her lips—at which point their tongues took over. They seemed to know how to slow dance all by themselves. It felt good, it felt right, it felt like she could do *that* all night.

It also felt too soon. It was still early in the summer, and Katie couldn't risk things moving too quickly. Besides, Nate might still be in the game—not that Brian knew it—and there were times, she had to admit, when her thoughts wandered to swapping saliva with him. Would he taste salty?

Tonight, she was having a mental threesome. Joss bothered her. She was still annoyed about last Saturday night. So what if she'd left the house in the middle of another of Ali's messes and Mandy's melodramas? Not her issue. Yet Joss had shot her this accusing look, like she was leaving the scene of a crime. Who was he to judge her (if that's what he was doing), anyway? He was hardly without secrets of his own. Maybe the others were clueless—Harper certainly was—but Katie knew what was going on between Joss and Mandy. If only she could remember how she knew him from before the share house.

Wednesday, the Beach Is Back.

Mandy was jazzed. After three frustrating weeks, *finally* something was about to go her way. That her good fortune was coming courtesy of the slobo next door was an unexpected twist. But she was used to adjusting.

Mandy could barely stand to look at her—let alone her repulsive rodent—but Alefiya Sunjabi was about to become Mandy's bestest friend. At least until Porky Pig delivered a well-connected client capable of jump-starting her career.

Wednesday, Ali's day off, Mandy called in sick to Duck Creek Catering and invited her NBF to hang out with her. "I'm going to Craigville Beach, the meatpacking district. If you know what I mean."

Alefiya did not.

Mandy winked conspiratorially. "An all-you-can-eat buffet of grade-A prime, guys with packages you would not believe. A girl could get lucky."

Well, *she* could get lucky—if she wanted. In her uplifting white-and-gold-studded bikini, Mandy was a guy magnet. Whereas Ali, she guessed, would be lucky not to be mistaken for a beached whale. It was win-win.

"Sounds like good times," Ali had said agreeably.

Mandy's description of Craigville Beach may have been crude, but it was accurate. She'd heard locals call it "Muscle Beach," one of the few on the Cape not designated "family friendly." For the buff and the beautiful, the predators and their willing prey, it was packed with hard bodies wearing smooth tans and skimpy swimwear. It was scope-out, hook-up city. Where better, Mandy thought, for the new "girlfriends" to get all confidential?

Along with her lip gloss, Mandy packed several bottles of water, a Ziploc bag of celery stalks, the latest issue of *Us* magazine, sunscreen, and an umbrella for herself—she burned easily.

Ali lugged a big picnic basket filled with messy mayonnaise-y salads, tuna sandwiches, and iced tea. Obviously, she hadn't gotten the memo that Mandy didn't do carbs. Ali had also toted some ginormous, scratchy-looking blanket, as if they were going to share. Yeah, right.

Mandy snagged a strategic spot for them, midway between two groups of guys, tricked out with beer cooler, MP3 players, wandering eyes, and appreciative smiles. As she shimmied out of her cover-up, she watched Ali peel off her elastic-band shorts and T-shirt, hoping the plump girl hadn't committed a fashion fiasco by wearing a two-piece. Even one of those old-lady types with a skirt would be better.

Surprisingly, Ali wore a black V-neck maillot, as flattering to her figure as a girl her size could get. "Not what you expected, huh?" Ali said, reading Mandy's mind. "Better, or worse?"

"I . . . uh . . . ," she stuttered. "You look . . . good."

"For someone my size, right? That's what you were thinking?"

"No way!" Mandy lied.

"Forget it. I don't have body issues the way a lot of girls do. I'm lucky."

Looking to change the subject swiftly, Mandy nodded toward a toned and taut twosome on the next blanket over, one in a slinky Speedo, the other in tantalizing trunks. "Speaking of bodies, check it out."

Ali licked her lips. "I wouldn't kick either one out of bed."

Mandy was, what, scandalized? Even knowing Ali brought home every stray on the Cape, Mandy didn't believe she actually slept with any of them. A girl of her heritage and heft was more likely to be a guy's friend, not his squeeze.

Ali laughed, going all mind reader on her again. She laughed. "I'm Hindu, and big—so people assume I'm sheltered, a virgin. But"—she put her finger to her cheek—"I'm guessing people make wrong assumptions about you, too?"

No way was Mandy going there—especially not with Buddha. There were limits to this newfound friendship.

"It's okay." Ali shrugged, rubbing sunscreen onto her ample arms. "We're all guilty of stereotyping, even me."

A perfect segue to gossiping about their housemates, and Mandy was just about to, only "Beep, beep!" Her "guy-dar" went off. The incoming hottie was mouthwateringly broad-shouldered, slim-waisted, and tousled-haired. She shifted position to pose languidly for optimum cleavage effect.

He was still several feet away when he waved. "Yo, Alefiya! Howzit hangin'?"

Mandy nearly fell out of her top. He . . . knew . . . *her*?

"Jeremy!" Ali jumped up and ran to hug him.

Jeremy. Mandy did a mental Google. Wasn't he the one who'd worked at Cove Landscaping for several years, knew all the celebs? She leaped to her feet.

Ali made the intros. Mandy purred, "A pleasure to meet you, Jeremy Davis. Ali has told us so much about you. Come join us. We'll make it worth your while."

A slow, if surprised, smile played across Jeremy's lips. "You guys are friends?"

Mandy laughed. "As of today, we are!" Then she added, "Seriously, we've got eats and drinks, way too much for the two of us."

Jeremy unscrewed a bottle of iced tea and settled on Ali's blanket, which now seemed inviting to Mandy, and she squeezed in. She politely allowed them a few minutes of flower-speak, or whatever lawn-yawn stuff they were yapping about. Finally, she interrupted. "It must be so exciting in your job, getting to meet celebrities and important people."

Jeremy gave Ali a sideways glance and shrugged. "Uh, sure. I mean, they're really just like everyone else. Once you get to know them."

Animated now, Mandy leaned closer to Jeremy. "That's what I always say! I know I'd hit it off with them. I mean, take me, for example. . . ." She paused, lightly resting her hand on his muscled forearm. "You could probably tell I'm a model. But I have so much more to offer. Only, breaking into acting is so hard! It's all about connections, who you know. That's how everyone gets started."

After that, it hadn't taken much time for Jeremy to agree to introduce Mandy to some guys he hung out with, friends of friends, sons of the quasifamous and connected.

That was all she'd wanted. Her "bonding" with Ali? Over it. She sure didn't need what came next. Ali, clapping her hands and bouncing up and down like a blubbery seal. "We should have a party! For the Fourth of July—you bring your friends, I'll invite some other people from Cove, and we'll mix it up. Saturday night at our place—you can introduce Mandy to everyone at the same time."

"But the Fourth was over a week ago," Mandy noted.

Ali shrugged. "It's always the right time to celebrate independence, no? Fourth, fourteenth, twenty-fourth—what's the difference?"

"Works for me." Jeremy was enthusiastic. "Give me the address, we'll bring some fireworks."

"Three-four-five Cranberry Lane," Ali told him. "Come around ten."

With a peck on the cheek for Ali and a nod to Mandy, Jeremy got up to rejoin his friends.

When he was out of earshot, Mandy said, "You really think a party's such a good idea? It isn't really necessary, I could just—"

Ali waved her away. "As long as we don't tell Mitch. The poor guy is so uptight. What he doesn't know won't stress him." She started rambling about baking Brie, making tostados, and stocking the fridge with beer, when Mandy tuned out. What would she wear?

Mandy got up and stretched. "I'm going for a swim."

"In the ocean? For real?" Ali looked doubtful.

"No, not for real. In the movie," she deadpanned, turned, and ran toward the surf. The foamy water swirled around her ankles and, like always, made her feel safe. She rushed in and began strong, swift strokes that carried her out into the ocean. Mandy flashed back on the pool at the Dorchester Boys and

Girls Club, where she'd learned to swim. The one silver lining in her otherwise crappy childhood: The exercise had peeled layers of fat off her.

Thursday, Mitch Showers with Worry.

Creeping worry. The knowing that something's wrong—or about to be . . . only you don't know what it is. It had plagued Mitch all his life. He'd learned to cope by swatting it away, peeling it off, beating it into submission until he could figure out what it was and deal with it. Right now, as he took his post-jog shower, he tried to scrub it away like dirt before it got under his skin and infected him.

This worry-bug had a name: Leonora. The morning his girl had shown up at the house had been such a sweet surprise. En route to a tennis game, she'd stopped off to see him first. She never did say why she needed to see him. Later, on the phone, she got angry and accused him of never giving her the chance to talk. "I came by because I needed to see you alone," she'd said, growling when he'd chuckled suggestively.

"Not for that reason!" she growled. "I didn't have a lot of time, and you totally wasted it by showing me off to those people you live with, like some prize."

Wincing at her condescending tone toward "those people you live with," Mitch nevertheless conceded. "You *are* my prize. Of course I want to show you off. I love you. What's wrong with that?"

"Your timing, that's what!" She hung up on him.

Lee was normally sweet-tempered, so he figured the outburst might be PMS-related. Growing up with a twin sister, he knew about female moodiness. Leonora's had not been pretty. She stayed annoyed with him, punishing him by canceling their date that night. That same night, the stupid ferret had broken the lamp, which led to his own outburst. He'd charged Ali for the damage, but felt guilty all the same.

Ah well, another weekend was a couple of days away, and Lee had softened, promising to spend it with him. She did need to talk to him, she'd said.

"About what?" he'd asked.

"About us."

Creeping worry. Mitch scrubbed harder. Whatever she was mad at, he'd make it right. He was her boyfriend, soon-to-be fiancé. Making things right with her was his job. And his joy.

Friday, Harper Runs Into Leonora.

TGIF! The Rebel Grllz had decided to have a weekly "Thank Goddess It's Friday" event. The idea had been Katie's—big surprise—but they had done the democratic thing and voted on the plans. Katie's crew always united in opting to shop every week. Harper had tried, and failed, to urge her bunch to widen their horizons, see a play, attend a concert, a trip to Provincetown: some culture.

"Shopportunities." Katie coined a word, and won. Again.

Today marked the third Friday they crammed into the resort's minibus and headed out to satisfy the primal needs of the eager little consumers. Harper was still holding out hope that eventually she'd have some positive influence on the group, but times like these, they were all about the tops, the shoes, the 'cessories.

Harper *had* won the smallest of battles. At least they weren't going to another brain-numbing Galleria, but into the town of Dennisport, checking out funkier shops, vintage clothing, local arts and crafts.

On the bus, Harper sat next to her favorite camper, Gracie Hannigan. Shy Gracie wasn't as superficial as the others, but that wasn't the real reason Harper took to her. The child had issues: self-esteem, body, braces, geeky glasses—the usual tween traumas—only she wasn't very good at hiding them. Which made her prime prey for the others, who delighted in making themselves feel good by making her feel bad. Gleefully, the baby fashionistas pointed out that stripes, tights, baby tees, or flip-flops were so over! And didn't Gracie know—hello!— that capris were played? And who cut her hair, the lawn guy?

The taunts weren't new to the kid; she'd suffered verbal

poison darts in school, too. But that didn't make them hurt less. If only, Harper caught herself thinking, Gracie was thin. She wasn't.

Gracie reacted by trying to blend in. As Harper had read in a book somewhere, she'd turned self-effacing to self-erasing. She never spoke up for herself.

Harper's strategy was to bring out Gracie's talents, her artistry, her musical chops. Good idea, in concept. In the real world of eleven-year-olds? The only way Gracie could hope to survive was to fight with the same ammo: Harper secretly hoped they'd find something on this excursion—some necklace, or top, or hair accessory—that'd boost the kid's self-esteem.

Luck was with them. Just a few hours into the shop-op, Harper scored better than she'd dared hope. She'd found Gracie this boho retro outfit—cute top and pants—and it fit! All the girls complimented her, told her how rad she looked. Harper spent her own money to add a necklace, and bracelet to match.

The little girl was truly aglow for the first time all summer. And so was Harper.

On the bus ride home, two of the other campers decided to style Gracie's hair so it'd go with her new look. So psyched, Gracie could barely wait to get back to the Luxor. "I can't wait to show my mom. Harper, you have to come with me!"

Harper didn't want to—she was tired, and what if Gracie's

mom didn't approve or something? But she couldn't say no to Gracie's pleas. "You have to be there when my mom sees me. Pleeeze, puleeze, pretty please."

What ensued was neither, Harper would think later, pretty nor pleasing. When they got back, she followed the kid into the hotel and waited outside the ladies' room in the lobby while her camper put on her new outfit and accessories. Counselor and camper took the elevator up to the ninth floor, down the corridor to Suites 909–910, the executive area where Gracie's family resided for this summer. Because she wanted the surprise to be total, Gracie didn't knock, but used her key.

There was a surprise all right—on them.

Gracie's mom wasn't in. Her dad was. In bed, undressed, and uh . . . cuddling. With someone who wasn't Gracie's mom.

But who was Leonora.

Alefiya Gets This Party Started—
The Fireworks Go Off!

"I'm comin' up, so you better get this party started. . . ."

The sky over the ocean outside 345 Cranberry Lane was clear and quiet. Its annual gig as host to the big fireworks display was over weeks ago.

This night, the fireworks were indoors.

It was close to midnight, and Ali's Not-the-Fourth-of-July party was off the hook, slammin'! There were easily, she calculated, a hundred people—and their dancin' feet—crammed in. Music rocked the rafters; food and drink flowed generously. Everyone was dancing, drinking, eating, and socializing. Interesting combinations of legs, arms, and other body parts intertwined as people squished together on the couches, chairs, tabletops, fireplace mantel, any inch of space they could find. The kitchen, where the bar had been set up and where she'd stashed most of "Alefiya's Incredible Edibles," was just as crowded. Hook-ups were happening in the bedrooms—she'd seen couples sneaking off—even the bathrooms were "occupied."

Ali, wearing a traditional sari with a red, white, and blue do-rag on her head, was sandwiched on the sofa between Jeremy and Sharif. She had never been this ecstatic—or, for that matter, stoned—in her entire nineteen years. This, she thought, deeply inhaling the joint the trio were sharing, is exactly how she'd imagined her summer, back when she'd planned it. "Schemed" was maybe the better word.

For the first time, she'd been able to get away from her parents, grandparents, uncles, aunts, cousins, siblings—her great big, colorful, opinionated family. She loved them all to death, and basically, totally respected their values, her heritage. But there were certain issues. Like the fact that her family insisted she become a doctor, and forbade her from fraternizing with any boy who wasn't Indian.

What could a wholesome, assimilated girl do? She was all about helping people, but preferred buds and stems to blood and stem cells. As for guys, she fell in and out of love every day; she was color-blind.

When the time came, maybe she would marry a "respectable" Indian boy, as her parents wished. But the time wasn't now. These three delicious months she'd fashioned into her own personal *rumspringa*, an Amish concept she'd brazenly co-opted. This was her first true Independence Day, her taste of real freedom. It tasted better than anything she'd ever tried. Even hot-from-the-oven Cinnabons.

"*. . . Pumpin' up the volume with this brand-new beat . . .*"

Jeremy's arm was flung around her shoulders, and Sharif was leaning into her side. Ali felt incredibly connected to every single person in the house, especially her roommates.

The one twinge of guilt: Mitch. She'd pulled this fiesta off behind his back, and against his big-ass rules. She wished she hadn't had to go covert, but he wasn't likely to show up tonight. He was finally spending the weekend at Leonora's.

Neither Katie nor Joss had arrived yet, but Ali was sure they'd dive right in. How much fun was this? She noticed Mandy, swathed in some hot pink confection with a daringly deep V-neck, animatedly chatting up someone she assumed was Jeremy's friend. Ummm . . . chatting up? More like brushing up against, curling herself around. Soul-patch dude seemed familiar, but Ali was in no shape to nudge a brain cell awake and attempt recall.

Ali saw Harper leaning against the far wall, surveying the room. Her fists were shoved inside the upper pockets of her cargo pants. She was wearing a T-shirt with the slogan, PAIN WAS TOO GOOD FOR HIM. It matched her sour expression. Uh-oh, Ali ought to go see what was wrong, but du-u-u-ude, as Jeremy would say, she was just soooo comfortable exactly where she was.

"It's gettin' hot in here . . . so take off all your clothes."

Jeremy licked her ear, which made her giggle. And Sharif—or "Reef," as he liked to be called these days—had just made room on his lap for his girlfriend, Lisa. Ali leaned over Jeremy to pass the joint, when something disturbed her full and total inner peace moment.

"Al*ee*-fee-ya." Someone was calling her, someone whose bouncy tone belied a disapproving 'tude.

"Excuse me, but what exactly is going on?" There it was again. Through her sweet and savory haze of marijuana, she realized (a) that line was not part of Nelly's party anthem, and (b) she should know the person asking the question.

Only she wasn't sure. She sighed, threw her head back on the couch, and closed her eyes, letting a satisfied smile spread across her face.

"Earth to Alefiya. I repeat, what's going on here?" The voice again, rising, trembling now. Ali tried to figure out who it was as she took hold of the joint Jeremy passed to her.

"Mix a little bit a ah, ah . . . with a little bit a ah, ah."

"Ouch!" Someone had kicked her in the shin? She coughed out the choking smoke, nearly gagging, her eyes tearing.

"Alefiya! What's going on?"

More puzzled than perturbed, Ali looked up and tried to

focus. She registered long, straight strands of gossamer hair brushing bare shoulders. Then, round baby-blue eyes, clouded over in rage, reddened cheeks, and rosebud lips pressed together tightly.

Katie! *That's* who it was. Katie standing above her, hands on her tiny hips, feigning curiosity about the party. A little vein in Katie's forehead was throbbing—Ali had never noticed that before. Did it mean Katie was actually angry, even though she didn't want to sound mad? Why? Had she forgotten to invite her? But that was impossible! Katie lived here. She was invited by default. So why was—

"I need to speak to you, now." Katie forced a smile.

Ali mustered, "Cool! Jeremy's lap's available. Sit yourself down!"

"Alone," Katie clarified.

"Yo, Leaf," Jeremy whispered, using the nickname he'd made up, "she looks serious."

His whispering tickled her ear, and she burst out laughing. Sharif stilled her. "Come on, I'll help you up." He nudged Lisa off his own lap.

Why was Katie squeezing her elbow so hard? Who knew the elfin girl was that strong, anyway? She was practically pushing her through the packed room, not even letting her pause to hug her friends from work, Jason and Eddie, and that nice guy she'd met at the bar the other night whose name escaped her.

Ali wanted to ask Mandy if the guy she was draped around was the famous photographer. And oh, Harper! She totally needed to talk to her. But Katie wasn't slowing down, just kept forcing her forward, through the throng, shouting, "Excuse us, move, please, excuse us." They were headed toward the kitchen. Ali was trying to tell Katie that that was not the place to find privacy. Dude! That's where the kegs were! And the lime shots and the vodka, tequila, rum, and fruity drinks. Didn't Katie realize it'd be even more crowded there?

Katie eased her vise grip when they did hit the kitchen— and then, only because the floor was slippery. And Katie sort of . . . went flying. Landing on her . . . what was that word Ali found so hilarious? Keister! That was it. Meant butt, tushy, derriere. She doubled over laughing. She couldn't help it. The sight of composed, can-do Katie, flat on her keister in the middle of the kitchen floor, tickled her funnybone. A few people reached to help her up, but Ali was laughing too hard to be one of them.

Upright, Katie dropped all pretense of control. "You find this funny? You think this whole disgusting scene is some joke?"

Ali blinked. "No. I'm sorry you fell," she said—and started to laugh all over again.

"You're stoned!" Katie accused her. "I can't believe you! I

can't believe you'd do this! Do you even know who these . . .
degenerates are?"

Ali stopped laughing. "Please don't call my friends degenerates. Besides, this party is for you, too. It's for everyone in
our house."

That didn't placate Katie. "Look at this mess! It's . . . it's . . .
a shambles! How could you do this?"

"What crawled up your butt?" Mandy was in Katie's face,
shoving a shot glass at her. "Here—have a drink, chill out.
It's the Not-Fourth-of-July, f'chrissakes, or are you snooty
Bostonians still upset over the tea party?"

Katie looked petrified. Like Mandy might take a swing
at her.

"We're having fun," Ali put in. "Really, it's just a party. I
was sure I told you about it."

"You didn't, because if you had, I would have made sure
Mitch knew. I assume he's not here." Katie's arms were crossed
defensively, but Alefiya heard a tremor in her voice, like she
was struggling not to cry. Instinct kicked in. Ali sobered up
and put her arm around Katie's birdlike shoulders. "Hey, look,
I'm really, really sorry. I didn't know it would upset you. I
thought I told you, and you were cool with it. If you want, we
can tell everyone to leave, okay?"

Katie's lip was trembling now, and Ali tried to shield her
from Mandy and the others in the room, now a rapt audience.

"So, uh, why don't we go outside, where we can talk? I don't think there's that many people in the back."

Katie took a deep breath; it seemed to calm her. "Forget it. I'll just go to my room—"

"Change into some jeans or something and join the party—I made baked Brie, and spinach dip, and baba ghanoush, if you're hungry."

Katie turned and took a step toward the bedrooms. Ali tapped her shoulder. "Hey, I mean it. I'll chase everyone out if you want me to. "

"Never mind." Katie slumped away, looking defeated.

Ali grabbed a couple of beers and made her way back to the den. If she'd learned anything about Katie, it was this: The girl could, and would, adjust. It'd be fine, and if not? She'd try to help her through whatever had made her such a wreck tonight.

Back on the couch now, she threaded her arm around Jeremy's waist. "Is that your big-deal celebrity photographer friend Mandy's talking to?"

Jeremy craned his neck. "I have no idea who that dude is. The one I was talking about is over there." He pointed toward the alcove near Mitch's room. "He's hanging with some chick in the T-shirt that says something about men and pain. I don't really want to know!"

Ali lit up. "Harper? Awesome. She's my favorite person

here. You've gotta meet her, come on—and you *promised* to introduce your photographer friend to Mandy. Do. Not. Forget. On pain of . . . ah, you've met Mandy!"

Jeremy laughed, and pecked Ali on the cheek. "You're the best, you know that, Leaf?"

She punched him lightly in the stomach. "Don't tell anyone—that's our secret."

Ali was aglow—only partly, she knew, from the pot, and the booze, and her handling of Katie. She was the happiest she'd ever been. As she crossed the room with Jeremy, she felt absolutely dazzled by everyone who'd shown up— admittedly way more than she'd assumed—and still more people were arriving. Everyone seemed to be "kickin' it," as Jeremy would say.

Jeremy made good on his offer to introduce his friends to Mandy. Ali didn't catch all the names and their connections, but she did catch Mandy's megawatt smile. That was the best thing about tonight. Mandy was so desperate for help with her career. Maybe these people could help her, maybe not. But Ali knew that just having a friend, someone who supported Mandy's dreams, might end up being just as good.

"Hey ya', hey ya' . . . shake it like a Polaroid picture . . . shake it . . . shake it . . ."

Dutifully, Alefiya shook her booty.

The music rocked. Joss had said they could use his CD

collection, and he had everything from Prince to the Beatles, from Outkast to cheesy 70s Bee Gees, who were warbling "You Should be Dancin'"; from the Pixies to the guitar God himself, Jimi Jones. Like the eclectic music, the partiers were this amazing cross-section of sentient beings: people of color, tattooed motorcycle dudes, goth girls, preps, locals, college kids, visitors, just everyone. And all because of her. She'd done this.

"This is ALL YOUR FAULT! You dumb-ass LOSER!"

This time, Katie came out *thundering*. Someone cut the music. Everyone froze.

Ali's jaw clenched, only Katie wasn't bellowing at her, but at . . . Harper?

"You're blaming me?" Harper hissed. "For what, your own stupidity? Give me a break."

"Yes, I'm blaming *you*. For this fucked-up summer," Katie spat. "You're too dumb to even know why."

Jeremy advanced toward them, but Ali put her arm out to stop him. It wasn't his place to be peacemaker.

"I may not be up to your standards of snottiness, but I do know this," Harper continued. "If you got shafted by some guy tonight, it's your own fault. Memo from the twenty-first century, kitten: Guys are not saviors. You'll just have to buck up and do that yourself."

"*You're* the expert on guys?" Katie trilled. "Oh, that's rich."

Harper folded her arms defensively—as if she intuited what might be coming.

Katie was afire. "Three words, holier-than-thou Harper: pussy trumps poetry. Ask any guy. Maybe if you'd put out, Luke Clearwater wouldn't have kicked you to the curb, and neither of us would be in this shithole!"

"What the hell are you talking about?" Harper shouted.

Katie smirked. "Oh, you didn't know, did you? Your soul mate, Luke, left you for my best friend! Lily McCoy!"

Katie Kicks Butt, but . . .
Harper Self-Destructs Anyway

"Hey, sweet cheeks, you're lookin' good, know what I'm sayin'? Drink up!" Some random guy trying to sound ghetto was all over Harper, burping vodka fumes in her face. In response, Harper snatched the bottle from him, boozily agreeing, "I *am* lookin' good. I'm *doin'* good. I am doin' grrrr-ate! Just like Kate. Oooops! That rhymed." She giggled and guzzled from the bottle. "Hey! I am a poet. An' don' I freakin' know it!"

She followed with another swallow, only she missed her mouth. Using her arm to wipe the vodka off her chin, she stood on tipsy toes and craned her neck to peer around the room. "Am'int I a poet, Jozz? Hey," she demanded, "wheere's Jozz? Why in't he here?"

Katie felt her cheeks redden. She was beyond mortified. Harper, obviously hammered for the first time, had done a complete 180, trading her patented emo-sarcasm for crude, lewd, loud, and proud. Like she'd channeled Mandy on the sauce. Drunk, Harper was self-destructing.

It was all Katie's fault. She'd had a humiliating, thoroughly heinous day. Her mood—her life!—was plummeting downhill, and she could not stop it. Worse, she'd dragged Harper down with her.

How could she have screamed at Harper like that? In front of a room full of people? She'd never, *ever*, let herself get out of control like that. What was happening to her?

Okay, so during the day she and Brian had run into that heinous Taylor Ambrose from school—who delivered the bulletin that she knew Katie was a counselor. When Brian blabbed that Katie was only working for her mom's charitable organization, Taylor laughed evilly. "Believe that if you want. I hear otherwise."

Katie had been freaked. What did Taylor know, and what would she take back to Boston with her? So far, Katie was pretty sure the indictment against her father had not come down yet. What inside info was Taylor privy to? She could not stop shaking all afternoon, and for the gazillionth time she cursed Lily for not being there, for not having her back.

Brian hadn't pushed for an explanation.

That was because, it turned out, he had other things to

push for. He thought going out with her for a month entitled him to "more." Sure, they'd hooked up, fooled around—a lot. But he wanted to go further. Why wouldn't he? He also thought she was twenty (that's what she'd told him), and experienced. He was too well bred to come out and say it, but clearly he wasn't far from accusing her of teasing him.

He'd issued a not-so-veiled ultimatum: "Sleep with me, or I'm moving on."

Katie rejected both scenarios, only she didn't know what to do. So she'd pretended to be offended, and demanded he stop the car right that minute—she wasn't going another mile with him, she'd pouted.

Well, who would've expected he'd do just that, even lean over to open the door so she could get out? She was miles from the house, on four-inch heels, literally being kicked to the curb.

She *assumed* Brian would follow, apologize, and at least drive her back.

He chose "none of the above."

Over an hour later, feet killing, ego crushed, she'd come home to this disaster! What kind of idiot was Ali, anyway? Anyone who ever had a house party knew how this would end. The cops would be called. The last thing she needed was to be caught in some stupid roundup of underage drinkers. If word got out she was living in this dump, she'd be the total laughingstock of Trinity!

She had, as Ali suggested, retreated to her room, only to come upon one couple thrashing around on her bed, and a threesome on Harper's side of the room.

Shit! (Without parentheses!)

If Lily were here, none of this would be happening. If Lily were here, she'd help her handle Brian (from whom at least she'd managed to snare some cash: some he willingly lent her, some he didn't know about). Lily would have advice; they'd have figured this thing out together, the way they always did.

It was all Harper's fault that Lily wasn't here. Harper's own fault that Luke had dumped her and taken up with Lily; Harper's fault that a hundred strangers were tearing apart her house, that she had nowhere to turn, no one to turn to.

That she didn't know what to do.

She'd lost it. And by doing so, she set in motion a total disaster. After the runaway words had sped from her mouth, they'd crashed through Harper's chest, piercing the girl's heart. Ali—who else?—had rushed to her, and soon Jeremy, a bunch of other people, and even Mandy had joined in, helping to dull Harper's pain with alcohol. Oodles of booze.

At first, Katie had rushed outside, panting—the verbal assault had taken the wind out of her—then forced herself to walk the streets, take deep breaths, calm down, and assess. What she'd just done to Harper? It was the most hurtful thing she'd ever done to anyone (to their face, that is). She'd just made innocent Harper pay for Lily's betrayal.

That realization finally forced her back to the party. At the very least, she would apologize. At most, she thought, surveying the scene now, she'd try to save Harper from herself.

Harper wasn't going to make it easy.

Katie watched helplessly as Harper, arms swaying in the air now, wove suggestively through the room, purposely bumping into as many boys as she could, like a Missy Elliot backup dancer: *"Work it, now reverse it, put my thing down, and reverse it . . ."* She accosted Sharif, who'd been dancing with Lisa. Harper shouted above the music, "Are you dancing, or having a seizure?"

Then, she grabbed him and planted a full openmouthed kiss, with obvious tongue, on his surprised lips. Further down the sinkhole of bad behavior, Harper leered at a shocked Lisa. "You should thank me. 'Cause he'll leave you, just like that." She punctuated by snapping her fingers, and moving on.

Katie tried to grab her, but Harper wasn't having it. "Unhand me, Princess Poopypants!" she yelled, flouncing away, bumping into more guys and rapping loudly, *"Keep ya' eyes on my bomp-a-bomp-bomp."*

"Harper, you need to come with me!" Katie's pleas were drowned out as Harper blurted, "Let's play charades!" as she bounded into the kitchen, grabbed the scissors, and cut her

T-shirt around the collar, then pulled it over one shoulder, doing the worst *Fame* impression ever, singing at the top of her lungs. *"I'm gonna live forever, baby remember my name! Fame!"*

Katie needed help. Ali—or even Mandy, at this point. But at the moment, she could find neither. She pushed through the throng, some clapping and encouraging Harper, others caught up in drinking, dancing, and canoodling, and oh God, Katie saw two people with their noses to the kitchen counter, sniffing. She went back into the living room, just in time to catch Mandy's backside as the house skank headed up the stairs, arm in arm with the guy she'd been circling.

"Mandy!" Katie called out. "Wait, I need you."

Mandy stopped, turned, and grinned cruelly at her. "No, you don't. You're Katie-I'm-So-Above-It-All Charlesworth, you don't need anyone."

Katie turned on her heel and redoubled her efforts to unearth Ali. But when she found her, Ali was sitting on the floor, with Clarence in her lap. She'd tied her red, white, and blue do-rag around the ferret and was singing "America the Beautiful" to him, backed up by Jeremy, Sharif, and Lisa.

Okay, she'd do this herself, physically remove Harper from the house. But when she turned around, the way was blocked: A circle three people deep had formed around the middle of the den, where Harper had decided that since charades wasn't working, a new game was called for. She'd run down the steps leading to the basement and had come upstairs with a board game.

Twister.

"Let's get naked and play!" Her shouts were greeted with hoots, woo-hoos, and squeals.

Which Harper took as a cue to remove her T-shirt. Instantly, she was joined by dozens of happy partyers. Someone cranked the music up louder; another shouted, "Lime shots here! Come 'n' get them!"

The game had begun, and unsurprisingly, got out of control quickly. Harper's leg wound around a guy's, and they fell. Others got to the floor to help them up. In the process, someone opened Harper's jeans—aided and abetted by another guy, who pulled them down.

She protested incoherently. "Hey, whatcha doin'? I wuzzin' out."

"Yo, this isn't strip poker, sweetcheeks, it's naked Twister! You said so y'self! We're just helpin' ya get nekkid!"

Katie panicked. She was responsible for this and she had to fix it, with or without anyone's help. But just then, her stomach lurched. Whirring sirens screamed up the block. Flashing red strobe lights lit the living room.

The cops.

Katie raced into serious action. Her four-inch heels good

for something, she kicked and punched and bit, and grabbed handfuls of hair to get to Harper, who, by that time, was pinned on the floor, a dozen guys pawing her. Katie dove on top of them, and with all her strength, managed to get most of the guys off her. Katie grabbed Harper's hands, and—now, finally, with Jeremy's help—pulled her upright. Together, they tried to get her outside, but Harper wasn't having it. Dazed and confused, but conscious enough to try and get away from Katie, she broke loose. At that second, the door flew open. Harper lunged into the arms of the first guy through the door.

And promptly threw up all over him.

Hangovers, Heroes, and Hope

Joss

Joss moved stealthily and swiftly. Barely one step ahead of the sirens, he flew into the house, tossed the hurling, half-dressed Harper over his shoulder, and ran. He dodged out the back door, betting the cops wouldn't bother to come after him. Breaking up house parties packed with underage kids drinking and doping had to be routine for them. They'd haul in a bunch of them and call it a night. He didn't worry for Katie and Mandy; they were survivors. They'd get out.

Ali was most likely to offer herself up on the altar of confession, in a backward attempt to prevent trouble for the others. He could only hope someone had talked better sense into her. Otherwise, dude, she'd be in for one hell of a sobering night. Ali had mentioned something about a party, but it hadn't really registered. In her spacey way, she said a lot of things. Didn't mean she'd actually do it. Make that, overdo it.

This was a bad scene; yet, running down the beach, a heady sense of adventure filled him, as if eluding the fuzz with a helplessly hammered chick was something he did all the time. It was like James Bond, only he was the antihero. For the first time since he'd ditched his life of privilege, he wasn't just free, he felt unshackled.

If only he could stop the spinning wheels in his head. He knew what would happen next. After the roundup, after parents had been notified, and some kids had spent the night in the clink, the police would find the person whose name was on the lease.

That would suck. Mitch, the poor slob, would be blindsided, and since he was over twenty-one, held accountable. Joss was sorely tempted to intervene. All he had to do was make one call, and the whole incident would be erased, like it'd never happened. That, however, meant calling his father, using his family connections. And he'd cut those ties, man.

Harper, who'd stopped upchucking, now kicked and punched him. "Put me down!" she managed to belch out.

Turning to be sure they hadn't been followed, Joss slowed enough to let Harper slide off him. He didn't free her completely, though. He kept a grip on her slender wrists so she wouldn't run off.

"Let me go!" she cried, fighting him, pulling away.

"It's okay, it's okay, it's gonna be okay," he said soothingly.

Then Harper looked up at him, and he wanted to die.

What had happened to her? She was ravaged. Her innocent, beautiful face was stained, scratched, smeared; her hair stuck in clumps to her wet cheeks. Her eyes were red and puffy. Were those bruises on her neck—or maybe hickeys? It was hard to tell in the dark. Her bra hung off her shoulder; her pants were down around her ankles. Joss hoped they'd fallen while they were running. He didn't want to even think of the alt-scenario, that they'd been removed during the party.

His heart ached as he folded her into his arms and kissed the top of her head. "Let's go over to the water, get washed up a little. Okay? It'll be all right, little one, I promise."

In his entire life, Joss had never welshed on a promise.

For once, he was glad the bartending gig forced him to wear a jacket over his shirt. He'd need both. Peeling them off, he soaked his soiled shirt in the surf and used it as a towel, cleansing Harper's face, arms, and neck. Eventually, she stopped fighting him, refastened her bra, closed her trousers, and accepted his jacket as cover-up. She wrapped it tightly around herself. She looked like a wet, bedraggled wire-haired terrier, all big, baleful eyes. And Joss wanted to hold her, to tell her she could confide in him, that he could make it go away.

He knew better than to say, or do, anything. It would be up to Harper to tell him what had happened—if she ever wanted to.

Katie

Katie had escaped the roundup by tailing Joss out the back door, then hiding behind the fence, watching others pour out the house. Only the first wave had managed to avoid capture. The two squad cars on the scene had apparently called for backup and, within five minutes, enough cops were at 345 Cranberry Lane to escort dozens upon dozens of partygoers into the paddy wagon and off to the precinct.

No way could Katie allow herself to be caught, even if only to be let go a few hours later. From sporadic e-mails back and forth to her parents, she knew nothing had gone down yet—they were on their cruise, all was well, and they assumed she and Lily were ensconced in the McCoy mansion in Chatham. The FBI had not come calling on the Charlesworths, nor would anyone be looking for her yet. Even though Taylor Ambrose might have some intel about her working at a drone job, Katie needed to be under the radar until she could figure out a scheme.

Katie had waited a good half hour after all the squad cars had gone before slipping back inside. So far as she could tell, she was alone.

The place was trashed. Bottles, butts, and smashed glass littered the living room floor. Lamps had been kicked, or had fallen over; two of the couches bore the scars of cigarette burns. And one thought pounded at her: Lily.

If Lily were here, Katie wouldn't be.

If Lily were here, Katie'd never have driven a stake into poor Harper's heart.

If Lily were here, Katie wouldn't be scared shitless.

Just then, something skittered across the floor and Katie jumped, screaming. Clarence. The stupid ferret—dragging the do-rag on his foot—had smelled food and had scampered across the room to feast on it. Slowly, Katie's heart settled back to normal.

Sure that the kitchen was in worse shape than the living room, she didn't even want to check it out. She needed to do something, call someone. She found her cell phone and dialed Mitch.

Mitch

It was nearing dawn when Mitch, tossing and turning on the couch in Leonora's den, got Katie's panicked call. He was only surprised it hadn't happened sooner. Of course there'd be a party—he was a veteran of too many summer shares to know it was inevitable. Didn't matter what rule he imposed. It was like the Cape Cod fog, or the windswept beaches, its own force of nature during a summer in a house shared by six young strangers. This time, he'd likely be held accountable since his name was on the lease. But it was useless to stress. Until the cops came for him, there was a ton of work to be done.

He took charge, like always, and without whining, placing blame, blowing a gasket, or otherwise giving in to his emotions, Mitch methodically got everyone aboard the cleanup train. He sent Joss to the twenty-four-hour Meijer in Centerville for mops, buckets, industrial-size garbage bags, and other supplies. He taught Katie how to use a vacuum cleaner, and after calming a guilt-ridden Ali, set her to scouring the kitchen. "Go slowly and carefully," he cautioned the whimpering girl.

Then he rolled up his sleeves. Until Joss got back, the heavy lifting was his alone. Of the two housemates not participating, his concern was only for one. Not Mandy. In the beginning of the summer, at his sister Beverly's suggestion, he'd programmed his cell phone number into her Nokia. Since she hadn't called, he assumed she wasn't in police custody—nor was she alone.

He was nervous about Harper, who, despite her stinging sarcasm, he'd become really fond of. He wondered what had caused her to get so drunk, so out of control. Joss, who'd rescued her, claimed not to know.

Mitch believed the guy. His suspicions lay with Katie and Ali. He was sure something had precipitated it, and they knew what it was. But no one was saying. As he hoisted the remains of another smashed lamp into a black garbage bag, he rewound to the real reason for his own quiet freak-out.

Leonora hadn't bailed on him, as he'd feared. She'd been ready, on time, when he came to pick her up—Lee, the girl who always kept him waiting. Maybe that should've been his first clue. The rest of the evening she'd been, what? Contrite? Wary? Jittery? Too quick to laugh at his seriously lame jokes. Too chatty over dinner, too interested—if that were even possible— as he blathered about his tennis clients at the Chelsea House, listening without hearing. She was flushed, fluttery, and kept looking at him weirdly—guiltily, even. As if she was searching his face for a clue to something. But what? That he loved her? That he wanted to spend the rest of his life with her? She knew all that.

Her bizarre behavior made him squirm. He kept asking if anything was wrong. After saying no several times, she asked, carefully, "Should there be? I mean . . . is there something you think . . . ?" She'd trailed off.

After dinner, they'd gone back to her parents' house, empty for the weekend. He didn't know what was bothering her, but he thought he knew how to make it better. Mitch had gotten romantic, drawn her into his arms, and begun kissing her in that way—their way, the way that usually led to lovemaking.

Not so much. "Mitch," she'd murmured, pulling away. "I can't. Stop."

"But we're finally alone," he'd countered, hurt and surprised.

She hung her head, then looked up at him with pursed lips. "I know. But . . . I just . . . I'd rather not. Not tonight."

Scared, Mitch coaxed: "Baby, we've barely seen each other. We've waited so long to be alone together. What's wrong? Whatever it is, I can fix it. You know that."

Leonora began to sob. "I'm sorry, Mitch. I'm so, so sorry."

He never did find out what she was sorry about. She fled into her room and locked the door. He lay on the couch. And then Katie called.

Harper

Harper awoke the next morning sick to her stomach. Her head killed, her body throbbed and ached. But there was something more, something else that felt sour, and painful. It had happened last night, during the party. But what was it? She tried to sit up, but her head was too heavy for her body. She couldn't raise it off the pillow.

Her cell phone rang—damn, had she set it on "Blast"? Without checking the caller ID, she managed to reach out and hit the "Silence" button. That movement was all it took to set her stomach to churning, and she knew she'd better move. Fast.

Harper barely made it to the bathroom. After washing herself off, she braved the mirror—which set her stomach in motion again, forcing her once again to kneel by the toilet and heave. When she felt sure there was nothing left inside her, she brushed her teeth and washed up again. Suddenly, the freakin' roar of a motorcycle engine revved up right outside the bathroom. What the—?

She flung the door open.

There was Katie, cute-as-you-please, running a vacuum cleaner along the hallway.

Snap! Everything came back to her, played out in her head like a video set on rewind. She saw the shock in her own eyes, felt the horrible hurt as Katie spat that vile thing about pussy trumping poetry. She saw her "friends," Ali and company, rush to her; remembered the metallic taste of the tequila, hot down her throat, drink after drink until it obliterated everything. All she remembered from the devastating humiliation of what had happened afterward was a purple-and-white-striped shirt that Joss had used to clean her up, his warm jacket, his pitying face.

"Harper, are you okay?" Katie asked tremulously. "I feel so awful, I never meant—"

Oh, she'd meant it all right. Every sickening word of it. That Luke had dumped Harper because he wanted to have sex with someone else. Worse, that someone else turned out to be Katie's best friend, Lily McCoy, a stupid, superficial, self-absorbed slut.

Because of Luke, Lily had abandoned Katie—left her stranded this summer.

Because of Luke, Harper had abandoned Boston—and ended up stranded with devious, mean Katie this summer.

It really sucks when you're the *I* in irony.

Harper got right in Katie's face. The only thing left inside her was bile; she managed to spit it at Katie.

Mandy

Mandy was p.o.'ed. Why was everyone in the house so freaked? By the time she returned on Monday morning, the place was sparkling. Spanking clean; looked better than it ever had. The floors shined, the counters gleamed; the rugs had been shampooed—dude, even the bathrooms had been good and disinfected. Place looked better than when they'd moved in, f'crissakes.

She expected no less of Saint Mitch, who was born with a PhD in TCB: taking care of business. Even as a kid, he was all Mr. Responsible. For his sister, Beverly, his mother, Dora, and sometimes, going way back, for Sarah herself.

So a bunch of random rich kids had gotten arrested. Big deal. Not one of *them* had. As far as she could tell, Ali, Katie, and Harper had eluded the cops. Joss hadn't even been there.

As for Mitch, guess what? Queen Leonora's well-connected daddy had come to the rescue. It just proved it was all who you know, not what you know. Daddy Leonora had made a call to the Hyannis police, and poof! No arrest, no record for Mitchell Considine. Homeboy was off the hook.

So what was with the scowling, the stomping around, the flying accusations, and, from Mitch to her, the scolding. All she'd done was enjoy herself, accent on the j-o-y. She'd had a blast at the party, and thanks to the fat cow Ali, had been introduced to the man of her dreams: one Timothy Johnson—Timmy-Cakes, to her—who ran with the showbiz crowd; worked as a best boy on movies and TV shows filmed on the Cape. Who, ta *da!*, right now, after their weekend of fun, fun, fun, was back on the job with *Skinny Dipping*, the movie starring Jude Law and Scarlett Johannson, being filmed on Martha's Vineyard.

Tim knew *everyone*. He lived right here in Hyannis—partied with the Kennedys, even—but, more important, stud-boy was tight with directors, agents, producers. He hadn't introduced her to anyone yet; Mandy was working on it, using her personal powers of persuasion. Soon, he'd be at her beck and call and she'd be on her way. Woo-fuckin'-hoo! Mandy was feeling so generous, she even resolved to clean the frickin' bathroom next time it was her turn.

Heal, Harper, Heal!

Harper removed the plastic bowl from the fridge, gently lifted the lid, and sniffed. Ewww. Nooo, tabouli salad did not last forever, contrary to popular myth. Holding it at arm's length, she dumped the whole concoction in the garbage, plastic container and all. Bad Harper, she chastised herself for her un-eco (antirecyclable) action. She couldn't drum up enough feeling to care. She hunted through the messy cabinet and, finding a bag of wheat pasta, put up a pot of water to boil.

It was around seven on Saturday night, and, clad in her worn flannel pj's, she'd decided to scrounge up some dinner and curl up with her journal, fairly sure she had the place to herself.

Katie, who'd rebounded seamlessly from the Brian boot-off—*quelle* shockeroo!—had claimed her next victim. Nate

Graham was another young, rich, and restless hotel guest. Although, Harper thought, astoundingly raffish for conservo-Barbie. But they'd been out every night this week, including tonight. Nate and Kate. Out on a date. Flirt, Katie, flirt. Retch, Harper, retch.

To be sure, her righteous roommate kept trying to apologize for her vicious, humiliating outburst during the party. But ya know what, Harper thought, pouring Katie's beloved orange juice down the drain—oooh, too bad, all gone—screw her. Except when a verbal exchange was absolutely necessary—mostly at camp—she was all stony silence toward Katie.

Harper ripped open the bag of pasta and dumped it into the now boiling water. She found the wooden spoon in the sink, rinsed it, and began stirring.

The post-party doldrums pervaded the house; everyone was either "in a mood" or not around. Even happy-go-slobby Ali was mopey, blaming herself for the disastrous turn the night had taken. Her friends, especially Jeremy—who was definitely into her—were taking her out tonight to lift her spirits.

Mandy pretty much slept the days away, and never alone. The guy she'd attached herself to at the party seemed to have moved into her room.

Just as Mitch, for all intents and purposes, had practically moved out. His gig at Chelsea House, he'd explained, had gotten more intense: He was now giving weekend and evening tennis lessons. After work, he generally saw Leonora, running every time she snapped her betraying bling-fingers.

How could Mitch not see what was going on? She wanted to shake him. Guilt, guilt, guilt! It was out of guilt! she wanted to scream at Mitch. Your beloved is sleeping with someone else, someone married! And dig, no doubt girlfriend was walking on eggshells, wondering if Harper would tell. But Harper hadn't had the heart.

But how blind could Mitch be?

How blind had she been? She never saw Luke's betrayal coming either. Had no clue he'd leave her for "Katie-Lite": that thimble-brained slut, Lily.

That arsenic-laced diatribe Katie had thrown about "putting out"? It was just wrong. Luke wasn't like other guys. That's why she'd fallen for him. They'd opened up to each other in ways far deeper than sex. Luke had said so!

Whatever. Harper lifted her chin. Making the same mistake twice was not gonna happen.

"Harper . . . ?"

She whirled. Joss was pointing at the stove.

Joss. Oh God, she'd been avoiding him. What was he doing here? He was supposed to be at work.

"Turn the water off. You're boiling over."

"I am?" Harper repeated, confused. She looked at the

stove. "Crap-damnit!" Bubbling waves of white-hot pasta foam erupted like lava spilling from mini-volcanoes, covering the pot, seeping into the burner, over the counter, heading for the floor.

She quickly killed the heat just as Joss went to remove the pot from the stove.

"Don't!" Harper grabbed his arm to stop him. "You'll get burned. Wait—I'll get a dish towel."

Chagrined, he gave her a loopy smile. "Yeah. Good idea."

Harper blushed, and got to work mopping the mess of soggy spaghetti and water. She didn't know if she was more embarrassed or ashamed. Twice now, Joss had seen her make a fool of herself. Once, she'd been half naked. He'd been gentleman enough to not bring it up. She'd been the coward—never even thanked him.

"Lucky for me you're here," she managed, furiously sponging off the stovetop. "How come you're not at work?"

"Donated my shift to another bartender—guy's desperate for dough." Joss handed her a roll of paper towels. "Here, use this. I'll get the floor."

"Thanks," Harper murmured. She wanted to say, "For everything, for saving me from further humiliation." But the words didn't come.

"Well," Joss mused as he wiped up, "hope you weren't jonesing for pasta. This dinner is beyond saving."

"No big," she said. Then her stomach growled. Loudly.

Josh laughed. "Hey look, I got the night off. So why don't we just chuck it . . . as it were . . . go out to dinner instead?"

Harper shook her head, more adamantly than she'd meant. "No! I mean, thanks and all, but . . ."

"But what? I know this place, you'll dig it—a real Cape Cod experience, on the beach up in Wellfleet. Been there?"

"I'm a vegetarian." And she'd blurted that, why, exactly?

"Then don't get a hamburger. Chill, it's just dinner."

It wasn't. Just dinner, that is.

It was the best time Harper'd had in weeks! Joss had nailed it. The Beachcomber was her kind of place: kick back, outdoor, a bar-restaurant, with an awesome view. It was snuggled atop a dune, overlooking a wide, pristine beach. They got there just at sunset. The sand seemed to be bathed in hues of rust, orange, red-clay; and the ocean, a dark navy.

The Beachcomber wasn't visible from the road; you had to know about it. Hence, the place was filled with locals: a homey mix of singles, couples, families, in their faded denims, Old Navy tees, sandals, and flip-flops. Not a Katie-type in sight. Harper and Joss bypassed the green-and-white-awninged bar, and settled at one of the few tables still empty.

"This place has been here for decades," Joss told her. "It's famous for its authentic Cape Cod oysters, and after dark, it's a big music scene. Concerts on the beach: jazz, rock, punk, reggae—you name it. Everyone's played the Beachcomber."

"You've been here before," Harper noted.

"Once—which makes me qualified to order for both of us."

Harper couldn't suppress a grin. Joss was so sure of himself, he just took over. He'd picked the place, driven them here in his cute rented convertible—he'd even maneuvered their seats so they'd both be facing the ocean. Was it because he was older—at least twenty-one, she calculated—or was he hardwired that way? Both, she thought.

"We'll have a dozen bluepoint oysters on the half shell to start," he told the waiter, "a mountain of your greasiest onion rings, and a couple of beers." He turned to Harper. "Uh, unless you don't want beer?"

"Sounds like it's part of the oyster/onion ring Cape experience."

Joss conceded, "It is. You kind of have to."

"Then I kind of want to," she said with a real smile.

To the waiter, Joss joked, "The lady is an oyster virgin, so we'll start her on the classic, then build to more exotic varied types. If she's up to it, that is." He winked.

Harper leaned back, clasped her hands behind her head, put her feet up on the extra chair. "How'd you know I've never had oysters?"

"Just a guess. Not many neighborhood hangouts in

Boston—or New York—that serve 'em. It's not like HoJo's fried clams, or The Original Ray's Pizza, if you know what I mean."

"What do they taste like?" Harper was suddenly hyper-aware that Joss was sitting really close to her.

He ran his fingers through his long curls. "Hard to describe. I think you're just gonna have to decide for your-self."

When their order arrived, Harper was about to decide to order something else. Oysters weren't much for eye appeal. She knew what they were: plump bivalves—muscles, really—in simple juice. Only they looked like pearly gray lumps of quivering phlegm-y slime, set in a ragged shell. Dude, it looked like something you'd send flying *out* your throat, not down it. Not that Harper would dare say that.

She didn't have to.

"Not much of a poker face, are you?" Joss grinned. "Don't be grossed out. Here, I'll show you how it's done."

Harper watched, transfixed, as Joss demonstrated. "First, we dab a little cocktail sauce just here." He spooned a drop of the red sauce onto the fat middle of the oyster, then, with his thumb and forefinger, lifted the ringed shell. "You hoist it up to your lips, open your mouth, stick your tongue out, tip your chin up . . . and let it slide down your throat. Hmmm . . ." He winked at her and took a slug of beer.

"I don't know . . ." Harper was dubious. What if she

choked on the thing? What if it got stuck in her throat?

"Don't be a wuss," Joss needled good-naturedly. "Nobody respects a wuss."

"A wuss? Did you just call me a wuss?" Harper attacked the oyster, drowning it first in cocktail sauce. She shut her eyes—and just did it. The slippery *thing* slid down, sort of like a log flume ride. She tasted mainly the cocktail sauce—that was a relief!

"Beer chaser," Joss advised, handing her a bottle. "Next time, slow down so you can actually savor it. By the way, chewing is acceptable too."

Harper reached for a comeback, only seeing herself—the fading sun glinting off her blond streaks, the mile-wide smile, her dimples—in the mirror of Joss's swimming-pool-blue eyes, she forgot what it was. Then she noticed what he was wearing. A purple-and-white-striped button-down beneath his jacket. "That's not the shirt—"

"You threw up all over?" He finished her sentence with a laugh. "Nah, that one didn't make it."

The elephant dropped onto the table. Time to do the right thing. Haltingly, Harper did. "About that night . . . I'm so very sorry, so ashamed, I don't usually—"

"Get hammered and hurl over the first guy who comes into the room?"

Harper fixed her gaze straight ahead, to the line where

the water met the sky: the horizon. A lone boat tossed on the choppy water, and a lone tear wiggled its way down her cheek.

Joss leaned over and pulled her to him. "I'm sorry, I didn't mean to trivialize it. I figured something monumental must have happened."

"You could say that," Harper whispered, tempted to let herself go, lean into his chest.

"You don't owe me an explanation," Joss said sincerely. "It's cool, really, we're good."

Harper swallowed and pulled away. "Katie got in my face with some nasty stuff. I reacted badly."

If Joss knew more—and by this time, he probably did—he didn't let on. He did empathize, though.

"I get it. I'm slow to burn, but push my buttons, and man, all bets are off. Back in high school, this jerk ripped into me, talked real trash about my dad cheating on my mom. I didn't even know I had it in me, I just hauled off and dropped him."

Harper quipped, "Put the 'fist' in pacifist, did you?"

"Oh, yeah. Didn't go unnoticed. Our school was right across the street from the police precinct. New York's finest earned their rep that day."

Harper lit up. Joss had just said the magic words: "New York."

Katie Whispers in the Wind

Had Harper or Joss been looking out at the water as keenly as they were eyeing each other, they might've spotted a small luxury yacht called *Lady Blue* cruising Cape Cod Bay. But by the time Nathan Graham's family-owned ferry passed by the Wellfleet inlet, the two were animatedly comparing experiences in New York and having an oyster eat-off.

It was just around 9:30 that night, and Katie stood at the railing, Nate's arms locked around her. She took in the shoreline, dotted with restaurants, souvenir shops, surf shacks, beaches. Her eye settled on a cute place with a green-and-white-striped awning, tables situated just at the top of a dune. How sweet is that? she thought, never guessing that Harper and Joss were sitting there. Nate leaned in and nuzzled her neck. "You cold, cupcake?"

Katie burrowed into him. "Not anymore."

"Mmmm, 'cause we can go inside the cabin anytime you want," her date pointed out, in that sweetly suggestive way of his.

"I like being out on the open water, under the moonlit sky," Katie replied. "There's something so romantic about it, like possibilities are limitless."

She'd gotten romantic with Nate Graham in record time, even for her. But what choice had she had? Brian had bruised her ego, rushed her, all before she'd had a chance to ask him for help.

She could try again. Brian had called repeatedly, tried to woo his way back into her good graces. Was it worth it? Though she'd met Brian and Nate the same day, Katie had chosen Brian first because he seemed like the better bet. Brainy, brawny, an old-money blue blood. The type she understood, and thought she could manipulate.

But, no—Katie's mind was made up. Brian's ship had sailed.

Nate, though he'd demonstrated squeal appeal for her prepubescent campers, had stalled at number two, because he wasn't really Katie's type. Short and wiry with blond bed-head spikes, Nate had grown up here on the Cape, vaulted from high school straight into the family business, which was boating.

His family came by its money via the fleet of ferries they owned and operated all over New England, an empire that had started with Nate's great-granddad and continued to flourish under the helm of his parents, himself, and his siblings. They had docks at Hyannis, Provincetown, Wellfleet, and Barnstable Harbor and did healthy business taking tourists to and from Martha's Vineyard, Nantucket, and, of course, on scenic cruises around the Cape itself.

The vessels reserved for the family's personal use went beyond ferries to sailboats, skiffs, schooners, motorboats, yachts—all fully staffed. There was, Katie quickly calculated, quite a cache of cash at Nate's disposal. He'd do quite nicely at the keeping-up-appearances game. Aside from that, he really was a nice guy.

"Sure you want to stay outside?" Nate asked. "I think we can be pretty romantic if we go inside."

"In a little while," Katie answered. "Let's go around the tip of the Cape one more time, okay? I want to see Provincetown again."

"If that'll make you happy, Katie," Nate said, suddenly serious. "You know, don't you, you're the kind of girl a guy would do anything for. Why you're wasting your time with me, that's the mystery."

Katie softened. "You're sweet, you know, really sweet. Hey, could you bring me another drink? A wine spritzer, or just sparkling water, either one."

"Hi-yi, Captain." Nate gave her a mock salute. "But

there'll be a charge for that. You have to pay in advance."

Katie threw her arms around his neck and pressed herself to him. "What's the toll?" she asked coyly.

"I'm thinking one of your special sweet kisses should do it," he murmured.

"And I'm thinking I can do better than that," she told him, moving her hand down his back, sliding it under the waist-band of his briefs. It was a promise of more to come, though she felt secure that Nate, unlike Brian, would not push her. This beau was younger, just eighteen to Brian's twenty-two. *Vive la différence!* She didn't have to pretend to know more than she did, to have experienced more than she had.

Maybe she would sleep with him, and maybe even confide in him. Maybe Nathan Graham would give her the life raft she longed for, something for her to hold on to, to save her from drowning in disgrace along with her family.

Or maybe not. She wasn't lying when she told Nate how much she loved being out on the open water, seeing the world from the sanctuary of a private yacht. Maybe she wouldn't think about the end of the summer.

But as she waited for Nate to return, Katie stood perfectly still at the railing, letting the ocean breeze blow her long hair back. "What's gonna happen to me?" she wondered, whispering into the wind.

Mitch and Mandy
Take It Sweet and Sour

"Hey, Mandy, hold up a minute." Mitch stopped her as she sashayed out of the house, her stilettos clicking.

She waved at him. "No time, chico. My ride's almost here."

It was just past 10 p.m. on Saturday night. Both had been out all day, only returning to the cottage for a quick shower before heading out again for the night. Mitch, who'd worked late, was meeting up with Leonora, hoping to finally understand what was tearing his beloved apart. By now, he'd diagnosed severe unhappiness in his girl. But if he didn't know the cause, he had no hope of fixing it.

He wasn't sure what Mandy was up to, only that he didn't like it. Admittedly, he hadn't seen a lot of her post-party, but to his eyes, she looked more and more like a cheap . . .

you-know-what . . . every day. Tonight, she'd squeezed herself into some way-too-low, too-tight tank top that practically pushed her boobs up to her chin.

"Make some time," he urged. "Five minutes—you can spare that much for an old friend, can't you?"

Mandy snapped her gum and winked at him. "Oh, Mitchell, you always did have a way of persuading the girls. Hang tight." She flipped open her cell phone, hit speed dial, and after a few seconds, said, "Hi, Timmy-cakes—yeah, it's *moi*. I'm running a little late. Be ready in ten minutes." After listening for a second, she added, "I'm always worth the wait, aren't I?"

Suddenly feeling like an eavesdropper, Mitch cleared his throat. "Sounds like someone you care about. I'm happy for you."

She regarded him warily. "Care about? Yeah, I'm a regular Care Bear. Especially tonight, since he's taking me to the *Skinny Dipping* set!"

"The *Skinny Dipping* set?"

"Yeah, that new movie—haven'tcha heard about it? It's got Jude Law, been filming over on Martha's Vineyard. Timmy's the best boy."

Best boy? Mitch scratched his chin. He'd never heard Mandy refer to anyone that way.

She threw her head back and laughed. A cascade of brassy red curls caught his eye, and instantly took him back to the time when those ringlets were strawberry-blond pigtails, and this overly made-up woman a chubby, bright-eyed girl named Sarah.

"You have no idea what I'm talkin' about, do you, Mitchell? You don't know movie-speak."

He flushed. "Educate me."

A "best boy" described Timmy's job, not Mandy's feelings about him. Those pretty much began and ended with his contacts. "Timmy's friend is the still photographer on the set. D'ya know what that means?

"Not the cameraman, but the guy who takes pictures of the actors?" Mitch guessed.

"A-plus for Saint Mitchell," Mandy said without sarcasm. "So his name is Joe Lester, and after they wrap tonight, Tim's gonna introduce me. And," she continued, her spirits high, "if all goes well, he's gonna book time for my photo session. My first professional photo session. Whatcha think—Mandy's not doin' too bad for herself. A fat girl from the projects?"

Mitch had a soft spot for that twinkle in her eye. It had always attracted him, made him believe in her, even though he had no real reason to. The odds of Mandy Starr—née Sarah Riley—of the downtrodden Dorchester Housing Projects becoming a movie star were pretty much slim, and none.

Yet still she believed in herself. Mitch couldn't find it in himself to contradict her.

"So what'd ya want to talk to me about?" Mandy asked.

Mitch scratched his head again, uncomfortable. "Well, it's . . . I don't know. That guy, that Tim. He's been spending an awful lot of time here."

"Your point?" The twinkle in Mandy's eye had disappeared.

"Well, I just mean, how well do you even know him? Is he trustworthy?"

She bristled. "How well does anybody know anyone? As far as you or anyone in this house is concerned, he's my boyfriend. That's all you need to know. End of story."

"Whoa, slow down, Mandy. I'm just asking a question. I see him—we all do—hanging out here even when you're at work. And I just want to make sure you're okay with that."

"Just spit it out Mitch, okay? You think, what, he's gonna rape and pillage if I'm not around to keep an eye on him? Have you had this finger-wagging scolding with Alefyia? She brings home anything that isn't nailed down."

Mitch frowned. This was not going the way he'd hoped. "My concern isn't for the house. It's for you. I don't want to see you being used. Or getting hurt." There, he'd said it.

The hint of a smile returned to her freckled face. Tenderly, Mandy cupped his chin. "We're not in Dorchester anymore, Mitch. You're not the cops and you don't have to protect me anymore. We've both come a long, long way. So trust me, okay?"

Impulsively, he hugged her. "Take care of yourself, Sarah."

She pulled away. "Right back atcha, Mitchell. Sometimes I think it's you who needs taking care of."

Mandy always did have good gut instincts. Mitch was very not okay. And he could not, for the life of him, figure out why. Okay, the summer had gotten off to a shaky start, but he was proud of the way he'd adjusted, put together the house share. That was something. It showed versatility, adapting to adversity. It showed he was resilient, strong, a leader.

They were just the attributes a girl like Leonora admired, needed, wanted. The qualities that would make him the husband she deserved, the father of her children, if all went well.

And the fact that he loved her desperately, would do anything for her, forgive anything. Didn't that count? So what had changed?

The night of the party, he'd called Leonora—not to ask for her father's help. Anything but. He was his own man, and if he had to be held accountable for the damage, so be it. At least no one had been injured, or gotten really sick or anything. When Leonora immediately offered to have her father call the county police commissioner, he told her it wasn't necessary. But she kept pressing, insisting she let Mr. Quivvers help. And Mitch interpreted: Leonora wouldn't want her future husband to have a black mark on his record. Only because it meant she still loved him, still cared about their future together, had he swallowed his pride and allowed himself the benefit of Lee's well-connected dad. For her sake.

It hadn't changed Lee's attitude toward him. Still, she ran hot and cold, overly solicitous one minute, the next, pushing him away. He hadn't told any of the house share people about his Lee issues. Which made it all the weirder that Harper kept obliquely referring to it, slipping in snide comments like, "Have you ever considered you'd be better off without Leonora? Maybe you should rethink this. Relationships all go sour."

Inserting herself in his love life was so inappropriate, Mitch reminded her, sometimes really angrily. For a microsecond he wondered if she was into him, and therefore jealous? But any nincompoop could see how she looked at Joss. Nah, not jealousy. Then what? From what he'd gathered, Harper's meltdown at the party had something to do with a cutting remark from Katie. About a boy who'd obviously broken Harper's heart. So maybe that was it.

What ate at him wasn't Harper, though. It was just now, the look in Mandy's eye when she told him to take care. Was there something she intuited he should be mindful of?

Mitch finished shaving, put on a clean shirt, khakis, and Docksiders, and banished Mandy from his mind. He checked beneath his mattress for the envelope and carefully counted. The engagement ring fund was now just past the $5,000 mark. Just another few weeks, that was all he needed. Once she saw that sparkler, dude, he was there. Reassured, Mitch locked up. He resolved to redouble his efforts with Lee, no matter what it took.

Harper and Joss:
Treble in Paradise

"Rockin' night!" Joss exclaimed, looking up at the sky. He breathed in deeply: The stars winked at him, the salt air filled with heady promise. And all he wanted was for the night not to end. He'd just treated Harper to her first authentic Cape Cod experience: oysters, onion rings, and beer, sucking in the sea breeze, gazing out at the ocean. It'd been awesome. Once they got past her stammering apologies-slash-gratitude about the party; once he finally told her, yeah, he grew up in New York, too, they grooved. Just as he knew they would.

She'd lived downtown, in TriBeCa, she told him, had gone to the Little Red Schoolhouse on Bleecker Street, and had grown up an independent, strong little kid raised by an extremely cool single mom. While Joss stopped short of telling her he'd grown up on the Upper East Side, attended pricey private schools, and grown up a sheltered little rich kid, with a Donald Trump–like, only-worse, father, there was enough of a common vibe to keep them laughing, reminiscing, connecting. And for the first time in eighteen months? Damn, he missed the city!

When they reached the car, he asked, "So, where to now? Dancing? Movies? Sports bar? Minigolf? Night court?"

"Don't quit your day job," she quipped. "You are so not the last comic standing. You know where we both want to go."

She wasn't suggesting—?

Harper crossed her arms, amused. "While slurping down oysters, have we not been ogling the most amazing beach ever?"

Joss grinned. "That was my next idea." Dude, it'd been his *only* idea, from the moment he'd found a hapless Harper in the kitchen, distracted by her woes, almost burning the place down. He wanted to rescue her, wanted to take her here, cradle her on the warm sands of the beach.

"So, there's a path down there," she said. "Obviously you've been here before. Which qualifies you to lead us."

Girl was right. Joss knew where they would go, how to get there, and what he needed to bring. He flipped open the trunk of the car, retrieved his black Taylor acoustic. He'd taken this guitar down to the beach multiple times, and let the songs find him. Cheesy much? But who was he to question a creative rush, where it had begun—or why?

Harper arched her eyebrows when she saw the guitar. "A beach concert?"

Joss motioned for her to follow him. He led her down a wooded path that began at the back of the Beachcomber. It sloped downward, looped around, straightened out for a stretch, only to curve again. Without warning, Harper broke into a run, shooting down the dunes as fast she could. Joss didn't need an invite to join her, nor did he ask permission to grab her hand as they ran in step. The wind flew in their faces, Harper's hair fanned out, wild and free and untamed as the girl herself. The path became steep as it neared the beach, but no way would Harper slow the pace. They hit the sand hard, winded and laughing at their childish silliness.

At the shoreline, Harper panted and bent over, hands cupping her knees. "Dumb fun. Bummer you had to do it dragging your strings." She dug into her pocket for a scrunchie and tied her hair back.

Joss flung the guitar over his shoulder. He wondered if, by the moonlight, she could see the decals on his guitar strap. Backstage passes of the groups he'd toured with in the past year and a half. Would she recognize the one that belonged to Jimi Jones? And if she did, would she react?

Harper kicked her sandals off and declared, "I gotta feel the sand between the toes."

They meandered down the beach, following the shoreline

as it curved westward, until they came to the cove that had been his destination all along. The dune scoop beneath an overhang formed by an outcropping of rock, a cozy shelter he'd discovered a few weeks ago that had become his songwriting haven.

Joss and Harper sat in silence until he corralled his courage and began to strum the lustrous guitar. He played "Better Things," an old chestnut written by the Kinks' Ray Davies that this cover band, Babylon Sad—the one Joss had toured with just before his Jimi Jones gig—used to sing every night. It wasn't a real mainstream song, but Joss had a hunch Harper knew the words.

She chimed in: "Here's wishing you the bluest sky . . ."

Joss smiled. Not only did she indeed know all the words, she had a strong, sure voice as well. He could compare it with a Chryssie Hynde, or . . . to a female version of Harper's father. But he didn't. Instead, they harmonized and ended with: "*I hope tomorrow you'll find better things. . . .*"

Joss told her, "When I was on tour with that cover band, dude, they sang this every night. I should be sick of it. Only I'm not. It still gets to me."

"Well, sure," Harper said. "It's unselfish. It's about what you want for someone else."

It didn't escape Joss that Harper took him for an unselfish kinda guy. He kinda liked it.

Harper continued. "Anyway, that's what good music is all about. It's more than happy-go-hooky lyrics and a count-to-four backbeat. There's truth in them there words. When they hook up with soul-stirring music—that's gonna haunt you."

Josh lit up. Bingo. He'd been right about her all along. Harper Jones had inherited way more than her famous father's quirky half-smile, wiry build, sarcastic wit, and bedroom eyes. Whether she even knew it or not, she had his musical genius. It lay deep in the DNA, no escape, though Joss suspected she'd been trying, probably her whole life.

Now. He might not get another moment like this. To tell her all, not just that he knew who she really was, but to come clean about himself. And knowing that, hope she could still be into him. He was just about to spill, when Harper interrupted.

"Do you know 'The Freshman'? By Verve Pipe?" she asked.

He did, but would rather have played "Your Body Is a Wonderland," by John Mayer. However, "The Freshman" it would be. *"For the life of me I cannot believe we'd ever die for these sins, we were merely freshmen."*

And so, they music-melded, Joss (née Joshua) Wanderman (née Sterling) and Harper Jones. An eavesdropper, someone crouched on the cliff above them, would have heard snippets of songs, attempts at harmony, convivial conversation that coiled and wound around itself like a helix, punctuated with lighthearted laughter and groans of "Eww . . . cheesy!"

And Joss never got to say what he knew he ought to.

But dude, it wasn't just vocal cords and guitar chords at play here. His heart—if that didn't deserve an "eww . . . cheesy!"— *that's* what was singing.

Joss didn't dare play a Jimi Jones song. Instead, he went into a riff Harper couldn't possibly know.

Only she did. "That's an original. You wrote it, didn't you?"

"What do you think?" He looked up hopefully.

"I think"—she paused and drew a treble clef in the sand— "it's amazing. Not that it doesn't need work!"

Joss crossed his arms over his guitar. Right—let her just try to keep lying to him.

She gave it up, palms raised in an "I surrender" gesture. "So what, yeah, I'm somewhat musical. I have a feel for it. At least I know what's good when I hear it, and what sucks."

"You know more than that. You also know how to fix what's not working."

"Maybe," she conceded. "It needs a full D with a seventh for accent. There, after the A minor. Build the chorus and finish with the power chord. Right now, you got it all in minors."

Whoa. She'd been schooled, and he was more impressed than he thought he'd be.

Harper continued, "Anyway, what are the lyrics?"

She'd opened the door, and Joss blasted through. "There aren't any. I'm neither lyricist nor poet. But I know someone who is. Fortuitously, she's right here."

Harper chuckled. "And so, ladies and gentlemen, we come to 'the agenda' portion of the program."

Joss feigned bewilderment, but couldn't keep up the ruse. He didn't want to. "Harper Jones, will you write something for this?"

She pressed her lips together, dug up a stone, and tossed it toward the ocean. "Maybe I already have."

Silence.

"But?"

More silence.

Joss put the guitar down. He got it. The poem she'd written, the one that would fit this song? She wasn't sharing. "Not ready to trust me with it," he speculated.

"Not so much," Harper conceded, now drawing a wavy musical staff in the sand with her forefinger. "But don't take it personally. Trust is overrated."

"Like relationships?" he guessed.

"Dude"—Harper threw another stone toward the water—"relationships are like cotton candy: all pretty and sparkly and sugary and tempting. But the minute you take a bite, what happens? They dissolve and leave you with tooth decay. Relationships that involve trust are bad for you."

"You can't really believe that." Joss bristled.

"Can't I? What more proof do you need than the saga of the lovebird living in the share house with us? Tell me *that's* not fucked up."

Joss tensed. "You mean Mitch? He's still crazy about Leonora. So what do you know that no one else does?"

"You know it too. The difference is, you intuited it, and I saw it. I saw *her*."

Harper drew her knees into her chest. She spoke softly, recounting the scene she'd walked in on, Leonora and Grace Hannigan's father under the sheets. Joss's stomach sank lower with each word. He pounded the sand. "Oh, man! I knew somethin' wasn't cool the first time I met her. Shit, poor Mitch."

"Do we tell him?" Harper's voice was barely above a whisper. "We can't, right? I mean . . ."

Joss shook his head sadly. "No choice. We have to. It sucks that he's the one to get his heart carved up. Leonora is his dream girl. She represents everything he's worked for. Everything she offers, it's the life he wants."

"The trick," Harper said, lifting her chin defiantly, "is not to want."

No! That's not it at all! That can't be it. Because right now, Joss wanted. Oh, how he wanted. Badly. Harper Jones was the most enchanting girl he'd ever seen. She was not just stirringly beautiful, but profound, and proud, and poetic, and . . . and . . . funny! God *damn*, she was funny.

She was also closed for business—she'd just said as much. Once upon a time she'd wanted—the boy's name was Luke— and look where it had gotten her. Once burned, forever scorched. This decision, irrefutable, made at age seventeen. Joss gazed into her astoundingly light blue-gray eyes. She was melt- ingly beautiful, this "sweet child o' mine," he thought lyrically. He loved the way the little tendrils of curls escaped her every effort to tie her hair back, how they brushed her temples, framed her cocoa face. Who could hurt a girl like this? Who could rip her heart apart, so she'd never give it away again? Joss couldn't understand.

Like the tide that can't stop nature's pull back out to sea, Joss could not help himself. He pulled her close, drew his arms around her, tipped her head up, and kissed her. He wanted to be gentle, tried to be, but God, she tasted sweet. And Joss had never been this hungry.

She didn't reject him. In spite of what she said, Harper parted her lips, and at first simply let him kiss her. When she tentatively began responding, her passion, her hunger did not match his. But it was enough. Enough to let him know he wasn't stranded here in head-over-heels land, alone with these feelings.

If she would ever acknowledge them, if they'd ever share

another kiss like that, Joss could not predict. As soon as they pulled apart, they got up and retraced their footsteps back through the dunes, climbed uphill until they reached the restaurant and the car.

Joss slipped a Death Cab for Cutie CD in to cover the strained silence between them. It wasn't until they were turning onto Cranberry Lane that Joss found his voice. "Hey look, I didn't plan for that to happen, but I'm not sorry it did. It was just a very cool evening, and I got caught up in the moment, in you."

Harper wasn't even looking at him.

"It won't happen again, not if you don't want it to," he said, unconvincingly.

Still no response. He leaned over and tenderly brushed her hair behind her ear. "Just don't hate me, okay?"

Harper pointed straight ahead, to the share house. "Something's wrong," was all she said.

Violated

"I've been violated!" Mandy shrieked, jerkily stomping around her room and clawing at her hair. Hysterical and hammered, she came off more comical than convincing. "The fuckers freakin' stripped me!"

Alefiya had come flying in. The scene mirrored the one in her own room. Drawers and closet doors yanked open, their contents rifled through and flung all over the floor—even the mattresses pulled off the beds, and turned over.

Ali took a deep calming breath, as much for herself as for the drama queen. "You weren't personally violated, Mandy. It's bad karma to exaggerate."

Mandy fired bloodshot daggers at her. "They pawed through my personal belongings! Like"—she hiccuped—"animals! They took my stuff!"

"Exactly," Ali reasoned. "Your *stuff*. Not you."

Mandy ramped up her rage. "You don't get it, do you? You . . . you . . . third-world freak! They raped my room. What would you call it?"

A robbery. Because that's exactly what it was.

What it *wasn't*, Alefiya deduced, as she tried calming the caterwauling girl, was random.

It was rare that all six of them were out at the same time. Whoever was responsible for this home invasion either knew that, or had been watching the house. She shivered.

By coincidence, Ali and Mandy had returned home roughly the same time, around 1:30 a.m. "Leaf," as Jeremy liked to call her, had been out with him, plus Sharif and Lisa. After weeks of trying, the trio finally succeeded in cheering Alefiya up. She still felt guilty about the way the party had ended, but as her friends kept reminding her, she was starting to accept that her intentions had been pure and, in the end, that no one got seriously hurt, or sick, or actually arrested.

"No harm, no foul"—an expression she'd learned over the summer—seemed to apply.

More importantly, Jeremy pointed out, it was over. Time to let it go, cheer up, enjoy the rest of the summer.

Still, Ali shied away from inviting them in that night. Her once carefree *mi casa es su casa* open-door policy didn't feel right anymore. So Jeremy settled for walking her halfway up the gravel drive and leaving her with a sweet, lingering kiss. She responded in kind, draping her arms around his shoulders and holding him close. Ali knew this: Summer's end would not mean the end of them. This boy was a keeper. That's when real problems would kick in. Ali shuddered, imagining her strict father going apoplectic at the sight of the very *not* Indian Jeremy LaSalle.

It was the taste of Jeremy's full lips on her own Ali was replaying when she turned the key in the front door. It didn't click. Hmmm. Harper was the only one who'd said she'd be home tonight—so why wasn't the door locked? Harper, being from New York City, was kind of paranoid about that.

Nervous, Alefiya gently pushed the door open a few inches. Clarence streaked through her legs, and in a flash, was down the driveway and into the street.

Ali dropped her purse and bolted after him. She didn't see the car rounding the corner—only heard the sound of tires screeching to a sudden stop.

"Clarence!" she screamed. No! No . . . please . . . don't let him be hurt, she prayed, running into the street. Clarence was inches from the car, but thankfully, unharmed. Beyond grateful, she picked the errant ferret up, wondering how he'd gotten out of his cage.

Tim Johnson, Mandy's "live-in" boyfriend, was at the

wheel. Mandy, in the passenger seat, leaned out the window. "Your pet rat wuz almos' roadkill. We gotta try harder next time, don' we, Timmy-cakes?"

Mandy was drunk. Well, at least she wasn't driving—that was something. Cradling Clarence, Ali turned away and strode back to the house. Behind her, the car door opened, Mandy toppled out, and Tim drove away. Before she could inquire why Tim wasn't staying, Mandy snarled, "Wus this crap on the front lawn? Who left the upstairs windows open? What'd you do, dump your discards out the window?"

Ali hadn't even noticed the lawn, still scraggly despite her efforts to spruce it up. What was her tapestry beach blanket doing out there? And her embroidered peasant blouse? Whose sandal was that?

"Pisshead!" Mandy drunkenly blasted. "What'd you do, throw my shoe out with your garbage? That's 'n expensive shoe, you numbnut!"

Ali was annoyed, borderline panicky now. The unlocked door, Clarence out of his cage, clothes hanging out the window and on the lawn. She grabbed Mandy by the elbow. "Sober up. We better see what's going on."

Mandy yanked away from her. "Are you kidding? I'm not goin' in there."

"Then stay outside and call the police. I'll go in."

Ali braced herself, afraid of what she might find. Something had happened—oh God, what if Harper was in there?

She wasn't.

Nor was anything else.

The living room was bare; the only clue that furniture had once been there, the indentations in the carpet from the coffee tables and lamps. Unless the stuff had been repossessed or something, they'd been robbed. Big time. Ali's hand flew to her mouth, her eyes went wide. She dashed into the kitchen— same story: table and chairs, coffeemaker, microwave, gone. Only the refrigerator remained, but like the cabinets, the door was open, its contents strewn all over the floor.

Mandy noisily trotted in, calling out brazenly. "Who- ever you are, we got a rat! A poisonous big ol' rat—and we're not afraid to use him! He's got teeth! Come out with your hands up!"

Ali rolled her eyes. If Mandy wasn't so ludicrous, it'd be funny. "No one's here," she told her. "They took everything. Did you call the police?"

"They took our stuff?" Horrified, Mandy lurched toward the stairs, groping for the railing. She stumbled several times, anyway, on her way upstairs.

Mandy was on her hands and knees, wailing now as she attacked the hills of sartorial wreckage. "They took"—hiccup— "my good stuff. My lingerie! I saved up for all that stuff! Even my scrapbook." She turned her tear-stained face to Ali. "What'd they want with that? It's personal—it's my dreams. . . ." She trailed off, her nose running, and sobbed into her hands.

"It's just material possessions. They can be replaced." Ali searched for a tissue.

"No they can't!" Mandy shrieked, and ran to the bathroom.

Ali guessed Mandy, drunk and distraught, had not summoned the police, so she went downstairs to use the landline in the kitchen. She had one hand on the phone when she heard Katie come in squealing. "Oh my God! What happened in here?"

"We got robbed," Ali yelled to her.

"We got robbed?" Katie repeated dumbly. "Who'd want to rob this dump? There's like nothing worth taking."

Ali shook her head. Maybe to Katie, there wasn't—the roomie upstairs would beg to disagree. As Alefiya gave the address to the cops, she heard Katie make a decision.

"I better call Mitch."

Calling Mitch was Katie's default reaction to anything that required a responsible adult to take over. It was at that moment Ali realized Mandy had probably been right about Katie all along. She *was* underage. And more: had been sheltered, pampered, taken care of all her life. It begged the question, already asked by the others, what was Katie doing here?

Katie flipped her phone shut and reported, "Mitch'll be

here in a second. He was just turning onto the block. He'll handle everything."

Ali squeezed Katie's shoulders lightly. "The damage has been done, and thank god, no one got hurt. The police are on the way. There's really nothing for Mitch to handle."

That turned out to be a really good thing. For this time? Mitch was incapable of handling anything. For the first time, in the face of crisis, their can-do den dad suddenly could *not*. Their lean-on-me hero became unhinged. Neither calm, nor cool, and far from collected, Mitch raced through the living room, directly into his bedroom, and very noisily freaked out. "My money! They stole the ring money. Every cent I've made this summer is gone!"

Ali and Katie, who'd followed, stood in Mitch's doorway, paralyzed. Just like in the other bedrooms, it looked like a tornado had touched down: The mattress had been turned over, sheets stripped off, pillowcases gone—used to haul away anything that could be stuffed into them.

Steadfast Mitch was in full-frontal meltdown, pounding the walls, screaming like a Mandy-banshee. "The bastards! The rotten, fucking bastards! I'll kill them!" He kicked the bed. "How'd they fucking know? How'd they get in? Through the fucking window?" He railed at the window, drew his arm back, and before anyone could stop him, smashed his fist through the glass.

"No! Stop it! Stop!" Summoning her prodigious strength, Ali pulled Mitch away from the window. Katie rushed to the bathroom to grab a towel to wrap around his bloodied wrist.

Mandy came thumping down the stairs. The glass-shattering commotion must have pulled her out of her personal pity-party. One look at Mitch, she sobered up. Pushing Katie aside, she barked, "Give me the towel. Let me do that."

Ali was almost impressed.

"Mitch! Get a hold of yourself!" Mandy commanded. Then her voice softened to a nurturing cajole. "Come on, honey, let's see if I learned anything from all those first aid lessons we got at the Dorchester Boys and Girls Club."

Ali registered surprise. So did Katie—for a microsecond. Then, the petite powerhouse leaped into action. "I'm getting duct tape, or whatever Mitch said he bought. All that stuff's in the bathroom, right?"

Eventually, Mitch succumbed to Mandy's ministrations, though it took all three girls to hold him down and stem the bleeding. If only, Ali mused miserably, they could have a similar effect on his psyche. Stalwart, unflappable Mitchell James Considine was falling apart before their eyes.

"You don't understand," Mitch whimpered. "How am I going to propose? How am I going to get her to marry me? My life is ruined!"

Worse than devastated, Mitch looked defeated. He sat on

the edge of the bed, head in his hands, sobbing inconsolably. There was nothing Alefiya and Mandy could do but sit on either side of him, stroke his back, and try in vain to console him.

Katie asked what no one else dared. "Why was all that cash in the house? Why didn't you put it in a bank?"

Bad move. Mitch freaked all over again. "Because, Missy McMoney-bags, I got a better deal from a jeweler who only takes cash. Not something *you* would understand! And besides, I didn't think we had anything to worry about living here—why would robbers pick this shithouse to target?!"

Mandy, Ali, and a stunned, red-faced Katie teamed up to soothe Mitch, tried to get him to settle down, until the cops arrived and they could take him to the hospital.

Such was the scene when a stunned Joss and Harper blasted in to find them a few minutes later. The sight of Mitch so pathetic stopped them cold.

Ali wiped away tears as she filled them in. "I called the police. They're on the way. I don't know what else to do."

Mandy began to bark out orders. "Finally! You managed to show up. Now make yourself useful and take Mitch to the emergency room. His hand's gonna need stitches."

With lightning speed, Joss took hold of Mitch, ignoring his distraught housemate's cries to "Let me go, you asshole! I have to get my money back!"

"Now you, Princess!" Mandy turned to Katie. "Your type

always has some prescription drugs around—go get something for Mitch."

Katie looked scandalized. Ali was about to intervene, when Mandy shrieked, "Just do it!"

Katie returned with two orange pills in her palm. "Xanax," she told Joss. "That should do the trick."

"Good," Mandy said condescendingly. "Princess isn't such a pea-brain after all." She turned to Joss. "Force him to take them. He needs sedating."

The cops arrived just after Joss left for the emergency room with a still-protesting Mitch. The Hyannis Police had sent two detectives, who went through the share house with the four girls, helping them catalog what had been stolen.

It was a long list. The thieves had been equal opportunity: They'd hauled off anything of even remote value. Aside from all their furniture, among the missing was Mitch's money, his laptop, Mandy's "designer accessories," trinkets, and, strangely, her scrapbook; Ali's embroidered silk sari—she had no idea what she'd tell her parents about its loss—and Harper's last paycheck. Joss, at the emergency room with Mitch, would fill in his missing items later; though Mandy was positive he owned several guitars, not a one remained in his room now.

The detectives repeated Ali's words of wisdom: "Just be glad no one was hurt.

"Besides," they added, "*could* be the owners of the house even have insurance. You could get the furniture replaced right away." They took everyone's statements, and copious notes. By the time they were ready to leave, they confirmed Ali's worst fear when she'd first discovered the robbery.

"No sign of forced entry," determined the young-looking detective, who'd introduced himself as MacMillan. "If you're absolutely sure the last person out locked up, then we're left with two scenarios." He paused, and let his partner spell it out.

"The thief was one of you, or it's someone with access to your keys," said Detective Ronson with a shrug. "So you gotta be asking yourselves, is anyone's key missing? Did one of you duplicate a key and give it to someone? What about the two guys you live with? One of them a little shady?"

Ali, Harper, Katie—even Mandy—said absolutely nothing.

Naturally, the detectives promised to do everything they could to find the perps and recover the stolen belongings. Before leaving, MacMillan wagged his finger at them. "Know what I think? One of you knows more than you're saying. This was an inside job."

Ali felt herself crumbling. It didn't take a sage or seer to know exactly how this was going to play out.

The Blame Game

Mitch could not look at Alefiya without glaring. He didn't bother to hide his disgust with her. Or with himself.

Saturday afternoon, he jogged along the shoreline, his bandaged right hand still throbbing nearly a week later. Damn! Why hadn't he trusted his instinct instead of convincing himself that Ali's slovenliness was just a minor nuisance? Her laissez-faire attitude was a major character flaw; he should have nipped it in the bud before it led to disaster.

Mandy had nailed it, right from the jump. But Mitch had convinced himself he wasn't judgmental like that anymore. Just because they'd grown up in poverty and the small-minded attitudes of the city housing projects didn't mean *he* still was like that. He'd gotten out. He'd earned a scholarship to Harvard, he'd evolved, he didn't make snap judgments about people based on one character trait. He was worldly, worthy of Leonora and her family, primed and poised to jump into that life, as if he'd been born to it.

And now that was gone. Slipped through his grasp like sand through his fingers. All because the money he'd put in the "Engagement Ring" envelope, all that he'd saved by living in a cheapo place, by playing janitor so he could pay less in rent, everything he'd so carefully put aside to buy his better life—all of it was gone, stolen.

All because Ali had been sloppy. He was convinced of it. How many keys had she lost? Like he didn't know Harper had replaced them. Katie had snitched.

How many keys had Ali—despite her denials—given to her "friends"? She used the place as a damn crash pad, which *he'd* tried to curtail. But Joss, the big strong silent hero, had defended her, insisted she had the right to as many guests as she wanted. Mitch wondered how Joss, who'd lost two precious guitars in the robbery, felt about Ali now?

Mitch cursed himself for not dealing with her right after the party. That's when he ought to have shut her down, kicked her out for breaking the rules. She'd have gone, too, ridden her guilt on the next bus back to Tufts.

But no, he hadn't handled it that way. He was bigger than that. Any fool knew there'd be a party; he just didn't know who'd break the rule first. When it turned out to be Alefiya

Sunjabi, he was secretly glad. By taking it all in stride, he'd shown that he bore her no prejudice, treated her as he'd have treated Katie had she invited a hundred strangers to trash their house.

Good call, he chastised himself bitterly as he finally ran out of steam, panting for breath. Schmuck.

Without the money, he couldn't hope to buy a ring. Without use of his right hand, he couldn't even work for the next couple of weeks. Let alone take on a second job, which he contemplated. So much for building the ring fund back up. Without it, what did he have to offer the ever-more-distant Leonora?

Katie knew this was Ali's fault. Unlike Mitch, she couldn't show her contempt since, comparatively, she'd barely lost anything in the robbery. Just her Vera Bradley suitcases, which the thieves probably used to carry out their booty. Which sucked, since she'd planned to sell them. But it was a far cry from having your money, your guitars, or, like Mandy, your jewelry (tacky as it was) stolen.

The cash Katie had been saving was every bit as crucial to her life as Mitch's was to his. (So were the prescription drugs she'd been hoarding, which she could totally sell.)

But she'd been cagier than transparent, trusting Mitch. She hadn't left her currency in an envelope underneath her mattress! Hello? Her Charlesworth brain was always working:

Even her oblivious mother knew that much about her.

True, the low-class losers who'd ripped and slashed their way through the cottage had come close, ransacking the closet she and Harper shared. But even they wouldn't bother with a pile of extra rolls of toilet paper—let alone, think to look inside the hollow cardboard tubes of the Charmin. All four triple-ply were stuffed with bundles of cash, every bit of what she'd earned and/or snagged from Brian had been squirreled away. She'd outfoxed the robbers.

Katie sat on the floor, legs pretzeled beneath her, and counted her cash. She was up to $3,000. She felt relieved, if not safe. She'd ducked the cops the night of the party, but the investigation of the robbery—they'd taken the names of everyone in the house—meant there now existed a police record of exactly where she was. Anyone could find her now, anyone could find the truth. The diva was in a dive, partying on someone else's dime every night, while she toiled in some drone job during the day. Not for charity or social causes, but because she needed the money.

Her parents could find her, if they wanted to. Anyone could.

Here it was, August, and she still had no real plan to escape the spiderweb, the mesh of lies her stupid parents had woven, to elude being punished along with them, for nothing she had done.

So maybe Nate? She didn't know exactly how he could help, but he was smart, as well as rich. Maybe if he understood her predicament, he'd think of a way out.

As for Alefiya Sunjabi? If Katie never saw her again, it would be too soon.

Harper stuck up for Ali. "You have no proof," she scolded Katie.

"It's circumstantial," she told Mitch.

Those two made no secret of their guilty verdict. Privately, though, as she sat on the beach writing in her journal, Harper conceded there was more than a good chance Ali's sloppy habits, and open-door policy, had indeed led to the robbery. She'd personally replaced Ali's lost keys twice.

Ali's denials counted for something, Harper reminded herself. She'd taken full responsibility for the party, had even ponied up as much of the damage-repair expenses as she could afford. If this robbery had been her fault, Harper believed Alefiya would own it.

But just because she hadn't intentionally handed her keys to one of her guests didn't mean it hadn't gone down that way. Who, aside from Alefiya, had so many random guests, anyway?

Harper gazed out at the ocean. A lone jogger stopped to catch his breath.

Mitch.

She'd lived with him nearly two months now, and stood by her first impression: J.Crew-guy was stand-up, square-shouldered, straight-laced, and . . . pure. Her heart broke, he was so misguided in his misery.

What she wouldn't do to run up to him now, take him by the shoulders, and shake some sense into him. "Dude, you should thank Ali. Good you can't buy the cheating bitch a ring. Leonora's not worthy of you!"

Harper sat still. No way could she crush him now—even Joss agreed. Now was not the time to tell what Harper had seen.

Thinking about Joss, she went back to the poem that'd go with Joss's music. She was into him, no matter that she didn't want to be. She almost wished he'd do something crappy, reveal his inner asshole.

Only, not. Joss had remained amazingly cool. He'd lost two of his precious guitars, which he so didn't have the money to replace—and yet, had not rushed to judgment, had sided with her in defending Ali.

"Hey, Shakespeare, ever thought-a writing a movie? That's where the money is."

Harper looked up and frowned. Mandy, in a barely there bikini, slinging a towel over her shoulder, plopped down in the sand next to her.

Crude, rude Mandy had been strangely subdued after the robbery, neither blaming nor supporting Ali. It had come out that she and Mitch were childhood friends—which now made a lot of sense to Harper. It explained tons about why these two opposites were so alike. And explained why Mitch's meltdown had pulled Mandy out of terminal self-absorption.

"How come you're not at Muscle Beach?" Harper inquired. "Isn't that where the daily manhunt takes place?"

Mandy slipped off her bikini top, exposing herself to the sun. "I need to get an all-over tan. My photo shoot is in a few days."

"You're not posing nude, are you?"

"Why? Ya worried about me?"

Harper found that she was. "I just wouldn't want to see you—or anyone—being exploited, or taken advantage of. That's all."

Harper was partly right about Joss. Losing his guitars *had* bummed him out, but not nearly as much as Mitch's behavior did. Joss had witnessed more than his share of meltdowns in twenty-one years, but he felt worst about this poor dumb housemate. All that pent-up good-guy rage had just spontaneously combusted! Mitch had not recovered emotionally—and he didn't even know the truth about Leonora yet.

It was Joss who went ahead and contacted the owners of

the house. It hadn't surprised him that they didn't, in fact, have theft insurance. Nor did they care to replace the furniture. The summer share clients would just have to deal. Soon enough, it was all good riddance, anyway. They should count themselves lucky the owners of the shit-shack weren't suing them!

Joss had hung up on the sleaze bags, knowing they'd be living in a bare house. The likelihood of the police recovering the stolen items was slim. Of course, he could easily replace everything—including Mitch's money. It'd mean nothing to him, really, his trust funds, all the other accounts in his name? They'd barely register the withdrawal. It would mean, of course, alerting his father to his whereabouts and risking being pulled back home.

Joss would've done it, anyway—running from that life seemed less important to him now—but if he did, he'd have to expose himself to the group. To Harper. She'd find out he'd been lying about who he was. Worse, if he replaced everything that'd been stolen, Mitch would go buy Leonora's ring. He couldn't let that happen.

Mandy was fuming. But not at Ali. She wasn't sure whether Miss Piggy had done anything or not. She simply couldn't be bothered sticking up for her. She had a photo shoot to get ready for.

Why had the thieves stolen her lingerie? What kind of sick pervs would do that? That was the big puzzle, she thought, as the sun's afternoon rays caressed her topless body. Of course they hadn't taken Alefiya's ugly, oversize garb, or Harper's ratty hippie chick rags—but why not Katie's exorbitantly expensive designer duds? Why *her* cherished collection of teddies, and thongs, and push-up bras? Why her accessories? Her jewelry had been costume, cheap stuff, but it was all she had.

Once she got famous, she thought, closing her eyes, she could afford the real things: those chandelier earrings, bejeweled belts, Judith Lieber beaded clutches, even real Manolos. Mandy licked her lips, picturing herself decked out royally. Like the outfit Paris Hilton wore, the one she'd cut out and put in her scrapbook.

Unexpectedly, a tear slid out. Why the scrapbook? It was a piece of her soul, the one thing that truly was irreplaceable. But, she rationalized, using a corner of her towel to dry her eye, the scrapbook chronicled her dreams. Once they became reality, she'd have tossed it out herself. So maybe the thief had done her a favor. Saved her the trouble.

What she didn't need was the distraction of Mitch. But she could not help herself. Mandy was worried about him. The dumb fuck was talking about taking on a second job! Like he wasn't wearing himself down as it was, doing that hoity-toity bitch Leonora's business. He told her he was think-ing of applying for a weekend lifeguard gig at Craigville Beach, soon as his hand healed.

"That, *plus* the tennis thing?" She'd been disbelieving. "What're ya, nuts? No one's worth killing yourself over, Mitch."

He brushed her aside. "You go to that beach all the time. All I'm gonna have to do is sit up in the chair and relax. No one goes in the water. Everyone's too busy hooking up."

Mandy wanted to believe that. But she didn't.

"Into each life, a little rain must fall." That was one of the meant-to-be uplifting clichés Ali's mom said to cheer her up. "The purpose of bad things happening," she'd remind her daughter, "is to make you appreciate the good things even more." When Ali was a child, she'd believed that. She was no longer a child.

It took a lot to unhinge Ali, make her question her beliefs, but the climate at 345 Cranberry Lane, the "scorn-fest," as Harper had called it, was making her come awfully close. The amount of animosity aimed at her weighed her down. It threatened to crush her spirit. She had misplaced a key here or there, that much was true. But she hadn't *given* anyone a key.

And okay, she hadn't done a background check on the few people—not that many!—who'd slept over. But Alefiya trusted herself: She was perceptive about people. Those she befriended, those she'd been generous to, were not thieves.

No way was the robbery her fault.

Not one of her housemates believed her. Some were open-faced hostile; others said things behind her back. Didn't matter. She knew they all blamed her. The words "We want you to leave" had not been said aloud, but it was all over Mitch's face. Of all the share house people, his contempt was the one she could bear least. When a week had gone by and the anger toward her had not abated, she seriously did consider packing up and going home early.

Jeremy talked her out of it. "What if we search and dig up the missing keys?" he'd suggested. "If they're in the house, which I bet they are, maybe the others will at least *consider* it wasn't your fault."

Ali didn't think that would help.

The next day, Jeremy had done the oddest thing. He'd arrived at the share house with a lantern. Ali was bewildered. "If you've come to help me search for the keys, a flashlight might work better."

Jeremy set the lantern down on her dresser and recited: "'From falsehood lead me to truth, from darkness lead me to light. . . .'"

Ali's hand flew to her mouth. A direct quote from Hindu scripture, usually recited on the festival of Diwali, on which people lit rows of lamps along walkways and gardens.

Jeremy blushed. "It's a little early for your holiday, but I thought maybe you needed this now."

The glow, from deep within Alefiya's soul, was brighter than a block of lanterns.

Happy Birthday, Katie!

"Surprise!" Two voices, a guy's and a girl's, rang out, accompanied by the sudden opening and shutting of the screen door.

Katie froze. Sunday afternoon, she, Harper, and Ali had joined forces to clean the kitchen, since Mandy was primping for her shoot, Mitch was at his weekend lifeguard gig, and Joss was still asleep. An uneasy truce had been reached since the robbery three weeks ago. Ali had found the missing keys. It had not convinced anyone of her innocence.

"Sur-PRISE!" The tandem voices again, coming from the living room now.

Katie, in scraggly cutoffs and a baseball cap, had been sponging off the stove. Harper, in overalls, was cleaning the refrigerator shelves, and Ali, in a long boy's T-shirt, had just started sweeping the floor.

"Anybody home?" the female visitor called out as two sets of footsteps came closer.

Katie knew the voice all too well. Her heart lurched. It was at that moment she truly realized how much she'd missed Lily McCoy, who had materialized, out of the blue, willowy, tan, toned, absolutely beaming—right in the kitchen archway.

Lily had arrived neither alone, nor empty-handed. A tall, angular hottie, blond hair brushing his forehead, was at her side, holding a huge Ziploc bag of live lobsters in one hand, a bottle of Cristal champagne in the other.

Lily herself was decked out in a Marc Jacobs mini, matching tank top with designer shrug. She carried a Dooney & Bourke clutch as her armpit accessory, and swung a plaid Burberry shopping bag in front of her. "Happy Birthday, Katie!" she sang out, running to embrace her. "I missed you so much!"

Katie stood rigidly, allowing Lily to hug her (while the swinging shopping bag grazed her butt). She let the soaking wet rag in her hand drop to the floor (instead of staining Lily's half-cardigan top, like she should have done).

Lily backed off and tilted her head sympathetically. "I know I'm not your favorite person right now, but best friends do *not* let birthdays go uncelebrated."

Katie murmured, "Best friends don't abandon each other for—"

"This is Luke," Lily said brightly, her arm snaking around

the cruelly thin (for a guy) waist of her boyfriend, the guy she'd deemed her "better offer." Lily started to say something about "It's time you two met" when, jarringly, a pair of earsplitting noises rocked the house.

The refrigerator slammed shut and with such fury, the bottles in the door crashed into one another. At the same moment, the Cristal champagne smashed to the floor along with the bag of lobsters. Everyone jumped.

That's when Katie realized, to her horror, that Harper was right there.

And when Luke learned, to his horror, that Harper was right there.

The exes stared at each other, Harper's eyes full of fury, Luke's wide with the fear of the guilt-ridden.

Ali stared at the floor. The lobsters had crawled out of the bag.

Lily stammered, "What's going on? I don't get it."

"You wouldn't," Katie practically spat. "It involves human emotions."

"Harper?" Luke advanced toward her. "What are you doing here?"

Harper pressed her back against the fridge and raised her palms defensively.

Ali, now clutching a lobster in each hand, inserted herself between Luke and a quivering Harper. "I don't know who you are," she said, not unkindly, "but I get the sense that Harper doesn't want you coming too close. Maybe you and your friend should visit with Katie in another room."

"Harper, I'm so totally sorry—" Katie began, but Ali shooed them out. "Give her a chance to get herself together," Ali whispered. "I'll clean this mess up—call me if you need support."

"Thank you," Katie managed to whisper.

"What happened to all the furniture?" Lily asked, surveying the bare living room. "Is it out being cleaned or something?"

"It's just out," Katie answered.

Settling herself on the only place to perch, the low fireplace mantel, Lily crossed her long legs and patted the cold stone for Luke to sit next to her.

Like a well-trained puppy, he obeyed.

"Well," Lily exhaled dramatically, "that didn't go exactly as I'd hoped."

"Lily, what are you doing here?" Katie hissed, standing over her. "And how could you bring . . . him? Well, I guess neither of you knew. . . ." Katie sighed. Luke squirmed guiltily.

Lily widened her eyes, affecting a wounded look. "I want to make up, Katie. You haven't answered a single one of my calls, my e-mails, texts—nada. You act like I don't even exist."

You should have thought of that two and a half months ago, Katie thought bitterly, her hands on her hips.

"It wasn't exactly easy to find you," Lily complained, "just so you know. I went through a lot."

Not easy? Katie thought. It *would* have been impossible if not for the robbery and, probably, the big mouth of Taylor Ambrose.

Lily whined, "Who is that girl, anyway, in the kitchen? What's her saga?"

"Harper." They said it together—Katie angrily, Luke still in shock, softly.

"Her name is Harper Jones," Katie said, "and in case you didn't get the subtext of the little drama, she and your boyfriend used to be involved. Very involved. Very recently."

Luke coughed self-consciously, unsure if he should confirm, deny, or bail.

"Fine." Lily brushed her lustrous hair back. "Now I know her name. But I don't know why your thong is in a knot. I'm not some villain."

Katie stared at Luke. It wasn't hard to see what Harper had fallen for. Luke Clearwater was obviously of mixed heritage. As in Harper's case, it worked. Luke's full lips, high, wide Johnny Depp cheekbones, and slight build hinted at an American Indian father (as did his last name). His height, swimming-pool-blue eyes, silky blond hair screamed Scandinavian. The total effect *was* admittedly doable—if you were into the whole soft-spoken sensitivity vibe.

So what was Lily was doing with him? Lily was all about status conquests, jocks who rock, studs with style, popularity princes, and, lately, older guys just to piss off her parents.

What Luke saw in Lily? Duh. Katie herself had shouted the reason to a house full of partygoers:

Lily put out.

"I like sex, so what?" she used to justify her behavior to Katie, who had cautioned selectivity. Lily had called her bluff: "Pul-eeze. Sex is currency with you. You'll give it up, but only when you can get something you want badly enough in return. I'm not calculating like that."

Katie suddenly felt stupid standing over the treacherous twosome. She settled on the floor against the wall and folded her arms. She spoke to Luke. "You never told Lily about Harper?"

Lily spoke for him. "Luke might've mentioned it. Did you, sweetie?" Lily ran her finger along his thigh. "If he said her name, it totally didn't register. It's not like she's someone I even knew."

Katie's stomach twisted. Once, she would have said the same exact thing.

"Anyway, how were we supposed to know she was here? It's not like you gave me a clue," Lily challenged.

She had a point, Katie supposed. Still, the damage was done. Katie couldn't imagine what Harper was feeling right now. But her heart went out to her roommate.

"So would you like us to leave?" Lily posed the obvious question.

The sad truth was that Katie did not. She'd missed Lily desperately, their friendship, their "best of breed" lifestyle. That's what she was fighting to hold on to! That's what this summer was all about. If not for the Luke/Harper complication, she might have welcomed the olive branch visit, after a few grumbling minutes forgiven Lily, even asked for her (belated) help. Katie's capacity for holding a grudge just wasn't that large. Not unless there was something to be gained by withholding.

Lily saw Katie caving. "So how ya like being seventeen so far?"

Katie grimaced. "I barely noticed the date." Which was a lie. Being alone (and still poor!) on her birthday made her sad, so she'd chosen not to think about it. If Plan A had panned out, she would've bagged a kick-ass boyfriend with cash and cache by now, would've worked out a way to recoup her old life, secure her future. There would have been a reason to celebrate.

Lily nudged the shopping bag at her feet toward Katie. "Don't you want to see what I got you?"

Before Katie could answer, Luke rose. "I'll go hang in the car. Probably better if you two talk without me."

Lily sprang to her feet and wrapped her arms around his

neck. "You don't mind, baby? You are sooo sensitive!" She kissed him openmouthed, way more suggestively than the scenario deserved. It was a very Lily moment.

"You want to know what I'm doing with him," Lily declared, like that was the most important of the million things on Katie's list.

"He's hardly your type," she acknowledged.

Lily smiled wickedly. "Oh, but he *is*. I'm in a new phase, and he's just so young and delicious. So . . . mmmm . . . innocent. So *summer*. Y'know?"

Katie did, nauseatingly. Lily had lured this boy, was toying with him, playing the bad girl to his adoring naïf/virgin. She was test-driving a new power role, nothing more.

"I'm teaching him everything he needs to know," she confirmed with a wink. "It's so fulfilling. And—bonus: He writes me love poems."

"You're going to dump him after the summer," Katie stated.

Lily shrugged. "He goes to Boston Latin. Public school. What do you think? And don't go all righteous on me. Denial does not become you—you'd do the same exact thing."

Katie reddened. "I have something more serious on my mind just now. Hello? Do you even remember why I'm here?"

"Of course I do."

"Then how could you just leave me stranded like that? And then, show up suddenly, expecting me to forget all about it?"

Lily shrugged, and pulled a cigarette from her bag. "Don't put me on the defense, Katie. You know it doesn't work with me. Luke showed up at my door one day, delivering pizza. And what can I say? You saw him. It was lust at first sight. And the . . . ahem . . . heart"—Lily patted her heart, but cast her eyes in a more southerly direction—"wants what it wants."

"That's your reason for abandoning me? You wanted to get laid?"

Now it was Lily's turn to pump up the volume. "How long have we been friends, Katie? And when, during the entire duration of our friendship, have we not put guys ahead of our plans? It's unspoken, but it rules: A hookup with a guy trumps plans you had with a girlfriend. I thought you'd understand."

"I didn't just hear that, Lily, because if I did, I don't even know you. This is not the same as canceling a trip to the mall for a hookup. There's a little more at stake here."

Lily leaned in toward her. "Don't push this, Katie."

"Don't *push* it? Consider yourself shoved. How could you turn your back on me like that?"

Dramatically, Lily lit her cigarette and inhaled. On the exhale, she said, "Maybe I gave your whole situation some thought. And maybe I realized that this summer, this whole getting-out-of-Boston thing was all about you. All about

The Kick. And not for nothing, Katie? Maybe I got tired of being 'The Side Kick.'"

Katie gasped. She'd never known Lily was jealous of her. And that envy had led her to screw Katie the very first time she really, really needed a friend.

Katie sprang to her feet and yanked the cigarette from Lily's grasp just as the girl was exhaling, causing a coughing fit. She threw it into the fireplace.

Lily recovered quickly. "Look, I know you think your life is about to be over, your dad's business dealings and all that. But hello? You're Katie Charlesworth. I knew you'd figure something out. With or without me, you'd deal. So it's not like I was worried about you."

Katie thought her head would explode. She'd wanted to know how Lily had found her—had someone blabbed?—but at that moment, she was too enraged to care.

"Anyway, I really thought you'd have forgiven me by now," Lily said softly.

Katie barely heard her; she was screaming now. "How could you have the gall to think I would forgive you? You walked out on me the first time something serious in my life happened. After promising you would help. You swore! And you changed your mind, left me flat, because all this time you've been jealous of me? Impeccable timing, bitch!"

Oh shit, Katie was crying. Bawling.

Harper Hears Some Tuff Truths

Harper's brain curled up into a fetal position. It would not allow her to process what she'd just seen. Unfortunately, she couldn't erase it either.

Luke—her Luke.

With Lily—Katie's bff Lily (*that* figured).

Luke and Lily, together as a couple, at the share house. Her hideaway.

After slamming the refrigerator, she'd fled, raced out the back door, down the beach to the water's edge.

Back in Boston, the awful day Luke had told her he'd found somebody else, Harper believed that if she saw him and his new "soul mate" holding hands and swapping saliva, the sight would send a knife to the heart. A pain so deep, death would be welcome. So she'd left Boston, avoided any possibility of running into them. Apparently, escape wasn't in the cards.

But a funny thing happened on the way to death-by-heartbreak, or maybe it just happened on her sprint from the house to the beach: She didn't die. She didn't even feel like dying. She'd seen her ex, she'd taken in Lily's skinny arm coil around his waist, and yeah, it reminded her of the way she and Luke used to walk with their hands slipped into each other's back pockets. That sight alone should have *flattened* her. But here she was, still standing. Digging her toe into the muddy sand, kicking it into the water.

She could breathe just fine. She could breathe *fire*.

Harper turned her back to the water and stalked toward the house. She needed a word with Luke, a little face time. She needed to barge right in on their reconciliation scene, Katie's and Lily's—and yank the boy away. "You don't mind if I borrow him?" she'd ask, not intending to wait for an answer.

Somehow, some way, Luke was going to give it up, explain to her what went wrong, why exactly he'd dumped her. What had she done to make him leave without warning, to render undone everything they had together?

And for Lily? How had this spoiled superficial bitch become his soul mate, his muse, forcing him to discard Harper like some crumpled-up verse that'll never be a poem, that isn't working?

It almost didn't matter what he said, she reflected, stomping onto the backyard deck. Just getting him to admit he'd shafted her was enough—and that the reason could *no way* have been sex. That would be just so trite, such a cliché! The Luke she knew and adored was just deeper than that; their relationship had meant so much, hadn't needed sex to prove it.

Harper had her hand on the back doorknob when she stopped suddenly. There was music playing. Norah Jones's jazzy romantic song: "Come Away with Me." The song had been this huge hit, could've been coming from any radio, anywhere. But Harper knew exactly where it was coming from. This was the live version, from the CD she'd bought for Luke.

She walked around the side of the house, to where Lily had parked her gas-guzzling status-symbol Esplanade SUV. Luke was in the driver's seat, his head bent forward, fiddling with the CD player. Had he meant for Harper to hear it? Was he summoning her?

No, this was *her* deal now. She flung open the passenger door and climbed in the car. She was confronting him—not the other way around.

"Harper!" His voice caught in his throat. Good, he hadn't seen her coming. The next thing he'd do was run his fingers through his silky hair; it's what he always did when he was nervous. That much hadn't changed.

But she had. Once, Luke's lopsided smile would've sent

her reeling. Now, it just looked dumb. He mumbled, "I had no idea you were here. That was so not cool. I'm really sorry."

Not, "How are you?" Not, "I was such a shit." Not, "I've made a huge mistake, and now that I see you, I realize it." What had she expected? Harper was in shapeless, oversize cutoffs and a ratty T-shirt; Lily, decked in a sexy designer mini that left little unexposed. When she'd been with Luke, it had been a total mind-meld, the solace of true understanding of each other, combined with the rush of creating something together.

Lily offered him . . . ? Obvious, much?

What she'd needed to know only a few minutes ago— What are you doing with her? How could you leave me for her? What does she have that I don't? What did she use that I didn't?—was painfully clear. As transparent as Luke's trite little heart. Sex. All along it had been sex.

Harper's eyes flitted to the dashboard, to a piece of folded-up paper. It was familiar-looking, the orange crinkly border distinctive. Funny Lily would have the same kind of paper as her old journal. Harper's heart seized as understanding dawned. Before Luke could stop her, she grabbed it.

Some people come into your life,
and are gone forever.
Some people come into your life
and stay forever.

Some people come into your life
and leave footprints on your heart,
and you are forever changed.

He'd used . . . Wite-Out? At the top, where she'd written "Dear Luke," he'd substituted "Dear Lily." And where she'd signed it, he'd whited out her name and signed his own.

"Wait!" Luke frantically tried to wrest the poem from her. "That's not—"

Harper didn't know whether to laugh or cry.

And then she knew everything she needed to know: Luke Clearwater wasn't worth wasting any emotion on whatsoever.

Mandy's Big Break

She was shivering. It wasn't just the goose bumps raised on her bare arms and uncovered shoulders, or her fight to keep her teeth from chattering; Mandy Starr's chills ran to the bone. Something was not kosher in downtown Denmark, or whatever that expression was.

"Perfect! Oh, per-*fec*-tion, you are de-*lec*-table!" Joe Lester, the photographer Tim had introduced her to, was practically salivating as he ogled her through his camera lens. The emotion—if you could call it that—was seconded by Joe's "assistant," Skeever, who leered on approvingly. "Ain't she sweet," drooled the balding lump of lard, staring at her from the corner of the room. "Ain't she a treat."

Mandy stifled the urge to march up and drop him.

What was this mound of shit doing, anyway? Weren't

assistants supposed to adjust the lighting, futz with those umbrella-things? Or at the very least, brandish a hairbrush, offer her a bottle of mineral water, or hello, lip gloss, anyone? Weren't they supposed to be assisting? The schlub leaning against the wall, hairy belly protruding from his too-short T-shirt, was a just a pig.

"Hey, Joe," she called to the photographer, "I'm freezing. Can we take a break so I can put a sweater on? Change outfits? I brought a real cute shrug."

"Not now," he responded, his eyes never leaving the digital camera. "Can't interrupt the creative process. Now, lower the strap on your other shoulder."

For the first set of photos, she'd chosen to pose in one of her favorite dresses, a designer copy of a lime green silk and satin sheath. The color brought out her eyes, the style—fitted bodice with a layered ruffle skirt—hinted at her curves. The shoulder straps were dotted with faux crystals, and Mandy liked them just the way they were. "If I pull them down," she pouted, "it changes the whole style of the dress."

"For the better, I assure you," Joe replied cheerily. "Now, be a good girl and walk toward me. Play to the camera."

Mandy did as instructed, tilting her chin up, keeping her gait slow and steady, like a model on the catwalk.

"Nice, nice," the photographer murmured. "Now, raise the dress up on one side so we can see some thigh."

I don't think so, she wanted to say, but didn't dare. Instead, she hoisted the hem a skooch. Enough to satisfy his "creative process."

"You're a natural, you know that?" Joe favored her with a smile. Mandy tried to gauge the truth in his eyes, this skinny dude with the soul patch and longish sideburns. "You're gonna go far in this industry, I can tell."

Mandy had longed to hear those words, yearned to hear them, rehearsed hearing them, her whole life. Back in the housing project, she'd stare into the mirror. There, she saw the classy, slim beauty inside the layers of childhood fat. She'd close her eyes and hear the fawning compliments, instead of the angry arguments between her parents on the other side of the apartment wall.

"I know talent when I see it, sweetheart, and you're the real deal," Joe reiterated.

So why wasn't she tingling with delight right now?

Joe came up to her and ran his fingertip across her shoulder blade. If he noticed her cringe, he didn't show it. "You're gonna be a big star one day. And you can take that to the bank."

Skeever put in, "Listen to the man. He's a star-maker."

Mandy tried to shake the unease, and the chills. "What other stars have you discovered?"

Joe grinned and stroked his soul patch with his thumb.

"Not so sure you'd know their names—they changed 'em for showbiz—but you'd know their work if you saw it. You seen the movie *Double Trouble*? Or *Fly Me to the Moon*? Or *Ride 'Em High*?"

Mandy knew the name of every movie she'd ever seen. These weren't among 'em. Still, she tried to relax. Joe was a professional. He worked with Tim on the crew of *Skinny Dipping*, the big movie filming on Martha's Vineyard.

Tim had told her that photo gigs for aspiring actress-models were a side business for Joe. And he had connections. If these pictures came out well, he'd show them to the producer of *Skinny Dipping*, or, even better, to casting directors.

Mandy admitted, "I could do reality TV, you know, like as a stepping-stone to a career in movies."

Picturing herself as the next Bachelorette, maybe America's Next Top Model, both of which she totally qualified for, Mandy only half heard Joe respond, "Reality TV? I dunno. Videos, *that* I can promise."

The studio was sparse, very little in the way of props or furniture. A raggedy plaid couch was set against an exposed-brick wall, and an aged cracked-leather beanbag chair sat under the one window. Joe decided to pose her in various positions on and around the chair, which Skeever moved to the center of the room. After half an hour of this, Mandy was growing bored, and colder. "Any chance we can raise the thermostat here?"

Joe shook his head and kept on shooting. "We need to keep the studio chilly."

Skever put in, "Might ruin the picture if you warm up too much, y'know?"

Mandy shivered. Asshole.

World Photos was located several streets off the main drag in Hyannis and, to Mandy's chagrin, up three flights of stairs. She'd had to lug all her own changes of clothes, makeup, and hair stuff since Tim had freakin' bailed on her at the last minute, citing a just-scheduled night shoot that apparently had required the services of the best boy.

She'd whined, begged, cajoled, even offered a special "reward" if he came with her, but Tim insisted she'd be better off, less introverted without him there. Which made no sense. Wasn't she more apt to really shine with a supportive boyfriend around?

"Look, angel. I introduced you to Joe—just like you asked me to. When the pitchers are done . . ." Mandy winced. Tim had many fine qualities. Pronunciation was not one of them.

"Joe's gonna show them around to the right people in the biz. This is gonna get you started, just like we said." He learned over and gave her a kiss, and cupped her breast. "Knock 'em dead, babe. You got what it takes."

• • •

Mandy was ready to change into another outfit, even though the photographer seemed perfectly content with the lime green ensemble. Citing the need for a bathroom break, she grabbed her tote, along with a few of the clothes she'd brought, and headed to the ladies'. As she slipped out of the dress and reapplied her makeup, her cell phone went off. Had to be Tim, saying he was on his way back after all. With her free hand, she fished it out of her purse.

"Sarah?"

"Doesn't live here anymore." Mandy didn't hide her disappointment or annoyance.

Beverly Considine laughed. "I'm sorry. Mandy. How are you?"

"Kinda busy, Bev. Can I call you back later?"

"You can, but you know as well as I do that you won't. Look, Sar . . . Mandy, this is important. It's about Mitch."

Sighing, Mandy tucked the phone under her chin, freeing her hands to twirl her hair into an updo. From outside the bathroom door, she heard Joe call, "Tick tock, c'mon Mandy, we're waiting."

"I'm in the middle of a photo shoot, Bev. I'll call you when I'm done."

"I haven't been able to reach Mitch, and I'm really worried that something's up with him."

"Is that what your Spidey sense tells you?" Mandy cracked.

"Don't be cruel," Bev reprimanded her. "It's what my twin sister sense tells me."

"Sorry," Mandy apologized. She doubted if Mitch had shared the disastrous details of the robbery with his sister.

"Call Mitch," Beverly urged. "You have his cell phone, right? Just call him and tell him to call me. Tell him I'm really worried about him."

"Got the number programmed in," Mandy assured her. "I'll call as soon as I'm done here."

Joe summoned her again. Mandy checked her look in the mirror, and satisfied, flounced out. Skeever leaned against the wall nearest the exit, Joe paced the room. Neither seemed thrilled by her new ensemble.

She, however, wanted a totally different look, one that said "casual hip," in case she was being considered for the part of a teenager in a TV show. So she'd chosen low riders, accessorized with a chain belt, and a sparkly cami beneath a sequined shrug. "What do you think?"

Not much, by their dour expressions. Finally Joe said, "Ditch the half-sweater, lower the pants, and let your hair down. We'll try it."

Mandy frowned. If there'd been an actual stylist here at her session, she was sure her look would prevail. She hesitated, but Joe tapped impatiently on his wristwatch. "Time's a-wastin'. We got a lot of shots to get in."

Mandy took a deep breath and forced herself to think rationally. Who was she to act like she really knew from professional photo sessions, anyway? Wasn't like she'd ever done one before. Maybe this was exactly what they're like, not the slick, doctored-up behind-the-scenes photos in her glossy magazines. Besides, she scolded herself, eyes on the prize. She was here, tonight, for a reason. And it had nothing to do with how low her jeans were, or letch-a-lump over by the door.

"Okay, hint of a smile, now, just a tease," Joe cajoled, keeping an eye trained on the lens.

Teasing, she could do. Mandy pivoted and lavished her most excellent come-hither pose on Joe's camera. The one that whispered, "Hey, hottie. Yeah, *you*, with the paunch and the pencil holder. Hella yeah, I think you're sexy. Come closer and I'll prove it, baby."

It was a total act—well rehearsed, too.

Joe was spectacularly unimpressed. "No, honey, I didn't say turn your body."

"But you said a teasing smile," Mandy noted.

Exasperated, he sighed. "If you turn away from the camera, you miss the whole point."

"Yeah, and them points are some-a your best assets," Skeever added.

Mandy glared at him. But he only laughed.

After several rolls of film in her now dangerously low

jeans, Mandy suggested another change of clothes. "For a more sophisticated look."

Joe put the camera down and feigned wiping his brow. "More outfits?"

There was the chill again, creeping up her spine. She played it cool. "I brought, like, a dozen."

Joe scratched his chin. "Didn't Tim explain what to wear?"

Her stomach began to churn, but she swallowed her mounting doubts. Smiling brightly, she said, "I know how this works. The pictures have to display different looks, so casting agents can visualize you in a whole variety of roles. You know, like, sultry, cute, romantic, serious, comedic, tragic."

A stony silence filled the room.

Then, a sickening smirk spread across Skeever's face. "We only want one look. And you got that down pat."

Infuriated, Mandy had to hold her tongue, lest she gave this subhuman a verbal whiplash he would not forget.

Joe clarified, "You won't be needing any of the clothes you brought."

"Why not?"

"Because we're ready to get serious now. And you'll find all the . . . costumes . . . you'll need in the closet." He nodded toward a door she hadn't noticed before.

Warily, Mandy strode over to it, trying to think positive. Maybe there really were class outfits inside. But knowing, in the way you sometimes just do, that that wasn't true. A peek inside was enough to know what they had in mind.

Hands on her hips, she swiveled to face Joe. "Uh-uh. No way. I'm a real actress. All I need is a chance to prove myself. And your pictures are the first step. I thought you were professional."

"Oh, that I am, darlin', that I am," Joe agreed, cocking his head.

Mandy's heart thudded so loudly, she could barely hear herself. "Then what's with the slut-lingerie in there?" she challenged. "What's that gonna do for my career?"

It wasn't the sneer Joe gave her as much as the nauseating guffaw that belched from Skeever's fleshy throat. "Oh, ain't that a juicy one," he finally managed after he finished laughing. "'What's it gonna do for my career?'" he mimicked cruelly.

Joe was suddenly all business. "Enough. Let's not play coy here. As you said, I *am* a professional photographer. And the photos we take today will most certainly advance your career. But how do you expect to get hired if you don't show us your real talent?"

"I don't know what you mean," Mandy lied, praying he didn't see her shaking, and already formulating an exit strategy.

Joe came up to her, took her hand, and led her toward the couch. Stiffly, she acquiesced.

"There's a lot of money to be made in . . . uh . . . acting," he explained gently. "Especially for someone with your looks.

And if you let us do our job, we can help you get started." He reached out, ran his fingers through her hair. "Natural red-head, huh?"

Mandy flinched and leaped off the couch as if she'd been launched. She growled, "No way. This is so not what we agreed to. I'm outta here."

Skeever moved swiftly for someone of his girth. Suddenly behind her, in one swift motion, he pulled her camisole top down, exposing her strapless bra. Mandy kicked him—hard, and right in the crotch.

"Eee-yow!" he yelped, holding his privates. "You bi—"

But Mandy had raced across the room, was within arm's length of her bag. In which her cell phone lay.

Joe was faster. He blocked her way. "We paid for the studio time," he said sternly, "and we will need some photos to sell to recoup our investment. I suggest you finish undressing, and let us get underway."

Skeever recovered, and grabbed her elbow. "And just for that little karate kid move, you're gonna have to give us more than a pose. In fact"—he leaned in so she could smell his letch-breath—"I hear you're a cocktail waitress. I'm hungry for my *whore* d'oeuvres. Joe, here, he's entitled to the main course."

Mandy was trapped. Joe was on one side of her, Skeever on the other, going for her bra.

The door banged open, and quickly slammed shut.

All three whirled. Tim! Mandy tried to rush to him, but Joe and Skeever held her back.

"Timmy, oh, baby!" Mandy cried with relief. "They're trying to—"

With a dismissive wave of his hand, Tim headed over—not to her, but to the closet?

Mandy was dumbfounded. Was she hallucinating? Why wasn't Tim coming to rescue her? Why was she still in the vise grip of the tawdry twins?

And then Tim, her supposed boyfriend-slash-hero, did the weirdest thing. He pulled something off the hanger and held it up. "You look good in this. Put it on."

Mandy nearly passed out. It was her teddy. Her black, lace-up teddy. Which she'd paid a week's salary for, which had been . . . oh shit . . . stolen. In the robbery. Mandy's stomach sank, and she started to hyperventilate. This couldn't be happening.

Tim balled it up and threw it at her. "Catch."

"Why are you doing this, Tim?"

"To help you, baby, of course. You want a career, don't you? You think porn stars are born? Course not. They have to work hard for the money. You like working hard—I know that from experience," he snickered.

The color, what was left of it, drained from Mandy's face. A voice played in her head: Mitch's. "You're an actress: so *act.*"

She might not get an Oscar, but if she succeeded, she might get away unharmed.

Game on.

Mandy forced herself to laugh. "Um, well, okay, I guess I do understand now. I mean"—she faced Joe—"Now that Timmy's here, I guess it's all right. He's my man. . . ." She nearly vomited, saying that. "And he knows what's best for me."

She must've been better than she thought. Joe and Skeever let her go. And Mandy shimmied into Tim's arms. Pressing herself against him, she whispered in his ear, "You should have told me, baby. This whole thing took me by surprise."

"You never were the brightest," he said testily. "Now go be a good girl, pick up your Victoria's Secret special, and put it on."

At that moment, Mandy knew that if she ever got the chance, she would kill him. And it would not be a pretty, or easy, death. She retrieved the teddy, fetched her tote bag, and flounced—practice made perfect, after all—toward the ladies'. "Be right back, gentlemen."

"Not so fast." Joe's voice. "You won't be needing your bag in there. Hand it over."

Fear washed over her, but she shook it off. "My makeup's in there, I need to freshen up."

Joe rolled his eyes. "No, your cell phone's in there. Like I said, hand it over."

Mandy's legs turned to jelly. As she closed the bathroom

door behind her, she struggled to breathe. There were no windows in here. How could she escape?

Then, she spied the sink where she'd been standing when Beverly Considine had called. She'd left the cell phone on the basin top. With a silent, yet fervent, prayer of thanks to the Considine clan, she punched in the number eight: the one Mitch had programmed in for her, to reach him in an emergency. There wouldn't be much time—seconds, at most—and no question, they'd be listening outside the door. She had to be smart: she text-messaged the address of World Photos, and this: "There's three of them. Hurry!"

And then she prayed. Hard.

When Mandy emerged from the ladies' room, she did the finest bit of acting in her limited career so far. She focused, and pictured the three thugs as her audience instead of her captors. In the mirror of her mind, *they* were naked and cowering. Lowlife Joe, all pale and concave, unequipped to please a woman, no doubt. Fatty-rat Skeever wasn't hard to imagine: all blubbery, hairy, and quivering. And then there was Tim—well, she knew him well enough. He'd already exposed himself for what he was: a small-time, no-talent, double-crossing hustler.

What a trio! What a joke. If she weren't in so far over her head, it'd almost be funny. Mandy had one goal right now: distract them, keep them busy, keep them at bay. She had to give Mitch time to get there. If it meant nude pictures, it'd be shameful, but nothing to compare to the hurt they could inflict on her.

In her lace teddy Mandy went to work, not only taking the directions Joe gave her, but playfully suggesting a few poses of her own. She had to make them believe she was down with this. That she could simply adjust all her red-carpet dreams to the sleaze-fest they had in mind. It seemed to be working. Jim snapped away exultantly, and Tim and Skeever played book-end voyeurs. Each moment that passed brought Mitch one moment closer. Mandy absolutely trusted that to be true.

Finally, Joe stopped clicking away.

"Reloading?" she asked, hoping to engage him in some stalling chitchat.

"You could put it that way," he said, motioning to Skeever. "Why don't you help the little lady into her next . . . costume?"

"Or," Tim chortled, "out of it."

The thug lunged toward her, and Mandy lost it. Lost her actorly concentration, lost her cool. Just as Skeever clamped a sweaty paw over her mouth, she extended her forefinger and middle finger and thrust them harshly into his eyes—a disabling motion that allowed her to scream at the top of her healthy set of lungs.

When the door burst open, the three stooges were taken completely by surprise, and by an enraged Mitch coming at

Skeever, just like in the old days, fists first, and furiously flying.

Joss, right behind him, took on Joe with a well-placed left hook. And in a scene more surreal than when she'd been stoned and watched *2001: A Space Odyssey*, Harper, Ali, and Katie went for Tim.

"No, he's mine," Mandy cried. "Let me at the bastard."

Ali was all over it—all over Tim, that is. She sat on the skinny, squirming worm while Harper held his legs down and Katie pinned his arms.

And with all the pent-up rage of an accumulated nineteen years of feeling shafted, Mandy whaled on her betraying rat-bastard of a "boyfriend." She punched, and she kicked, and she clawed, and she cursed, and she never once let him see her cry.

And later, when the police had come and gone, when the toxic trio had been hauled off to the clinker, the housemates of 345 Cranberry Lane piled into Mitch's car and went home. After they'd pulled into the gravel driveway, Mitch asked the others, would they mind? He needed a private moment with Mandy. He folded her in his arms and allowed his childhood friend to finally break down. "Mitch," she croaked, "I don't know what I would have done if you hadn't been there."

Mandy had been humiliated in every way a girl could be, exploited, shamed, and pawed—but thanks to pluck, luck, and mostly Mitch Considine, the worst had not happened. Still, Mitch fretted over her like a mother hen. She almost laughed when he pleaded, "Will you talk to the girls, at least?" He thought she might confide in them. Right.

It was the only way Mandy could get him to agree to get some sleep—it was nearly two in the morning! So after a long, hot, cleansing shower, she sat on the floor of her room, gratefully wrapped in Ali's large terry-cloth robe, and surrounded by the other girls. Ali toted mugs of decaf tea, and a basket of what she called "comfort munchies."

Mandy searched each one of their faces: cocoa-colored Harper with the clear blue-gray eyes; compact Katie, with the little girl bow lips and mind like a steel trap; and round, dark, easy-does-it, motherly Alefiya. At various times during the summer, she'd sneered at all of them. She'd been contemptuous, she'd been downright mean. Yet when she got into trouble, every one had come to her aid. No one had said, "Screw her, she deserves whatever happens."

Had the tables been turned? If Katie, or Harper, or especially Ali, needed to be rescued, would Mandy have bothered? A lump formed in her throat. She was not about to let it stop the words from coming. "I owe you guys, big time. I screwed up."

"What happened?" Katie asked. "I don't understand how you got into that . . . situation."

Harper shushed her. "You don't owe *us* an explanation.

We're just relieved you're okay—and . . ." She paused to chuckle. "And not for nothing? You gave that asshole what he had coming. Righteous kick to the groin, dude."

The others laughed, which made Mandy tear up. "It was my fault."

"No way," Harper countered hotly. "Just because you were gullible enough to believe the photo session was on the level doesn't give anyone the right to exploit you."

Mandy focused on the threadbare carpet. "It was my fault the house was robbed."

Silence.

Finally, Ali said, "But you didn't plan it. I got there the same time as you, remember? You were completely freaked out."

"I made Tim a key," she confessed. "That slimeball. He tricked me, used me, and even left me a clue—taking my lingerie? And my scrapbook? I should have realized it was him, making fun of me all the time."

More silence.

She turned a tear-stained face to Alefiya. "I let them blame you."

Ali shrugged. "It's okay."

Mandy shook her head furiously. "It is *far* from okay. The whole summer I treated you like shit. I was such an asshole. And I'm so, so sorry."

Katie was curious. "Can I just ask, maybe this is a stupid question. But I wondered why you picked on Ali. What'd she ever do to you?"

"Simple." Ali surprised everyone by answering for Mandy. "Every time she saw me, she saw herself—the way she used to be."

Mandy's jaw dropped. "You . . . you knew that all along?"

"I knew you weren't a racist. And your body language, the way you hold yourself, the way you—"

"Preen?" Harper put in.

Katie giggled.

Mandy flushed. "I was a fat kid, a really fat kid. 'Six-ton Sarah,' they called me. Sarah—that's my actual given name," she confessed. "Or 'Fatty Fat, the Gutter Rat.' I was this little flabalanche with big dreams of being slinky, of being gorgeous, of being admired. No one took me seriously. Except—" She paused.

"Mitch," Harper finished. "You guys grew up together, didn't you?"

Mandy nodded. "Only we hadn't seen each other for years. His sister—you know he has a twin, Beverly?—ran into me at McDonald's, and told me Mitch was looking for renters for the share house."

"You didn't want any of us to know you grew up together?" Ali said.

"Force of habit. Neither of us really wants to be reminded of the circumstances," Mandy conceded. "We were raggedy housing project kids. Mitch had brains, he studied his way out. Me? Not so much."

Harper said gravely, "I have to ask you guys a question. It's really serious. It's like, if you know something that will hurt someone else, really rip their guts out, do you tell them? You know it's for their own good. If they like, live through it."

Mandy eyed her, nervous suddenly.

Ali said, "Sounds like this is about someone we know."

"It's about Mitch."

Harper inhaled sharply and unloaded. The housemates reacted predictably. Katie was shocked, stunned, disbelieving. Ali was near tears.

It was Mandy whose slow burn exploded like an earthquake. It was Mandy who went, to put it mildly, bat shit. It occurred to each of them, independently, that a restraining order—to keep Mandy away from Leonora— might not be a bad thing.

Hang On, Harper— Katie Coughs Up a Truth Ball

"Seriously, mom, I'm *fine*." Harper let her mother babble on, all the while keeping her legs moving, eyes on the narrow trail ahead of her.

"No, I don't want to come home early. I'm gonna finish out the summer. There's only a week left, and I'm not just leaving the kids at camp," Harper reminded her mother.

She was thinking of Grace Hannigan, the camper whose dad had the affair with Leonora. Her family had been ripped apart after that, and these days, Grace clung to her counselor for dear life. No way Harper could abandon the kid, no matter what. Not that she wouldn't have liked to come home, she was so over the reason she'd left. A Luke sighting would be as meaningful as a cockroach sighting.

Sometimes? She saw the benefits of not being so close

with your mom. Susan always intuited if something was wrong—and did her best to console and comfort her, which in Susan-world translated to: talking about it. Lots of talking about it.

No matter that Harper was hundreds of miles away, and could handle things on her own. Or that Harper'd had, like, enough yapping this summer to last a lifetime.

Her hair was up in a scrunchie, and the last rays of the day's sun tickled her neck. She pedaled eastward, back toward the share house. "Okay, Mom. Yeah, I really gotta go now. Bye. Yeah, love you too."

Harper pulled the hands-free earphone out and flipped the phone shut.

In the days following the stealth Luke attack, and the whole Mandy-goes-confessional-drama, Harper had taken frequent bike rides after work along the old railroad tracks, now converted to a bike trail. With each upward pedal-push, she'd chastise herself for being such a stupid little fool, falling in love with someone like Luke. With each downward push, she'd strengthen her resolve to not let it happen again. She ought to have known better. Shit, she did know better! "Won't Get Fooled Again"— wasn't that the classic Who song? Right on, bro.

As for Joss Wanderman? He'd arrived in her life bearing gifts of music, gifts of the soul. Sucks for you, dude, she thought. You're not getting in.

Cutting out after work served a purpose beyond a mind-rewind. Harper got to keep her distance from Katie, who was like an annoying Chihuahua chasing the bottom of Harper's pants. Katie just kept tugging at her, trying to "explain things."

Explain my tush! Like she cared to hear why Katie had really lashed out at her, why she'd allowed the backstabbing Lily to visit. She and Katie had coexisted all summer, even pulled together to help Mandy. They'd return to Trinity, and Katie would probably go back to treating her like she didn't exist. That'd be fine.

By the time she returned to 345 Cranberry Lane, the sun had set. Neither Mitch's nor Joss's rental car was in the driveway. She hoped Katie, still dating Natey, might be gone for the evening too.

No such luck. Instead, she found her roommate the only one home. Perfect time to pounce, which the platinum princess took full advantage of; woeful doe eyes included, free of charge. "Please, can we talk now? You have to believe me, Harper. I had no clue Lily would show up—let alone bring Luke!"

"Whatever." Harper wheeled her bike through the kitchen toward the basement door.

Katie followed, even as Harper guided the bumping two-wheeler down the steps. "You have to understand," she whined, "Lily wasn't supposed to even know where I was! I've been ignoring her phone calls and texts all summer. I didn't want her, or anyone, to find me *here*."

Harper nudged the kickstand, set the bike against the wall, and tried not to be intrigued by that last little nugget. Too bad she actually was, and Katie caught on quickly.

Besides, she was hungry, and intuitive Katie flipped open her cell phone and—before Harper could decide what to do—was saying, "Is this Mystic Pizza of Hyannis? I'd like to order a large pie, half veggie, half pepperoni, a Dr Pepper, and, hold on." She turned to Harper. "What do you want to drink?"

A half hour later, the two sat cross-legged on the living room floor, hunched around two upside-down wooden crates Joss had brought home that served as the coffee table.

Still, Katie used silverware to daintily cut her pizza slice into bite-size pieces on a real plate. Harper eschewed utensils, just folding a slice whole and devouring it, letting the cheese drip where it may.

"So, look," Katie said, "what I'm about to tell you is very, very private. You have to swear you won't tell anyone."

Only because she was mid-chew did Harper not retort, "And yet? I'm willing to bet it's very, very superficial and insipid." Wiping her mouth, she went with the gentler, "So why are you sharing now?"

Katie hesitated. "Maybe I care what you think of me."

Right. Maybe George W. Bush will learn to pronounce "nuclear."

"And maybe," Katie continued, sipping at her soda, "I care that you got hurt because of me. Is that so hard to believe?"

"Pretty much," Harper acknowledged, slurping spring water from the bottle.

That wasn't entirely true. Even *she* had to admit Katie'd displayed some true grit, especially that night they all schlepped to that godforsaken warehouse to rescue Mandy. Being a stuck-up Boston blue blood hadn't sucked up her soul. Not entirely, anyway. Still, Harper was wary of Katie's confession motivation.

"C'mon, cut me some slack. If I explain stuff, maybe you won't hate me so much. Besides . . ." Katie drew a breath and closed her eyes. Like even she couldn't face what she was about to say.

"Yeah?" Harper prompted.

"I could use a friend. I don't seem to have very many."

Harper knew she should just shut up and let Katie vent. Sarcasm trumped manners. "What about Lily-the-boyfriend-slayer? Is the vapid vixen no longer on the VIP list for your debutante ball?"

"Harsh." Katie's voice broke.

What? Katie, on the verge of . . . an actual tear? Harper would not have thought her capable. Pinched by a twinge of guilt, she concentrated on her pizza slice.

Katie's eyes misted. "For one thing, there probably won't be a debutante ball."

The crust nearly flew from Harper's mouth. It was all she could do to keep from bursting out laughing. Oh, no! Poor Katie-pooh. No deb ball? This was The Kick's big trauma?

"I don't have any money. I'm not sure there's enough to make it through Trinity next year."

Intriguing, thought Harper. "Okay, I'll play. Where's all the moolah? Mom and Dad cut you off or something?"

A tear slid from Katie's manga-like eyes. "Not Mom. She doesn't even know."

"Know what?"

Katie pushed her plate away and cut a glance toward the door. "My father made some bad deals at the bank. He's being indicted for fraud."

Whoa. Serious stuff.

"When it happens," Katie continued, "it's all over. The money will be gone, the house seized, everything—my trust fund, college savings—my credit cards totally cut off. It'll be very public, all over the TV. Everyone will know."

Harper lost her appetite suddenly. Is that why Katie-bird had ended up in this dump? She asked, "Is it going down this summer? Is that why you're here?"

Katie tensed. She swiped her plate off the makeshift coffee table and started to get up, but changed her mind, set it down. "It hasn't happened yet. My parents are on a cruise, and Lily told me the staff is still running the house. I don't know when it's going to happen, only that it will."

It's like, thought Harper, when you blink your eyes and everything blurry turns painfully sharp and clear. Like a code unscrambled, a stuck-between-stations radio dial finding a clear signal, a missing puzzle piece found. A picture formed, neither pretty nor cool, and least of all "Kick-y."

Katie lifted her chin. She didn't appreciate being pitied. "This was supposed to be my summer to deal, to salvage my life. With Lily's help, I would've figured something out. I'm sure of it."

Ouch. One-two punch. First her dad blindsides her, then her flinty friend bails. Harper almost felt sorry for her. No wait . . . Harper *did* feel sorry for her.

Until Katie answered. Harper's carefully worded, "I'm not doubting you, but how can you be sure of all this?"

Turned out—hello!—to be the way Katie uncovered all sorts of dirt, including how she knew the history between Luke and Harper. She spied, eavesdropped, read people's journals, and in this case, hacked into her dad's private computer files. "My whole life is over," Katie whined.

To Harper? It seemed like Katie's *parents'* lives were, in fact, the ones taking a dive. Katie wasn't thinking about them. All she cared about was resuming her rockin' life as queen bee of Trinity High. The imminent downsizing of her social-slash-economic status clashed with her life plan.

So, ladies and gentlemen, Katie-acolytes of all ages, mused Harper, we can do the one thing The Kick cannot do: hack it when reality bites, when the going gets genuinely tough.

Katie was trying, though.

She detailed Plan Awesome for Harper. While living the high life in Lily's aunt's freebie mansion, they'd be piling up coin, earned by the counselor job, tips, plus what Katie could scam off rich boyfriends. If "the fraud thing," as Katie called it, didn't go down anytime soon, she could make it through most of her senior year at Trinity, head held high. No one in school would be the wiser.

Then, she could split, pay her own way to college if she had to, and not be around when shame came down on the House of Charlesworth.

And if it happened before high school graduation? Maybe, Harper offered naively, Katie could get a scholarship, financial assistance for senior year? The school, she knew well, was generous with that sort of thing.

Katie was shocked, stunned, furious at the temerity of the suggestion. "Are you kidding? Are you insane? Me—an object of pity? People looking down their snooty noses at me? What are you thinking?"

Harper was thinking that karma was real. That Katie had

spent the past three years sneering at "pitiable" people, at the losers, the feebs, the "fringe." She could dish it out all right, but the prospect of being on the other end was unfathomable. This wass the petty world Katie had created at Trinity, or at least perpetrated. Harper thought this was pretty much justice.

But Harper wasn't dumb enough, or mean enough, to say that to Katie's face.

Katie whined on mournfully. "Our house is as good as gone. If it happens while I'm at Trinity, I'll have to go live in some apartment or something. And everyone will know."

"So, that'd be the worst of it?" Harper dared inquire, picturing the cozy crib she and her mom shared.

Katie's face got very, very red. "What part of all this don't you understand? I will not have my entire life ruined because my stupid father turns out to be a thief! I've worked too long and too hard. I deserve the best clothes, the best crowd, the best"—she fumbled, pausing to think—"accessories!" she finally blurted.

Harper was astonished. You really could not overestimate Katie's superficiality.

Warming to her subject, Katie's whining intensified. "I deserve to make my debutante ball, to wear Vera Wang to the prom, to show up with someone worthy, in college and rich, like Brian or Nate. This is my senior year! I refuse to let my parents' shame be mine."

Snap! *That* was the moment Harper stopped feeling sorry for Katie. She had to ask, "What about your mom? She knows nothing?"

"She lives in perma-denial." Katie waved dismissively.

"So you'd just abandon her? When the thing goes down, you'd skip out?"

"Maybe I can rack up enough credits to get into college early—or something—I am so outta that scene. Whatever it takes, really."

"Your mother would be alone," Harper couldn't help pointing out. "It doesn't sound like coping is her strong suit."

Coldly, Katie responded, "She's never had to cope. She's all about the lifestyle, and it hasn't failed her."

"Knock, *knock*!" Harper said sharply, banging her fist down on the crate. "Mirror, mirror on the wall, who's the most deluded of them all? You have no respect for your own mother, yet you're all about following in her Manolos. Socialite, heal thyself!"

"You're mocking me?" Katie challenged. "You think this is some trite thing? You think it's no big deal?"

"That's the saddest part, Katherine. I think it *is* a very big deal. And the way you're reacting to it? Makes you as shallow and self-serving as any human being who's ever pranced across the planet."

Katie's Got a Sinking Feeling

The Kick's knee-jerk reaction was to kick herself for confiding in Harper. The frizzy-haired freak wore her fringe label like some badge of honor. Katie's first impression of Harper had not changed a whit all summer.

Except for this: what Harper had said to her? It *killed*. Killed in the way only the truth can.

"Denial much?" she asked herself as she furiously scrubbed the dishes in the kitchen sink—a few were her own, but never-thoughtful Ali had left an impressive pile of pots, plates, and silverware. How sad was it that Katie welcomed even this diversion? She didn't bother putting rubber gloves on.

That was supposed to be a bonding conversation with Harper. Katie had finally decided maybe Harper could help her. Her whole confession should have drawn her quirky roommate to her side! But no! Like everything with that girl, it had turned into a confrontation. Much as Katie took pains to explain, Harper stubbornly refused to see things her way.

Okay, so maybe Katie lost her cool more than once, maybe her voice betrayed her frustration. "You don't get it!" she'd railed at Harper. "Why would you? Unlike you, I'm *someone* at Trinity. I've earned the crown of homecoming queen and prom queen. I'm going to an Ivy League school, and then I will marry very, very well. I refuse to let anything change that."

But Harper had only cracked, "So your goal in life is to become a Desperate Housewife, a total cliché."

"No!" Katie had countered, kicking the cabinet beneath the sink now. "I won't be my mother. I'm the smart one. I won't be hoodwinked."

How could she think someone like Harper would get her? No matter how much Katie tried to make her see the righteousness of her cause, Harper was like a broken record. "What about your mother?"

"What about her?"

"Don't you think she'd need you?" Harper stared with those unnerving gray-blue peepers.

"Need me? What could I do for her?" Katie had shot back.

"You could be her daughter. You could be supportive. Besides, you're the brilliant Charlesworth, you know how to cope. Why not use some of that kick-ass talent when it counts?"

Katie's bow lips formed a straight line. "Save the Disney Channel schmaltz for some naïf," she'd advised Harper. "My mother boarded her private jet a long time ago—and the cabin doors have closed. It's too late to go all 'me and mom against the world.'"

Harper just kept shaking her head. "You're a piece of work, Katie Charlesworth,"

"You think I'm horrible."

Harper's response cut. "I think you've been so busy spying on other people, you haven't taken time to figure yourself out, and what's really best for you—the real you."

Katie'd countered miserably, "You still don't understand. When it happens, I won't be able to face anyone—Lily, the kids at school."

"That doesn't matter. As long as you can face yourself. Can you?"

She stared into the sparkling clean, albeit stained and cracked, porcelain sink. That was a question Katie could not answer.

It was late when Katie returned to the share house. She'd borrowed (without asking) a pair of Harper's broken-in sneakers and had trolled the neighborhood, circled the tiny boxlike houses, noted the (eww . . .) cheap cars parked in neat drive-ways, and observed, when the window shades weren't drawn, the other residents of Cranberry Lane.

She'd never thought about them before—just random Cape Codders whose lives would never intersect with hers. Now, she was facing the possibility of being one of them. How did you even do that? Katie wondered. What do you do if you're without credit cards, designer duds, Escalades, and cool parties? How could you live in a house like this, so cramped you'd be too ashamed to invite anyone over. She couldn't wrap her brain around it.

Lily understood the terror Katie felt.

Harper did not.

Katie wasn't finished trying to force Harper to get it.

No cars were in their lame excuse for a driveway, which meant Mitch and Joss were out, but Ali was obviously home, evidenced by her pilly sweater on the floor by the staircase. If Mandy was around, you'd know it. Katie didn't hear her.

Katie marched into the room she shared with Harper, found her sitting up in bed, reading by the lamp on her night table. She'd meant to say something deep, to force Harper to understand what she was going through. But all that came out was, "What are you reading?"

Harper held the book up. *The Color Purple*, by Alice Walker.

"Any good?" Katie asked, not having heard of it.

Harper closed the book and drew her knees to her chest. "Did my sneakers fit you?"

Katie said sheepishly, "I didn't think you'd mind. I took a long walk, and I didn't have anything appropriate. Turns out we're the same size."

"Who'da thunk it?" Harper quipped. "So, what do you want?"

Katie twined her fingers and stretched her arms out. "I said I needed a friend. Why can't you just be one?"

"I assume this is your normal strategy—if you don't get what you want, or like what you hear, you just keep at it."

Katie smiled at her ruefully. "It's worked in the past."

Harper couldn't suppress a grin. "And yet? You need to be so over the past. We both do."

Katie smiled—maybe Harper was warming to her after all. "Lily and Luke?" she dished. "Just so you know? They deserve each other. If your ex really is into her, he's headed for a crash-and-burn. Lily's wicked, already planning on kicking him to the curb. And if you take him back"—Katie wagged her finger at Harper—"you're a fool."

Harper widened her eyes. "Never. But—whoa, why would I take advice from you? Do you even like the guys you've been going out with this summer?"

Katie considered. "Not Brian, he turned out to be a bore.

Nate? Maybe. He's got the whole kindness vibe, and he wears it well. But I don't . . . exactly see . . . the two of us together. No matter what happens."

"So basically, you're just using him, too," Harper concluded.

"God, Harper, everyone uses everyone. How do you not know this by now?" She flung back her head, exasperated.

"I won't—can't—believe that."

"Oh right. You believe in love for its own sake. Oh, wait, didn't that get you in trouble already?" Katie gave her long look. "You're going to do it again, aren't you?"

Harper's eyes flashed dangerously. "What are you talking about?"

"Joss. You're crazy in love with him. It's totally obvious."

Harper abruptly switched off the bedside lamp. "Darkness falls. Night-night, roomie."

"There's something you might want to know about him," Katie said.

Harper flipped the light back on.

At that exact moment, a voice startled both of them. "What, Katie? What would she need to know about me?"

Katie whirled around, Harper sat straight up.

From the doorway, Joss took a tentative step into their room. "You're about to tell Harper that I'm not who I say I am? That I've deceived her?"

"What are you doing here?" Harper and Katie said as one.

"I live here, don't you remember? So go on, tell her," he goaded Katie.

From the day she'd first seen Joss Wanderman, standing in the doorway of the share house—not unlike his studied-casual pose right now—Katie knew she knew him from somewhere. It'd come to her, she'd been sure of it. And then just the other day? Two and a half months later? It had.

It was from a feature article in the society section of the *Boston Globe Sunday* magazine. About J. Thomas Sterling, one of the richest businessmen in the country, a savvy venture capitalist who'd built an empire to rival the Trump Organization. Many times married and even more sought after, J. Thomas wielded power like an ax, using and abusing it to cut down his enemies and threaten those who might be. The only reason she'd happened upon the article was that Lily had e-mailed it to her, suggesting she check out the "number-one son" in the article's family portrait. "Josh Sterling," she'd written, "*Apprentice* material, hottie, and available. Someone to meet, don'tcha think?"

The photo, maybe two years old, showed a young collegiate, conservative and preppy, short brown hair, wearing an argyle sweater under a Zegna sports jacket. Patriarch J. Thomas was smiling broadly, his arm around his son's narrow shoulders. Joss—or Josh—looked massively uncomfortable. Like he'd rather be—

"Anywhere but there." Joss was telling his story to Harper.

"That life was never what I wanted. So I split, stayed under the radar, haven't looked back."

"I take it," Harper speculated, "your father wasn't exactly down with the music thing." She nodded at the guitar Joss held.

"Not so much," Joss confirmed. "I'm the only son, heir to the throne. I'm supposed to ascend, run the organization, not haul equipment in exchange for getting to play backup for—"

"Does your father know where you are?" Katie interrupted.

Joss had been staring at Harper, trying to gauge her reaction to the exposé, but he switched his attention to Katie. "I'm sure. J. Tommy has the resources to find anyone. I'm guessing he's lying back, giving me my space—confident I'll come crawling back."

"Will you?" The question came again, from both girls.

Clutching the neck of his guitar, Joss sank slowly onto Katie's bed, the unoccupied one. "A month ago? Two months ago? I would've said never. No way, José. Keep the money, drive the limos off a cliff, I don't need any of the perks. To quote an old rock guy, 'It ain't me, babe.'"

"And now?" asked Katie cautiously. "You would go back? Did something change?"

Joss had returned to trying to read Harper's face. But she wasn't giving it up. He lifted the guitar into his lap, flicked his fingers across the strings. "A lot has changed, actually, in the past three months."

Katie crossed her legs and shifted her position. Harper remained still. She wondered if Harper hated Joss for lying, for deceiving her about his background. She wondered if Harper had been waiting for something like this, something she could use to convince herself that Joss was just another Luke, an unworthy jerk.

Joss finally said, "I didn't mean to deceive you."

An expression crossed Harper's face, and Katie read it perfectly. She was more in love with him than before!

"You didn't deceive anyone," Harper confirmed. "I think we all got to know who you really are this summer. I think that's what you wanted all along."

Deep, Katie thought. And then wondered, what now? Will Joss unburden himself and tell Harper his other big secret? The not-so-worthy one? The one Harper would find truly contemptible, and hurtful.

"There's something else you should know." Joss leveled his gaze at Harper. "Something I'm not proud of."

Katie jumped up, pivoted, and dashed from the room. He was gonna do it, stupid fool. She so didn't need to hear it.

Only, due to the thinness of the walls, the silence in the rest of the house, and—okay, if she had to admit it—her own keen interest, she heard everything.

Joss outed himself about sleeping with Mandy.

Harper outed her real feelings. Disgust, jealousy, rage. And now—the excuse she'd been looking for for cutting him off.

Joss fell all over himself explaining, apologizing, trying to make Harper understand that it had happened, and was over, before he'd realized his feelings for her. That he'd been a jerk.

Katie had to strain to hear the rest. From Harper, it sounded like, "Of course."

From Joss, it was all about, "I gave in to temptation, but then I met you. And no one tempted me after that. Harper, wait . . ."

The light went out in the room. Katie heard Joss's defeated footsteps heading away. Despite the darkness and the distance, she could absolutely read Harper's mind: close call.

She Rescued Him Right Back

Mitch's life flashed before him. Only not the way it's always described in books or shown on TV—that moment when you know you're dying. Not like a movie on rewind, or a comic book strip of halo-lit snapshots, and certainly not, as he'd heard more recently, a PowerPoint slide presentation in the great beyond, hitting on his accomplishments, defeats and goals.

He'd have chosen any of those above what was happening now! Mitchell James Considine's autobiographical death scene was coming at him as a rush of ocean waves—cold, overwhelming, disorienting, inescapable.

A scene would appear—he and Beverly, six years old, being chased by playground bullies—then, roar up in front of him like a Scooby-Doo monster with its claws extended, before simply curling in on itself and enveloping him.

One after another they came at him, relentlessly. The day his father, grizzled and drunk, kicked them out of the apartment. Mitch, at eight years old, scared and shaking, climbed up the fire escape, and snuck in through the window to let his mom and sister inside.

A moment in the puke-green school cafeteria, when third-grader Sarah Riley didn't have her food stamps, and chose to go hungry rather than let anyone know. Mitch gave her his sandwich, insisting he wasn't really hungry, anyway.

His lungs screamed and he couldn't breathe. He was so cold.

Next, the pants were too short, his red socks were sticking out, everyone was laughing at him. Splash! A wave of shame hit as he watched himself now, self-consciously crossing the stage to receive his high school diploma. He knew, but did not see, his mom in the back row of the auditorium, beaming with pride as he was named class valedictorian.

His arms strained, ached with the effort of keeping up with the waves. More were coming.

An image of his mom, returning home late, haggard from scrubbing other people's floors—the name DORA stitched to her gray uniform; the pinkie pact he'd made with Bev, swearing they'd get out of the projects, and then, from far away, another image was coming toward him. But who was that? A girl, her face blurred, because she was twirling like a ballerina, swirling around him, faster and faster, crashing down now and sucking him under.

"Mitch! Mitch! Can you hear me?"

He heard only in gasps and gurgles, "Mitch, I'm almost there!" He strained toward it, but it was too faint, and he was too far away.

"Mitch, I'm coming! Hang on!"

Who was coming? What could he hang on to?

The other swimmer! Instantly, Mitch flashed to the present. He was the lifeguard. And he'd seen someone out there, a child, arms flaying, needing him. How many times had the boy gone under? He remembered being panicked, scampering down the lifeguard post, racing into the water, and swimming out as far as he could. He thought he'd called out, "Where are you? Hang on, I'm almost there!"

He couldn't find the drowning swimmer. The boy was too little, and the ocean was too big; it was all too much. He was the lifeguard, and he was lost.

An innocent kid would die today, maybe had already. Because Mitch Considine hadn't been fast enough.

Another wave. But, unlike the others, this was just a white, foamy screen, no snapshot of his life appeared on it. This wave was far more powerful than the others, sucking him into blackness. So was this it, finally? He'd gone under for the last time.

Mitch felt a new sensation, something tough and sinewy,

yet soft and familiar. If this was death, it was more comforting than he'd thought it could be. It felt like someone's arm— God's?—strong and sure, bent at the elbow, wrapping itself halfway around his chest, locking in under his armpit.

It was pulling him, tugging him, yanking him, even . . . not down, deeper into the cold, black pit . . . but up. Pulling him back.

"No, I have to save him. I have to save . . ." Mitch wanted to say, "Stop! Forget about me, there's a child out there who needs to be rescued first." But no words were actually leaving his mouth. It was dark where he was now.

Her lips were soft, lush. Not like Leonora's, whose kisses felt like little pecks, teasing, perfunctory, always leaving him wanting more.

Whoever was kissing him now *was* giving him more— Breathing life into him.

He coughed. Blinked. He looked straight into the sun, and saw the outline of an angel, a halo suspended above long waves of copper hair. "Mandy? Is that you? Are we . . . ? Wha . . . wha . . . happened?"

He heard someone, not her, respond, "She saved your life, man."

Other voices chimed in, so many that they overlapped each other, broke into one another, confusing him.

"How lucky can a guy get?" "Mouth-to-mouth from the hottest babe on the beach?" "Oh, man! It's like *Baywatch*, only real!" "You one lucky sumbitch, y'know?"

Mitch wanted to get up, but his head was too heavy to lift. He managed to turn his cheek onto the soft sand. Kneeling next to him was another lifeguard, Doug or Drug or something—Mitch had never been sure—seriously freaked. "Got here as soon as I could, Mitch," he panted, "you are lucky this chick was here. I wouldn't have made it."

This chick? He didn't mean Mandy? That wasn't possible. So who was she? Where was she? Mitch tried to turn his head the other way, but it was too much work.

Doug gripped his arm. "What made you go out there, man?"

To rescue a drowning swimmer, why else? He'd seen small arms waving, going down, being sucked under. Had he been hallucinating? "There wasn't . . . ?"

He coughed. "No one was drowning?" he finally spit out.

"Just you." Consciousness had returned fully. He'd know that voice anywhere. It matched the vision he saw, the haloed redhead. Mandy ran her fingers through his hair. Then she handed him a towel. "Here, blow your nose, you'll be fine."

Mitch exhaled and felt his body uncoil. He was safe now.

"Okay, show's over, you can all leave." Mandy booted the looky-loos, then whispered, "You fell asleep, you dumb lug."

"You were here?" Mitch asked stupidly. "I didn't see you."

"I was sunbathing next to the lifeguard station. I waved, but you were asleep, so I let you be."

"You should have woke me up," he said weakly. "It was irresponsible."

"Yeah, well, I made an executive decision," she cracked. "You needed your sleep more than I needed an even tan. I sat on the beach and took watch for you. No one was even in the water."

He felt like a total idiot. She confirmed it too. "Suddenly, you jerked up—probably in the middle of a nightmare—and you ran out there like your pants were on fire."

His throat hurt when he laughed. "Remember the time my pants really were on fire?"

It'd been back in the bad old days. Mitch, Bev, and Mandy were walking home from junior high school. They turned a corner and saw black pillars of smoke coming from the Dorchester Housing Projects. Turned out some lunatic on the fourth floor of their building had decided to make a bonfire of his ex-wife's apartment. Mitch had broken into a run, terrified that his mom might be trapped inside the burning building. Luckily, she hadn't been home, but he'd exited the building spewing smoke and fanning flames off his behind.

Laughing transformed her, he thought, brought back the bright-eyed freckle-faced kid he'd known, and maybe crushed on. Just a little. "I was always trying to be the hero," he admitted. "Old habits die hard."

"Yeah well . . ." She cut her eyes away from him, out to the ocean. "Some of us appreciated it. Still do."

It was a struggle, but Mitch pushed himself up on his elbows and grazed her fingertips with his. "I don't know what would've happened to me if you hadn't come."

Mandy shot him a rueful grin. "Died, I suppose."

Mitch grinned. She always did tell it like it was.

"I *told* you this was a bad idea," Mandy chastised him. "You're a great guy, and a hero, too, but you're not Superman."

"Cut me some slack, okay? I had no choice."

Mandy's face clouded. "There's always a choice, Mitch. Someone real smart told me that once. Mighta even been you."

Look where "real smart" has gotten me, he thought.

"Do you think," she asked, "it's this sickness people like us have? This obsession to have money, be famous? Do any stupid thing just so people will look up at us, instead of look down—like they did when we were kids?"

Not so long ago, Mitch would've been righteously offended at the trite suggestion, and the comparison of "Mandy Starr" and her hackneyed pipe dreams with Mitch Considine and his lofty goals and worthy ambitions.

"We both made some real asinine moves this summer," he conceded, "trying for a better life than the one we had. I never thought it would be this hard."

She agreed, stroking his arm. "I worked like crazy to lose

all that weight. I thought just by being sexy, like in the magazines, I could be a winner, you know?"

He did know. All too well. He, too, thought he could lose the scruffy little outside-looking-in boy; if he worked tirelessly, he could launch himself right into another life. Leonora's life. With effort, he put his arm around Mandy's shoulders, and together, they lay back down, her head resting on his chest.

"I knew better than to go to that photo studio. I knew it was a sleazy setup. But a part of me believed it would turn out the way I dreamed. The pictures would like, dazzle 'em. I would be famous, special. You know?" She tipped her chin up so she could look into his eyes.

He had to close them. Otherwise she'd know exactly what he was thinking: You *are* someone special. You always were.

Much later, he and Mandy sat outside, on the deck, a six-pack of beer and a bag of chips on the little table between their chairs. Mandy had managed to talk Mitch's boss into believing she and Mitch had been kidding around and things got out of hand. That this lifeguard—how ridiculous!—hadn't nearly drowned. That Mitch shouldn't be fired.

Funny, he was no longer sure he still wanted the second job, or even the tennis gig anymore. He'd been so single-minded all summer—hell, all his life, really—that to not be sure of something, to not have a goal, felt strange. And yet, it was less unsettling than he'd imagined.

He took a long slug of beer and eyed her. She'd put on an oversize football T-shirt and slipped into a pair of well-worn jeans. She was barefoot, and he noticed her toes; the sparkly pink polish reminded him of the first night at the share house.

He hadn't planned to ask, but couldn't help himself. "You didn't just 'happen' to be sunbathing, did you? You were keeping an eye on me, making sure I was okay. Weren't you, Sarah?"

She smiled ruefully. "Like you didn't just happen to program your cell phone into mine that first day? You wanted a way to save me—if I needed it."

Why this girl ever thought herself stupid was a mystery to him.

"Mitch?" Her voice was hesitant suddenly. "I *was* keeping an eye on you, but for more reasons than you thought. I knew taking on two jobs was gonna kill you. And"—she paused, uncharacteristically—"I was trying to find a way to show you that it wasn't worth it. That *she*"—another pause, pointed this time—"wasn't worth it."

That's when Mandy broke the news, told him what everyone at 345 Cranberry Lane already knew but had been afraid to tell him. Mandy told Mitch the truth about Leonora, exactly what Harper had seen last month.

She'd gone to Chatham herself, Mandy informed Mitch,

sat in the grand foyer (she pronounced it foy-YAY) of the Quivvers mansion, told the maid she'd wait for Leonora to come home. "I had to confront her," Mandy explained. "I was gonna make her confess. I was gonna punch the slut out for cheating on you."

"But you didn't?" Mitch said quietly. He was hearing this from afar, it seemed, catching maybe every other word she said. It didn't matter. Mandy was to the point, and clear. She repeated exactly what Leonora had told her.

His sweetheart, his beloved, the woman he lived and almost died for, had been cheating on him all summer long. She felt guilty, sure, but not enough to stop! That's why she'd been so weird, so hard to get through to. Leonora had come to the share house that day to break it off, to tell him she was ending their relationship. But he hadn't let her get a word in edgewise, he'd been so busy showing her off, like his big trophy. And then she got so angry, she didn't want to talk to him at all!

It was right after that, Harper had caught her in bed with little Gracie's dad. That's when things got really complicated. Leonora had freaked out, didn't know what to do, or how to act. If Harper blabbed, her whole life would be ruined! The sad truth was that Mitch was only a small part of it. If Harper told, her parents would find out that their twenty-year-old daughter was having a sleazy affair with a married man—doing it in a hotel room?! No one did that sort of thing. Or if you did, you certainly didn't get caught! She was fairly sure her parents would've booted her out of the country somewhere.

Leonora didn't know how to handle it. She'd spent every day trying to gauge Mitch, to guess what, if anything, Harper had told him. One minute, she'd be lavishing attention on him; the next, completely disengaged. Now Mitch knew why.

Yes, Lee admitted to Mandy, she did insist her father intervene with the cops, get Mitch off the hook so he wouldn't have an arrest record. At first, she'd truly thought the incident would serve to remind her how good she had it with wholesome, worthy Mitch Considine.

Just the opposite. It had only proved what Leonora had suspected: She was bored with Mitch, the knight in shining armor. She wanted out of the relationship, but didn't know how to end it.

Hours earlier, Mitch had been a drowning man. Now he was into a serious beer buzz. Finally, everything was crystal clear to him. It would not ever matter how much money he made, what kind of career he'd forge, how big the ring would be that he'd give her as an engagement gift: Leonora was never going to be his.

Mandy held him as he sobbed. When it was over, when his tears had been spent, he couldn't say if they'd been tears of rage, regret—or relief.

The Clambake: Everyone, Out of Your Shell!

Katie

Hot, hot, *hot*! Katie was surprised the sand beneath her bare feet still burned. It was, after all, the end of August, just before sunset. Carrying a pot full of just-cooked corn on the cob, she had to do this run-and-hop thing (how graceful!) from the backyard deck toward her beach blanket buddies—Mitch, Mandy, Harper, Joss, and Alefiya—who were all digging in for an end-of-summer big-ass clambake.

Mitch had said it was "tradition," but Katie so doubted it. She suspected he wanted to start a new one.

As she neared the human hodge-podge she'd lodged with, she had to laugh. The hippie, the hussy, the prep, the slob, the slacker, and yeah, the princess (that'd be her)—they'd accused each other of all of the above—somehow, the whole crazy quilt had worked. Today, the end of their last day living together, they'd celebrate the against-all-odds friendships—and love affairs, even—that had resulted.

In the middle of the clashing array of beach blankets, towels, flip-flops, T-shirts, and shorts tossed on the sand sat a ginormous steamer pot, courtesy of Clambakes-To-Go (no one wanted to risk Ali cooking: The house was clean!). The pot was full of orangey red lobsters, shrimp, clams, and oysters; next to it sat an uncharming plastic tub filled with clam chowder, and several smaller plastic containers with drawn butter, crackers, and horseradish-ketchup dip. A kid's beach pail was employed to hold nutcrackers, napkins, and paper cups—clambake accessories.

Ali had been put in charge of the music, and she'd toted speakers and an iPod to the party, which Katie was sure could be heard all the way to Chatham. Already, Ali was up and dancing, singing into a beer bottle-cum-microphone, "And I . . . yi . . . yi . . . yi . . . will always love . . . you-ou . . . ou . . . ou . . . ou!" Her Whitney impression was wanting, but Katie'd heard and seen much, much worse.

Mitch, working food patrol, was "Langostino-man"—so dubbed by Joss, who (naturally) had taken on bartending chores. Taken them very seriously! Beyond popping beer-bottle caps, Josh was tending to blenders full of frothy frozen margaritas and daquiris; the upended crate they'd been using as a coffee table since the robbery now served as a bar counter, on which he'd lined up shot glasses as well. Impressive!

Katie trooped toward them, shouting, "Corn here! Getcha corn on the cob!" She set the pot and her rear end down on someone's SpongeBob blanket and buried her toes in the sand.

It'd been a head-spinning week. Lucky her day camp gig had ended the prior weekend; she'd needed the time to execute her new plan.

This one she'd dubbed Plan A—for Amends.

Katie had more than a few to make. In doing so, she began to feel like her old self again: The Kick, large 'n' in charge, doing what needed to be done. Her exceptionally stylish (always adorable) way.

The day Joss had delivered the news had turned the tide. That day, she should have been destroyed, debilitated, beyond consolation. Instead, she felt empowered. How weird was that?

Joss had come through, big-time, for her. He'd reached out to his own family, the deep-pocketed and deeply connected Sterling Organization. It hadn't taken them long to unearth the Charlesworth scandal secrets. They confirmed her worst suspicions. Richard Charlesworth would soon be charged with fraud. The FBI had been building a case, waiting to pounce until they had every last shred of evidence, an indictment assured. They'd allowed Richard and Vanessa to go on their summer cruise; agents would be waiting when the ship docked back at Boston Harbor in another ten days.

Devastating as the details were, knowing *when* it would occur was a huge relief. It allowed Katie to let that boulder of doubt and fear roll off her shoulders.

Joss had gone completely above and beyond informant. He'd offered her money. "As much as you need, to get you through school, and after."

She'd broken down and sobbed. Not for her parents—not yet, anyway—not for herself. In her life, Katie had not known that kind of generosity, and it touched her deeply. Joss didn't want anything from her.

Yet? She was going to do something for him all the same.

Later that day, she'd sought out Harper, lazily reclining on the living room floor. Harper'd propped a bed pillow up against the fireplace mantel, and, while she didn't look all that comfortable, she was less than thrilled to be interrupted from what Katie termed a marathon read-fest. To her knowledge, Harper had done no writing since the day Joss admitted his fling with Mandy. Lately, all Harper did was take long bike rides and read books. She must've gone through a dozen hardcovers in the last week.

"Do me a favor?" Katie had said. "Pick your head up from the world of fiction and listen to something real. You need to know what Joss just did."

"I don't need to know, and I don't really want to either," Harper corrected her. "I'm over it."

"Too bad," Katie replied, plopping down next to her and proceeding to fill her in on Joss's bighearted gesture. Harper pretended not to care, but Katie had learned to read her roomie well enough by now. Harper was calculating what it had cost Joss to help Katie.

"He's not Luke," Katie kept repeating. "Joss is the real deal. They don't come around often. And"—Katie had put in before Harper could dismiss her—"he needs you."

"Not."

"You're not into his money—or his looks, even. You connect with him. The music thing—it's obviously what he's about. You get it. If he has to go back to Sterling, Inc., do you think anyone there will?"

Harper, stubborn as she could be, wasn't budging. At least not on the Joss topic. But, clearly, she was worried about Katie. "So it's really going down as soon as you get back to Boston? Before school starts?"

Katie nodded.

"If you want . . . ," Harper started, "I know I'm . . . what do you call me? Fringe! But if you want to stay at school, you can live with me and my mom. It's just an apartment, but it's big."

Katie smiled, and told Harper what she'd told Joss. She'd think about it. She had choices. She'd gotten something out of this summer she'd never expected: real friends. Who didn't give a hoot about The Kick, or what she could do for them. Harper, of all people, "fringe-girl," had forced her to examine exactly what it was she'd been so obsessed with holding on to. Her parents' life? How empty, and pathetic, was that? Look where it had gotten them.

Speaking of her parents, Katie had a responsibility, something she'd never ducked in all her life. Her mom, oblivious and flawed as she was, loved Katie as best she could. Vanessa needed her now. So Katie would go, stand by her, no matter where they ended up. Somehow, she would force herself to understand her father's side of the story too. That would come later.

As for the ridicule she would certainly suffer at the hands of the Trinity best-of-breed crew?

Bring it! They—Lily included—would meet the real Kick. She could, and would, deal. Without a credit card (pause for a real sob), if it came to that; without a debutante ball; without this season's designer best—with or without (she still hadn't decided) Nate Graham—but with her head held high.

Katie didn't have time to dwell on what would be. She did, however, have ten days until the news broke. Which meant she still had some clout on the Cape. She used it, one last time. As a favor to a housemate, who'd morphed into a friend.

His name was Whitford (really). He was freckled, friendly, sun-dappled, deep-pocketed—the real-life Kennedy kin she'd run into at Blend in Provincetown. Whitford was ripe for summer fun, and very open to meeting someone, especially when Katie described her friend as cute, carefree, and fun-loving.

But a funny thing happened when she told Mandy that she'd set her up with Whitford—the Kennedy connection. The redhead, who'd taken years off when she removed her makeup, had said, "Thanks, but no thanks. I'm kinda happy with the catch I made on my own. Oh, BTW: Mandy doesn't live here anymore. The name is Sarah."

Sarah

Sucking out the sweet meat from the tiny lobster legs was as delicious and satisfying as she'd always imagined. To Katie's "*Eeww*, no one eats that part of it," she'd laughed. "Now you know someone who does," she'd said, and cracked open another. Mitch took a slug of beer and draped an arm around her. Sarah did not think herself capable of this much joy. Funny that she should derive it from her fucked-up childhood, from the Considine twins, Mitch and Bev, friends she'd excised years ago, along with the excess poundage. If she were a literary type, like Harper over there, she might say she had reclaimed her soul this summer. But since she wasn't? She'd just let Joss pour her a frozen margarita and get up and show Ali, wiggling her bodacious booty to *The Best of ABBA*, what a real "Dancing Queen" looked like!

Sarah's soaring spirits had as much to do with the amends she'd made before leaving the share house. The first was a no-brainer. Hitching a ride with Mitch, she'd gone to the biggest pet store she could find, and picked up . . . jeez, who knew they even had special food for ferrets? Let alone ferret toys? Ali had been overjoyed, even though Sarah had stopped short of petting the thing.

On Katie's advice, and on Katie's cue, she then accosted Harper, who slammed her book down in frustration and demanded, "Does this bare living room look like a confessional to you? First Katie, now you, desperately needing to tell me something. What part of 'I don't care' don't you get?"

"A lotta stuff went down this summer," Sarah had said calmly. "If not for Mitch, and the rest of you, I'd've been in deep shit."

Harper folded her arms over her chest. "We already had our sista-friend bonding session. Gratitude extended and accepted. End of saga."

"Not quite," Sarah contradicted. "Before we leave, I really want you to know that I'm not the same shit heel I was three months ago."

"Fine! I get it! You've seen the error of your ways. So, can I have the big bedroom now?"

"In your dreams." Sarah feigned annoyance. "But you can have something better: the truth. Your choice to accept it or not, but here it is: I threw myself at Joss. I totally . . . I don't even know why . . . he was there, he was easy on the eyes, he was unattached. I wasn't into him, and trust me, he was never into me. It was random sex. Okay, so when I found out he was on tour with some aging rock star, I thought he could hook me up. Y'know, introduce me to the manager, the agent, make some connection. But we never got that far. Joss ended it soon after it began."

Harper sighed. "So you sent Mandy Starr packing, and what, you're going all Amish now? You're withdrawing from the Amazing Actress-slash-Model Race?"

"Of course not!" sniffed Sarah. "I have talent, a gift. Why squander it? But I'm going to do it right: take acting lessons, take it slow. And when I'm ready, sign up with a real agent. Legit. Mitch is going to help me."

Harper couldn't suppress a smile. "That's actually pretty terrific. He's an amazing guy."

"Yeah, so what am I? Liverwurst? Mitch *is* getting me—a big improvement over that prissy tight-ass Leonora," she asserted, sticking out her prodigious chest and tossing her wavy hair.

Harper laughed. "You go, sister."

Sarah lowered her voice. Earnestly, because this was really important, she said, "Listen, Harper. This isn't about me. I'm real sorry for the foul things I said this summer. And the worse things I did. But don't hate Joss because of me. That's a really dumb reason."

Joss

When he'd picked up the phone and punched in his father's office, Joss wholly expected some administrative assistant to answer. He was ready to say, "Please put Mr. Sterling on the line."

But after several rings, turned out J. Thomas *was* on the line. "Son?" his voice borderline-quavered. "Is that you?"

Of course his father had probably tracked Joss's new cell phone number a year ago. "Yeah, Dad," he confirmed. "It's me. Joshua."

His father harrumphed. "Not Joss? Took me a while to get used to that"—affirming Joss's suspicions that his dad had known all along where he was—"but now I rather like it. Helps me see you in a whole different way."

"What way's that?" Joss held himself in check, trying not to let the old resentment get in the way. He was calling to ask a favor, nothing more. Irritating the old man wasn't the best strategy. He asked after his dad's health, his sister and brother, anything else he could think of before revealing what he really wanted.

J. Thomas Sterling went along with it. Not once did he bark, "What the hell did you think you were doing?" Or taking that superior attitude: "So, I see you've come to your senses." Or some other condescending thing Joss imagined he might throw at him.

Instead, his father listened. Said he'd be happy to do Joss the favor—it'd be easy for him to get information regarding Richard Charlesworth. And took the moment to remind his son that his bank accounts—dormant since Joss hadn't touched them—were, as always, being well invested, and available to him.

The true miracle, Joss reflected, was that J. Thomas never once asked the reason for the favor. Nor did his dad want to know when he was coming home, nor mention that the corner office designated for him still sat empty. Instead, he said haltingly, "Son, it means a lot that you called. Every time the phone rang, I kept hoping it'd be you." Joss couldn't be sure if what he heard after that was the sound of J. Thomas Sterling, Esq., weeping. He wouldn't know what that sounded like.

The call had put him through the emo-wringer. But in a strange way, it gave him the courage to place another call, to another father. To ask another favor.

He was a little looped himself, when, pouring a second frozen margarita for Mandy—that is, Sarah—he felt someone come up behind him and slide an arm around his waist. Because it felt so sweet, and right, he didn't turn away.

"That was pretty amazing, what you did for Katie," Harper said, letting him wrap his arm around her shoulders. "You obviously told your dad where you were."

Joss laughed. "You make it sound like I turned myself in! Like I'm going to jail."

"Won't they expect you to work in the family business?"

"More than likely," he said, nodding.

"What about your music?" She stared up at him with those amazing light gray-blue eyes.

"What about yours, Harper Jones?"

She frowned. "When did we start answering a question with a question?"

Joss withdrew his arm from Harper's shoulders. "Let's get some oysters before they're all gone."

Harper pursed her lips. "Shrimp for me, oysters for you."

"That works too," Josh agreed, swiping a couple of beers and leading her to the outer edges of the clambake.

She peeled the shrimp gingerly, watching him slurp down the oysters indelicately. He handed her a beer. "You wouldn't rather a frozen drink, would you?"

"No way. I'm not about the hard liquor—learned my lesson at the party."

He laughed. "Don't remind me."

She kicked him gently. And he fell more deeply in love with her. Which is precisely why he had to risk it: "So, I ask you again, Ms. Jones, what about your music? When are you going to deal with it?"

Harper sighed, like she'd expected this. And was ready for him. She dug into the back pocket of her cutoffs, withdrew something obviously ripped from her journal, and handed it to him.

He looked at her inquiringly before unfolding the paper. "On the Beach," she'd written across the top. Joss swallowed, his heart clutched. He had trouble focusing on the poem. No, not poem: lyrics. *"We watch the sun sink slowly into the ocean/the yellows, the oranges, the fiery reds/fade into the pinks, blues and grays of dusk, fade into us. . . ."*

After a few lines he no longer saw just lyrics on a page, he heard them blend into the music—his music. He let the song play in his head; made a mental note that a bridge would have be written, where it would go.

"How badly does it suck?" Harper's voice jolted him back from creativity alley.

He put the song down, turned to her, and said what he knew he had to: "You're just like him, you know."

"Just like who?"

"Your father."

Harper

Harper freaked. She jumped up off the sand and tried to run away, but Joss was quicker. He blocked her way, locked her in his arms. She didn't fight as hard as she could, wasn't even sure what the instinct to run was all about. Yet, there it was.

The song blaring from the housemates' CD player was "Love Shack," by the B-52's, and the others were dancing, Mitch, Mandy/Sarah, Katie, and Ali—shouting out the chorus: *"We can get to-ge-ther, love shack, baby! Woo!"*

Pulling away from Joss, Harper finally managed, "How long have you known?"

"If I tell you, promise not to run?"

The breeze that accompanied the just-beginning-to set sun toyed with his long hair. Harper resisted the urge to brush it out of his eyes. She let him lead her farther away from the group. Of all the annoying confessions, the things people "had to tell her" this last week, this was the least expected, the least welcome.

Joss began, "When I first met you, I was intrigued. There was something about you I couldn't pin. You reminded me of someone—the way you move, your expressions, the dimples— and even though I just came from touring with Jimi Jones, I didn't make the connection. Then we got to know each other, and when you told me you wrote poetry, when I realized it was more than that, there was music in your soul. You never said a word, and I respect your privacy—I probably would've let it go, kept it to myself."

"But?"

"I fell in love with you this summer."

Harper pretended not to hear that. She had enough to process.

"I don't want to hurt you," he said earnestly, reaching for her now. "It's just that I needed to know if you knew. And if you didn't, would it be okay if I told you? And if you did, is it okay that I know?"

Joss was rambling. When he rambled, his cool quotient plummeted below zero, so she reached for him—how could she not? "I know Jimi Jones is my father," she said, just above a whisper. "I've known since I was twelve."

"You do?" Joss looked surprised. "Do you want to meet him?"

Harper couldn't resist raising her eyebrows and quipping, "So, you can hook me up, huh?"

Joss was too far beyond the earnest-edge to go with the joke. He colored. "Harper, please understand. You are the coolest chick I've ever met. I've already screwed things up. We have something. I don't want to lose it."

She wanted to contradict him. They did not, in fact, "have something." They wouldn't be having a thing. It was, had to be, No thing. There were a million ways to say it, and she swore she was just about to. Instead, she heard herself ask, "What's he like?"

Finally, Joss smiled. God, he was cute when he smiled. "Jimi's really cool. For someone in his position—to his fans, he's like a rock god—he handles it amazingly well. He's still all about the music, a perfectionist. Somehow he's managed not to let the money, the power—the temptations—corrupt him. I've worked for other bands in the last few years, and he's by far the most real. He didn't know who I was, some anonymous roadie, but he always took the time to comment on my playing, to answer my questions—give advice, even."

"So are we nominating him for sainthood?" Harper muttered.

Josh laughed. "Sorry. People around him say he's mellowed over the years—if that means anything. Anyway, yesterday, I called him—to find out if he knew about you. Just so you know? He does, but all these years he's honored your mom's wishes to not intrude. If you say the word, he'll come."

She did not.

Joss said, "You know the song he ends every concert with? 'Under My Skin'? It was written for your mom. But you probably knew that."

Harper had suspected as much. Without realizing she was doing it, she sang softly, *"You were always the one/Your laugh,*

277

your eyes, your arms still/comfort me on rainy nights/You're under my skin/lady of my heart. . . ."

He hadn't brought his guitar to the beach, so when Joss came in on harmony, it was a cappella. Harper, her own harshest critic, liked what she heard. Their voices wound around each other, blended, like that night on another beach. Only better.

Maybe Harper would meet Jimi Jones one day. With or without Joss's help. But never without her mom's knowledge, and her blessing. That, she could not, would not, do.

Mitch

Mitch kicked back, out of breath. All the jogging he did, he was still panting from dancing, singing, and laughing. The relief of just letting go, not having to be anywhere, do anything, or prove anything to anyone: This was as fine a feeling as he'd ever had.

He surveyed the scene. What a mess! Empty shells, from the lobsters, crabs, mussels, and oysters, lay everywhere, punctuated by beer bottles, corncobs, scattered napkins, and used utensils.

No matter, there'd be plenty of time for cleaning up later.

Now was the time for chilling, his lady at his side, his friends close by, and his belly full. He leaned back on his elbows and stared out to the sea. The sun seemed to be balancing on the water's surface, like a perfect sphere, reminding him of that song his mother used to sing: *"And I think it's gonna be all right, Yeah, the worst is over now, the morning sun is shining like a red rubber ball."*

He thought of her now, long gone. And he suddenly knew how proud of him Dora Considine would be. Not because he'd achieved wealth or status, or had married—her expression— "some fancy, dancy" girl like Leonora, but because he'd escaped it. Long on the road from the prison of poverty to the lock-up of having to live by other people's standards, he'd found his own path. He could just be himself.

And that's all she'd really ever wanted.

Impulsively, he kissed Sarah's cheek. Causing her to turn just enough so their lips locked. Mmmm . . . lusty and luscious.

And so very unexpected.

Just like, he thought, grinning at his disparate housemates, the scraps. The scraps had really made it after all.

Alefiya

Ali sat cross-legged on her blanket, Mitch and Sarah on one side, Katie on the other. She'd partaken of everything: from the thick, creamy clam chowder, lobster tail, two ears of corn; she'd even let Joss show her how to properly devour oysters, giggling as Harper merrily ragged on them both. Oysters might never be Harper's thing, but Ali could see now she'd have to teach Jeremy to enjoy them.

Jeremy! Her heart soared when she thought about him. She'd return to school in Boston next week, leaving Jeremy behind. Not for long, and surely not for good. She hadn't thought about finding a boyfriend this summer. That was a sweet, surprising bonus. She was seeing him later tonight, after the clambake, and they'd already made weekend plans to see each other in September.

She'd miss him until then, but needed time to work on her parents, anyway.

The *rumspringa*—to borrow that Amish phrase, since she still had none of her own—had turned out to be everything she'd hoped, and a whole lot more. She'd tasted freedom, found it sweet *and* bitter. The harshness of the scorn aimed at her after the robbery, the mistake of throwing the party, Mandy's taunts, and even Katie's thinly veiled contempt at the beginning of the summer, was hard. But on balance? It didn't come close to the joy she felt now. Alefiya would certainly return to her parents' world, honor their traditions. She loved them deeply, after all. But she would declare botany, not premed biology, as her major at school; she would be her own person. She would be with Jeremy.

"How're you doing?" It was Harper, who'd come to sit beside her now.

"Never better," Ali said. "The whole summer, the way everything turned out. I knew it'd be fun, but I didn't expect it to be this awesome. You . . . Joss . . . Mitch . . . even Sarah. Everyone's just exactly as they should be."

Harper put her arm around Ali, which started a chain reaction. Mitch and Sarah moved closer. Katie was squinched between Harper and Joss.

A snapshot from behind the group would show six friends sitting by the shoreline, close enough to touch, arms locked around each other's shoulders, silently watching the sun go down. Or, as Harper had poetically put it, watching the glorious array of yellows, oranges, and reds gradually fading into pinks, blues, and grays.

When it had just about set, Joss commanded, "Nobody move. I want to get something."

He returned not with a camera, but with six shot glasses, a bottle of tequila—the worm authenticated it—lime wedges, and a shaker of salt. Carefully, he divvied everything up, took his spot next to Katie, and instructed: "On my count. One . . ." Glasses were hoisted. "Two . . ." Chins tipped up. "Three!"

Down the hatch they went, first the salt, then the shot, and finally the lime-sucking ritual. The group's rhythm was off, but no one noticed. When the laughing, and coughing (Katie and Harper) died down, Mitch said it: "So, same time next year?"

Partiers Preferred

If I were to share a summer house, here's who my ideal roomies would be: the brilliant Bethany Buck, who had the original idea for the series; Sangeeta Mehta, who took this book to the next level; the agents extraordinaire, Jodi Reamer, Rachel Sheedy, and Elizabeth Harding, who all, in a game of e-phone, helped me reach my old friend, actor/producer Ralph Macchio, who reconnected me to the brilliant S. E. Hinton, who graciously allowed me to reference her classic, *The Outsiders*.

Without the contributions of these people, this book would not have been half as much fun as it is.

Thank you all so very, very much.

Jared's Sweet Deal

Jared Larson tingled all over. He was high on, and in, the heady hills of Hollywood. A wide smile of contentment spread across his classically chiseled face as he eased the Lexus convertible into the narrow driveway. The house it belonged to was empty and all his, all summer long. He planned to make excellent use of it. Rent out rooms, pocket a nice chunk of change, while spending the summer partying. Chicks, clubs, ka-*ching*—for a twenty-one-year-old free spirit, it doesn't get any better than that! Especially because his father would never find out. Ah, freedom: It's what this great country was built on.

Flipping his Oliver Peoples aviator shades atop his stylishly short hair, he glanced over at the familiar front door and grinned. Painted a garishly loud royal blue, it stood a few feet behind a leaf-and-vine-covered gate. Shoulder-high hedges encircled the house.

It was *so* L.A., he thought. In this town, good shrubbery makes good (i.e, *envious*) neighbors. When you build a tall, dense fence around your crib, you force passersby to wonder: What's on the other side? Some crazy-amazing mansion? Who lives there? A star?

Jared chuckled as he started down the path of terra-cotta stepping-stones leading to the backyard. Amazing? This place? In the eyes of a stoner, maybe. The blinding blue front door was only one of the odd color choices—the entire exterior had been painted a screaming pumpkin-orange color. Good thing this area of L.A. was considered artsy.

The neighborhood, officially Lake Hollywood, was a maze of eclectic houses on steep narrow streets that zigged and zagged so randomly, the only things you could be sure of were hairpin turns and blind driveways. A bitch to drive around, especially at night.

The part about a star living in the orange and blue monstrosity, however, was sort of true. A quasi-celebrity owned this house, an actor audiences knew by sight, never by name. Jared knew him as Uncle Robert, a character actor in his forties who had, as one critic viciously sniped, "a great future behind him."

Ouch. That'd hurt. Jared's uncle, the only relative he

actually liked being around, *had* weathered a long dry spell, career-wise. He'd taken roles in straight-to-DVD junk movies to pay the bills. But Rob's desert days were done, as over as yesterday's sushi craze. Robert Larson was currently making a killer comeback, in a career-defining movie. Already, there was buzz about a best supporting Oscar nomination for him. The movie was filming in Prague. When Uncle Rob packed up and left, Jared moved in.

So what if the bizarrely painted cottage wasn't like the spacious mansion Jared had grown up in?

It was funky.

"Rustic, cozy, tucked away, perched above the Sunset Strip" was the description Jared had put in the Roommates Wanted ad on Craigslist. From that posting he'd already netted a trio of roomies. Two guys, Nick and Eliot, were coming in later today from Michigan; tomorrow, a chick named Sara from Texas would arrive. The guys didn't know the chick, and he knew none of them. That was cool with Jared—as long as they knew how to pay the rent!

Seriously, Jared was positive the two guys and the girl would work out—he needed just one more summer-share tenant to fill that last bedroom. He was confident he'd snag one by week's end, if not sooner. After all, he was charging what was, for this area, a bargain-basement rent for an amazing location. He could afford to because he had no overhead; their rent was his profit. So his dad had cut off his credit cards? Yo, every establishment he knew took cash. It was all good. Jared was born without a self-doubt gene.

He didn't need it. His father had enough doubt in Jared for both of them.

"Shabby" was the word Rusty Larson used to condescendingly describe this "shack" on "the wrong side of the hills." Why his ne'er-do-well-enough brother insisted on living there was beyond him. Of course, anything outside the three-square-mile area that encompassed the Larson family compound in Bel Air, Dad's high-rise office in Beverly Hills, and the beach house in Malibu where his bimbette of the day was stashed, was "beyond" him. Rusty Larson rarely stepped out of his Jag if an anorexic palm tree wasn't swaying gently above.

Jared agreed with his old man on absolutely *nothing*, but as he turned the corner into the backyard, his eyes widened in surprise. "Shabby" would've been putting it kindly. Forget about manicured lawn or neat patch of green. Overgrown, never-mown grass, dotted with scratchy stalks of burned-out weeds, covered what was once a decent-looking backyard.

Lucky, thought Jared, it was only a small plot of land— just enough to surround the curvy natural rock swimming pool, abutting Jacuzzi, and barbecue pit. He strode over to the pool and gaped at what used to be sparkling blue, clean, welcoming. It was a sickening greenish hue. Dead bugs and other unidentified objects floated lazily on the surface, as if they'd moved in. It was the thick coating of muck that really turned his stomach.

At least Uncle Rob's neglect could not screw up the home's most kick-ass and valuable asset. The one thing that was free, always there, and breathtaking.

The view.

"Viewtiful," his horny teenage girlfriend used to call it. Even on a hot 'n' hazy Saturday in June, it was amazing. (Smog? What smog?)

Jared strode to the outer edge of the property and surveyed his summer fiefdom. Spread out before him, acres of lush, juicy Caliscape. The sky above, the valley below, the undulating dips and curves and turns and tiers of the hills were like surround sound, encircling everything. Ah, the famous hills of Hollywood.

His father was a shortsighted snob. There *was* no "wrong side." Here was the heart and soul of the Southland: mini-mountains into which hundreds of homes neatly pressed. Some were on stilts, others carved into the rocks; all blended in with the terrain. And within eyeshot? Only the most famous of all landmarks, the *Hollywood* sign.

Below were broad boulevards named Sunset, Melrose, Wilshire, and Beverly. At night their ginormous billboards blinked and beckoned, their hot clubs called. Down there, deals were waiting to be made, girls waiting to be flirted with, the pleasures of food and drink, all spread out before him like a never-ending smorgasbord. Ah, the possibilities. More than anyplace else on earth, Hollywood was about possibilities. They were as endless as the landscape.

This was where he belonged. This summer, he'd prove it.

Jared checked his sport Tag Heuer watch—it was nearly two. The roommates weren't due for several hours, but if the inside of the house were as wrecked as the yard, he'd have to deal—quickly.

He counted the stepping-stones, knelt next to the fourth from the right, and slipped his palm underneath the terra-cotta stone. Wedged between the stone and the dirt was exactly what he expected to be there. The front door key.

Once inside, Jared heaved a sigh of relief. Unlike the mess of the backyard, Uncle Rob had left the house in order. Just as Jared remembered it.

The large living room was warm, welcoming, and cluttered. It was, Jared often thought, the intersection of high-end and low-brow, where expensive and rare crisscrossed with junky, cheap, and marked-down everywhere. Hippie-meets-haute. Nothing matched, and everything worked.

Dark wood beams tented a vaulted ceiling, and a worn black leather couch abutted a blue-and-orange-striped sectional sofa.

A mirrored orange high-backed Moroccan wing chair and matching ottoman, which his uncle had shipped from overseas, sat by the brick fireplace.

A gallery of guitars (bass, electric, baritone, and acoustic) and other stringed instruments—sitars, mandolins, banjos, and violins—lined the pale tangerine walls, mounted like artful pieces of musical sculpture. CDs, vintage record albums, photos, and candles perched on shelves and bookcases tucked into random nooks and crannies. Between the albums, guitars, bongs, incense holders, aromatic candles, and bottles of Kabbalah water, the entire room was a hippie paradise.

Kitchen, bathroom, and a tricked-out game room completed the main floor.

Suddenly, Jared's cell phone rang. He checked the caller ID: his father.

Jared watched himself in a hallway mirror as he talked to his dad. Make that *lied* to his dad, who believed he was in summer school, making up for the disaster that'd been his senior-year grades.

"Hi, Dad, I'm good. I'm just walking into the dormitory now . . . it's fine, I'll survive. It's Ojai Community College, not the county lockup!

"Nope, don't need a thing. Just got done confirming my classes—they'll wipe out last semester's failing grades, like they never happened."

"Yeah, I got a private room, no pesky roommates to distract me.

"Totally, I understand why you cut off the credit cards. It sucks, but I'll have to deal, right? What's my choice?

"No need for you to visit—you've got business. It's cool, it's chill."

After he hung up, Jared raked his fingers through his hair. He would make good this summer—that part wasn't bogus. Just in a different way than he'd told his old man.

Jared picked up a huge copper bong from the old chipped oak coffee table and stared at his reflection. Smooth-cheeked, collar up, cool and confident, clear green eyes—he did not recognize the screwup his father saw him as.

Whose fault were those failing grades anyway? He'd made it clear he neither wanted nor needed college. Rusty Larson owned Galaxy Artists, the hottest talent agency in town. Why Jared wasn't there, working at the junior exec level already, was the mystery. Whatever. He'd play it the old man's way, promising to take make-up classes, which he'd pass with flying colors. The rent-a-brainiac he'd hired to take the tests for him would see to that.

His one regret regarding his summer scheme was the secrecy involved: He couldn't tell his friends what was really up. Someone was bound to blab. In Hollywood, gossip is precious currency, and he would not chance his dad finding out. That meant house parties were out. He'd have to socialize on neutral turf: the clubs, or some girl's apartment.

Speaking of . . . he punched in speed dial. But neither Caitlin nor Julie picked up. He left messages. "Hey Cait, it's Jared. See you at Mood tonight . . . ?" "Jules, Jared here. Be at Hyde later?"

Then he made for the liquor cabinet, poured himself a Stoli-rocks, and slipped out the sliding glass doors that led to the backyard. Standing on the stone lip of the pool, he sipped the smooth vodka, refusing to let the toxic crap in the water screw with his happiness. A simple call to a cleaning service would take care of everything. As he'd told his dad, it was all chill. It'd be a funky, functional, fund-enhancing summer. Accent on the "fun" part: Jared was determined to have keggers o' it this summer.

Inspired, he raised a toast to his absent relative.

"Here's to you, Uncle Rob—to bagging that Academy Award, and to the biggest favor you've ever done for me. Does a favor count any less just 'cause you don't know you're doing it?"

Jared knew the answer to his existential question was a resounding . . .

"Fuuu . . . !!!"

It happened so quickly he could not react—couldn't get

his mouth closed before sucking in a glob of foul-smelling, vomit-inducing algae garbage. Couldn't keep his balance, couldn't hold on to his drink. He'd been pushed from behind, shoved, rendered defenseless as a girl. He heard the smash of his vodka glass hitting the poolside pavement and felt a wet film of fetid slime cover his skin. He belly flopped, face forward, into the muck.

Lindsay:
"Didn't You Used to Be . . . ?"

Lindsay laughed so hard, she thought she'd bust a gut. The sight of Jared McPerfect—Mr. Pristine—caught unaware, blindsided, flailing, pinwheeling his arms as if he could turn them into propellers and fly . . . then, splash!, nosediving into the pool. It was too, too much. What a rush!

Shoving him had been pure impulse. She'd planned on surprising him, not turning him into the raging freak he now resembled, shaking his head furiously, like a wet dog. She clutched her stomach at the sight of Jared soaked, sputtering, and screaming obscenities as he tried to free himself from the gook-choke.

Lindsay had just arrived in Los Angeles. She'd come straight here, only to be greeted by Jared, his back to her, prepped to perfection from the tips of his alligator Tods to the top of his two-hundred-dollar designer haircut. The lad of the manor had been so engrossed in admiring his reflection in the pool, raising his glass to the splendor of himself, he'd heard neither the taxi door slam nor the thwacking of her flip-flops as she'd made her way to the backyard, dragging her wheelie behind. Jared might as well have had a target on his back.

It'd just been *too* tempting. And "temptation, resistance of"? Not a Lindsay Pierce strong suit.

"What the fu—!" Jared finally managed to splutter when he saw his stealth attacker. "Lindsay?! What are you doing here?"

She tossed back her gleaming copper hair and admonished him. "Jared Larson, this is exactly why you'd never make it as an actor. You can't keep the smile off your silly face. You want to be mad at me, but you're just too happy to see me."

He growled. "You forfeited any chance of a happy reunion by throwing me into the pool. Or should I say, the toxic waste dump?"

She shrugged. "Think of it as delayed payback. Last time I was here, it was you who threw me into the pool. Only," she amended, "it was cleaner. And we were naked."

"I don't remember you minding, especially since I jumped in after you. Anyway"—only Jared could manage a smirk while being humiliated—"we ended up in the hot tub." With that, he splashed down hard on the slimy pool surface, hoping to spray her.

Lindsay skipped backward. "I knew you'd do that. After all these years, you're still so predictable."

He glowered, taking long, painstaking strides through the gummy water, making his way toward the steps.

"Hang on," Lindsay said. "If Uncle Rob is as predictable as his nephew, the towels will be exactly where I remember them." She flipped around, executing a killer ass-swivel—she knew he'd appreciate the move, which she'd practiced in her floaty halter top and snug, low-slung Diesels—and flounced through the sliding doors into the house.

It was good to be back, Lindsay thought.

By the time Jared had stripped off his scum-soaked clothes, taken a quick turn in the outdoor shower, and toweled himself furiously, Lindsay had settled into one of the poolside lounge chairs, fingers wrapped around a cool, fruity-flavored vodka drink. She could still read him like a billboard above Sunset Strip: He was psyched and confused, couldn't decide whether Lindsay bursting back into his life was a good thing—or one he ought to be wary of. Given Jared's natural distrust of people (*Takes one to know one*, she thought), he was proceeding with extreme caution.

Calmly, confidently, she repeated her story, testing which parts he'd pick out as totally bogus. "Word on the street is, you're looking for tenants. You need cash, I need a place to crash. I'm back in town, I need to reconnect with friends. And who's the first friend I *bump*—oops, bad word choice—into, but you? It's bra*sheet*." She punctuated with a winning smile.

Jared attempted a scowl but came up with a barely concealed grin. "You can't even say it right. It's *beshert*—buh-*shirt*. Not that you're even Jewish."

Lindsay toyed with her big hoop earrings and tossed her ponytail defiantly. "I'm Jewish-by-Hollywood. I lived here long enough. Anyway, Jared, I *know* what it means: We each need something the other one has. And here we find ourselves, together again. It's perfect."

"It's *beshert*," he corrected. "It means fated, that something was meant to be. It does not mean that something came up and you figured how to take advantage of it."

He'd hunkered down on the lounge chair next to hers, shirtless, just a towel wrapped around his waist, cell phone in his lap. Lindsay felt a familiar twinge. It'd been three years, and time had been good to Jared. Always a looker, he'd grown taller, tanner, leaner, and smoother, if that were possible. It was all she could do not to reach over and touch.

In the old days, her fifteen-year-old self would have practiced no such self-control. She'd have twirled that towel right off his slim waist. Jared would have been the "something" she'd have taken advantage of.

And Jared would've said, afterward, "You're amazing, Linz. Let's do this. Move in. Forget about rent." The teenage Jared she used to know wouldn't have missed a beat . . . or stopped to ask what Lindsay was doing back in California after being away so long. Three years in which she'd not once responded to his calls, letters, and, later, e-mails. Of course, being Jared, he hadn't tried very hard to stay in touch with her. Just long enough to lick his superficial wounds. Then he'd probably gone on to some other young starlet.

Today's twenty-one-year-old version of Jared peppered her with questions. The full-on interrogation. When she'd lied and said, "Word on the street is, you're looking for room-mates," he freaked. Apparently, he hadn't wanted anyone he knew to find out.

He sat sideways on the chaise lounge, feet planted on the ground, hovering over her. Until she told him the truth, Jared wasn't letting his guard, or his towel, down.

"Chill out." She assured him she hadn't spoken to, nor heard from, anyone in Jared's circle. It wasn't the grapevine that'd outed him, but the *on*line. Plotting her return to Los Angeles, she'd been on Craigslist every day for months, waiting and watching for a listing both location-acceptable (near the studios, where she hoped to land auditions) and financially feasible. Lindsay had money, but no intention of getting ripped off.

A match popped up a few weeks ago, worded in her native tongue, Hollywood-speak. She could have written the ad herself.

She recited it to Jared, with her interpretation. "Everyone knows a 'cozy' house means it's miniscule. 'Tucked away' is code for 'not the best neighborhood.' And 'rustic' translates to *maybe* there'll be running water. Which reminded me of you— the prince of spin. And then I saw your cell phone number on the listing. Like I said, it's bra*sheet*."

"*Beshert*," he growled.

"Yeah, that." Lindsay drained her drink. Tipping her chin to the sun, she inhaled the sweet jasmine-scented air. She knew she looked . . . um . . . what was that other Jewish word? *Kvetching*? Something like that.

Jared noticed. Despite his wariness, he couldn't stop himself from admiring her. "You look . . ." He stumbled for the word.

"Luscious? Sexy? Sublime? *Kvetching*?"

A belly laugh escaped. Jared's whole body shook with obvious delight, loosening the towel. "You're somethin' else, Linz, you really are. Just off enough to be a hoot. *Kvetching* means complaining."

"You're not . . . complaining . . . that I turned up?" She pushed back on her elbows, raising herself up to face him.

The beginnings of a blush crept up his neck. Pink. It worked for him. "Memo to Lindsay," he said. "Stop trying to be such a Hollywood-speak insider. No one does that any-more. Anyway, you are quite fetching."

"Fetching? As in 'go fetch me another drink'?"

Jared sighed. "No. As in, our little Linz has grown into quite a fetching young lass."

Lindsay glowed. She'd worked hard to look this good.

There hadn't been much else to do in the middle of the Iowa cornfields, where she'd spent the last mind-numbing years, besides plot her triumphant return west. To the land of milk 'n' honey, the place of good 'n' plenty, where she'd once been plenty good, and plenty adored.

Lindsay had been a star, playing middle sister Zoe Goldstein-Wong in the long-running sitcom about a Chinese-Jewish family called *All for Wong*. She'd landed the role when she was only ten, a freakishly freckled moppet with huge golden brown eyes, a button nose, and Cupid's bow lips. Famously ticklish, she was best known for her throaty, staccato, hiccupy giggle-fits. A trait she came by naturally, alas. It always gave her away. One insensitive critic dubbed her the Woody Woodpecker of child stars.

The show had run for five years and rerun for all eternity, rendering her very public, unpretty puberty in perpetuity. She had not transitioned well—unlike an Olsen twin or the girl who'd played Rudy on *The Cosby Show*.

There'd been zits, bad haircuts, and that whole nasty

"plump" thing the producers had unkindly pointed out. It didn't help that Lindsay'd been a smart-mouth, purposely ad-libbing when the cameras were rolling.

The war between Lindsay's family, under the guise of "protecting" her, and the producers—who were protecting their show—had grown bitter, and public. Good thing the tabloids weren't as out of control back then as they are now. Not that she'd ever been as big a tab-magnet as today's young stars.

And there was this: The measure of her fame was not a direct connect with the measure of how much she liked being famous. Lindsay lapped up, thrived on, bloomed under every spotlighty ray of attention. She'd never gotten over the craving.

The family feud alone would likely have gotten her fired— "She's replaceable, you know," producers used to threaten— only *All for Wong* got canceled. End of feud, end of story; to Lindsay, it felt like the end of her world.

Once the gravy train stopped rolling, that is, once her income dried up and she could no longer support the family, they hauled ass back to Iowa. With her in tow. Towed her back like a broken car. Only she wasn't broken, and she didn't want to be dragged back. Grenfield, Iowa, was her family's hometown. Not hers. Never hers.

She'd spent her enforced separation from L.A. working on her looks, her ticket back. Lindsay wasn't deluded. She was far from Ms. Uber-talent, but close enough to the scene to know talent's limits. In this town, a rockin' bod combined with A-list connections were far more potent than any ability you might have.

Taking the looks route hadn't been easy. Denying herself in America's heartland, where the major food groups were corn-dogs, Krispy Kremes, and Dairy Queen shakes, was a bitch. Hitting the local YMCA instead of a real fitness center, work-ing by herself instead of with a trainer, had sucked. No one helped, no one encouraged her. Not the children of the corn, as she secretly called the kids at Grenfield High, not her cretin cousins, certainly not her parents. They thought she was nuts.

"Lindsay, sweetheart," her mom (who probably felt guilty liv-ing off her all those years) kept at her, "you don't have to be skinny; you're perfect the way you are. You don't have to be judged by how you look. You can grow up normal now."

What Mom never understood? Lindsay didn't *do* normal. Not back then, and not now. She'd turned eighteen in May, graduated high school, tucked in what was left of her stomach, and headed back to Hollywood, head, tush, and tatas held high. Slim and curvy where baby fat once rolled, defined cheekbones where chubby cheeks were often pinched, she'd grown tauter, totally tantalizing. And bore ambition to match. Forget the TV "sitcomeback." Or playing some drug addict in an indie movie to prove her acting chops.

Chew this! Her goal was no less lofty than icon. Lindsay Pierce aspired to be a brand. Complete with makeup ("Get the Lindsay Pierce look!"). And fashion ("The Lindsay Pierce line is sold exclusively at Bloomingdale's!"). And major accessories ("Bracelets, scrunchies, toe rings, designed by Lindsay herself!"). Of course, there'd be a fashion doll. And a fragrance. Everyone who was anyone did perfume. She read *Us Weekly.* She kept up!

Hooking back up with Jared Larson was a means to an end. Jared's dad owned Galaxy. Jared could get her a high-powered agent, who'd snag her star-making movie roles. Convincing her ex-bf to help? Let's just say that when she saw her ex-boyfriend's ad on Craigslist, it was a done deal.

"The truth, Lindsay—why are you really back?" Jared demanded.

Oy. Still with the interrogation. All she needed was crappy lighting and stale coffee, and this could be a scene from *Law & Order.* Why was Jared so jumpy? She attempted to peel away, if not the towel, the layers of lies he was bound to be telling. "Does Uncle Rob know you're living in his house—and renting out rooms while he's away?"

"Do Mom and Pop Pierce know where their oldest daughter is?" he volleyed back.

Lindsay laughed. She'd missed more than Jared's body: Swapping one-ups with him was one of the best parts of their relationship. They *got* each other. "I didn't run away. My folks know I'm here. Besides, I'm eighteen—legal. In case you hadn't noticed." For emphasis, she puffed her chest out, tossed her copper tresses back.

"Okay, yes, my uncle knows I'm here." Jared was pink again. Lindsay wasn't sure if her chest had caused him to blush, or he was lying.

"And Rob's okay with this?"

"Why wouldn't he be?"

Lindsay could think of about a zillion reasons but didn't press. "I take it your father doesn't know what you're up to."

"Not exactly."

"Hmmm." Lindsay narrowed her eyes. "We can safely assume Daddy Moneybags isn't financing you—otherwise, why the need to collect rent?"

Jared conceded that his father had cut off his credit cards—temporarily.

"And the crowd, our old friends? Tripp, Caitlin, Ava, MK, Julie B . . . ? None of them know the truth either?" That was a guess.

Jared held her gaze. "I'd appreciate it if you didn't tell them."

Lindsay licked her lips. *That'll cost ya,* she thought. But didn't say aloud. Instead, she closed one eye in pretend concentration. "So lemme get this straight. Your dad thinks you're at community college making up your failing grades. To be sure you don't screw around, he's cut off your credit cards. Your friends believe this hooey as well—except they assume you're plastic-fantastic, flush. It wouldn't occur to your uncle that you're squatting in his crib. Hence, you're living here for free, making money off other people. Is that about right?"

Jared's curvy lips tightened into a straight line.

"Whew! Keeping up with Jared's web of lies. Feels like old times. I love it!"

Maybe he saw the wheels in her head turning, maybe he realized her arrival here was gonna cost him, one way or another, but Jared obviously couldn't resist lobbing one back. "I'd be careful about worshipping old times, Lindsay. You can't go home again."

She stiffened. "What's that supposed to mean? Another convenient quote from the master of deception himself?"

Jared burst out laughing again. She'd been right. He couldn't stay mad at her. He shook his head, still chuckling. "I didn't think metaphors could get any more mixed up, but once again, you prove me wrong."

"Let's try basic arithmetic. Here's the math as I see it: You want four roommates. You've got two guys coming later today, one girl arriving tomorrow—and now there's me. Add up so far?"

"You want to move in. How are you going to pay the rent?" He folded his arms over his rippley-smooth chest.

Just for fun, Lindsay uncrossed her legs.

"In U.S. currency, I mean." Jared would not be distracted.

"No problem. I'm going to get a gig. But," she added before he could chime in, "no way I'm paying what the others are! Not if you want me to keep—let alone keep track of—all your little secrets."

Jared's jaw tensed. He looked even more luscious when pissed. "That's blackmail."

"You say blackmail," she chirped, "I say quid pro quo. Which is how this town totally operates. Anyhow, it's not like I'm gunning for a free ride. I'll pay for my keep. One way or another."

Ignoring her implication, Jared said, "Do you even have an agent?"

"I'm not currently represented." She delivered the line in her best Hollywood-speak. "I thought you could help me out. I had no way of knowing about your little spat with Rusty Larson, head of the biggest talent agency in town."

Jared sighed. "We'll find a way to get you an agent."

Lindsay lit up. "I knew it! I knew we'd get back on the same track. It's bra—"

He held his palm up. "Don't even try."

"Can I try something else?" She untied her halter top. If that didn't loosen his libido . . .

California, Here We Are:
Nick and Eliot Find Nirvana

"Holy crap! They're gonna do it . . . right here . . . in public!" Eliot's bug eyes nearly popped out of his head; the roadmap he'd been clutching slipped to the ground. "It's not technically public if it's a private backyard, but . . ."

Nick gaped, speechless. Right in front of them, better than big screen, more 3D than HD, was the most awesome scenic view they'd had the entire road trip. This skinny dude—gotta be Jared, the kid who'd put the Roommates Wanted ad on Craigslist—with this *bodacious* chick, sharing a chaise lounge in the backyard, sucking face, pawing each other, going at it, hot and heavy. A towel was slowly slipping off his butt and she was topless, man! The couple was oblivious to anything else, including the presence of the two best friends who'd driven out from Michigan to spend the summer in L.A.

Nick felt overdressed. Clearly, dude, life out here was *waaay* more casual than in West Bloomfield. He'd have to adjust.

Eliot, unsurprisingly, was in deep distress. "N . . . n . . . ni . . . Nick . . . I think they're gonna do it!" He gulped. "We gotta let them know we're here."

"Chill, E," Nick shushed him. "These are our roommates. And you never get a second chance to get your first impression. Somethin' like that."

"This isn't right," Eliot whispered frantically. "We shouldn't be standing here. Let's go back to the car . . . until . . . uh, they're done."

Neither moved.

Nick had spent most of the three-day drive wanting to pop his best friend. No more so than right now. Why couldn't Eliot just zip it, enjoy the show? The entire trip, Eliot had whined about "things that could go wrong." He'd conjured an encyclopedia of worst-case scenarios, everything from catching Legionnaires disease if they stayed overnight in "that flea-bag motel," to food poisoning from the freakin' Waffle House, to carjacking. "We're running out of gas. We'll be stranded in the middle of nowhere" was on permanent loop.

There were times he'd wanted to pull over and leave Eliot in the middle of nowhere.

You'd think by the time they'd reached Los Angeles, the

E-man would have chilled out. Not so much. The shotgun-riding worrywart was sure every other car on the freeway had targeted them for a drive-by. When they pulled off the 101 at the Hollywood Hills exit, Eliot had been convinced Nick was going either "the wrong way," or "in circles." Kept whining that the car, Nick's 1997 Chevy Nova, wasn't going to make it up these steep hills, they'd be killed in a head-on with an oncoming car, just around the next hairpin turn. "This can't be the right neighborhood," Eliot whined. "We're lost. We should call Jared, give him our cross streets. He'll tell us how to get there."

Call for directions? How lame would that look?

Nick didn't need directions. Let alone nervous Nelly the nail-biter on his butt. He needed his best friend to have a little faith in him. After eighteen years of friendship, Eliot Kupferberg still thought Nick Maharis was a reckless rebel, bound for trouble. Not anymore. Nick was bound for a career as a professional model. The Calvin Klein billboards, man! His gig with a top L.A. photo agency was the first step into his bright and brawny future.

"Her p . . . p . . . pants . . . She's pulling them off!" Eliot cried, alarmed. "And she's . . . oh, shit, Nick, I know her! I recognize her, she's . . ."

"*Sweet,*" Nick whistled under his breath.

The action on the chaise lounge ramped up. The make-out session got more heated. Arms and legs were wildly entangled now. Jared and the chick were bumping, grinding, breathing heavily, in their own space.

"I told you we weren't lost," Nick said.

There was nothing else to do. Nick was just gonna stand there and watch. Eliot had to take matters into his own hands. He'd noticed the cell phone that slipped to the ground along with Jared's towel. He dug into his pocket and retrieved his own cell. During the process of renting the share house, he'd already programmed Jared Larson's number in.

The Killers' "Mr. Brightside" rang out. Which apparently was Jared's ringtone. His head jerked up. And not a moment too soon. He'd been kissing her, caressing her breasts, and was headed southward. He stopped to get the phone, just as Eliot knew he would. Hollywood playas never missed a call.

Finally! Jared saw them, standing not twenty feet away, Nick gaping, Eliot with the cell phone by his ear.

The girl, openmouthed, flipped around, affording them a full-on topless view. Eliot nearly fainted. It *was* her.

"Jared Larson here," Jared said warily into his phone.

Huh? Who did he think was calling? Eliot was confused. Jared couldn't be that dense, could he?

Catching on, Nick shot him a murderous look.

Eliot cleared his throat. "Uh . . . Jared? It's us. Eliot. And Nick. From Michigan. We're . . . uh . . . here." Stupidly, he waved.

Jared shaded his eyes, kept a straight face, flipped the phone shut. "Dudes. You're seriously early."

Nick countered, "Nah, we're right on time. Sorry we kind of walked in on you guys."

Shit, Eliot thought: Jared had meant California time. They weren't expected for three hours. "We're still on East Coast time," he said by way of apology.

Wrapping the towel around his waist, Jared nodded. "S'cool. This day has already been full of surprises."

For a guy who'd just been caught with his pants down, this Jared character was smooth. A childhood rhyme caught Eliot by surprise—"smooth as the shine on ya' granny's ride." *Okay, I'm officially an idiot,* Eliot realized.

Jared pointed toward the sliding glass doors that led into the house. "You guys go on inside. The room upstairs with the twin beds is yours." He nodded at the girl, who hadn't bothered to cover up. "By the way, this is—"

"Zoe!" The name popped out of Eliot. "Zoe Wong! I'd know you anywhere. I mean . . ." He fumbled, feeling excessively stupid, "Not that I've ever seen your . . . uh . . . or even thought about you in that way . . . it's not like that."

Jared swooped in for the save. "Lindsay Pierce. She used to play Zoe on TV. Her real name is Lindsay."

And those are real too, Eliot caught himself thinking, and turned tomato red.

314

• • •

Nick thought he'd died and gone to heaven. A tune looped in his head. *I wish they all could be California girls.* . . . Maybe they all were! He was too macho to deal in superstitions, but this felt like a sign. Proof he'd done the right thing, coming out here for the summer. First thing they see? An R-rated scene, costarring a real, actual actress.

It didn't take a leap of the imagination for Nick to put himself in Jared's towel. He'd been a fly-guy in high school, a chick-magnet, teacher-charmer, trophy-winning athlete. With his dark good looks and buff bod, he was the guy other guys wished they looked like. In L.A., he'd be golden. This summer was going to rock harder than he'd dared imagine. He just needed Eliot to be there with him, not make them both look like hicks. He flexed a bicep.

Eliot nosed into the room at the end of the hallway. "Do you think he meant this one?"

Nick sighed, ran his fingers through his long, curly black hair, and elbowed his way past Eliot. "Yeah, bro, I'm pretty sure this is the room." On the second floor of the house, they'd passed an open loft area with a view of the living room, a tricked-out master bedroom with its own balcony, and another with a double bed and canopy. Theirs was good-size—twin beds against opposite walls, a couple of dressers, windows that faced the winding street.

Nick upended the bigger of his duffle bags, the one that held his weights, barbells, ropes and elastic pulleys, and a half dozen pairs of new gym shorts and matching bicep-baring tank-shirts. He was just about to shove them in the top two dresser drawers.

"Wait!" Eliot brandished a can of disinfectant like a weapon. "We have to spray and wipe the drawers clean first. Who knows what could be living in them?"

"A colony of rats? Or snakes? Maybe spiders!" Nick teased. "I'd say cockroaches, but I bet they're not allowed in this neighborhood."

"Germs! I meant germs, mold, dust," Eliot argued. "You know how allergic I am. And don't think you're immune either."

"Knock yourself out." Exasperated, Nick flopped on the bed.

Nick and Eliot had been next-door neighbors and best friends forever. They'd braved everything together, from the terror of the first day of kindergarten through cub scouts ("scub scouts," as Nick's sister Georgina used to call it), from confirmations and bar mitzvahs, braces, glasses, and zits; from the "Will I be cool?" fear of freshman year in high school through the triumph, relief, and excitement of graduation.

Didn't matter that they were so different—Nick, dark, hearty, handsome, and an up-for-anything adventurer, while

Eliot was pale, shy, gawky, terrified of his shadow. Didn't matter that Eliot was a reader, a thinker, computer savvy, observant, and cautious, while Nick was all about action movies, violent video games, wildin' out, impulse. Or that Nick was a babe magnet. Eliot? Not so much.

Early on, the two had forged an unbreakable bond, a protective shield.

No way was Nick ever going to suffer the humiliation of failing any classes. Not while Eliot had his back.

And anyone who even thought about bullying Eliot had to go through Nick first. No one was dumb enough to try.

Nick fronted that the upcoming year would change nothing, despite the fact that Eliot's grades and SAT scores had won him admission to Northwestern University in Chicago, while he (even with Eliot's tutoring) would be staying home, "stuck at State," as the Michigan saying went. If you were smart, you went to the University of Michigan in nearby Ann Arbor. If you weren't of that "caliber," a word Nick's father used, you went to Michigan State, in East Lansing. Stubbornly, Nick refused to believe that distance would cause a chink in the armor that was their friendship.

Eliot knew better.

Not that he'd dare say it out loud—'cause that'd be wimpy—but Nick sensed the real reason El had agreed to come with on this trip. Sure, the E-brain was taking classes at

UCLA with some science professor. But, dude, he could have done that anywhere. Eliot was here as a last act of solidarity, of support. One final give-in to Nick, who was on a quest—his chance to make it big, to change the course of his future.

Nick had the look—and the bod—to be a model. He was five-eleven, 180 pounds of serious ripped muscle, with dark, hooded eyes—"bedroom eyes," the girls used to say—a straight nose, and pillow-soft lips. He wore his dark curly hair long, behind his ears, just brushing his shoulders, and liked to sport a few days' worth of manly stubble. Gave him a sexy, dangerous vibe.

Nick had done some modeling in catalogues for stores like Meijer and Kohl's, as well as a TV spot for a Chevy dealership. It was time to trade up. The Abercrombie shopping bag, Calvin Klein jeans, posing with some hot babe in magazine spreads. It was all about being in the right place, with a tight butt, at an opportune moment.

He could have come out west alone, he wasn't scared or anything. He just thought it'd be more fun with Eliot along.

Eliot, who was now staring out the bedroom window, declaring, "This house is one mudslide away from death."

Maybe scratch the fun part.

Sara:
Stranger in Holly-Weird

Sara stood on the fabled corner of Hollywood and Vine, over-whelmed and underfinanced. The oppressive heat, though dry, had turned her shoulder-length, wavy blond hair into sticky, sweaty tendrils. Her loose-fitting T-shirt now clung to her. Embarrassed, she pulled at it self-consciously, and willed herself to stay calm.

Granted, she was—momentarily—lost. But she'd made it this far. She was in the heart of Hollywood, California! A place she'd spent her whole entire life dreaming about. The city that held, Lord willing, the key to her entire future. She should be tingling with excitement, not shaking with fear.

Things just hadn't started out as she'd expected, that's all.

Her dreams, fueled by magazines, movies, and the chit-chat of small-town beauty pageants, had not prepared her for this chaotic city, or even this street, choked with traffic, wider than the river that snaked through her rural Texas hometown. And the people walking by—it was like a carnival of faces, tourists with cameras, bikers, hippies, skinheads, freaky folks of all shapes and sizes.

It wasn't like she believed the myth about the streets of Hollywood being paved with gold. But she had expected a town radiating glamour, glitzy stores showing off designer fashions, famous restaurants packed with stars.

Not Big Al's Tattoo Parlor. Or Bondage Babes Leather 'N' Thongs. She shuddered.

No wonder she felt less like Audrey Hepburn in *Breakfast at Tiffany's* and more like Kate Hudson in *Almost Famous*. Setting her suitcase down, she stepped off the curb, shaded her eyes from the oppressive sun, and waved tentatively, hoping a taxi would stop.

"*Mira, mira, chica*—oooh, come closer!" A man with a scruffy beard and bad skin leaned out of his car window, leering at her.

She jumped backward, her heart thumping.

"You need a ride, sexy mama?" He crooked his finger, beckoning her. "We got room for you."

"N . . . no," she managed to squeak, thankful the traffic light had changed, and the impatient car behind honked, forcing him to move on.

No, this was not the Hollywood she'd fantasized about.

Guess that's why they call 'em dreams, she thought ruefully, *and not "real life."* Sara squared her shoulders, gripped her suitcase, and plowed on. She'd taken the shuttle bus from Los Angeles International Airport into Hollywood, thinking: How far could it be from Hollywood to the Hollywood Hills? Thinking it'd be easy enough to walk.

The bus driver had dropped her off at the corner of Hollywood Boulevard and Cahuenga, advising her to grab a cab to complete her journey to the Hollywood Hills. "You can't walk it," he'd told her. "It's too far, honey. And here's a tip: No one walks in Los Angeles."

Cab fare had not figured into her carefully constructed budget, so she skipped lunch. But darn if she could figure out how you "grab a cab." In the town that made movies, hailing a cab didn't work like *in* the movies, where all you had to do was step off the curb and wave into the street. All she'd netted with that gesture was a scary man trying to lure her into his hunk-of-junk car.

She walked west along Hollywood Boulevard. The oppressive desert heat forced her sweat glands into overtime. Now everything was sticking to her, the long flowy skirt, her bra and panties, even her jewelry—a simple cross pendant and her silver purity ring.

Two long blocks later, at the crazy-big intersection of

Hollywood Boulevard and Highland Avenue, she found a phone booth. The famed Grauman's Chinese Theatre, with its opulent pagoda roof, was only a few feet away; the brand-new ultramodern Kodak Theatre, home to the Academy Awards, loomed behind her.

She parked her suitcase on the curb and dug into her purse for the phone number of the only person she knew—though hadn't yet met—in Los Angeles.

Her panic accelerated with each one of the four long rings. Finally, a voice that wasn't voice mail: "This is Jared."

A long pause. Then, "Sara who? Do I know you?"

His tone caught her up short. What if the guy from whom she'd rented a room turned out to be unfriendly, or worse, a thief? What if he'd taken her money and there wasn't even a room? She swallowed hard. "Blind faith, that's what you're going on," her boyfriend Donald had said when she'd sent ahead the first month's rent. "And that's just not smart, Sara."

But Donald hadn't wanted her to go, would've said any-thing to stop her. And a few seconds later, when she explained herself, the voice on the other end of the pay phone softened. "Oh, *that* Sara! Of course!" Jared had told her to wait right there. He'd be by in a jiffy to pick her up. Not that he'd said "jiffy." Her word.

Heaving a sigh of relief, Sara hung up, closed her eyes, and leaned her forehead against the plastic receiver. A verse from a hymn popped into her head. *I once was lost, but now I'm found.* . . .

Yes, faith was a good thing. It would see her through. It would see her live the dream she and her mom had nurtured for so many years. And like her mom often sang, *Dreamin' comes natural, like the first breath of a baby.* . . . It would reward them for the sacrifices they'd made, for the scrimping and scraping by they'd endured for so many years. Pageants had been Sara's ticket to show business, only it'd cost a lot to enter them and make her costumes. Singing and dancing and baton-twirling lessons, it all added up! But she and her mom had persevered. Little Miss Texarcana. Little Miss Darlington County. Little Miss Country Dumplin'; Jr. Miss Bayou. She didn't always win the crown, but she usually made the top three.

Her mom was never disappointed. When she didn't win, Abby Calvin would remind her, "God has bigger plans for you. You've been blessed with talent. You're meant for better things than standing around, showing off some fancy outfit, twirling a baton. My Sara is going to be a star."

It wasn't just their silly pipe dream. Everyone at home agreed, from their friends and neighbors, to the teachers and kids at school, to so many pageant directors, she'd lost count. Becoming an actress was God's plan, her destiny.

By Sara's nineteenth summer, they'd saved enough money for one plane fare to Los Angeles, and one month's rent. The idea was to get a waitress job while calling on agents. You needed an agent to represent you, that's what all the pageant directors had said. Her first appointment was already set up by Ron Zitterman at Pageants, Inc. Sara had packed one suitcase with a few "audition" outfits. A bunch of addresses for other talent agents lay tucked into her most precious possession, her Bible.

Sara's dad believed in her, but his faith seemed to falter the nearer she got to actually leaving. Pop put the kibosh on her staying at "some sleazy rooming home, or cheap motel." He'd watched too many episodes of *CSI* to allow her to live alone.

They'd found the listing on the computer at the library. Her dad had just about grilled Jared Larson, who'd assured Virgil Calvin that the house was in a safe neighborhood, that it'd be like a college dormitory, with other girls Sara's age. Jared had mentioned that his own parents would be checking in.

"Miss . . . miss . . ." Someone was tugging on her skirt, whispering hoarsely.

How long had she been standing there, blocking the pay phone? She spun around.

"Miss . . . please . . . can you help me?" Sara's heart clutched. A child, rail thin, brown, and sweaty, thrust an open palm at her. "Please, for food," she croaked.

Sara stared down, a wave of compassion washing over her. The child's dark hair was a matted and greasy nest, her fingernails dirty, clothes ill-fitting and shabby. And she was just this little bitty thing, couldn't be more than eight years old.

"Where are your parents, sweetie?" She knelt down to get a better look, found herself staring into big brown puppy-dog eyes, ringed with thick black eyelashes.

The child seemed not to have an answer. "I'm hungry," she finally said. "Could I have some dollars?" Her eyes now fixed on Sara's purse, up on the shelf of the phone booth.

"Of course you can," Sara said without thinking. She stood upright and scanned the street, hoping to see some adult this child belonged to.

Instead she saw the back of a husky teenager in a white tank top and backward baseball cap—peeling down the street with a suitcase. Her suitcase.

"Hey!" She grabbed her purse and gave chase.

But the young thief was fast, and the few seconds it'd taken the child to distract her were costly. Undeterred, Sara sped down the block, yelling for the kid to stop. Back at Texarcana Regional High, she'd run track, been pretty darn good, too. Only she wasn't in her tracksuit and Keds—she was hampered by the long cotton skirt clinging to her damp legs and ladylike sandals. Her calves began to ache, she felt a sharp stab in her groin. Still, she was five-nine and all legs. Sara felt certain she could have overtaken the kid. She would have, if not for the car that'd suddenly swerved onto Cherokee Street and screeched up to the curb. In a flash, the boy—and her suitcase—were inside and speeding off down the street.

More outraged than scared, she panted, waited for her breathing to slow, her heart to stop pounding. When she hobbled back to the phone booth to dial 911, the little beggar girl was gone. No doubt the kid was already in the getaway car.

She'd been set up. Scammed. Mugged.

The sobs didn't come until after she'd reported it to the police, but when they did, she shook violently. She wanted to call her mother, but wouldn't dare. What could Abby Calvin do from a thousand miles away? Her pop would demand she turn around and come straight home. More than anything, she felt ashamed. She'd been such an easy mark—robbed by a couple of kids!

She'd just finished repeating her story to a policeman—Raimundo Ortega, his badge said—when the gleaming Lexus convertible pulled up. Its driver, a spiffy-looking guy in a bright lime-green polo shirt, crinkled his forehead worriedly. "Are you Sara? Did something happen?"

"You must be Jared. This is so embarrassing. . . ." She offered a rueful smile and told him what'd happened.

He pulled a business card from his wallet. "Officer, I'm Jared Larson. My father is Russell Larson, the head of—"

"Galaxy Artists." Patrolman Ortega, clearly impressed, finished the sentence.

"That's right," Jared said with a smile. "If you could retrieve Miss Calvin's suitcase as soon as possible, we'd be in your debt."

The cop, who'd only a moment ago advised Sara that petty theft was a low priority—discouraged her from thinking she'd ever see her belongings again—practically saluted Jared. The LAPD would get right on it! He would personally call with a status report in a few hours.

"I can't tell you how much we'd appreciate that," Jared responded politely.

What Patrolman Ortega did next could've knocked Sara over with a feather. "I know this is kinda strange . . . circumstances and all," he said haltingly, "but, if you wouldn't mind, sir, there's this, uh, screenplay I've been working on, and y'know how it goes. . . ."

Jared held his hand up. "Say no more. Just send it to my summer house in the Hollywood Hills, and I'd be happy to get it to my father right away—with a special note about how cooperative you've been."

Sara got into Jared's car numbly. What kind of strange place *was* Hollywood? "W-what," she stuttered, "was that all about?"

"Nothing that doesn't happen every day. Mr. Policeman needed extra incentive to find the thief who stole your suitcase."

She thought for a moment. "Incentive? Don't take this the wrong way—I'm grateful for everything—but wasn't it more like bribery?"

"No way. It's just how things work in this town. Quid pro quo."

"Quid pro what?" Sara was even more confused.

"You do something for me, I'll do something for you," Jared explained. "And let me tell you something—a cop with a screenplay to sell? That's just a cliché. Who doesn't have a screenplay to sell? Or a headshot to get to a casting director. A tape or DVD, a dream of fame and . . ." He trailed off, probably realizing he was about to describe Sara.

"So you really will send his script to your father?"

He shrugged. "Let's see how fast he comes up with your suitcase."

Sara was speechless.

"Anyway, at least they didn't get your money," Jared said, changing the subject. "Unless you had a cash-stash in the suitcase?"

Sara shook her head. "Something more valuable."

"Jewelry?" Jared guessed.

"My Bible."

This—*this!*—shocked him. Not that she'd been mugged. Not that he'd just bribed, and probably lied to, the police. He coughed, a poor attempt to cover up a laugh.

Sara wasn't angry. She had good instincts about people— well, if you didn't count that little girl at the phone booth— and she believed, deep down, Jared was a good person. She turned her head, sized him up as he drove. He was a looker, too, if you liked skinny boys with fancy cars who could sweet-talk their way out of any situation. They weren't her ways; she wasn't sure if they were virtuous.

But she felt safe, for the first time all day.

"You hungry?" Jared asked her now.

"No." Her stomach growled, giving her away.

He laughed. "Hang on, we're coming up to In-N-Out Burger. Best burgers in the West."

She brightened.

"With fries and a shake, that's what we'll get you," Jared was a mind reader.

"I'm on a kind of tight budget," she admitted, salivating.

"No worries, it's on me. Your trip got off to a bad start. This is comfort food—you'll feel better, promise."

He pulled up to a fast-food place that resembled a glossy country diner. IN-N-OUT BURGER, the sign above it, painted fire-engine red with a blazing yellow arrow, advertised.

While they waited on the ten-car-long line, Jared informed her, "This place is a California legend. People drive sixty miles each way for their famous double-doubles."

"What's a double-double?" Sara's stomach rumbled so loud, she was sure folks in the cars behind them could hear it.

Jared just grinned.

The minute she found out, she became an instant convert.

They sat at an outside picnic table for what Sara believed was the tastiest meal she'd ever had. The heat no longer bothered her, nor was she fretting about how her sweaty clothes were clinging to her. She felt sure her suitcase would be returned. Life was all about the burger—or, burgers. A "double-double" turned out to be two juicy cheeseburgers, lettuce, tomatoes, and onions stacked on a big ol' toasted bun.

She was too hungry to be embarrassed about the way she practically Hoovered it, washing it down with a rich chocolate shake. Not until she wiped her face and released a huge sigh of contentment and relief did she realize Jared was staring at her.

"Welcome to Los Angeles," he said with a wink.

Sara was charmed by the orange and blue house. "It's like a little gingerbread cottage, right out of a fairy tale . . . so colorful!"

Jared admitted he'd never quite thought of it like that.

Her appreciation grew when Jared led her into the living room. "This is just so homey!" she exclaimed. "It's like a huntin' lodge, only with guitars on the walls instead of deer heads."

A throaty, staccato laugh rat-tat-tat-tatted from behind her. Sara spun around. The cackling was coming from a pretty, freckled girl with long reddish hair. Tucked comfortably in the corner of the sofa, she balanced a thick fashion magazine on her lap and held a glass filled with ice and a clear liquid.

"If you're waiting for her to stop, best sit down and get comfortable," Jared advised.

"Is she laughing . . . at me?" Sara was confused.

"Guitars instead of deer heads! That's . . . priceless!" the girl squealed, slapping the cushion with her free hand.

Jared leaned over and took the drink away from her. "Sara, I'd like you to meet Lindsay. Tragically, she is unable to help herself. She's afflicted with TAS: Tactlessly Annoying Syndrome. Exacerbated by alcohol."

Tears were sliding down Lindsay's scrunched-up face as she continued to hoot. "Hunting lodge!"

Just then the sliding glass door from the far end of the room opened, and someone started toward them. Sara gasped and turned scarlet. 'Cause this boy must have jumped down off one of the billboards on Hollywood Boulevard. He was dark-eyed, curly-haired, and what a build! He was the hunkiest guy she had ever seen. The most naked, too. But for a teensy black boykini, he wasn't wearing a lick of clothing. She could not stop staring.

Above his swimsuit, his flat stomach formed a V shape. He was all ripples and muscles, biceps, triceps—what they called six-pack abs. He didn't have any chest hair. And he was dripping wet.

Something went flippity-flop in her tummy. She forced herself to look away.

So it was a moment until she could respond to his greeting. He walked right up to her, held his hand out. A large hand, she noticed, with slim, well-defined fingers. "Hi, I'm Nick," he said in a big, booming voice. "You must be Sara, right? I was just in the Jacuzzi. Welcome to Casa Paradise!"

Her voice wavered. "Thank you. This . . . sure is . . . some house!"

"Too bad it could skid down the mountain in a mudslide, be swallowed up in an earthquake, or flame out in the flick of a wildfire." The worried-sounding voice drifted down from a loft area that overlooked the living room. Sara peered up into the bespectacled, round, friendly face of another boy, this one skinny and frizzy-haired, leaning over the wood railing.

"Hi, I'm Sara—and I sure hope you're not the building inspector or anything?"

Nick interjected, "He's Eliot, our resident worst-case-scenario worrywart, and all-round pain in the butt."

Eliot. Nick. Jared. She gulped. She'd be living with three boys. Surely something Jared had not told her pop.

"You just get here?" Eliot asked. "I'll help you with your luggage. Is it outside?"

"You could say that," Jared responded dryly. "Very far outside."

A little while later Sara found herself on the low-slung striped sofa, between Nick and Eliot. Jared had settled into an easy chair, Lindsay'd fled to the black leather love seat. What surprised Sara was how friendly everyone seemed, even Lindsay—how comfortable they were with each other. And they'd only started sharing the house the day before.

What truly astounded her? She practically felt like one of them already. Completely the opposite of how she was only a few hours ago. Settled, secure, among folks all around her age. Everything was gonna work out just fine. Maybe being robbed her first day was God's way of testing her.

"What if you don't get your suitcase back?" Nick was asking her now.

"That'd be okay." Sara pictured the little girl who'd been used as bait. "They're just material things. Those people probably need those clothes more than I do. I've already forgiven them in my heart."

"You have?" Jared was astonished.

"You're taking this really well," Eliot put in, also surprised.

This time Lindsay didn't let loose peals of laughter but leaned forward and asked, "Are you one of those teens for God or something?"

"I'm a Christian, if that's what you mean."

Lindsay smirked and pointed to the bottled water on the coffee table. "Best not drink that. It's Kabbalah water. It'll turn you Jewish."

Eliot chuckled; even Nick couldn't hide his amusement.

Jared frowned. "You're being a jerk, Lindsay."

She turned to Sara. "Only if you drink the whole thing." Lindsay found herself highly amusing, but Sara didn't get it. What'd Lindsay find so funny?

Or why, a bit later, when she innocently said, "So are you fixin' to be an actress too?" Lindsay forgot to laugh. She turned purple.

The View from the Jacuzzi

Jared pressed his lower back into the pulsating jet of the Jacuzzi, luxuriating in the powerful water massage. He rested his elbows on the blue marble lip of the hot tub and inhaled the sweet, orangey California air. This was his real life, not sweltering in some pissant classroom in Ojai making up his loser classes. If he cared about medieval times, he'd rent *Gladiator*, not read *Beowulf*. Advanced calculus? And God created accountants . . . why?

Jared didn't need college, he needed to fast-forward to his real life. The one where he eventually ran Galaxy, where he made business deals from the Jacuzzi, swilling Corvoisier.

The bubbly in his glass today was beer. It worked for now; he was buzzed, and flush. The hicks from the sticks, Nick and Eliot, had ponied up their share of the first month's rent. Sara had paid for June in advance. He'd even guilted La Lindsay into giving up some coin.

He looked at his ex-girlfriend now, across from him in the hot tub. The Jacuzzi floozy, barely covered in a tiny string bikini, was flirting outrageously with red-faced Eliot, who was probably pitching a tent in his Boba Fett boxer swim trunks.

Eliot had to know he was out of his league, but better she cast her spell on this yokel than on Jared. He was relieved he and Lindsay had gotten interrupted on Friday—his resistance had been low, her persistence set on max. He was over her, over the hurt of unread e-mails, unreturned phone messages, unacknowledged gifts. He could duck and weave with the best of them, but backward was not a direction Jared ever moved. It was Lindsay who slammed the door on them three years ago, and Jared had no interest in ever opening it again. He ignored the twisting in his gut as Lindsay playfully flicked Eliot with water, regaling the bug-eyed yutz with tales of her glory days playing Zoe Goldberg-Wong.

She hadn't been quite so playful last night. That moment Sara had innocently inquired if she, too, was "fixin'" to be an actress? Priceless! Lindsay'd gone bat-shit. She'd taken Sara's cluelessness as a deliberate insult. Poor Sara. She couldn't know it, but she'd cut Lindsay in the worst possible way—(a) for not recognizing her! and (b) suggesting the two of them were equals, both trying to break into the business.

Sara's gaffes would not go unavenged. War had been declared at that moment. But was it truly war when only one side was playing?

Lindsay had refused to share a room with Sara.

Sara had graciously agreed to sleep in the loft. It lacked privacy, but she was a total Anne Frank, and believed no one would spy on her!

When Sara realized the landline phone in the house had been disconnected, Lindsay had refused to lend her a cell phone to call her folks.

Eliot came to the rescue, insisting Sara use his.

Lindsay wouldn't lend her any clothes to sleep in.

Sara had laughed it off. "That's all right, you're such a teeny little thing, they wouldn't fit me anyway."

That'd placated Lindsay for the moment.

Jared held out no hope for a lasting peace.

But at this moment, twenty-four hours later, all good. His third beer was icy cold, goin' down smooth. A soft southerly breeze caressed his shoulders, his hair. Neil Young's classic album *Harvest Moon* wafted through the outdoor speakers. The sun cast an orangey glow as it began its descent beyond the mountains.

Nick was stretched out on a towel next to them, letting what was left of the sun dry him. Pious pageant-girl Sara, in a borrowed pair of shorts from Nick and a T-shirt from Eliot, was sitting on the grass a few feet away, hugging her knees. And, he couldn't help noticing, totally devouring Nick with hungry eyes. Hmm . . . be interesting to see how that played out. No way had Nick not noticed blond Sara's ample curves and sweet demeanor.

Soon the housemates would be in for the ultimate Cali-sunset experience, gloriously dizzying, pinks, corals, and tangerines, a first for his newbies. Feeling generous, Jared picked up his cell phone and lazily ordered dinner from Tuk Tuk Thai for all of them. He was just about to recite his credit card number into the phone when Lindsay kicked, splashing water at him, and shook her head.

Reminding him that his credit cards had been cut off. "Wait, it'll be C.O.D. Twenty minutes? Great."

Lindsay grinned. "Have you thought about how you're going to pay for a pool-cleaning service? Or a lawn boy? It's a mess out here, in case you hadn't noticed."

Sara tilted her head. "You mean, hire someone to clean the pool? And to cut the lawn? Why would y'all do that?"

"Because that's how we roll in these here parts," Lindsay mimicked.

Coloring slightly, Sara said, "But why spend money when we can do it ourselves? There's five of us. If we all pitch in, we'll get it weeded, cleaned up in no time."

"Pitch in?" Lindsay was flabbergasted.

Sara shrugged. "I'll just go ahead and get it started. I cut the grass at home, anyway, and what's a pool if not a bigger bathtub? I can handle that. Besides, I've gotta have something to do between auditions and job hunting."

Lindsay, who'd moseyed over to Jared's side of the hot tub, was amused. "What kind of job will you be huntin' for? And will there be a shotgun involved?"

"Knock it off, Lindsay." Jared was getting bored with her snarkiness. Lindsay's deep-seated insecurities always came out as jealousy. But of Sara? That made no sense. To make polite conversation, he said to Sara, "You said you had an appointment with an agent. Which one?"

"It's the Wannamaker Star Agency in Hollywood. I'm set up for Thursday at three. I'm hoping to have a waitress job by then so I can pay the fee."

Jared blinked. Was Sara really that naive? "Don't do that! That's a scam. No reputable agent charges up front. An agent only gets 15 percent of what you make for a job he or she has gotten for you."

Sara's face fell. "Really? Mr. Zinterman didn't say that. Guess I should cancel the appointment, then," she said dejectedly.

Just then the sound of a car horn blared. "Tuk Tuk Thai delivery!"

"Be right there," Jared shouted. As he jumped out of the

Jacuzzi and made for the front door, he looked up: The sky was already painted with coral, pink, and tangerine stripes. Timing was everything.

A dozen empty Thai food containers and several downed beer and wine bottles later, the vibe was lighter, freer, the buzz shared by all as they ate al fresco, grazing, gazing into the sunset. Yeah, even Lindsay had mellowed.

Eliot, who'd settled next to Sara, sharing her towel, was trying to cheer her up. "Maybe Jared's father can get you an interview at his agency," he suggested. "That's one of the biggest in town. Very reputable."

Lindsay was about to open her mouth but Jared clapped a hand over it, silently declaring the hot tub a "no insult" zone. Then he got an idea.

"That's the suckiest idea I ever heard!" Lindsay exclaimed as soon as her mouth was freed. He hadn't even finished explaining it.

"Chill, Lindsay—and listen. You both need agents, you both need jobs. I need rent from the two of you. And I've got pull at Galaxy. . . ." He was about to say, "What's the downside?" but he knew: Lindsay didn't do "competition" well, perceived or real. Sara was the enemy. Enemies don't share turf.

"What's your plan?" she asked coldly, arms folded.

Sara said nothing. Hope was written all over her face.

Jared flipped open his cell phone. First, he left a voice mail for Amanda Tucker, one of Galaxy's senior, most respected, and most feared agents. "Hi, Mandy, it's Jared. I've got an amazing opportunity for you. That assistant position you've been looking to fill? Wait'll you hear who I got you! Call me."

Nick, Eliot, and Sara traded glances. They had a lot to learn.

Now Lindsay was grinning big. She got it. Jared was multitasking. Amanda would get an assistant with cachet, a name in this town; Lindsay would net a powerful agent. Once said powerful agent got her an acting role, buh-bye, shitty assistant job! So win-win.

Jared's next call was to Lionel Mays, a junior agent. His tone was assured. "You're gonna be kissing my butt for this one, Li—I'm sending you a fresh new talent. Every agency in town's gonna want her, and you get the first shot at repping her. You can thank me later."

Sara leapt up off the ground as if she'd been launched and threw her arms around Jared, practically burying his face in her bust. "You got me an agent? You could do that with one phone call?" she squealed. "Bless you! Bless you!"

"Down, girl," Lindsay warned, though her tone was mischievous, not malevolent. "Jared set you up with an interview. You'll have to prove yourself."

Nick put in, "But that guy you called—he has to take Sara on, right? You're the boss's son."

Lindsay grinned mischievously. "You gonna give"—she could not resist—"*Pop* a heads-up? Tell him you're sending over a proven superstar, and a chunky wannabe? Besides, isn't there some kind of disconnect between you two?"

"Nothing that would keep me from doing a favor for my friends. I'm golden at Galaxy. As always." He smiled smugly for her benefit.

Sara was beaming. She turned to Nick and Eliot. "Y'all never did say what you're fixin' to do this summer. Did y'all need Jared to make a call on your behalf?"

"I don't think there's anything Jared can do for me. I'm not what you'd call showbiz material," Eliot said, self-consciously toying with his glasses.

"Don't be hard on yourself," Sara scolded. "You can do anything you want, if you put your mind to it."

"Thank you. But both Nick and I are set. He's got an internship and I'll be at UCLA, taking a course taught by the science editor at the *Los Angeles Times*."

"The *L.A. Times* has a science editor? What for?" Lindsay was puzzled.

"You're spending the summer in school?" Jared was equally bewildered.

Eliot explained. "I'm going for journalism at Northwestern University in the fall, and UCLA offered this great summer course—it covers natural phenomena, weather, earthquakes, that sort of stuff. Who knows, maybe I'll learn something there that can help us—if a brushfire doesn't swallow us up first."

Nick shook his shaggy mane. "Couldn't resist, could ya?"

Jared turned to Nick. "Bro, what kind of gig did you get?"

"Tomorrow I start at the Les Nowicki Modeling Agency."

Sara clapped her hands together. "I just knew you were a model! I knew—"

Eliot broke in, "He's not a model. He got an internship as a photographer's assistant." He shot Nick a look and amended, "It wasn't an easy internship to score. A lot of people applied. But once they saw Nick's portfolio and video, he got the gig."

"E's right," Nick said, "but I'm thinkin' once I get a foot in the door, I got a good shot at a modeling career."

"Definitely!" Sara's face was alight.

Lindsay took a long pull on her beer. Soberly, she said, "You do know, Nicholas, that all male models are gay. You might want to start with another part of your anatomy in the door."

Nick's jaw dropped.

It'd gotten dark out, and Jared hadn't put the outside lights on. So he could only assume that the macho Michigan model-to-be was pale as a ghost.

Jared jumped in to do damage control. "That's a sweeping stereotype, Nick. It's like saying—"

"That all actresses have to sleep their way to the top?" Lindsay stared at Sara.

Sara's jaw joined Nick's on the ground.

Eliot grew uncomfortable. "Ah, c'mon, that's such an old saw, it can't be true anymore."

Her eyes trained on Sara, Lindsay responded, "Some old clichés are still true. Like this one: In this town, to get ahead, you've gotta give some head."

"I'm sure I don't get your meaning." Sara gulped, making it clear she obviously did.

"The casting couch, girlfriend—surely even *you* have heard of that." Then Lindsay made a lewd gesture, licking her lips suggestively.

"Oh!" Sara's eyes grew big, and Jared could guess, her face red.

"Not all actresses sleep their way to the top. Why are you making her nuts?" He pinned his ex-girlfriend with angry eyes.

"Of course not all! Did I say 'all'? I meant the ones trying to break in—you know, the ones from . . . some little town in Texas . . . hoping to snag their first role." Lindsay was positively gleeful.

"I believe that I will make it on my acting talent," Sara said, no longer skittish but composed, "because I have no intention of debasing myself for any reason."

"Well, good luck with that." Lindsay rolled her eyes.

The front door bell rang. Saved! Jared wasn't expecting anyone, but was more than happy to have this conversation interrupted. So was Sara, apparently, who jumped up to answer it. A minute later he heard her squeal with delight.

She came running back around the house, one hand holding her suitcase, the other holding that of Officer Ortega. "Look! They found my suitcase!"

"We put a few of our best guys on it and got it right back. You might want to check that nothing's missing." Officer Ortega smiled proudly.

Jared went to shake the officer's hand, momentarily forgetting about the deal he'd made—until the cop handed him a thick manila envelope.

"You remember," he said haltingly, "that, uh, screenplay I mentioned? Thought you'd want to have a look at it—y'know, send it on to Galaxy."

"Of course! I'll messenger it to my father first thing in the morning. With a note about your speedy recovery of Ms. Calvin's belongings." Jared recited the well-practiced lines.

"You really gonna read that, send it to your old man?" Nick asked when the policeman had gone.

Jared shook his head no. It was Lindsay who grabbed the manila envelope and cavalierly pitched it into the pool, reciting, "I don't think this is right for Pop . . . mean for Galaxy."

Sara, wearing Nick's shorts and Eliot's T-shirt, dove into the mucky pool to rescue it.

Lindsay was shocked.

Dripping with algae, Sara waded out of the pool clutching the soaked package. "I feel responsible. Would y'all mind if I read it?"

"Knock yourself out," Jared said with a shrug.

Much later, after everyone had gone in, Jared reflected. No one had asked him about his summer plans. He had them, all right. They involved doing exactly what he'd tried to tell his dad he could do: meet people, schmooze, network—bring Galaxy some amazing deal. He'd have to add another chore to the summer: peacekeeping. Refereeing.

More to the point: taking the knife out of Sara's back every time Lindsay plunged it in.

A full-time gig, for which he'd get *bupkis* in return: nothing. His head said, *Oh, Lindsay, what am I going to do with you?* His heart, if he let it, was already on the verge of saying something else entirely.

Is this what it would be—a battle between head and heart, all summer long? Jared hoped not.

Workin' for the Weekend

Lindsay Stoops to Scoop.

It wasn't the smell that grossed her out. Or even the act itself.
It was the way it *looked*. What if someone saw her? What if,
worse, someone *recognized* her?

"Isn't that Lindsay Pierce, scooping dog poo? Eeww!" She
could practically hear the snide whispers. "So *that's* what
became of her!" You couldn't stoop much lower in this town,
and yet, one week into her job as Amanda Tucker's personal
assistant at Galaxy Artists, *this* is what she'd been reduced
to—picking up after Amanda's miniature pinscher, George
Clooney. Yes, Amanda had named it after a client she'd
famously failed to land.

Lindsay flung the doggie bag into the trash. She used to

have "people" who did this kind of thing for her—she wasn't supposed to *be* people. Among her other daily duties for her piddly paycheck: filling the min-pin's bowl with bottled Smart water and fetching freshly baked doggie biscuits. For Amanda, she ordered soy lattes, picked up and delivered dry cleaning and laundry, went office-to-cubicle selling Girl Scout cookies for her niece. Twice so far she'd run to the Manolo Blahnik store on Rodeo Drive, switching the gold five-inch-heeled Manolos for the black lizard four-inch-heeled Manolos, then back to the gold again.

Answering phones would've been a promotion.

"Yap! Yap! Yap!" Worse, the pesky little poo-machine on the other end of the snakeskin leash suffered from Irritable Bark Syndrome and a nasty temperament—just like his owner. He growled at little children, nipped anyone who went to pet him, and loveliest of all, tried to mount any dog he could get close to. Which was a joke, since George Clooney weighed all of seven pounds. And yet, the rat-faced runt tried to go all alpha dog, literally, on their asses.

It hadn't surprised her that Amanda kept the tiny terror in her palatial office. At her level, executive vice president of talent, she could have an alligator in there if she wanted. Lindsay hadn't thought she'd have to deal with it. Her first day, Amanda barked instructions: "Put his poo in a plastic bag. If you're not near a garbage disposal, put the package in your pocket until you find one—he gets embarrassed if you're hold-ing it out where other people can see."

And there was this little gem: "He won't answer unless you call him by his full name."

"George Clooney, no!" she scolded him as he tried to mount a passing pit bull bearing a dangerous resemblance to its scary owner. She jerked the little rat-beast away and continued their drudge through Griffith Park. The park was huge, and way famous. It had a gazillion trails for hiking, biking, and horseback riding, places to picnic and play golf. Plus it was home to the Los Angeles Zoo and the famous Observatory, at which a very spe-cial episode of *All for Wong* had been taped. Sweet memories for Lindsay—but, hello, it was also really out of the way, high in the hills and nowhere near Galaxy's offices. On the upside, there was virtually no chance of running into anyone important. Everyone who was anyone took their Princesses and Baileys to the Hollywood Dog Park. The downside? Same thing.

In spite of her lowly chores, she was beyond grateful to have this job. Her thank-you to Jared was the air-kiss she'd blown at Rusty Larson, casually mentioning her visit to Jared at the Ojai Community College campus.

Amanda, her boss, was just under Rusty on the power chain, a classic Hollywood agent. Severely striking, short-tempered, high-strung, and prone to screaming hissy fits, she strode through the office in her Prada suits and towering heels, berating lowly junior agents and assistants, pitching pencils, notepads, and coffee cups at anyone she felt like—then doing a complete one-eighty, kissing up to casting directors, producers, directors, and studio execs.

Lindsay lapped it up, loved every second spent at Galaxy's gleaming, curved, all-glass structure in the heart of Beverly Hills. She already felt back in the game. If she wasn't playing the part she wanted, at least she was at the epicenter of the action. Inside every office, inside every cubicle, even, the hottest scripts were being read, power meetings set up, and best of all, deals were being made. Her big break could not be far away. The assistants networked incessantly, and any juicy tidbit, gossipy or gig-worthy, got transmitted instantly.

This, as opposed to Sara's craptastic junior gofer job at *Caught in the Act*, some *ET*-wannabe TV show. At least she, Lindsay, was picking up the dog shit of a power player in the biz; Sara was probably toiling for some camera grip. And that joke of an agent Jared procured for her? Maybe he could get her an audition for third banana in a commercial. Airing on cable.

Lindsay's agent, Amanda Tucker, represented practically all of Hollywood's A-list actors. It wouldn't be long before her days of running, fetching, pooper-scooping, copying, mailing, and filing were over. Besides, she had all day to eavesdrop and gossip.

What she'd scoped out so far? The gloss behind the gleaming glass structure was fading. Galaxy needed a hit. It needed a big new star, and a starring vehicle—i.e., a block-buster movie to which it could attach its clients, producers, director, screenwriters: The Package.

Her cell phone rang. Amanda, her most frequent caller, launched into a list: "On your way back, stop at Gelson's and pick up an order of edamame, two brown rice California rolls, and a half-caf, skim-milk, fat-free cappuccino." Another of Lindsay's chores was to remember which fad diet Amanda favored each day. "And tell them not to skimp on the wasabi—I'm famished!"

Lindsay flipped her phone shut and fished inside her purse for a pen and paper to write down Amanda's list while she still remembered it—she wasn't authorized to have a BlackBerry yet. "Sit, George Clooney!" she ordered the dog, who for once obeyed. She loosened her grip on the leash.

Bad move.

As soon as Devil Dog felt the leash go slack, he sprang into action—bolted up and away. The leash slipped right off her wrist.

Shit! Lindsay took after him, calling out his name, to the delight and bemusement of the park-goers. She dashed up a trail, around a tree, looking everywhere. Finally, Lindsay saw his tail wagging. "George Clooney! Stop!" she yelled—and promptly tripped, right into the azalea plants.

She cursed, banging the ground with her fists. She'd lost the damn dog, and with it, her job, her future, her hopes. She was doomed. She closed her eyes, lay on the ground, and thought about weeping dramatically.

"I think I have something that belongs to you." A voice—male, strong, assured—floated down from above.

Accentuated by a confirming "Yap, yap, yap!"

Lindsay opened one eye. It was level with the scuffed toe of lace-up Timberlands. Granola-guy, was her first thought.

"Miss? Are you okay? I've got your dog . . ."

She opened both eyes, allowed them to travel upward—the boot was tucked under rumpled jeans. A black Napster T-shirt came next. She was about to get to the face, only it got to her first. Scruffy cheek stubble, medium brown eyes, long dark hair. So not her type.

In bending to help her up, he dropped what'd been tucked under his arm.

She instantly recognized it as a movie screenplay.

He became her type in a nanosecond.

Lindsay poured on the grateful. "Thank you so, *so* much. I'd have died if I lost poor . . . George Clooney. He means everything to me. And he's so tiny. . . ." She trailed off, allowing actor-dude (for of course that's what he was) to lead her to a bench, where she made a great show of affection toward an obviously wary George Clooney, who growled and tried to bite her.

"So, I'm Lindsay Pierce, and you're—?"

"Mark Oliver," he replied genially.

"Are you an actor?" She nodded at the script, tucking her hair behind her ears coquettishly.

"Isn't everyone in this town?" Mark had obviously never watched *All for Wong*.

No matter. It was info, not a new fan, she was after.

What Lindsay learned: Mark, a relative newcomer who'd been in several failed TV pilots, was represented by the Endeavor Agency, one of Galaxy's rivals. The script he was reading was for an action comedy called *Heirheads: The Movie*.

The plot involved three splashy young heiresses who use their vast resources to solve mysteries. It was Paris Hilton-as-Nancy Drew-meets-James Bond, Charlie's Angels without Charlie. As Mark described the characters, Lindsay easily saw herself as the most glam heiress, Remy St. Martin.

Mark was reading for the part of Remy's wealthy boy-friend. He didn't think the main girls were cast yet, but had heard rumors that some big-name starlets were going to screen-test. Lindsay wiped away the drool before he could see.

She had found her first gig.

Nick Stands In.

"Unzip your pants, Nicky, another inch down. We're going for more tease in this shot." The middle-aged photographer, Les Nowicki, looked up from behind the camera lens. His tan lines deepened when he frowned. "You have to learn to relax, to make love to the camera. Let's try it again."

Nick *was* trying. But relax? Not happening. Especially when a bunch of weirdos, guys, chicks, and others of indeterminate gender were staring at him, sizing him up—and down. He took a deep breath and eased his pants' zipper down another notch. An assistant turned a giant fan up, blowing his unbuttoned shirt wide open.

"That's better, that's *good*!" Les praised him through the lens while snapping his fingers. "He needs more shine!" Keith, one of Les's assistants, dashed over to rub his chest with oil. Nick tensed.

He was well into his first week at the modeling agency. The gig was not what he thought it would be. As a photographer's assistant, Nick figured he'd be hauling equipment, setting up lighting, moving props, learning by watching, getting instruction.

His goal was to get his own professional photos done, then sign with one of the major modeling agencies in town. By the end of the summer, he'd have a kick-ass portfolio—and the bucks would roll on in. Bonus? Meet 'n' greet some hot model-babes.

He hadn't bargained for spending his days, and some nights, striking seminude poses for the camera, being slathered with oils, gelled, glossed, made up, and dressed down.

Nick's primary function was being a stand-in. Before the

actual models arrived for the shoot, he was the guy who posed while Les's freak-team of assistants worked on the lighting, backgrounds, wardrobe, and often, on him. There was a gal who sprayed fake-bake tans and body glitter on the models, a guy whose sole job was eyebrow plucking, a manicurist, a pedicurist, and even someone who waxed the male models. Breast carpets, considered manly by many, were verboten at the studio. It was all about slick and shiny, and especially ripped.

For hours on end Nick stood, sat, reclined, lay on his belly, squatted, leaned against the wall, the window, the bed, so the team could judge what would work and what wouldn't. Digital pictures were taken, studied by Les and his team, then retaken, with adjustments in lighting, props, and his pose. By the time the actual models arrived, the set would be positioned and the shoots good to go, swiftly and smoothly.

The cool part was when he got to wear samples of designer duds—tight D&G T-shirts, Boss shades, Zegna suits. The uncool part was that most of what he wore, he wore . . . open. Suggestively so.

Nick had been too excited when he learned he'd gotten the internship to bother checking it out, to do what Eliot called "due diligence." So he came west without the slightest inkling of what kind of modeling photo studio Les Nowicki ran. He knew now.

Les specialized in shooting models for calendars, posters,

and greeting cards. Hallmark was probably not a big customer. A glance at the framed portraits lining the studio's brick walls told the tale: These models, mostly male, weren't exactly in family-friendly poses.

"Sophisticated" was the word used in his interview.

"Soft-core" was his opinion now.

"Turn your face toward the window, Nicky, rest your left hand on your thigh," Les instructed him. "Excellent!" He snapped away.

Nick stared outside. The studio was located on the fourth floor of a funky building on Santa Monica Boulevard in West Hollywood, or WeHo, as Les's helpers referred to the neighborhood.

"Boys-town," Lindsay had flatly declared.

Whatever. From his point of view, it was a bustling, vibrant, glitzy, showbizzy part of town. Nick gaped at the towering billboards up and down the boulevard, touting the latest movies, biggest CDs, and slickest fashions going. He could easily picture himself on each and every one, especially the Calvin Klein underwear ads, Bulgari Fragrance for Men portraits, Armani shades, Tommy Hilfiger stripes, Izod polos, and Nautica stars. Ads he'd seen in magazines were supersized in Hollywood.

"Turn the other way now. I want a profile, with your right

hand on the thigh. Higher, Nicky," Les instructed, motioning with his hand while his eye stayed trained on the lens. "Yes, that's it!" he crowed, clicking away. "Nicky, you're a natural!"

The compliment made him feel queasy.

"Break time, ladies," called Alonzo, another of Les's assistants. Nick quickly buttoned up his shirt and rezipped his trou.

"Hey, Nicky," Keith called out. "A few of us are heading to Hamburger Mary's for a bite and a brew. Come with?"

Nick declined—politely, he hoped.

"Oh, the summer boy is too shy to go out with us," Alonzo teased, as a few others laughed. "Still hasn't warmed up, but he will."

Don't hold your breath, Nick wanted to say, but tilted his head in a friendly gesture, and headed out the door. He hated being referred to as "the summer boy." It felt condescending.

Hiding under his army green VH-1 baseball cap, he walked the several blocks to Pink's, "the most famous hot dog shack in Hollywood," according to Jared. Hungrier than usual, he ordered two man-size chilidogs and a jalapeño dog, and took his unhealthy stash to an empty table on the patio.

A leggy blonde walked by, arm in arm with a guy in a blue and maize Wolverines T-shirt, the University of Michigan football team. A wave of homesickness crashed over him. He checked his watch. It was just after 5 p.m. back home. If he'd stayed there, he'd have been finished with his shift at his dad's construction site, heading to the bar, wolfing down a brewski, flirting with the babes. He'd have been . . . home.

He flipped open his cell, about to call Eliot. Weird El, who was only here to humor Nick, was the one in pig heaven. Spending each day in a stuffy classroom in front of the computer with a bunch of other catastrophe geeks. And then coming home to feast his bug eyes on two outta-his-league babes, an actress and a virgin. Nick had just punched in Eliot's number when a tray landed on his table. He looked up—into the amazing eyes, dazzling smiles, and perky boobs of a pair of L.A. hotties.

"Is it okay if we sit here?" asked the darker-haired one.

"Go for it."

The redhead piped up, "We don't mean to pry, but you look so familiar. Are you an actor?"

"Or a model?" the other one ventured.

Nick folded the phone, and smiled a real smile for the first time that day.

Sara Gets Caught in the Act.

"Sara, can you escort Cameron Diaz from her dressing room to Hair and Makeup? They're waiting for her there. And then we need you to help pre-interview Orlando Bloom—he's in dressing room three." Wes Czeny, the assistant director of

Caught in the Act, waved a script as he passed her in the hallway of KABC studios.

"Sure thing," Sara answered brightly. "I'm on it."

A big man with bushy gray eyebrows, a bulbous nose, and the friendliest face in Hollywood, is how Sara described her new boss. Her first day, a couple of people had warned her off him. "He has an evil temper." So far, Sara hadn't seen that side of him.

"He's a teddy bear," she gushed to her roommates.

"Wait till he wants to cuddle with *you*," Lindsay said with a smirk.

Sara had learned to let Lindsay's snide comments slide— she was too busy to fret over them anyway. Her job took up practically all her time. *Caught in the Act* was a new show, hoping to join the ranks of such popular entertainment half-hours as *Access Hollywood*, *Extra*, and *ET.*

As a start-up, the show demanded lots of overtime. She'd been there only two weeks, and already some days Sara worked near ten hours. She did so happily, would've worked through the night if needed. It was all so new and exciting! She was getting to see everything up close, big stars and their "handlers"— her first showbiz word she hadn't learned from Lindsay and Jared!—seeing how the writers came up with ideas, watching the directors, and figuring out what all the cameras and boom microphones were for. Every single person on the set impressed her, especially the hosts of the show, John St. Holland and Susie Smiley. They were so friendly, so smooth!

"The bland, the blonde, the botoxed," she'd heard one of the crew snipe about the pair. John had that kind of stony square face like it was chiseled out of marble, and Sally had blindingly white teeth and not a wrinkle on her. But Sara was pretty sure viewers loved them.

She knocked on the door of dressing room one, and was soon looking into the swimming-pool-blue eyes of Cameron Diaz, who'd been relaxing on the couch, a fat fashion magazine in her lap.

"Ms. Diaz, they're ready for you in makeup whenever you are."

Cameron slipped into a pair of high-heeled slingbacks and stood up, signaling she was good to go.

The star was tall, really slim, and like so many people in Los Angeles, very friendly. To Sara's comment that she hardly needed a lick of makeup, the star insisted that all girls need all the help they can get.

Sara had to pinch herself. One of the world's biggest movie stars was talking to her . . . just like any other girlfriend. Wait'll Momma hears!

It wasn't just Ms. Diaz who'd been gracious and normal. Sara had met a bunch of movie and TV stars. A few arrived with big entourages—usually it was the hangers-on who ordered her around—but it was her job to get them lunch or whatever they wanted, to make sure they were comfortable. Some came with long lists of requirements, topics they would not discuss on camera, and at least one stormed off the set after agreeing to an interview. But mostly, she found, the bigger the star, the nicer and more gracious they were.

The notion cheered her. When she got to be a star, she wouldn't have to pretend to be a diva, or anything like that. She could still be nice, virtuous, down-home. And she'd get there on her God-given talent, not because she'd compromised even one single value. She'd show Lindsay!

Everything that'd happened so far was due to divine providence. Jared had snared her an agent, Lionel—who she adored!—and Lionel happened to be friends with Candy Dew, the producer of the show, who mentioned they were hiring assistants. The phrase "It's not what you know, it's who you know" was turning out to be true in this world.

The point of *Caught in the Act*, she'd been told, was to present a different side of celebrities, to get them to confess their secrets—silly, sinful, salacious, or sweet; as long as it was personal, it'd do.

Candy had put it this way: "The only reason anyone comes on the show is because they have something to prove, or promote. It's our job to let them promote their latest movie, album, TV show, perfume, or whatever, prove they're not sick, or gay, or married, or too old, or crazy, and get them to spill something juicy to us. It's pretty simple, actually."

Her job? Do whatever was required, from whoever asked.

Listening to stars promote their movies got her thinking about the screenplay written by Officer Ortega. Sara had rescued it from the filthy pool because it was the right thing to do. She'd only read a few pages, but it seemed interesting. It was about this rookie cop and a runaway.

Now she picked up today's *Caught in the Act* script from Wes's assistant and made her way to dressing room three. The star, thin, angular, with a mustache and soul patch, was on the phone. Waiting at the door until he motioned for her to come in, she caught herself thinking, *He's not nearly as good-looking as Nick.*

When he got off the phone, he asked what she needed. That accent! It just about knocked her out.

"Would you mind if we went over the questions that Sally would like to ask during your interview?"

For the next half hour, over bottled water and fruit, they did. She found out he did not want to talk about any of his rumored romances, but he'd be happy to comment on his latest movies. And she found out, quite accidentally, that he had the funniest story to tell about his first dinner in an upscale

Asian restaurant, where he mistook the heated cloth napkins for shrimp toast—and tried to eat them!

Darn if she didn't laugh as hard as anybody during the taping, as he described the looks on the waiters' faces as he bit into the steaming fabric. Wes came over and put his arm around her. "Great job, Sara," he said. "You've got quite a knack for getting people to open up to you. Maybe you should consider that as a career option."

"I'm determined to try my hand at acting. That's why I'm here," she reminded him.

He snapped his fingers. "Damn! I forgot to tell you. Marla said your agent called—you should call him back. And, Sara—get a cell phone, okay?"

As soon as she could, she returned Lionel's call. And screamed so loud, the whole crew probably heard her. Sara had her first audition a week from tomorrow. When she stopped screaming, Lionel said, "It's just a peanut butter commercial, don't get excited."

Don't get excited? How could she not? Sara practically skipped along Hollywood Boulevard that evening, thanking the Lord for her good fortune.

She was in that generous frame of mind when, passing Big Al's Bondage Boutique, she noticed a teenage girl squatting on the sidewalk, coffee cup in her hand. Sara flashed back to her first day in Hollywood. This kid was only a few years older than the child who'd scammed her—a child who was probably rotting in some juvie facility by now.

Sara strode over, opened her purse, and knelt down beside the girl. "What's your name?"

Jared's Spider Club Web

"'Cel-e-*brate* good times, oh, yeah'!" Lindsay, in no way a singer, belted the song at the top of her lungs. She bopped to her own beat in the passenger seat of Jared's convertible. She wasn't even drunk yet (he didn't think), yet full-on uninhibited—loud and off-key. Wasn't there a law against felonious assault of iconic bar mitzvah songs?

"'We're gonna celebrate and have a good *time*'!" She hollered out the lyrics. And had he mentioned, badly?

"Linz, take it down a thousand," he shouted.

She ducked into the oversize lavender Hermès bag at her feet—*Note to self: how'd she afford that?*—extracted a bottle of Patron tequila, and took a swig.

"Oh, no you don't." He shook a finger at her. "Put that away."

"Don't be a buzzkill, Jared," she bellowed. "'Ev'ry-*one* a-*round* the world, c'*mon*'!" She danced in her seat, waving the bottle in the air.

"We're gonna get pulled over before we even get to the club!"

"When'd you turn into such a wuss? I'm precelebrating. I got my first audition next week—whoo-hoo! And besides, it's not against the law if the passenger is drinking."

"What state have you been in, besides oblivion? It's illegal to have an open bottle of alcohol in the car."

Playfully, she leaned over and licked his earlobe. "Oh, but you have a way with policemen-hyphenates. Patrolman-slash-screenwriter, officer-slash-actor-producer, cop-slash-model. Really, Jared, what're the odds you'd be stopped by another one of them?"

He had to laugh. She was so, so, so cute. And so upbeat and so damn . . . hot! Sexier than ever, stylin' to the max, wearing a shoulder-baring halter top, sprayed-on miniskirt, and slouchy high-heeled suede boots. With that pricey Hermès Birkin bag over her shoulder, the ex-girlfriend was workin' it.

He slammed on the mental brakes. He was not—repeat NOT—falling for her. And whatever playful flirting she was doing? Meant nothing. She hadn't, after all, tried seducing him again since that first day, several weeks ago. They were friends, they were cool, and tonight Lindsay was reconnecting with his—their—friends. It'd be her first night of serious clubbing since returning to Los Angeles. They were headed for the exceedingly exclusive Spider Club at the Avalon Hollywood. Jared's posse would be there, along with a petting zoo of A-list celebrities, everyone from Ashlee to Paris.

Lindsay Pierce would blow in there and blow everyone away. She suspected it; he knew it.

Jared had been out clubbing nearly every night since the summer began. Booze and booty weren't the only reasons. This season, he had an agenda. Before Labor Day, he would make one major deal for Galaxy, his dad's agency. Using his connections, charisma, and charm, he would suss out the hot new screenplay being whispered about; which young A-list actor wanted to switch agencies; find up-and-coming new directors. In a business where information is currency, Jared would strike it rich. He would prove to his father that he was worthy. The clubs were where the connections were, where the buzz began, where the showbiz action really was. For Jared, the club scene was the motherland.

Lindsay, the distracting passenger riding shotgun, also had something to prove to the showbiz world: She was on the comeback trail.

Lindsay had repeated the story to anyone who'd listen, how she'd tipped her boss Amanda off to *Heirheads: The Movie*. Then how the high-powered agent had coaxed the screenwriter into e-mailing her a copy of the script, at the same time brow-beating her staff for not knowing about it.

Lindsay excelled at suck-up. To her boss, she modestly cooed, "If not for George Clooney, that itsy-bitsy sweetie poochie-pie, we'd never have known about *Heirheads*."

To her agent, she was quid-pro-quo girl. She'd found it, she deserved a chance to audition. "The part of Remy St. Martin, it was written for me."

Lindsay's audition was a done deal.

Jared had tried to curb Lindsay's enthusiasm. "Amanda will totally send other actresses to audition for this. It's not you exclusively."

"They can dig up Katharine-freakin'-Hepburn and send her, for all I care." Lindsay flipped her copper tresses defiantly. "This role has my name on it."

Woe to the dunderhead who tried to yank her off the grandiosity pedestal. Jared knew when to give up.

"Besides, this script is so good, it can be the one that saves Galaxy," she'd asserted proudly.

"What about my family's firm needing saving?" That'd been a scary newsflash to him.

She repeated the office scuttlebutt: Galaxy was losing out to the biggies—CAA, ICM, William Morris, Endeavor. Galaxy had not nailed a blockbuster deal in weeks.

That'd freaked him out. In a biz fueled by "What have you done for me tomorrow?" if Lindsay was right, the situation sucked. If Galaxy looked weak, they'd soon be hemorrhaging A-list clients. His dad needed him more than ever. Rusty Larson just didn't know it yet.

A perp lineup of bare boobs, of all sizes 'n' shapes, met them at the door—the nightly brigade of girls holding their tops up, hoping to impress the bouncers at the velvet ropes of the Spider Club.

Lindsay was scandalized. "Are they auditioning for 'America's Next Top Tit-Model'?"

Jared laughed. "Things have . . . evolved . . . since you've been gone."

"You call degrading themselves evolution? Give me a break. What ever happened to the good old reliable payoff? Or the haughty 'I'm on the list' line. Or just sneaking in . . . ?"

"Like *you* ever had to! You had an all-access pass to every club in town," he reminded her as the burly bouncer, recognizing Jared, lifted the ropes and waved them in. "You may find that decadence has trumped cleverness."

"Self-degradation? Bad. Decadence? Just the way I like it," Lindsay quipped, slipping her arm around his waist.

It felt like old times.

On the trendy carousel of clubs in L.A.—Hyde, Les Deux, Mood, Rokbar, and the Tropicana came to mind—the Spider Club was the Friday night scene to make. Officially, Spider was the VIP room at the Hollywood Avalon rave hall. Realistically, only the seriously elite ever got in. Other clubs had theme nights, Spider's theme was "You know what? Don't even bother."

Inside Spider, the def-est DJs ruled. Tabletops were the preferred dance floor for sexy girls. The club was anything you wanted it to be, a rowdy drink-and-dance-fest or a discreet canoodle cradle. The red, pink, and orange Moroccan love-den booths inspired make-out sessions *and* make-deal sessions.

Everyone was looking to score.

"Yo, Ja-*red*! Over here!" First voice he heard over the thumping beat belonged to Tripp Taylor, trust-fund son of a famous producer. The Tripster was decked out tonight in an up-collar D&G shirt and wide-brim fedora dipping over one eye, a look that was too skeevy for Jared. He had one arm draped around slinky Caitlin Cassidy, daughter of a cosmetics empress, the other on the thigh of Ava Golightly, resident anemic-bulimic of their crowd.

"Make some room, peeps," the already inebriated Tripp ordered. "Our man with the plan has arrived. And, looky-loo, he has not come solo!"

Stacked cushy red-leather cylinders formed the backrest of the booths, each side roomy enough to seat three or four depending on the coziness quotient, which usually went up as the night wore on.

Facing this tony trio was Julie Baumgold (or, as Jared secretly thought of her, Julie BBB—Beautiful But Bony), Austin Tayshuss, and MK Erksome. This sextet was Jared's core crowd.

Julie B. was the first to realize whom Jared had brought. She clamped one bejeweled hand over her glossed lips. "Lindsay?! Oh, my God, *Lindsay*! You look amazing!!"

Ava came in second. "When'd you get here? You look fabulous!"

Tripp extended his hand. "Jared said you were back, but he failed to mention the foxy-factor! What's in the water back in Indiana?"

"Iowa," Jared corrected him, unsure why he was annoyed.

"I knew it was one of those *I* states." Tripp clasped Lindsay's hand.

Lindsay lapped up the attention, "Thanks, you guys—it's great to be back. What're ya drinking?"

Austin, son of a socialite and an action star, rose. "Squeeze in here, Linz, we'll make room."

Jared snapped his fingers. A waiter materialized. "We need a couple chairs." Like he'd let Lindsay sit between obnoxious Austin and lecherous MK.

Once they were settled at the end of the booth, Jared was happy. Lindsay, Julie, Caitlin, and Ava traded fruity martinis and girl-talk—shopping, designers, and who-was-screwing-who gossip. Lindsay fit in as if she'd never missed a beat.

The guys, meanwhile, sucked down shots of Patron and debated cars, clubs, clothing, the Bruins, the Trojans, and who had seats nearer to Nicholson and Spike Lee for the Lakers this year. The winner should have been Jared: Galaxy owned an entire row. But since Austin's dad had a hit movie, and MK's banker-mom had just struck foreign gold, it was likely he'd be grubbing off them.

"How's summer school treatin' ya?" MK asked. "Making up those suck-grades?"

"I'm multitasking," Jared replied, "making up the grades and making deals for my dad's agency."

Hearing him lie so smoothly, Lindsay pursed her lips and playfully pinched his cheek.

Jared was about to kick her, but just then, Julie got their attention. "Guys, look who's on the dance floor! She never comes here. Must be celebrating something."

Eight heads turned. The *Sports Illustrated* cover model and a few girlfriends were dancing to the Black Eyed Peas' "My Humps."

"She's *so* had work done," catty Caitlin sniffed. "Check the forehead."

Ava wasn't sure. "No wrinkles, but isn't she, like, twenty-two?"

"Your point?" Caitlin was clueless.

Jared chuckled. Ya gotta love superficial, especially here in Hollywood, where it goes deep.

Lindsay, quaffing apple martinis, sparkled, burbling about her coup, unearthing this amazing script *and* going for her audition next week.

"You rock, girl!" Austin cheered her on.

"That's our Linz, right back in the game. You are so my hero." Tripp waved his arms worshipfully. Bro was drunker than usual. That's what ticked Jared, not the fact that a girl Tripp hadn't mentioned once in three years was suddenly "our" Lindsay. He ordered another Patron.

Julie, suffering attention deficit disorder *and* acute affluenza, was over the actress on the dance floor and on to the Birkin bag on the floor by Lindsay's feet. She gushed, "I am so all about that Hermès! That's the ostrich leather in African violet. It's, like, seven thousand dollars, but the waiting list is impenetrable. How'd *you* get it?"

"I actually got it for free, off my agent," Lindsay said brightly, ignoring the implication.

"Amanda Tucker just *gave* you a seven-thousand-dollar bag?" Caitlin said suspiciously. "No way."

Ava arched a designer-plucked eyebrow.

"Amanda used it as a dog carrier," Lindsay breezily enlightened them. "Yesterday, the fart-faced runt took a dump in it. She was gonna throw it out. Instead, I had it cleaned." She hoisted the bag onto the table and unclasped it. "Smell anything?"

The group burst out laughing, Lindsay the loudest. Jared hugged her impulsively. Only later would he figure out how she'd "had it cleaned." She'd talked Sara into doing it.

More celebs, starlets, rappers, hip-hoppers, heiresses, and scions arrived. Lindsay kept an eye on the door, making sure everyone who used to know her saw that she was back. And in fine form!

She was flirting when Jared got up to let Austin and Ava get by—they were going to table-hop, glad-hand everyone they knew—and a stab of dread shot through him. What the hell was Adam Koenig, the kid he was paying to do his school assignments and take his tests, doing here? He was a nobody! The nobody who, if he came over to their table, could blow his cover to all his friends who believed he spent his days in summer school.

Jared stalked over to him. Best nip this little glitch in the bud, keep his secret tucked safely away.

Austin and Ava were in the deejay booth by the time he got back to their table, the dance floor was jammed, the music crankin'. A couple of semiclad women had already begun high-stepping on the tables as the dance version of a Christina Aguilera song came on.

Lindsay, totally tipsy by that time, massaged the back of Jared's head with her fingertips, bleating her rendition of the song into his ear. "'You are so se-*duce*-able, baby.'"

Luckily, the decibel level had shot up to deafening, so no one else heard. Jared, a little sloshed and a lot relieved that he'd taken care of his problem—Adam and friends were gone— gazed into her smoked-glass eyes and touched her soft dusty-pink pillow lips. She licked his finger and giggled. "'Yes, just *so* se-*duce*-able, baby . . .'"

"Linz!" Julie bopped up on the booth cushion and hoisted her skinny bod onto the thick glass tabletop. "Come dance with us."

Caitlin followed, and soon the two of them were shimmy-ing to Rod Stewart's "Hot Legs." Lindsay was into it. Her skirt, Jared couldn't help noticing as he helped her up, was awfully short.

As if magnetized, their table was instantly surrounded by a dozen guys. "Shake ya tailfeathers," someone yelled out, clapping as the music morphed seamlessly into tunes by Mariah Carey, Akon, Kanye West.

"Go, ladies! Go, ladies!" MK stuck two fingers in his mouth and whistled.

Outkast's "Hey, Ya" came on, and a girl atop a table across from them shouted, "Hey y'all—what about us? Can we get some love?" She and her girlfriend, in matching booty-shorts and sky-high Jimmy Choos, bumped hips together as the room egged them on and the song encouraged. *Shake it, shake it, shake it like a Polaroid picture, shake it, shake it!* And to the guys' delight, the dancers did just that.

"Oh, yeah?" Caitlin crowed. "Watch this!" She, Julie, and Lindsay did a highly suggestive bump and grind.

"Chick dance smackdown!" someone yelled.

From the far side of the room, another trio wanted in on the action. The group on the dance floor didn't want to be left out. For the next frenzied half hour, Spider Club became an elite rave scene with the whole crowd sweatin', singing, doing shots, and mostly dirty dancing at the urging of dance club favorites.

Lindsay was having a blast. Her rat-ta-tat-tat howl pierced the room.

God, Jared had missed her.

Out of nowhere, a lace thong flew through the air. He grabbed it. Linz—? But no, it belonged to Julie, now crooking her finger in a come-to-me motion.

Never gonna happen, he thought, pitching the panties to Austin, who'd come back to support his "team."

Caitlin had ripped off her bra and tossed it into the air. MK caught it and hung it on his ear, like a doofus. Lindsay wasn't wearing a bra. Jared hoped she wasn't drunk enough to—

"Your ex-girlfriend is smokin'!" raved Tripp. "Just how ex is she?"

"What do you mean?"

"I mean," Tripp leaned in, "can I have a go?"

"No!" Jared exploded.

Tripp held his palms up. "Whoa, sorry, bro, no need to get your boxers in a knot. I thought you two were over—"

"We are!" Jared shouted over the music, "But . . . she's . . . plastered! I don't want her taken advantage of, that's all."

"Help me up, you guys!" It was Ava, a little late to the dance party, now wanting in on the tabletop action.

If he hadn't been so pissed at his friend, Jared might've thought twice about the wisdom of four girls on one glass table. Ava, it turned out, didn't "go lightly" at all.

A half second later, she was up.

The table? Not so much.

A loud crack blasted through the room, accompanied by panicked screams. The table split in half, as if someone had karate-chopped it down the middle. Shrieking, the four girls slid to the center, crashing into one another. Julie's heel hit the halved glass first and hardest, sending shards flying in all directions. Her left leg folded under her and she grabbed at the air, trying to stop plummeting. But Caitlin had already fallen on top of her, pushing her down farther. Ava grabbed at Lindsay's hair, causing Linz to holler even louder and topple right into the Julie-Caitlin tangle.

Amidst the flying legs, arms, and butts were martini

glasses, since the girls had been toasting themselves while dancing. Splinters of colored glass sprayed the room, nicking them even as Jared, Tripp, Austin, and MK rushed to extract the girls without embedding any glass into their skin.

The Spider waitstaff rushed over. They got Ava off first, then Lindsay, Caitlin, and finally Julie, who was sobbing hysterically. "My leg! I broke my leg! Get an ambulance!" Between sobs she managed to insist she'd only go to Cedars-Sinai, not St. John's.

Caitlin and Ava, suffering cuts and bruises, would accompany Julie in the ambulance. Cait was already demanding plastic surgery because a few splinters had scratched her face. Ava, feeling guilty that she'd caused the landslide, wouldn't stop crying long enough to see if she'd actually gotten hurt.

Lindsay was strangely subdued. Wrapped in Jared's jacket—her clothes had ripped to shreds, seemingly the worst of her injuries—wobbly on her feet, she refused medical care.

Jared was truly worried for her, but the best she'd let him do was carry her to the car. He seat-belted her in and took off. Spider had insurance, and there were enough "names" there to deal with any consequences. His didn't need to be among them.

"You sure you're okay?" he asked every few blocks.

Lindsay leaned back against the headrest and closed her eyes. He wanted to warn her that her head would start to spin if she closed her eyes. But when he glanced over, she was . . . smiling? "Some comeback," she mused.

He felt himself relax. "Some girls just know how to make a lasting impression. No one's ever gonna forget your first night back on the scene."

"Jared?"

"Yeah?"

"I really, really, *really*—"

"You really what?"

He signaled left at the light at Highland and went to face her, but Lindsay had turned her back to him. She was leaning out the open window. Hurling her guts out.

"Oh, my God, Linz, why didn't you tell me to pull over?"

After a few heaves, she turned back—wiping her face on his jacket sleeve. "I really am happy to be back."

It was the sloppiest smile he'd ever seen. "I am too, Linz," he said softly. And it was true. She had him at hurl-o.

Full House

"What were you *thinking*?" Jared's voice scaled up an octave as he leaned in over the poker table. "Bringing a homeless person into this house?" His disgust and fury were aimed at the one person *least* likely to cause controversy: Sara.

It was Lindsay, martini glass in hand, who giggled, "A homeless ho. Does that make her a ho-ho?" She slapped the table with delight; her pile of poker chips went flying.

No one amused Lindsay more than herself, Eliot realized.

Unamused, Sara raised her finger to her lips. "Shush! She has a name. It's Naomi Foster, and she can hear you!"

And no one was more righteous than Sara.

Eliot shuffled the deck of cards. The housemates, who'd been together just under a month, had fallen into weekly Thursday-night poker sessions. Lindsay had started it, which was ironic, since she was the worst player. And that was quite an accomplishment, since Sara had never played in her life.

Linz could not keep a straight face. When she had a good hand, she got so excited, the table shook. When she was trying to bluff, the giggles began. Signaling raises all around.

Eliot dealt two cards facedown, then an exposed card to each of them.

Jared's jack of diamonds was the high card, but his focus was squarely on Sara. "I want her out. End of story."

"You gonna bet?" Nick motioned.

Jared tossed a one-dollar chip into the center of the table. "And I don't care if she can hear me!"

"Well, you should," said Sara, coolly studying her cards. "I raise you a dollar."

"I raise both of you!" Lindsay, who was showing a lowly three of hearts, declared.

"Check." Nick tossed in enough chips to stay in the game.

Not Eliot. He wasn't getting into this pissing contest. He had crappy cards, and the chances of winning this hand were on par with those of the homeless girl staying at the share house.

Sara had brought home a "stray," as Lindsay callously declared. Jared may have been loudest in his censure, but truthfully, no one was thrilled.

"Naomi," Sara said steadily, as Eliot dealt another round

of cards, "is goin' through a rough patch right now. A little Christian charity wouldn't hurt any of you."

Charity, Eliot could have said, wasn't just for Christians. It was part of every religion. In his house at the Passover seder, the silver cup symbolized that the door was always open to anyone in need. But in his experience, it was theoretical. No homeless person ever came to his table.

"Charity?" Jared said. "Fine. We'll give her money"—he threw five dollars' worth of chips into the center of the table—"then she can leave."

Sara pressed her ruby lips together and raised Jared again. "Money isn't what she needs. She needs someone to care about her, help her get her life together. Why can't y'all see that?"

"We do." Nick stepped into the uncharacteristic role of peacekeeper, a role no one else, including El himself, wanted. "Jared has a point. This girl, this Naomi, could be a criminal. She could steal from us, or worse, hurt us."

Sara smiled. "Have y'all seen her? She's tiny. She hasn't had a hot meal in weeks. I couldn't just leave her out there."

There were many things Sara could just not leave. Like cleaning the house. The tall, shapely pageant beauty believed it was wasteful to spend money on a maid, so she assumed the responsibility.

No one *wanted* to help, but Eliot and Nick couldn't stand by and watch her go Cinderella. So they pitched in. Between them, they'd gotten the backyard lawn mowed, the garden weeded and replanted. Draining the entire pool and scrubbing that mother had taken a full weekend.

Jared and Lindsay? They were all about creating chaos. It never occurred to Linz that *she* was supposed to pick up after herself. The diva never had to. Where she tossed a towel is where it stayed. Where she left a dirty martini glass? It waited for someone else to pick it up.

It would've been easy for Eliot to dismiss Jared and Lindsay as clichés, spoiled, self-absorbed rich kids. But Lindsay'd spent her entire childhood working, and even now, in her drone job, she never missed a day at the office.

True, it'd turned all kinds of ugly the night Linz revealed that she didn't get the role in *Heiress: The Movie*, even though she'd rocked her audition. When Amanda informed her that the role had gone to "it" girl Sienna Miller, Lindsay'd been outraged. A pissed-off Lindsay put the "mean" in demeanor.

It soothed her wounds only a little upon learning that Sara hadn't been chosen for the peanut butter commercial, despite her brilliant reading of "Go crunchy, go smooth, go organic!"

But Lindsay was a trooper. A day later, she'd licked her wounds and gone on high alert for her next chance at an acting role.

Jared was another story. Eliot had already figured out that he was supposed to be taking summer school courses but instead spent his days on the phone, playing agent, attempting to make deals, collecting rent while house-sitting for his uncle. It was obvious to Eliot the kid was busting to work—in Daddy's company.

Nothing that'd happened so far had scuffed the shine off Jared McSmoothy. Until now. He raked his fingers through his hair and admonished Sara, "What gave you the nerve to bring her here—without even asking me?"

Eliot could've answered that one! What gave Sara the nerve was her sense of extreme righteousness.

Naomi—who couldn't be more than, what, sixteen?—had been in the kitchen slurping down a bowl of ramen noodles when Nick and Eliot had come home earlier in the evening. Nearly lost in Sara's fluffy terry robe, she'd stared at them with frightened saucer eyes—the biggest, roundest violet eyes he'd ever seen outside of a velvet painting, or an anime cartoon.

"This is Naomi. She'll be staying with us for a while." Sara had introduced her before the Michigan boys picked their jaws up off the floor

Nick had offered his hand. "Hi . . . uh . . . do you come from around here?" A stupid question, but at least he had manners.

Eliot hadn't been able to stop staring at her sunken cheeks, pierced eyebrow, and dark wet hair dripping onto the collar of the robe. Though Sara insisted otherwise, it was clear to Eliot that the girl was homeless, a beggar. Or a hooker.

Naomi had been asleep in the loft when Jared and Lindsay came home. They'd been arguing about her ever since.

Nick searched for a compromise. "What if we did a background check? If she doesn't have a police record, maybe it'd be okay for her to stay with us a few days."

"That won't be necessary, since she's not staying even one night." Jared glared at Nick.

This was one of those moments when Eliot totally hated himself for being such a wimp. But he couldn't help himself. "There are knives in the kitchen, Nick. . . ."

Lindsay put in, "What's she need knives for? She could take a guitar off the wall and bash your head in while you're sleeping—"

Sara slammed her cards down on the table.

Lindsay kept it up. "Or bring her badass friends into the house. Rob us at gunpoint—"

Sara cut her off with an angry look.

It took a lot to piss off Nick.

He'd reached "a lot." "Lindsay—shut up! Sara, you said you befriended her on the corner of Hollywood and Highland. Seriously, what do you know about her?"

Sara tipped her chin up. "She's a human being. She's hungry

and cold, and has no one. What else do I need to know?"

"How about"—Lindsay deliriously raked in the pot of chips, which she'd just won—"the location of the nearest homeless shelter?"

"Good idea." Jared flipped his cell phone open.

Sara reached out and swiped the phone from him. "Better ask if they have two beds available. If you kick her out, I go with."

A long pause. Finally, Jared muttered, "You're being ridiculous." But he didn't take his phone back from her.

Sara dealt the next round. She played five-card stud.

Nick took three cards, Eliot, two. Lindsay insisted that because she had an ace, she was entitled to four. Jared tapped his cards on the table, meaning he'd play the hand dealt him.

Sara, also playing her original five cards, softened a bit. "I'll take full responsibility for her."

"What does that mean?" Jared demanded.

"I'll keep an eye on her. She can come to work with me, and here in the house, she can help me with the cooking, cleaning, weeding the garden—you know, the stuff you and Lindsay are too good to do."

Jared didn't have an answer.

They played the round of poker, Sara raising the bet three times before the foursome stopped challenging her.

Then Sara turned over her hand: full house.

• • •

"California is the calamity capital of the world." Eliot, who'd never so much as mowed the lawn at home (being allergic to pollen, mites, and dust), found himself in the backyard late Saturday morning, on his knees, sharing gardening duty with Nick, Sara, and Naomi. Armed with something called a weeding trowel, he was trying to uproot a stubborn dandelion—and more important, yank his housemates' heads out of the sand.

"Between floods, fires, earthquakes, mudslides, and riots, more disasters have happened here than any other place," he told them.

"At least there are no hurricanes," chirped Sara. She was planting seedlings, determined to clean up the backyard, and pretty it up, too, with a new garden.

"The rains sometimes lead to massive floods, which can become landslides. I don't have to tell you that homes like this one"—Eliot paused to nod at theirs—"are at big risk for that."

Three sets of eyes stared at him: vacant (Nick), wary (Naomi), and the worst, indulgent (Sara, humoring him). Gamely, he plowed on. "I know you think I'm being paranoid, but—"

"You? Paranoid?" Nick, working an edging spade in the ground, quipped. "Why would we think that? Just 'cause you're wearing a gas mask and gloves to weed the yard?"

"It's not a gas mask!" Eliot pulled the surgical mask down to his chin. "It's for my allergies, but you all should be wearing them. Who knows what kind of poison might be in the ground? I don't want to breathe it in. And you all should be wearing gloves."

Sara said soothingly, "We're not making fun of you, Eliot."

Naomi, who'd tried to settle in as unobtrusively as possible, giggled.

He blurted, "We're all in imminent danger!"

"Danger, Will Robinson! Danger, Will Robinson!" Nick cupped his hands around his mouth like a megaphone and did his best *Lost in Space* voice.

Sara squealed with delight.

That wasn't even remotely funny. Eliot scowled at them.

Nick poked him in the ribs with his edging spade. "Okay, we *are* making fun of you. But the alarmist thing is wearing thin, dude."

"I'm being a realist. This is science."

"My bad, man—I forgot that course you're taking at UCLA. What's it called, Disasters-R-Us?"

Again, Sara giggled. But when she looked up at Eliot's serious mug, she stopped. "Eliot, sweetie, come on. Nothing bad has happened here in a long time."

He could not help it. "Well, only if you consider nineteen

ninety-four a long time ago—one of the worst earthquakes hit just a few miles from here. Fifty-five people were killed."

That's when Eliot noticed a flash of something—fear? memory?—scud across Naomi's heart-shaped face. He was moved to ask, "Are you from California, Naomi? Were you here when that quake hit?"

She paused, and shook her head. "We traveled all over the country, so I'm not exactly from anywhere."

Eliot totally didn't believe her. Nor did he challenge her.

"Fifty-five people?" Nick was back on the earthquake subject. "That's nothing compared to hurricane deaths, or tsunami devastation. I'll take my chances at fifty-five."

"You wouldn't say that if one of those poor souls was someone you loved," Sara pointed out. "But I believe in my heart we'll be fine."

Eliot kept on point. "A range of natural disasters, from brushfires to rockslides, collapsed bluffs, and earthquakes, have all hit L.A. at one time or another. The next time could be any time!"

Sara put down her watering can, folded her long shapely legs under her. "If we really are in imminent danger, do y'all think my momma would have allowed me to come out here?"

What Eliot thought: Her momma was a zealot waiting for her own life to begin when Sara got famous. What El said was, "I think we need to take this seriously, so we can be prepared if something does happen."

"You cannot fix what you refuse to see," Naomi mumbled, brushing her jaggedly cut jet-black hair out of her eyes. "I heard that somewhere."

Eliot gave her props. "There! I couldn't have said it better."

"So what have they been saying in that class you're taking?" Naomi, sitting on the crabgrass, pulled her knees in close to her body.

"The natural disasters we're seeing—mudslides, brush fires, earthquakes—are gonna keep happening."

"Oh, stop it," Sara said. "You're just tryin' to scare the pants off us." Catching Nick's smile, she turned a deeper shade of red.

"What does your boyfriend back home say about your being here?" Eliot demanded. "Has he ever heard of the San Andreas fault line?"

Sara looked wounded; Eliot felt like a heel. "I'm not sure what Donald has heard of," she said quietly. "He didn't want me to come."

"Hey, I'm sorry, that's none of my business. I just . . ." Eliot reached out and took her hand.

"I understand. You're worried something bad's gonna happen. And even if we don't agree, we're friends, and we should listen."

Nick stood up and peeled off his tank top. Eliot caught

Sara's reaction. Look up "lust" in the dictionary: That'd be her picture.

He stuttered, "The . . . the . . . thing about wildfires and floods is that you have some warning. Earthquakes can tear your life apart, without warning."

Naomi suddenly bolted up, wordlessly, and headed inside the house.

Eliot continued, "Like I was saying, that earthquake in the San Fernando Valley was a six-point-seven magnitude. It would've been way worse if it had hit during the day, when people were at work, out shopping, in school, if more cars had been on the road. As it was, the tremor toppled chimneys and shattered windows all over Southern California. A dozen people were killed when an apartment building collapsed. An entire highway was destroyed; a freeway overpass collapsed in a busy intersection."

"But if there's no warning, what can anyone do?" Nick asked.

"Be ready. I'm putting together an earthquake preparedness kit—I bought a transistor radio, flashlights, gloves, gas masks, bike helmets, and a first-aid kit."

"Transistor radio?" Sara asked.

"We'll lose electricity in an earthquake—no TV, Internet, nothing. It's the only way we'll have of knowing what's happening, when help is arriving."

"What's with the gloves? In case of snow?" Nick teased.

"Not snow: glass. It'll shatter all around you. You don't want it embedded in your hands when you're trying to crawl out."

"You bought all this stuff already? Where is it?" Sara asked.

Eliot smiled. "I'm putting it all in the kitchen cabinet by the microwave. One more thing: Nick, you gotta get Jared to show you where the main gas line in the house is. We'll need to shut it off at the first tremor."

He got them to agree to everything, except to practice drills like ducking under something sturdy, a heavy table or doorframe, and getting as far away from windows or anything made of glass. But Eliot was happy with the progress he'd made. At least they were listening. "It's possible the next one will be, like, an eight on the Richter scale—that's what they're calling 'the big one.'"

"Who's got a big one?"

Lindsay, and her scathing wit, materialized. Leave it to her to make a crack that'd arouse *and* annoy them. Eliot shielded his eyes from the sun and looked up, hoping no one saw his face: the combination of lust and livid was embarrassing. Lindsay was luscious, bedecked in bangles, hoop earrings, toe rings, and ankle bracelets—and not much else. Her red string bikini was as tiny as a Kaballah bracelet. She'd come outside to sun herself, and deigned to stroll over to the garden.

"We were talking about earthquakes." Eliot's voice squeaked.

"Not that you couldn't cause a few quakes, looking like that," Nick noted.

Delighted, Lindsay dropped anchor—her towel and her barely covered butt. "Is Eliot making everyone nervous?"

Not as much as you are, he thought . . . nervously. "I'm just explaining—"

She cut him off with a dismissive wave. "Native Californians don't worry about that stuff. So-called experts have been going all alarmist, predicting massive death and destruction for decades. Chances are, hurricanes will destroy the Southeast before we get even another tremor. We just get all the press."

Native Californians . . . Eliot thought about what she'd said. People like Jared and Lindsay thrived on calamity— drama queens and princes *lived* for life on the edge. To them, it's like a disaster movie they've been cast in. They really did live in a dream world.

Lindsay interrupted his musing. "Anyway, if you're so sure of impending disaster, why don't you leave? What's keeping you here?"

Another question he'd asked himself.

Nick answered for him. "El, leave?" He looked meaning-fully from near-naked Lindsay to shapely Sara, and shook his head. "Snowball, meet hell. This place is as near to heaven as my boy is likely to get."

Lindsay chuckled. Sara laughed nervously.

Eliot colored but didn't dispute his friend. He got up and strode into the house for a cool drink. He knew the real reason he'd stay. It wasn't about the hot babes living under the same roof. Eliot had no shot with Lindsay, no matter how much she flirted with him.

And despite Nick's encouraging him to go after Sara, she was a real long shot, what with the boyfriend back home and the way she looked at Nick. Besides, she'd confided in him about some purity pledge she'd taken, had shown him a ring that symbolized her commitment to stay a virgin until mar-riage. So no, Eliot wasn't staying in the hopes of getting lucky. What kept his feet glued to the shaky California terrain was Nick. Something wasn't right with his friend.

"You okay?"

He spun around. Naomi was settled in the corner of the striped couch, with what looked like a screenplay splayed over her knees.

"Yeah, I just came in for a cold drink. Can I get you some-thing?"

She shook her head and returned her attention to the script.

Out of curiosity he asked, "Are you trying to break into showbiz too?"

She didn't look up.

Naomi: Fear and Fireworks on Independence Day

Crack! Boom! Pop!

The house rumbled beneath her. It sounded like the deep growl from the belly of a beast—or was that her own body? Naomi was quaking, shivering, despite the blanket she was snuggled under. She hugged her knees, squeezed herself farther into the corner of the sofa between the pillows. As if that could protect her.

She tried to focus on the dialogue of the script Sara had given her to read, hoping to blot out the loud commotion just outside the sliding doors. Why Sara insisted Naomi read it, she couldn't figure out. It wasn't a part Sara was up for; this was some random story about a policeman and a runaway. Sara probably thought Naomi related to the plot: That's how little Sara, or anyone, knew.

The story wasn't half bad, but the part of the runaway, Moxie, was not one she related to at all. Naomi had not run away.

She put her head back into the script, but it was no use. The blasting fireworks panicked her, brought up memories she'd worked hard to forget. As for the burbling buddies in the backyard hot tub, they just distracted her.

"Awesome!" She heard Nick reacting enthusiastically to the fierce display of a Fourth of July sky pageant. "Oh, man, that *rocked*!"

"Look at the stars, those colors!" Sara marveled.

"That's what it's like every time Jared and I hook up," Lindsay teased Sara. "The earth *moves*, we see stars! You should try it." Word had spread quickly through the share house about Sara's moral convictions. Naturally, Lindsay took every opportunity to taunt her.

"Quit it, Linz," Jared interjected. "Sara Calvin will be our first virgin movie star."

Naomi knew Jared was still furious that Sara had brought her into their house. And since the high and mighty Jared was chief pooh-bah, it was a wonder Sara had prevailed. There were moments, like now, she wished Sara had not. It wasn't for lack of gratefulness. She was plenty thankful to Sara. She just wished she didn't have to be.

Pop! Pop! Crack!

Another chorus of fireworks exploded, louder. Naomi jumped. Whoever was launching these was close to the house. Too jittery to sit in one place, the formerly homeless girl sprang off the couch and strode over to the sliding doors, where she could now see, as well as hear, the show going on outside.

It was after nightfall on July Fourth. The five housemates had squeezed into the hot tub. She could almost see the fireworks reflected in their shiny, happy faces, their unscarred eyes. From this rarefied perch high in the Hollywood Hills, they did have an amazing view of spectacular light shows, above and below them.

There was room for her in the hot tub. Sara had offered her a bathing suit.

No way. The idea of hanging out with this bunch freaked her out.

The feeling was mutual.

They tolerated her. It'd been a little over a week and she hadn't assaulted anyone, stolen anything, smoked or snorted any illegal substances, nor snuck any lowlifes into their house. Moreover, she helped Sara with the chores. Didn't mean she was now welcome.

It was easy to know what Jared thought of her. Garbage. Trash. Human debris. Not that McSmoothy said as much to her face. His act was neutral, but he wasn't much of an actor.

Jared still wanted her out. Lindsay wanted what Jared wanted, and gave him all he asked for—and judging by the frequent noise from his bedroom, they were making each other very happy.

Jared and Lindsay, too impressed with themselves for words, were glued at the hip in the Jacuzzi, lasciviously feeding each other bits of sushi. Lots of tongue action, putting on a show for everyone to see.

Eliot was mooning after Sara, who was lusting after Nick, whose dark eyes were focused only on the spectacle in the sky. Naomi chuckled. The pious girl was havin' all sorts of trouble with that temptation law, or commandment, or whatever it was. Every night, during her prayers before bed, she kept praying that she wouldn't fall into temptation.

Naomi didn't think He was listening. Not that she believed much in God, or in any higher power. Maybe she had once, a long, long time ago. But that belief had long ruptured, had gotten buried beneath the rubble of what was once her life.

Compared to what she'd been through, the little domestic dramas playing out here were laughable. These five had no idea how lucky they all were. Naomi checked herself: She'd been pretty lucky too, that Sara had come into her life when she did.

The good-hearted country girl was the real deal, a rare

deal, a true believer. Doing the humanitarian thing, befriending Naomi instead of what most people did: avert their eyes and walk by the beggar girl, or toss a few coins in her cup and continue walking. Worse were those who wanted something from her.

Sara didn't want anything. She wasn't trying to proselytize, pimp, or procure her services in any way. Sara never pressed her to find out what had happened to Naomi, why she was on the streets. The tall girl with the wavy blond hair was naive enough to just want to help.

Still, no way would Naomi have come home with her. But the day she finally said yes was the day the street had gotten too dangerous: Some low-life skinheads had threatened her, and she'd been terrified.

And despite the roommates' resistance, things were okay so far.

During the day, she went to work with Sara on that *Caught in the Act* TV show. No one asked her who she was or why she was there. They just took her for another lowly intern and piled drone stuff on her—Xeroxing, filing, fetching coffee, taking notes. She was too smart to get comfortable, though.

Her "pay" for working on the TV show with Sara and helping around the house? Food, clothing, shelter. Naomi had her own room of sorts: the basement of the share house. The most important compensation, however, was safety. For now, Naomi was safe. And now was all she, or any of them, really had.

Naomi put the script down and wandered back into the kitchen, where a sink full of dirty dishes awaited. She didn't really have to, but she needed to keep her shaking hands busy, so she began to scrub and dry each glass, spoon, fork, dish, and coffee mug.

Her eyes wandered out the window over the sink to the backyard. Nick was slurping down a Bud Lite from the bottle, leaning against the back of the hot tub, eyes closed. He had that model pose down. He was harmless, she thought, sweet, dumb, and meaty. He'd been friendly from the start, and now regarded her as a mere curiosity. He didn't ask a lot of questions or stare at her relentlessly like his roommate.

El-geek, as she secretly thought of him, peppered her with "kind" questions. She was supposed to think he cared, but she saw right through him. In his mind, she was some runaway, a poor, pitiable soul who'd come to Hollywood looking for fame and fortune, falling instead into a life of drugs, prostitution, homelessness, hopelessness. A cliché.

If only they really knew.

She'd give the himbos from Michigan one thing: They were devoted to Sara. Whatever the tall, tawny Texan asked, they'd do. Like hauling a couch from the game room to the basement, clearing and cleaning an area for her to sleep.

Sara brought out the best in those boys.

And the worst in that Lindsay creature.

Around Sara, Lindsay was snotty, superficial, jealous, and bitchy. Putting her down at every opportunity. Lindsay was supposedly trying to mount a big "comeback," but so far, she hadn't gotten any acting parts. The only thing that cheered her was that Sara hadn't either. Chuh! Even the homeless girls on the streets were more supportive of one another.

Sara had another audition coming up this week. Naomi had been helping her rehearse.

"You're up for the role of who?" Lindsay's loud question pierced the air. Instinct kicking in, Naomi stealthily made her way back into the den and opened the sliding doors so she could see what was going down. She wanted to be there, in case Lindsay's claws came out. "How come I don't know about this?" she charged. "Are we keeping secrets now?"

"Tomorrow I'm reading for a guest role in that new HBO drama. Didn't I tell you?" Sara's tone was even.

Boom! Crack! A thunder of fireworks split the sky, and Naomi flinched.

"How'd you even find out about it?" Lindsay wanted to know.

"Lionel, my agent, sent me up for it. It's just a little bitty guest role, only two scenes. That's probably why you didn't get sent for it. It's not important enough for you."

Appeased, Lindsay relaxed, shrugged her bare shoulders.

Naomi's eyes went wide. Lindsay bought that? Geez, she's so high on herself, she can't see through the bullshit clouds.

Sara should have left it at that. But she didn't. "Got any tips for me?"

"Yeah." Lindsay tilted her head back, poured a shot down her throat, and wiped her mouth with her arm. "Lose twenty pounds. You'll never work in this town lugging around that much weight. Real women have curves, but there's nothing real about Hollywood. Girls who get work in this town look like Nicole Richie at her boniest."

Sara's Body Works

The muscles in his stomach crunched tightly, then smoothed out again, tightened, then relaxed. Nick Maharis, lifting weights while doing knee bends in his bedroom, was almost more than Sara could stand. And yet that's exactly what she was doing, standing in his doorway, afraid to breathe, watching those abs and quads tighten on the down motion, then biceps, triceps, and pecs stretch across his dark, hairless chest when he straightened up.

Breathing out as he pushed down, breathing in as he came up. Up, down, his gym shorts riding up his thigh, his biceps bulging. She was hypnotized.

The crunch of his muscles when he dipped down, the smooth pecs when he stood upright. Crunchy, then smooth. Like peanut butter. Licking it off his chest, how tasty would that be? That's the ad campaign they should have gone with.

She gasped, clapped her hand over her mouth. How could she have thought that?

Nick flicked his dark eyes toward her. "What's the matter?"

"No-nothing . . ." she stammered, swallowing hard.

"You made a noise like you saw something scary."

In her head, she was hearing her boyfriend's admonitions: "Don't fall for any slick lines, Sara. All those guys out there want only one thing from you."

"Anyway, welcome to my makeshift gym." Nick grinned.

The night Lindsay made the rude comment about Sara's weight, she'd been more startled than hurt, but it'd led to a shouting match. Eliot argued that Sara didn't need to lose any weight; Jared agreed with Lindsay that maybe her "heft" wasn't helping during her auditions.

"That's crap," Eliot had said heatedly.

"What do you know?" Lindsay had challenged. "Ever been an actress? I don't think so." She'd turned to Sara. "You have three choices. Starve yourself, throw up after every meal, or snort coke. Ask any model or actress—that's how we roll in this town."

"No way! Don't you dare!" Eliot had been scandalized. "Either of you!"

Nick had genially offered to show Sara a workout routine. "To tone you, keep you in fighting form—that's all you need."

Too quickly, she'd said yes, please, and thank you.

Now that she was here? In sweatpants and her brother's old cutoff T-shirt? Now that her eyes were glued to Nick's glutes? Her thoughts sinful? Sara Calvin knew this was a bad idea.

She was going to do it anyway.

Nick's workout equipment consisted of a set of weights, a barbell, ropes, and a huge red rubber ball that reminded Sara of a giant inflatable beach ball.

"Not exactly state of the art," Nick conceded, "but it'll have to do for now. Can't afford membership in an L.A. gym."

"Not yet. But when you're up on a billboard modeling for those famous designers, you'll be able to buy your own gym."

When he laughed, his eyes crinkled up so all you could see were those long, thick black eyelashes. All she could feel was her tummy tumbling.

She should leave. Now would be a good time.

"So how do you want to begin? Stretching? Aerobics? Curls? Lunges? Weights?"

Donald's voice popped into her head. "Once you start, it's impossible to stop—you just keep falling down the well. Remember your purity pledge. Remember me. I'll be waiting when you get back."

She didn't want to go back. She'd been in California over a month, and so far, though she'd only been on one failed audition, she loved her job, she loved the people she'd met, she was learning so much!

But she only had until the end of August. Then her mom's money ran out, her job ended, she'd have to give up the house-share and move someplace cheaper. Or move back home, defeated. Back to Donald, who didn't want her to succeed.

Her voice wavered. "Nick, do you think Lindsay's right? If I don't lose weight, I'll never get any acting jobs?"

Nick shrugged. "I'll tell you what I know. Those skanky types who starve themselves? Not hot."

"Not attractive?"

"No way. Guys like girls with a little meat on their bones, you know? Working out isn't about getting all skinny. Exercising helps shape and tone you. It's good for your heart, lungs, every-thing. But if you wanted to lose weight—and I'm not sayin' you should—anything that increases your heart rate burns calories."

Could he not hear her heart racing? She could lose weight watching him.

"We'll start with some simple stretches." He bent over at the waist, so his fingertips touched the floor.

She watched.

"This is a great stretch for the back of your thighs, glutes, and lower back."

She bent over, wondering what he thought of her glutes.

"Do you feel it?"

"I think so." To tell him what she really felt would incriminate her.

Nick demonstrated stretches for the calves, inner and outer thigh muscles, arms, and shoulders. It was when he came up behind her, putting one arm gently around her waist, bending with her to show her an abs stretch, that Sara felt her legs turn to jelly.

He laughed. "Balance. That's what half of working out is about."

Next was weight lifting, for underarm toning. He demonstrated first.

"Okay, Sara, your turn." He came up behind her and proffered two small barbells. "These are fifteen pounds. Might be a little heavy at first."

He stood behind her. Very close behind. He lifted her right arm and placed the barbell-shaped weight in her hand. "Here, curl your fingers around it. Take the other one. . . . Now pretend like you're Popeye, showing off your muscles."

She laughed nervously and did as told. Tried to, anyway. She couldn't do it more than once; after that, the weights pulled her arms down to her sides.

From behind, Nick bolstered her arms. "Try again. Don't be discouraged. Just do as many reps as you can. You'll improve, you'll see."

He was so close, she could practically feel the beads of

sweat transfer from his body to hers. She inhaled him. Sweat and soap: The combination was intoxicating. She had to do something. Say something. Conversation would take her mind off what her body was saying. "How's your modeling going?"

"Slow," he admitted. "Not exactly the way I thought it would." He explained that he, too, had a deadline. Three months to make it before he had to concede defeat, go home. Just like her.

"When's the audition?" he asked, demonstrating lunges.

"Friday." She tried to follow, taking a long stride, bending her knee, stretching forward at the waist.

"Nervous?"

She was hyperventilating for other reasons entirely.

"Lunges are good for keeping your thighs taut and your butt tight," he explained. He continued to demonstrate, unaware that his shorts rode up even higher with each stride.

Her tummy and butt tightened without her moving a muscle.

"Do you feel it in your thigh?"

When he cupped her quads, she jumped.

"So what exactly is the part in the drama?" he asked, amused at her nervousness.

"It's for a girl named Victoria, a friend of the cheerleader's, out to betray her."

"A bad girl, huh?" He tilted his head and rubbed his chin. "Not exactly how I'd cast you."

"You see me as the good girl." She laughed uneasily.

"I guess I do. But that's why they call it acting, right? You make the audience believe you're something that you're not."

"You be a good girl," Donald had reminded her. "Don't let them change you out there. Don't compromise your morals."

Keep talking. Stop thinking. Stop feeling. Any topic would do. "Nick, do you remember that script written by the policeman who found my suitcase?"

"The one you rescued from the pool?"

"I've been reading it. I admit I don't know much, but it's every bit as interesting as the ones the stars talk about on *Caught in the Act*."

"The cop's is better? No kidding!" Nick seemed genuinely surprised.

She'd just about finished it, and was having Naomi read it too. It was called *Hide in Plain Sight*, and it was about a girl forced to go into witness protection with her mobster parents. She runs away, the bad guys go after her, and this young cop gets involved.

"Sounds cool," Nick agreed. "Why not give it to Jared?"

"I'm not Jared's favorite person right now, remember? He'd probably make fun of me. And really, what do I know?"

"As much as anyone, I'd think."

"Maybe you want to read it?"

"I'm not much of a reader. If not for Eliot, I might not have made it through high school."

"I don't believe you. You ever think of acting?" Sara asked. "You've got the looks for it."

"Me? I have no talent whatsoever—and I think you need more than looks to make it in this business. And someone like you, you've got both—you're a knockout and a natural talent."

She blushed. He thought she was a knockout? "There are so many beautiful people here, I'm nothing special." He thought she was a knockout! "What I have is grit and determination."

"And me."

"You?" Sara's heart went into serious flutter.

He grinned and rolled the huge ball toward her. "With the help of my rockin' training, and this balance ball, you'll snag the next role you're up for."

She laughed. "I was wondering what that ball was for."

"It's for stretching, pull-ups, and stomach curls. Come on, I'll show you." He rolled it into the center of the room. "Lay faceup on it."

She giggled. "I'll fall off."

"I'll hold you steady, don't worry."

That's exactly what she was worried about.

Cautiously, she followed his instructions, draping her back on the ball, legs slightly apart, touching the floor.

"Arms straight out," he said. "Now use your stomach muscles to pull yourself up, just enough to curl yourself."

Nick stood over her.

She couldn't move.

He took her hands. "Use me as resistance, and pull."

She did as told. Maybe a little harder than he'd expected. Because she pulled him right down on top of her.

"I have good news, and bad news. Which do you want first?" Lionel, the sweetest man ever, Sara's agent and friend, called her at work.

"Might as well be done with the bad news first."

"You didn't get the part on the HBO show."

She swallowed nervously. "Is it because I was too . . . big?"

There was a pause on the other end of the phone. "Not big enough of a name. They went with Nicole Richie."

"I'm ready for the good news, Lionel."

"You sitting down?"

"You know I'm not. Go ahead. Lay it on."

"Just got word that they're doing a remake of *The Outsiders*."

Sara's eyes widened; she squealed. "Oh, my gosh, I just love that movie!"

"It's a classic," Lionel agreed. "Made names for Tom Cruise, Matt Dillon, Ralph Macchio, Rob Lowe, Emilio Estevez—they all went on to bigger and better after that. There's one important female role, Cherry Valance. It's pivotal, it's perfect, it'll make a star out of whoever gets it."

Sara flashed on a scene from that movie. "Cherry. Was that Diane Lane who played her in the original?"

"Good girl! You know your classic movie history. You have a week to prepare. This is a biggie."

"You really think I have a shot? I haven't gotten anything so far—not even that dang peanut butter commercial."

"All the better, my smooth and crunchy one," Lionel quipped, and Sara's belly flip-flopped.

"They want an unopened jar. An unknown, a fresh, talented looker who'll blow 'em away. In this case, not having any credits is a definite plus."

"Just what we knew would happen," her mama crowed when she called with the news. "See, I told you, Sara, every time you tried for something and didn't get it? It's because you're bound for real stardom. I know this is the one."

Lionel sent "the sides"—a few pages of the script with Cherry's scenes—by messenger that afternoon. By evening, both she and Naomi had read it and had shared the news with Nick and Eliot.

Eliot was pumped. "That's my favorite book from junior high! I'll go online and order the original for you from Amazon."

"It was a book?" Sara asked.

Eliot booted up his laptop. "Required reading."

"In our school?" Nick scratched his head. "I don't remember it."

"That's because I did your report." Eliot was on the Amazon site. "You had to say if you'd rather be a greaser or a soc. You picked greaser."

"S. E. Hinton," Naomi murmured. "She wrote it when she was sixteen."

Eliot complimented her. "That's right."

Naomi had offered up nothing about herself. Sara wasn't sure the girl even had an education. "I guess it was required in your school too?"

Naomi shrugged. "I guess."

Eliot was all about it. "You *have* to read it, Sara. You'll understand the character better and ace the audition."

"I'll go out and get the DVD. We'll help you rehearse," Nick offered.

Sara was overcome with emotion. Everyone wanted to help her! She threw her arms around Eliot. "You have no idea how much this means to me. Y'all are . . . my best friends." She started to cry, and Eliot stroked her back, holding her tightly. She wasn't sure, because she was crying, but she thought Eliot whispered into her ear, "You smell sweet."

Sara wept. Eliot grabbed a tissue and blew his nose. Even Nick, notorious noncrier, sniffled. They'd settled around the big oak coffee table in the living room, lit candles, ordered dinner in, and watched the DVD of *The Outsiders*.

"Johnny Cade gets to me every time," Sara said between sobs. "His life was so sad, and he was a hero. And Ponyboy, you just can't help loving him. . . ."

Nick leaned back on the couch, stretched his arms out. "Forget about them. It's Dallas Winston—Dally—that Cherry is supposed to be in love with."

"No she isn't," Eliot corrected. "She says she *could* love him—"

Naomi picked up the pages of the script from the coffee table. "Should we start helping Sara rehearse, while it's fresh in our minds?"

Nick volunteered to read Dally's lines, Eliot shoved his hands in his pockets, doing Johnny. Naomi played Ponyboy.

Sara alternately sat, stood, walked around—and eventually, after several readings, lay down on the carpet to stretch her back and her imagination. She wasn't real happy with any of her readings, and wanted to try again.

"'What's a nice, smart kid like you running around with trash like that for?'" She sounded like a sweet, syrupy kindergarten teacher. That wasn't right.

Naomi responded as Ponyboy: "'I'm a greaser. Same as Dally. He's my buddy.'"

Eliot clapped. "Naomi, that was good!"

Nick added, "Dude, if you were a guy, you could totally nail this."

Naomi ducked her head down, embarrassed, and mumbled, "Let's keep going. Sara? Do Cherry's next line."

She did, and tried it completely differently.

"That was better," Eliot decided.

It was just okay. Cherry was a complicated girl—she could be sensitive and sweet, but also sarcastic and confrontational. She didn't have that many scenes in the movie, but she made you remember them.

"Let's go over the part where Dally brings her a soda at the drive-in," Nick suggested. He read Dally's line, pretending to hand her a drink. "'This might cool you off.'"

Sara recited, "'After you wash your mouth and learn to talk and act decent, I might cool off too.'"

Darn, that was bad. Sara closed her eyes.

Eliot tented his fingers. "In this scene, Cherry's being sarcastic, Sara. You need to read it . . ." The room went silent.

Naomi spoke up finally. "As if you were Lindsay."

"That's right, like this," came another voice, oozing with snarkcasm: "*After* you wash your mouth . . . and learn to talk and act decent, I *might* cool off too.'"

Sara, prone on the floor, looked up just in time to catch the full impact of the ice-cold Pepsi flicked in her face. She was aghast.

The pointy toe of Lindsay's boot was on her stomach before she could get up. "By the way, Cherry throws the soda at him *before* she says the line."

Lindsay turned theatrically and whirled out of the room. Exit, stage left. Jared, clutching a few pages of a script marked "The Outsiders," wore a dumbfounded expression. He followed her.

Jared Plays House, Lindsay Plays Games

"Why is *she* auditioning for Cherry?! That role is mine, and I want her off!" Lindsay was steaming, stomping around the elegant, expensively appointed great room at the Larson family mansion in Bel Air, waving her cell phone around like a weapon.

"Put the phone down, Linz. You can't call Amanda; you're not calling Lionel." Jared, resting his elbow on the marble fireplace mantel, tried to dissuade her. "You got the audition too. And we're not asking them to cancel Sara's audition."

Lindsay pouted. "I thought you were on *my* side."

Jared reached for her, drew her into his arms, and kissed her tenderly on the neck. "Always, baby, always." He stroked her hair, reassuringly. "But—"

"But what?" She pulled away. "You think she's better than me?"

"Of course not! Linz, listen. Every young actor in Hollywood is up for a role in *The Outsiders*. It stars seven guys—"

"And one girl," she pointed out. "The one who'll be remembered over everyone else."

"It has the potential to be a star-making role," Jared conceded.

"Or the comeback role of a lifetime! No one will ever think of me as Zoe Wong again. Cherry is my Charlize in *Monster*, my Scarlett Johansson in *Lost in Translation*, my Kirsten Dunst Mary-Jane moment in *Spider-Man*. Sara, who's never done anything, cannot get that role!" In frustration, Lindsay grabbed a pillow off the Armani/Casa sofa and threw it at Jared.

Jared caught it, then caught her in his arms again. "Linz, look at me."

She tried pulling away again, but he gripped her tightly.

"Seriously, babe, you have to hear me."

The sun filtered down through the tinted skylights, reflecting like kaleidoscopic glints in Jared's emerald-green eyes. A girl could get lost in them trying to find his soul, Lindsay thought, if she let herself. He parted his lips, and something inside her softened. His kiss was sweet, sensual, not overpowering. It didn't have to be: Lindsay understood.

Jared had spirited her away for the weekend. His dad, Rusty, was on a business trip. The twins, Brooke and Brynn, were on a spa/shopping weekend somewhere in Santa Barbara. Glynnis, their mom, hadn't lived with them in years.

Which left the mansion on Stone Canyon Road in Bel Air empty, but for the staff. They were thrilled to see Jared, had happily placed his order for a huge bouquet of white calla lillies, had delightedly sprinkled the majestic staircase leading upstairs with a blush of rose petals.

He'd done this for her. He'd taken her for a few stolen days of luxury away from the funky—and crowded—share house in the hills, a weekend's break from her craptastic job and the ever-more-contentious roommates. Jared had been neither romantic nor sensitive when they were together the first time. Either someone had given him lessons—or, this time, the boy was just a goner for her.

Lindsay didn't want to think about the second thing. Her focus had to be on her career—that is, on *having* one. Slowly, she extracted herself from his embrace and sank into the enormous Italian leather armchair.

"Jar, I so totally appreciate what you're doing for me. The house, this weekend, it's . . . amazing. It's just that getting this role is imperative."

"Why this one? Acting gigs are like buses—you miss one, the next comes along."

"This one is here now. It could redefine me, show the world my real talent. But first, I have to eliminate—"

"Sara?" he interjected. "Give me a break, Linz. She's one of dozens of actresses in Hollywood going for this role, why obsess about her?"

"In some ways, she's exactly what they're looking for," Lindsay explained. "Sara's as unknown as unknown gets. She's got that corn-fed, freaking Oklahoma thing down. She's tall, blond—"

"Cherry's a redhead," Jared reminded Lindsay, "more like you. I don't think Sara has any shot at this."

"Can we make sure of that?" she said in a whisper.

"No, we cannot. And we should not."

Despite his unwillingness to cooperate, Jared's confidence made her feel better. More so when he reached into the bar and poured her a raspberry Stoli.

"Anyway . . ." Lindsay licked the rim of the glass, inhaled the flavoring, and closed her eyes. Mmmm, it was good. "Cherry Valance is a soc. I'm a soc. I can look down my nose at anyone!"

Jared grinned and settled on the wide armrest of her chair. "Yes, and that's what I love about you. But—"

"What but? No buts!" She sipped her Stoli.

"In this script, Cherry's not a typical soc. She sympathizes with the greasers, too."

Lindsay pulled away from him. "So what are you saying?

421

Miss Proud-and-Pious does sympathy better than I do?"

Rhetorical much? Jared drained his scotch and soda. Wisely, he kept that thought to himself.

"I'm an actress. I can do anything. She hasn't proved she can do anything, besides win Texas beauty pageants!" Lindsay sniffed.

"Then why are you worried about her?" Jared slid into Lindsay's chair so their thighs rubbed against each other's. He put his arm around her, drew her even closer. "You know how to do this. Make the part yours. Forget Sara, and everyone else going up for it."

She knew he was right. But she needed this role. She was running out of time—and maybe even faith in herself. A little.

If she didn't get it?

It would prove she didn't have the chops, the talent to stretch beyond being in a dumb sitcom.

It would mean her family was right: She ought to have stayed fat and barefoot in Iowa, not tried to claw her way back into the biz.

Her whole life, all she'd be remembered for was Zoe Stupid Pimply Wong. And that giggle.

If she lost to Sara? Unthinkable, the ultimate humiliation. She'd be laughed out of the share house, hooted out of the hot clubs, kicked out of her crowd, ridiculed out of Galaxy. Worst of all? She'd be pitied.

Lindsay tucked herself into Jared's chest, looked up at him with big, sad eyes. "You really think I have a chance?"

Jared refused to humor her. "Here's what I know: You are Lindsay Pierce, and what Lindsay wants, what Lindsay goes after, Lindsay gets."

This time, she initiated the kiss. There was nothing slow or sweet about it.

It was his smile, she thought when they pulled apart, not his eyes. If you could read that smile, you'd know Jared Larson. You'd see the vulnerable boy inside the slick exterior, the insecurity and yearning behind the McSmoothy facade. She had hurt him by ignoring his letters, e-mails, gifts. She was capable of hurting him again. She didn't want to—especially not at this moment. But what did it say about her that she couldn't account for tomorrow?

"Listen, baby," he was saying. "This weekend, we'll work on the sides, we'll do Cherry's scenes together. After we pamper ourselves with room service, massages, movies, and ultimate pleasure."

The rose petals were meant to lead them upstairs, to Jared's posh bedroom. The twosome never made it off the armchair. Good thing it was sturdy.

Lindsay swung her leg over his, turned her body toward him. Jared encircled her; he parted her lips with his tongue, and they kissed passionately. He pulled her onto his lap, let his hands wander under her T-shirt. "God, you're beautiful," he whispered between caresses, soft squeezes, and more kisses.

Gently, Lindsay loved him back, lightly massaging his chest, kissing his shoulders, his neck, blowing little puffs in his ear. She knew what he liked. And what would come next.

First she unzipped him while continuing to stroke his chest, then he repaid the favor. Their caresses were practiced, familiar, and tender, his on her thighs, hers on his abs, her fingertips skimming his belly just beneath the elastic band of his briefs.

They knew each other's rhythms, and though they were sweaty, excited, and panting, they moved with deliberate, delicious slowness, each more interested in the other's pleasure than in their own. He licked her neck, she bit on his earlobe, drew little circles around his nipples, while he let his fingers travel the length of her body.

Jared was quiet in his lovemaking; Lindsay, not so much.

Would they have heard the car pull up, the door open, and the footsteps entering the room if she'd been a quieter lover?

Moot point.

Rusty Larson probably had cleared his throat loudly, maybe coughed a few times as he caught sight of their naked, entwined bodies on the Roche-Bobois double-arm chair. And Lindsay wasn't really sure how many times he'd had to shout "Jared!" before they looked up.

"Yummy! Mr. L., these garlic noodles rock!" Lindsay, slurping the tasty cellophane noodles, was beyond pumped. And the savory lunch, which also included Dungeness crabs and tiger prawns, courtesy of Rusty Larson, was really only part of the reason.

"Nice to see you enjoying yourself, Lindsay," Jared's dad said, winking.

Someone else's dad, in someone else's mansion, walking in on his son in a compromising position with an ex-girlfriend, likely would have reacted somewhat differently than Rusty Larson had. The powerful Hollywood mogul was neither horrified, embarrassed, furious, shocked, indignant, nor bewildered. He didn't shout "How dare you?" Or "What the hell do you think you're doing?" Or worse.

Rusty Larson was bemused.

Instead of recriminations, there was a reward: lunch! And a lovely spread it was, catered by the trendily precious Crustacean of Beverly Hills, and served al fresco on the patio that overlooked the koi pond in the Larsons' Bel Air backyard.

Oh, sure, there was an obligatory exchange about the awkward situation. Jared acted chagrined. "Man, I'm so sorry you had to walk in on that."

Rusty did the "understanding dad" thing. He chuckled, "That dorm room at Ojai isn't exactly the way to impress

Lindsay. Not very comfortable, I imagine. And you assumed you had the house to yourself. I get it. If I were you, I'd probably have done the same thing."

That's when Lindsay got it. In some twisted alt-reality, walking in on them reaffirmed Russ's belief that Jared really was spending the summer as he'd promised, making up his courses, living in the dorm. Why else would Jared seize the opportunity to sneak back to the mansion when he believed it empty?

"By the way," Rusty said, "I heard from your uncle the other day."

Jared tensed. "How's it going over there in . . . where is he again?"

Smooth, Lindsay thought. *Like Jared doesn't know.*

Rusty confirmed that Uncle Rob was in the Czech Republic, and likely to be there through September. "I hear the buzz is strong on his performance," Rusty added. "Maybe this one will finally be his big break."

"Yeah," Jared added snidely, "an Academy Award does wonders for family relationships. Maybe you'll finally stop looking down your nose at him."

There's no shit like family shit, thought Lindsay, as Jared and Rusty went into the same verbal tussle she'd heard years ago. Jared absolutely believed Rusty saw him as a slacker—just like his uncle—an unworthy heir who'd practically flunked out of college. A son who needed to be taught a lesson: a tough-love summer spent at school with no credit cards.

Without planning to, by getting caught, they had just lent credence to his dad's assumption. How weirdly wonderful was that?

Indeed, Rusty was abnormally ebullient, nothing like the gruff, all-business head of the agency she saw at the office. His reddish hair was graying at the temples, he had the look of a tanned, fit, supersuccessful mogul totally down. No one would guess from his demeanor that he was at all worried about the future of Galaxy. No one who wasn't an insider.

Over forkfuls of roast lobster and shot glasses of sake, he was relaxed, expansive, confiding. "I give you credit, Son. I had my doubts you would stick school out. I figured you for a week or two before you'd start asking me to cut you a break. But I promise, you do things my way, make the best of it, it will pay off."

If Jared snared a deal, as he'd been trying to, maybe this summer would change Russ's opinion of his son after all, Lindsay mused. And hey, if there was a little sumpin' sumpin' in it for her, so much the better!

She smiled sweetly. "Take my word for it, Mr. L., Jared's totally made the best of things." Her hand strayed under the table, stroking Jared's thigh.

Rusty regarded her. "Jared didn't tell me you two were back together."

"The secret's out now," she conceded, moving her fingers beneath the hem of his shorts, drifting up his thigh, rendering him excellently silent. To his dad, she gushed about how she commuted to Ojai on the weekends, just to see him—but the "shlep" was so worth it.

Jared dropped his napkin. Purposely. In diving under the table to get it, he managed to fish around Lindsay's lap. Which is the reason she squeaked, sounding like a chipmunk, when answering Russ's question about where, exactly, she was living this summer. "With fr-friends!"

She started to laugh. The Lindsay laugh. Lightly, she smacked Jared in the head as he came back up from under the table.

"Ah, the Zoe giggle. Who could forget that?" Rusty's eyes crinkled when he smiled.

Lindsay sobered up swiftly. "Actually, Mr. L.? I'm hoping everyone will. . . ."

He looked at her quizzically.

She took a deep breath, ignored Jared kicking her. "I don't know if you're aware, but I'm up for Cherry in *The Outsiders*."

"Are you?" His eyebrows arched. "That's terrific. Amanda is sending you out?"

On this subject, Lindsay could no sooner be coy than she could bluff at poker. She hammered her point: "Can you do anything to help me get the role?"

Jared warned, "Linz, don't go there . . ."

But Rusty chuckled. "I like a woman who just comes out with it."

"She's not asking you to do anything underhanded," Jared put in.

Lindsay kicked him hard now.

"I know," his dad agreed, "but, Lindsay, you understand that I don't have any real influence over who gets the role. That's a decision made by the director, and the producers."

"Well, can you at least tell me who else is going up for Cherry? I heard that Ashlee Simpson and Nicole Richie campaigned for it. Is that true?"

Before his dad answered, Jared jumped in thoughtfully, "Isn't the director of *The Outsiders* with Galaxy? Maybe you could just ask her a few questions—y'know, what they'll be looking for at the auditions."

Rusty leaned over and mussed Jared's hair. "Okay, I like your thinking, Son. No dirty pool, just something to help your lady. Hang on. . . ."

Rusty stood up, flicked open his cell phone and punched in the speed dial for one of his star directors. After a minute, they heard him say to the big-name female director, "Sweetheart, how's it going? No, I'm back on the West Coast—yeah, got in early. So listen, about *The Outsiders*. You start casting this week, right?"

Lindsay bounced up and down in her chair, completely unable to contain herself. A couple of times during the conversation, Jared put his palm over her mouth to keep her from squealing.

"Spill! Spill," she shouted as soon as Rusty hung up.

"They're testing some of the biggest teen stars for Ponyboy—actors and rock stars."

"And Cherry?" She prodded.

"They're only seriously looking at unknowns."

Lindsay bit her lip. "Or someone making a comeback?"

He studied her, pressed his fingertips together. "Sure, Lindsay, that's possible."

"Dad," Jared said, "anything you can tell her, any insider tips that you know—it'd be a real favor. More than anyone, Lindsay's helping me get through my classes. She's been so supportive, helping me with my papers and stuff. That oughta be worth something."

Rusty looked surprised.

Lindsay melted.

"I asked for the entire script to be sent over. If you read the whole thing, you'll see what they're going for—an updated version, not as close to the book as the nineteen eighty-three movie was. They want the greasers tougher, more like hip-hop kids, and the socs to have a little more meat to them, not so one-dimensional. As for Cherry, they're thinking of a sexier type, more sultry than syrupy. And instead of mourning her boyfriend Steve, she's making an obvious play for Dally. But anyway, it should all be in the script."

Lindsay's heart soared.

Jared said, "Dad, this is . . . really cool of you."

Rusty said, "I gotta warn you, Lindsay, all the insider info in the world won't help if some actress just comes in and blows them away. Scripts change all the time. It'll be up to you to win the role by yourself."

"Oh, don't worry, Mr. L. I will. I will so get this on my own. It's . . . *beshert.*"

"Hi, Sara." Lindsay was leaning over the kitchen counter Sunday morning, sipping coffee and pretending to read the *L.A. Times.*

Sara, wearing some heinous puffy-sleeved thing out of the Frederick's of Purity catalogue, regarded her warily. "What are you doing up so early?"

"Early? It's after nine." Lindsay acted borderline chipper.

"And yet this is the first time I've seen your face before noon on a Sunday." Sara slung her fake leather bag over her shoulder.

"I couldn't sleep. I'm nervous about the audition next week." Which wasn't entirely a lie.

"Me too," Sara acknowledged.

Lindsay turned toward the fridge. "So, I'd offer you coffee, but you don't do caffeine, right? How about some OJ?"

"Thanks, but I don't have time."

"Off to church, huh? And I guess your little shadow isn't going along."

"No, Naomi doesn't go to church." Sara headed toward the door.

"Hey, Sara, wait up. Mind if I come with?"

Sara's clear blue eyes went wide—then quickly narrowed. "Why?"

Lindsay heard Jared's voice in her head. *Do not pull any-thing with Sara. Take the high road. Win the role because you're the one best for it.*

Lindsay shrugged. "Because it's Sunday. And I'm feeling"—she pressed her lips together—"well, a little prayer couldn't hurt, right? A little inspiration?"

Sara hesitated. Clearly she didn't believe a word of this hooey, but no way would Sara refuse. Especially after Lindsay greased the wheels: "We can borrow Jared's car. Beats the walk and the bus. You'll get a front-row pew."

A few moments later, after Lindsay had changed into the longest dress she owned, only a couple of inches above her knee, she carefully backed out of the driveway and headed down the hill toward Cahuenga Drive. "You know, Sara, I've been thinking—"

"About getting religion so you can get a role in a movie?" No mistaking it: Sara's tone was sarcastic. Lindsay guiltily wondered who she had to thank for that: her influence, totally.

"Didn't take you very long to get jaded," Lindsay remarked.

Chastised, Sara mumbled an apology.

Lindsay laughed. Waiting for the light to change at the corner of Sunset Boulevard and Doheny Drive, she admitted, "Anyway, I do have sort of a confession to make."

Sara eyed her suspiciously. "Save it for church."

"I think *you'll* find this confession useful. With all due respect to the higher power."

Sara crossed her arms, distrustful.

"Here's the thing: I had lunch at Jared's family's house yesterday. His father, Rusty Larson, was there."

"Mr. Larson, who owns Galaxy. You asked him about the movie," Sara guessed.

"I got insider info."

"And you're taking this opportunity to share it with me? Even I'm not that much of a hayseed. Not anymore, anyway."

Lindsay exhaled slowly. Here it was; Sara would either buy this or not. "Hear me out before you turn me down. Rusty—I mean, Mr. Larson—told me that dozens of actresses are going for it, but they need to make a decision within the next three weeks. So I had this brilliant idea. Why don't we work together in this first round of auditions, eliminate the competition?"

"How are we going to do that?"

"By using the rest of the info he gave me."

As All Saints Baptist Church came into view, Lindsay launched into her plan to give Sara the wrong info.

"They're totally playing it old-school, a faithful adaptation of the nineteen eighty-three Francis Ford Coppola movie. So you should watch it again, totally imitate Diane Lane's performance, but sweeten it up. They want Cherry to be so sweet, she could cause an insulin attack. Really sensitive. Really moony for her dead boyfriend, Steve, and for Ponyboy."

A small pang of guilt stabbed her. And surprised her. Why should she feel guilty? Hollywood was cutthroat. Better the girl learned it now. Still, she was feeling borderline crappy now that she was totally turning Sara in the wrong direction. Lindsay forced herself to swallow the guilt, and stay on point.

Sara still didn't trust her. "You're saying you know this because Mr. Larson got it straight from the director, while you listened in?"

Lindsay wavered. Sara was staring at her with her big blue eyes. She pushed on. "Can you keep a secret? Jared and his dad have . . . issues. And Rusty kinda thinks that I'm a good influence—"

Sara chortled. "*You're* a good influence?"

Lindsay was miffed. "Believe it or not, there are worse

influences than me. It's not like I'm some doped-up loser, like your little friend Naomi."

Before Sara could defend the homeless girl, Lindsay said, "Rusty cares about Jared's well-being, and helping me is his way of helping Jared. It's all good."

Even Sara could see the logic in that.

"So will you work with me? We get rid of the competition, and when it gets down to the two of us, as it will, the best one will get it. That's fair." Lindsay pulled up to the church and shifted the car into park. She held out her hand. "Deal?"

Sara hesitated, then took it. "It's not fair at all. But it's Hollywood."

"When do services end? I'll pick you up." Lindsay gestured at the imposing stone structure

Sara was puzzled. "Aren't you coming in?"

Lindsay waved her hand dismissively. "Not necessary. I made my confession. I feel so much better. My soul is cleansed, knowing we're in this together. Besides, Barneys is having a sale."

Nick and Eliot
Get Really Nervous

Nick felt nauseous. It wasn't something he ate, more like something he'd bought into. This whole deal. Except for the part where he got to live in a cool Hollywood place with sexy roommates, the summer was turning out to be one serious bust. He stared at the pot of coffee sitting on the burner at Nowicki studios. No one had brewed fresh; this'd probably been sitting here since the weekend. He poured himself a cup anyway, tasted the grinds in his first sip. His stomach lurched.

It was the end of July, and he didn't even have a portfolio yet, let alone appointments with reputable modeling agencies. Which Nowicki's was not. The stuff being shot at his studio was so not his cup of bitter coffee. No matter how you sweetened it.

"Nicky—"

God, he hated being called Nicky. Especially by the boys here.

"Nicky, darling, they're waiting for you in the back room. They've got the camera set up. Chop, chop." Alonzo, one of Les's personal assistants, clapped his hands.

"Be right there," he called, tossing the coffee into the garbage.

They were shooting a calendar called "A Year of Boys," and Nick was on stand-in duty for the twelve models, one pictured for each month. The poses were all, needless to say, shirtless and suggestive.

Yesterday, he'd posed as Mr. January: naked except for fur-lined briefs. When the real model came in, they'd had to stuff the briefs—at least Nick hadn't suffered that humiliation!

Today, they were doing Mr. February.

"Nicky, Nicky." It was Les, summoning him to the set they'd created, the facade of a fireplace. Nick would be posed lying on his side on a fluffly rug, bracketed by long brass fireplace tools. Les frowned when he saw him. "Didn't anyone tell you? We need you stripped down."

Stripped down?

Alonzo advanced, thrusting a cardboard cutout of a red heart at him. The Valentine's Day prop. "This is all you're wearing, Mr. February."

Nick gaped. The prop was just big enough to cover

him . . . maybe. He shook his head vehemently. "No way. I can't do this one."

Keith, the one member of Les's posse Nick could deal with, strode into the studio and assessed. "What's wrong?"

"Nick is being shy. And we're running late." Alonzo tapped his wristwatch.

"Find someone else. I'm not standing in front of everyone—"

"Hang on a minute," Keith said. "I'll be right back." When he returned, he was holding a beige thong. He grabbed the cardboard prop from Alonzo.

"Here, man," he said to Nick. "Go behind the screen over there, put this on, and use the heart to cover yourself. No one will see anything."

Nick grimaced. He hated every second of this. But at least Keith had been cool.

Impasse overcome, the rest was routine, if no more comfortable. He lay on his side, stretched out on the carpet, propped himself up on one elbow, cupped his chin. In his other hand, he held the red heart in front of him, positioning it wherever Les told him. "A little to the right. No, a little lower. Try it higher." Wearing the thong, girly as it was, helped. He felt somewhat secure. Even as Les bellowed, "Wait, what's he got on? He's supposed to be naked. It's in the shot."

Keith reminded him. "Don't worry, Les. The real model

won't be wearing it. Forget it's there. Let's get the lighting right and be sure he's positioned where we want him."

Nick breathed a sigh of relief.

Short-lived, as it turned out. Les decided his faux model needed shine, a full-body layer of gloss. Alonzo and Alain—privately, Nick thought of them as the Twinkle Twins—raced to apply it. No fans of Nick, who'd refused every one of their social overtures, no matter how innocent, they did everything possible to make him squirm.

They slathered it on with long, sensual strokes. He tried to bat them away. "Cut it out," he barked.

"Oh, but we're not done," Alonzo purred. "Les wants you slicked up good."

Nick'd had enough. He took a swing at Alonzo, who ducked just in time.

"Oooh," Alain squealed, "a rough one!!"

Keith strode over. "Cut the shit," he ordered Alonzo and Alain. "You two are done here."

When the shoot was over, as a way to say thanks, Nick invited Keith to lunch.

Keith Sternhagen, Nick learned over pizza, subs, and beer, had come to L.A., as he had, from the Midwest. "Racine, Wisconsin. Nice city."

"Hoping to be a model?" Nick asked.

"An actor," the young man confided. "But it's a hard nut to

crack. I left right out of high school, had no connections, and my savings didn't last very long. I needed to get a job, and I was lucky that Les took me on. I've been with him, making a good buck, for going on seven years now."

"So you just gave up on the acting? You don't go out on auditions or anything?" Nick took a bite out of his ham and cheese sub.

"Not lately. My last agent dropped me. It's disheartening. You keep putting yourself out there, only to keep getting rejected."

Nick understood. He lived with it. Sara and Lindsay—who had plenty of connections—had been striking out. Last week, they'd gone for their *Outsiders* audition: Neither had heard a word since, and both were on pins and needles. It wasn't fun.

"With Les," Keith was saying, "I got a steady income, a trade, a family. I might not be famous, but I'm not getting rejected every day."

Nick gulped his soda. He gathered his courage. "Keith, can I ask you something?"

"Sure," Keith put his pizza down.

"I'm not . . . I don't want to offend anyone. Y'know, I'm cool with live and let live. But that's not my lifestyle—"

Keith threw his head back and laughed. "You're kidding! You've made that very clear, my friend."

Nick blushed. "Sorry, I'm just . . . this is hard for me. It's a new situation. I thought maybe with time, it'd get easier, but it's the opposite. I'm thinking about quitting." There, he'd said it.

"Don't."

"Why not? I'm . . . man, I'm miserable here."

"Look, you came out here to be a model—"

"Not that kind."

"Dude, everyone starts somewhere. And no matter what you think of Les, or the studio, it really can lead to that billboard up there." He pointed through the restaurant window to the billboard of a man and woman posed sexily for Armani cologne.

"You think so?"

"You've got the look all right, you've got the determination, and the work ethic. You need to pay your dues, and then you need a break. From where I sit, you're on the right road."

Nick considered. "So you think this internship, this summer, could really lead to something big? I should stick it out?"

Keith's brow furrowed and he leaned in over the table. "Do you mind if I give you some advice?"

"Mind? No, I'd really appreciate that."

"You need to get closer to Les. You do that, he'll shoot the portfolio for you, and he'll hook you up with the best agencies in town. I've seen it happen. But right now, you're not exactly making friends at the studio, and that influences Les."

Nick's stomach clenched. Was Keith saying what he thought he was? 'Cause no freakin' way, man.

Keith continued. "You're a lust magnet. I'm not telling you anything you don't already know—why else would you be here? You made it this far, you put yourself in the right place, right time. Now you gotta play it for what it's worth. Otherwise, you can take those pretty pecs and sculpted abs back to Michigan. Open a gym or something."

"That can't be the only way to break into modeling," Nick groused.

"It's your call," Keith said carefully. "No one will ever force you to do something you don't want to. But you know that famous saying, 'The lady doth protest too much, me thinks'—and you know what that means."

Nick had no freaking idea what that meant. He put his cards on the table. "Look, Keith, I'm not gay. And I'm not gonna do anything . . . like that. If making friends with Les means what I think it does, forget it."

"You'd just as soon go home a failure, huh?"

Nick swallowed hard.

"Let me ask you something. Been dating a lot since you got here?"

"Why do you ask?" In fact, he hadn't dated at all since getting to L.A.

"Haven't seen you with any girls, you haven't talked about anyone. Just curious, that's all."

"Well, don't be. I could get any chick I want. . . ." He trailed off, and for some reason, began to sweat. "I've just been really busy this summer. I haven't had time," he mumbled.

Keith shrugged. "How much time do you need? All I'm saying is, don't close the door on something you've never even tried. At the very least, it might be a means to an end. At best? You might like it."

Nick went all drill sergeant on Sara that evening, just hammering away as she grunted and panted through her push-ups. "I want to see ten more reps!" He was angry, and knew it was wrong to take it out on her, but couldn't seem to stop himself.

"No, not . . . possible," she moaned. "Too hard." She flopped on the floor.

"Let's get those arms toned—let's try twenty-pounders." He brought over the weights.

Sara sat up. "Nick, is everything okay?"

"Why wouldn't it be?" He attempted a smile, but missed. "We've been working out for three weeks; it's time to ramp things up. That's how it works."

"Okay, let me put my hair up, and we'll do weights." She

pulled a ribboned one from her pocket and pulled her wavy hair into a ponytail.

"Here." He gave her a titanium barbell-shaped weight.

Instead of taking it, Sara slipped her arm around him. "I can tell when something's wrong, Nicky."

He tensed. "Please don't call me that. Now, come on. If you get a callback for *The Outsiders*, you want to look lean and mean."

Sara took the weight.

"Pump it up," he coached. "Come on, up, down, up, down. Feel the burn?" he asked as she struggled with the barbell.

"All I feel is burning tired. Nick, this is too hard," she grunted.

"No pain, no gain," he recited, feeling like a heel but unable to stop.

"These weights are too heavy," she complained. "I can't do it."

"Sure you can. Build up that muscle."

"I'm gonna pull a muscle first." She dropped the weights on the floor.

He exhaled. "Let's do aerobics, then. Here's a jump rope. Think you can manage that?"

"Why are you being so mean?" Sara began to cry as she took the rope and started the routine he'd taught her.

"I'm being real. You're being too sensitive," he growled.

"You gotta toughen up in this biz, or you'll never get any-where. I thought you learned that."

Ten minutes later, Eliot walked in. He grabbed a water bottle from the nightstand and handed it to Sara. "Nick, give the girl a break. She's sweating bullets here. What are you try-ing to do?

"I'm helping her. She's gotta tone those muscles if she wants to make it."

"It won't help if she's dead."

After Sara had left to take a shower, Eliot confronted Nick. "What was that all about?"

Nick dropped down on the bed, kicked his sneakers off. "What?"

"Why were you pushing her so hard?"

Defensively, Nick replied, "I ramped up our workout. What's it to you?"

"The girl was practically in tears, Nick. What'd you say to her?"

"Get off it, Kupferberg. If Sara's got an issue, she's a big girl, she can tell me. Or do you speak for her now?"

Eliot's jaw dropped. "What's going on, Nick? This is not you."

"When did you appoint yourself expert on me?" Nick said defensively.

Eliot scratched his head, then turned to leave. "When you're ready to be normal, I'll be outside in the hot tub. Sara and I are going to rehearse there."

Five minutes hadn't gone by before Eliot stomped back into the room, slammed the door, and accused him, "You like her. That's what it is. You want her for yourself."

Nick bolted up. "What the—?"

Eliot pointed his finger accusingly. "You're hot for Sara. Only you can't have her, so you're being nasty to her, and to me, instead. I'm right, aren't I?"

Suddenly, Nick burst out laughing. Leave it to Eliot to take a situation and bring it to a whole new level of ridiculous.

Eliot's face turned beet red. "Nice to see your mood shift, but I wasn't aware I was being so funny."

Nick got off the bed and threw his arm around Eliot. "Sorry, man. For everything. I just had a really rotten day at work, and I guess I was taking it out on Sara. And you."

Eliot was unconvinced. "You know I like her. . . . I mean, I really like her, Nick."

"Well, go for it, bro. The coast is clear—except for, uh . . . well, there's Donald." He ticked off his fingers. "There's the purity pledge. And there's"—he looked skyward—"the big guy upstairs. I don't think she's giving it up for anyone."

Eliot smiled wanly. "She looks good when she's sweating."

Nick grabbed a comb from the dresser and looked in the

mirror. "Got a question for you. This guy at work said some mumbo-crapo about some lady is protesting too much. Like I was supposed to know what he meant."

"What guy at work?"

"What's it matter? Just tell me what it means. If you know."

"'The lady doth protest too much' is a line from *Hamlet*. You remember a little of tenth-grade Shakespeare? It means that if you keep saying no to something, the opposite is true. Like if you keep insisting, over and over, that you're not into Sara, the opposite is true. You really *are* after her."

And how'd we get back there? Nick was confused. He was not after Sara.

"Why not?" Eliot broke in like a mind reader wielding a sledgehammer. "How could you not be attracted to her? She's sexy, she's gorgeous, she's sweet . . . she's the whole deal. I'm having a hard time just being friends."

Nick worked hard to not let his panic show. Sara was hot, anyone could see that. So was Lindsay. Yet he wasn't really interested in either of them. Was it possible that the job was changing him? Turning him gay? Could someone turn gay?

Carefully, he said to Eliot, "Look, bro, I know you like her. And even though I think she's a challenge—Religion Girl's got baggage, like we just said—I'm just stepping out of the way. Not to sound, you know, obnoxious, but I can get any girl. I don't need Sara."

"Good," Eliot said. "Step far out of the way. 'Cause if she does decide to ditch Donald, I want to be the guy, y'know? And even though I'm not that great-looking, I think I have a chance with her. I really do."

All Nick could manage was, "Keep the faith, dude."

The following Thursday night, everyone except Naomi settled around the poker table in the game room. It'd been ten days since Lindsay and Sara had auditioned, a fact Lindsay made everyone aware of . . . every minute. "I so know that phone's gonna ring," she burbled, getting up to refill her glass and Jared's with vodka. "It's gonna be Amanda. And she's gonna say, 'Call back tomorrow, Linz, for your second audition for Cherry. The casting directors love you!'"

She gaily winked at Sara. "And then, Eliot's phone is going to ring—that's the number they have for you, right?"

Nick growled, "Can you just deal the cards, Lindsay? We're here to play poker, not be the audience for your nightly monologue."

Lindsay smiled sweetly as she carefully dealt a card to each person. "And Eliot's gonna answer his phone and go, 'Sara, it's for you. It's Lionel . . . you've got a call back, you're still in the running for *The Outsiders*!'" With a flourish, she threw a dollar into the pot. "Who bets I'm right?"

Jared raised her a dollar. "I bet you lose this hand."

"I hope you're right, Lindsay. I raise both of you," Sara said with a grin.

Eliot won the round. He chose his next words carefully, having planned this for a while. "I have a wager. I bet not a single one of you will know what to do when an earthquake hits. And I'd like to—"

Jared rolled his eyes. "Would you stop with this already? It's August. You'll be gone in a month. Then you won't have to worry."

"You wouldn't either, if you knew what to do," Eliot responded sagely. "I'm going to teach you."

"Like hell." Jared pushed his chair back, went to refill his glass.

Lindsay hopped up too. But she was too stoked, in too good a mood to be annoyed. She strolled behind Eliot's chair, draped her arms around his neck, and playfully kissed the top of his springy hair. "As long as we can keep playing cards, I say, let the El-man go all 'Earthquakes for Dummies' on our asses."

Eliot flushed copiously.

Jared whirled around from the bar, gave her a look.

But he wasn't gonna mess with a deliriously happy Lindsay. And Nick wasn't gonna bother putting a cork in the Catastrophe Kid, either. When El was on a tear, nothing was going to stop him.

Over several hands of Texas Hold 'Em, five-card stud, and high-low, Eliot gave detailed preparedness instructions. "First, there are over three hundred and fifty earthquakes a year in L.A."

"That's like one a day—no way," said Nick dismissively.

"They're just so small you don't feel them, except for maybe a gentle wave in the middle of the night. That's the other thing: ninety percent of earthquakes happen in the middle of the night."

"Why's that?" Lindsay, suddenly interested, asked.

"There's a theory about seismic activity triggered by geological temperature changes that happen at night."

Lindsay snickered. "I can see why temperatures definitely rise at night."

Eliot got flustered. Damn, that girl could make pure snow blush. He plowed on. "There are generally two kinds of quakes. The first is a rolling quake; it rolls through in a waving motion and you feel like you're on a boat. That's the ground bending. The buildings actually sway and move. The wave rolls through and is gone in about four or five seconds."

"What's the second?" Sara asked nervously.

"The shaker. It hits like a bulldozer. You feel like you got slammed by a WWE wrestler. The shaking is so intense, windows blow out and buildings pancake—implode. The nineteen ninety-four quake lasted over forty-five seconds!"

"Doesn't seem like that long," Nick noted.

"It will when you're going through it," Eliot responded. "Anyway, we won't have much warning, but if you start to feel a wave beneath you, get moving. Whoever's closest to the kitchen, grab the preparedness kit and distribute the contents. Then get out of the kitchen fast! It's one of the worst places to be during an earthquake. If you're downstairs, duck beneath this table; it's the sturdiest one in the house."

Jared was astonished. "You weighed it?"

"I didn't have to. It's made of solid cherry wood, and we'd all fit under it. Unlike the low coffee table in the living room."

Lindsay grinned wickedly. "But it'd be cozier under the coffee table . . . and there's water there." She looked at Sara. "Oops, it's Kaballah water—you can't drink it. You'll have to go Jewish, or stay parched. 'Cause everyone knows in the event of an earthquake, don't drink the tap water."

Nick started to scold impish Lindsay, but Sara put her hand up. "It's okay. In case of an earthquake, I think I could make an exception. Anyway, what if you're upstairs when . . . I mean . . . if it happens?"

"Bend over and kiss your ass good-bye?" Nick suggested playfully.

"Stay upstairs," Eliot said. "The stairs could collapse, and falling debris could hit you in the head. Stand in a doorway, or against an inside wall. And wherever you are, get away from all windows. By the way, Nick, did you ask Jared where the main gas line is?"

Nick had not.

"Okay. We can check it out tonight. We have to know how to turn it off. Where's it located, Jared?" Eliot asked.

Jared threw his hands up. "How am I supposed to know? This is my uncle's house. And somehow, the subject of the freakin' gas line never came up."

Eliot banged his fist on the table. "Well, it should have. We've got to find it. Unless, in the event of an earthquake, you want to take the chance of being blown sky high."

"Whoa, chill out, E. After the game, I'll find it," Nick said soothingly.

"How will you know where to look?" Sara asked.

"My old man's in construction; I'll figure it out. And," he added, with a stern look at Jared, "I'll show you, in case the subject does come up."

Jared pressed his lips together. "You guys are taking this way too far. This is ridiculous."

Eliot shrugged. "Dude, you want our rent money? There's a few things you're gonna have to deal with—we should have figured this out back in June. Since we're talking about your life too, maybe you want to take it more seriously."

"You go, E-man!" Lindsay, borderline sloshed, clapped her hands.

Jared decided to push Eliot's buttons. "What makes you so sure it'll be an earthquake, anyway, not a wildfire? Or a tsunami?"

"I'm not sure," Eliot responded. "I bought gas masks for all of us, and helmets, in case of that. They're in the cabinet with the earthquake preparedness kit."

It was all Jared could do to keep from pissing his pants. Tears of laughter rolled down his face. His question had been facetious.

Eliot was steaming.

Lindsay put her forefinger to her lips and tilted her head. "Eliot, when's your birthday?"

"What's that got to do with anything?"

"I bet you're a Leo. 'Cause, baby, you are a passionate one. You roar, boy! Am I right? Are you a Leo?"

"His birthday is August twelfth," Nick said.

Lindsay squealed, "Oh, my god! I was right! And that's next week—we are so having a party." She jumped up and pirouetted around the room, "Par-*tay*! Par-*tay*! I say—par-tay!"

"Lindsay, sit down and deal the cards. It's your turn," Jared said.

"Only if you say okay to a party." She plopped into Jared's lap and kissed the tip of his nose.

No way could Jared resist Lindsay. Who, Eliot wondered, really could? So when, as dealer, she insisted on a "new game," they all went along with it.

"Here we go," she grinned maniacally. "Only one card each. I deal it facedown. You can*not* look at it!"

They indulged her.

"Now," she said. "I want each of you to take the card—don't look—and stick it on your forehead so everyone can see what you have, only you can't."

"You're making this up," Nick said skeptically.

"I am not!" Lindsay protested, "It's called Schmuck Poker. Am I pronouncing it right, Jared?"

Jared was laughing too hard to speak, but he nodded his head as he pressed his card, a five of clubs, on his forehead.

"Come on," Lindsay urged, "everyone do it."

Eliot shook his head in disbelief. Lindsay had a jack of spades; Sara, a seven of hearts; Nick, a queen of hearts. He had no idea what he had.

"Now we bet," Lindsay declared.

"On what?" Nick asked incredulously.

"On our cards, silly," she answered. "This is poker. Jared, you start."

"I bet five dollars." He tossed his money into the pot.

Which sent Sara into a whirl of laughter.

"You think you have me beat?" Jared challenged, "with that piddly card on your forehead?"

"I raise to ten dollars!" was her feisty response.

Lindsay, sure she had the table beat—'cause after all, she

was Lindsay—capped the betting at twenty-five dollars—but not before everyone had dissolved into hysterics and finger-pointing. By that point, Nick, Eliot, and Sara had folded, believing Miss Thing the probable winner.

Which is how Lindsay scooped the pot away from Nick and Eliot, who, it turned out, both had her beat. She'd bluffed.

Triumphantly, she crowed, "I win! I win! Now we have to have a party. We'll celebrate Eliot's birthday, and callbacks for the audition. Sara's and mine."

Sara, giggling at Lindsay's antics, finally managed to say, "You're gettin' ahead of yourself. No one's called—"

Precisely at that moment (she could not have staged it better), Lindsay's cell phone rang.

A half second later, so did Eliot's.

Lindsay and Sara:
Two Auditions

Pumped or pissed. Lindsay couldn't decide what she was more of. Getting the callback meant she'd made it to the next round of auditions, trounced hundreds of Cherry-wannabes. Yesss! She was smokin'! Lick fingertip, raise it high in the air!

But so—*damn*—had Sara! What was up with that?

For the benefit of the housemates, she'd fronted "knowing" they'd both get callbacks, when naturally, she knew nothing of the sort.

Wait . . . take that back. She did know one thing: She'd kicked *ass* at her first audition. 'Cause that's the kind of thing, as she'd joyfully recounted to Jared, you just "know" when you're doing it, and get confirmed by the looks from the casting directors when you're done. They lean over, whisper in each other's ears, write on their notepads, nod encouragingly, and say—this is key—"We'll be in touch."

As opposed to the dismissive "Thanks for coming." The English-to-Hollywood translation: "You sucked." Forget about a follow-up. Only good news nets the phone call.

So when Amanda herself rang during the poker game, Lindsay shot off her chair as if she'd been launched.

When Eliot sang out that Lionel was calling for Sara, Lindsay crash-landed, her good mood up in flames.

How'd *that* happen? She'd personally seen to it that Sara gave the wrong kind of audition. Told her to do the reading all sugary and saccharine when the full script confirmed they were going for Cherry Bomb, not Cherry Vanilla.

So what'd happened? Had Sara only pretended to believe her, and gone balls-out the way the casting directors wanted? Or worse, had Sara read Cherry's lines dripping with toothache-inducing sweetness, and won the judges over anyway?

The second scenario was Lindsay's total nightmare.

'Cause if that'd happened, it meant the girl from nowhere had "something"—the indefinable unquantifiable charisma. The "thing" that must not be named.

The dark art Lindsay had no defense against.

She couldn't share her insecurities with Jared. She'd sort of not told him about deliberately trying to undermine Sara. Jared played by Hollywood rules—winning at any cost, that is—but there were some things he was stupidly stubborn about.

Like wanting Lindsay to win the role fairly. Like it was okay to procure the script and insider info, but not okay to screw up someone else's chances. Especially when that someone else was rent-paying Sara?

Lindsay had played her own game. It'd backfired. Somehow, Sara Calvin, a nobody from nowhere, now had the same exact chance of nailing this role as Lindsay had. Where was the fair in that?

Lindsay's stomach churned. She really, really didn't want to lose out to her own housemate.

The first round of *Outsider* auditions had taken place in the casting directors' offices in Beverly Hills. It'd been a cattle call, the waiting area jammed with dozens of would-be Cherrys. They came in all stripes: blondes, brunettes, redheads, African Americans, Asians, Latinas, tall, tiny, short, stocky, curvy, stick-thin. Some wore cowboy hats (did they think this was a remake of *Bonanza?*), others decked out in prim 1960s dresses. More than half the girls had anxious stage mamas and papas at their sides. Several paced, others perched, many couldn't decide how to calm their stomach-churning nerves. Silently or out loud, all were going over the audition scenes in their heads—and overtly or covertly, wishing the worst to every other person in the room.

They waited an excruciatingly long time to be called in, one by one, for their tryout. Then they got five minutes to make a lasting impression on the casting directors with a stellar reading. And then, coming out, one by one, by turns hopeful, dejected, deluded.

Two weeks had passed since the heinous cattle call, and the field had been whittled down considerably. According to reliable sources—i.e., Galaxy office gossip—there were now about twenty girls in contention. Eighteen others besides Lindsay and Sara.

This second round of competition took place at the Warner Brothers studios in Burbank in front of the movie's director and producers. The crop of actresses who made it through would then have a final audition for the studio boss. Rusty Larson had a weekly tennis game with the head of Warner Brothers studios. Should Lindsay be Galaxy's only client in the finals, she was in.

She had to make it through this round. Two obstacles stood in her way: the director, Katherine McCawley, and Sara Calvin. She didn't know the director at all, didn't know what card to play to win her over. She knew Sara all too well.

To better her chances with the first, she'd rented the DVD of the director's first movie, and rehearsed a gushing suck-up speech about it.

To better her chances of beating Sara, she planned to sneak

into the girl's audition: Whatever Sara did in her tryout, Lindsay had to do it better. Slipping in unnoticed was the easy part. She needed one piece of luck: for Sara to be called before her.

"Lindsay Pierce, you're up first!" A clipboard-clutching assistant summoned her. Clue number one that the good luck goddess might not be smiling on her plan. Sara, from across the room, gave her a fingers-crossed signal. Which was, she had to reluctantly admit, sweet of her. Which Lindsay had deliberately not been toward her. She prayed the karma gods weren't out today.

Her stomach churning, she managed to wave back.

Gamely, she followed Assistant Lady from the waiting area to the set, which turned out to be the one that used to be the stage for TV's *Smallville*. Made sense, Lindsay conceded, as that show took place in small-town America, as did *The Outsiders*. She smiled inwardly: Being tested in this setting reinforced her instinct about what to wear. In the 1983 movie, Diane Lane had done most of her scenes in buttoned-up blouses and skirts. Today's Cherry, at home in this setting, would be clean-cut, prepped up, in Lucky jeans, midheel boots, layered pink polo, carrying a Kate Spade bag.

Lindsay Pierce? Check!

She'd used a curling iron to give herself long, loose waves, brushed her bangs to the side and clipped hem back with a ribbon bow—her one homage to the beribboned actress in the original.

The casting agents, director, producer, and random assorted assistants huddled in a row several feet from the stage, to which Lindsay had been asked to ascend. Huge spotlights from the overhead beams lit the area, an instant reminder of her days spent on a stage not unlike this one, as Zoe Wong.

Her stomach settled. She no longer worried about the good luck gods. She waved at her audience. "Hi, I'm Lindsay Pierce, and I'm a big fan of—"

"We know who you are," one of the producers interrupted her. "We know how thrilled you are to be here, and we're running late."

She gulped. Okay, so they'd heard this all before. Whatever. She lifted her head confidently, and smiled graciously.

"We're going to do two scenes," he told her. "We'll start with Cherry and Dallas at the drive-in movie, then we'll move on to Cherry and Ponyboy. Are you ready?"

She drew a breath. "Locked and loaded."

He called the actor who'd be standing in for Dallas Winston: Lindsay was caught off guard. He was tall, scruffy, rugged . . . omigosh! The boy from the park! What was his name—Mark? For a moment, she forgot herself, gave him a huge smile, and started to ask how he'd done on that other movie. The young actor saved her from what would have been a huge gaffe. He got his Dallas on immediately.

Caddish, cocky, sexy, he pretended to offer her a soda. His

reading was half sneer, half come-on. She knew the lines, knew when and how to toss the soda at him . . . she also knew she'd gotten flustered. Had screwed it up. She'd meant to play it haughty, righteous, and cool. Instead, she knew she came off unsteady, unsure of herself.

Mark-as-Dallas did his next line.

Cherry's comeback to him was supposed to be flippant, a one-up. Only she didn't do it right! Another half-assed reading— Lindsay was starting to panic. Where was her inner nasty when she needed it most? Lindsay so wanted a do-over. Otherwise, based on that stinky reading, it'd be *all* over.

"Okay," called the casting director, "now we'll do a Ponyboy scene." The actor called on to read with her this time turned out to be Tom Welling, the actor who starred in *Smallville*. Lindsay didn't know him, was surprised he was reading for Ponyboy: He was much too pretty for the part.

She did the line pointing out what an original name Ponyboy was. She did it without any sarcasm. She then told him everyone called her Cherry because of her hair color. She'd planned on tossing it, but didn't.

The next scene they were asked to do was further on in the script.

A strange sensation came over her as she read with the handsome young actor. Gazing into his chiseled face, his jade-green eyes, she saw not an actor, but . . . but . . . Jared? She didn't have time to think about it. Instinct said: Go with it.

And she forgot, just forgot—she'd later say—how she'd planned on reading Cherry's lines, how the script called for a mean girl. Ponyboy smiled Jared's smile, and she knew in an instant that no matter what the script called for, no matter what the director's "vision" was, it was wrong. It wasn't Cherry. The key to finding the character wasn't in the book, the movie, the screenplay, or insider info. It was right there, inside her all along.

Cherry wasn't some random cardboard snob, no matter what era the movie took place in. She was a teenager—impetuous, flirty, feisty, but also sweet, soulful, and sensitive. With enough foresight to understand she was stuck in a world that wasn't fair to the greasers or the socs.

Some of Cherry's characteristics fit her, Lindsay, like a glove. Others were such-the-Sara. She ended up doing the reading as neither: She did it as Cherry.

Her last line of the reading was, "Just don't forget that some of us watch the sunsets, too."

The actor gave her a surprised look. She thought: I can't believe I did that. I did exactly what I shouldn't have. I blew it. I blew—

"Lindsay—is that your name?" The director spoke first. "That was an interesting take."

The casting director coughed. "What happened between

the first reading and this one? You went in an entirely different direction." Translation: "If I knew you were going to read this way, you would not have been called back."

Lindsay had nothing to lose. "I didn't plan it. I'm not sure what came over me. I think it was just . . . that's Cherry. It's who she is. It's who I was at that moment. I know that's not the way you wanted it. I'm sorry, but . . ."

The director stood up, her round face made pretty with a genuine smile. "Lindsay, I know you were in a sitcom several years ago. But today? You blew me away."

Lindsay lit up like the Las Vegas skyline.

"Of course," the casting director quickly threw in, "we have more actresses to see. But I think it's fair to say you will be hearing from us."

Lindsay flew back to the waiting area and called Jared. And Amanda. And Caitlin, Julie, and . . . pretty much everyone she had on speed dial.

Then she snuck into Sara's reading.

Sara was reading with Tom Welling. She stood tall, her hand on her hip, her chin up. She'd worn dusty blue jeans, loafers, a button-down shirt, and a blazer, her hair caught in a ponytail.

Lindsay watched silently. Sara didn't suck. So far.

Then Sara came to one of the most famous lines in the movie. Diane Lane had done it rushed, in a whisper, almost as though, if she said it fast enough, it wouldn't be real.

Sara's delivery was slow, dreamy. "'I could fall in love with Dallas Winston. I hope *I* never see him again, or I will.'"

She's thinking about Nick, Lindsay realized with alarm. Worse, she's . . . she's . . . fucking brilliant.

Lindsay had been so busy on the phone, congratulating herself, she hadn't heard the rest of Sara's reading. Was it as amazing as what she'd just heard? Would she torture herself by listening in to the reactions of the judges?

Is Paris Hilton a spotlight-slut?

"What's your name again?" the director asked, interested.

"And you've never done any acting before?" This from a clucking producer. "And you're from the Texas panhandle? Near Oklahoma?"

When they got to the question "How would you feel about dying your hair red?" Lindsay vomited.

Beautiful People Partying

Naomi: Saturday Night, 10–11:00 p.m.

Oh, yeah, we're goin' to a party, party!

Naomi knew the song. "Birthday," by the Beatles. Sara must have asked the deejay to play it in honor of Eliot's birthday. She was one of the few who remembered the reason they'd thrown a party. Naomi watched from her corner of the living room as Sara planted a kiss on Eliot's cheek and wished him a happy nineteenth birthday. Eliot blushed. Profusely. He tried to return the kiss, aiming for her lips, but Sara had already turned the other cheek.

Naomi chuckled inwardly. A snapshot of Eliot: His aim is true, but his target keeps moving.

None of the other partygoers, mostly guests of Lindsay and Jared, even noticed the song, or its honoree: They were too busy reveling in the fabulousness of themselves. They were packed into the living room, game room, overflowing into the backyard.

In a twisted way—she was the only one in the room, or the zip code, who'd think this—it was like the homeless shelters, crowded and loud. Just switch designer for destitute, laughter for tears, and hope for hopeless. As Sara says, we're all children of God. Just some are more favored than others; more or less entitled. The haves and the have-nots.

Tonight was all about the haves. To wit:

A night of short skirts and long beers, buff bodies and bare skin, roaming eyes and brushing fingers, teasing, flirting, the rush of being young, hot, and born to the high life. All over the house, inside and out, there was dancing—dirty and otherwise—singing, raucous laughter, clinking of glasses, kissing of asses, touchy-feely-gushy and phony. All fueled by an open bar, uppers, downers, alphabet drugs, and, she guessed, simply the kind of bubbleheaded joy that being rich and worry-free gets you.

How does it feel to be, one of the beautiful peo-*ple . . .*"

It was the Beatles song "Baby, You're a Rich Man." Had the deejay read her mind? Naomi skulked back into the kitchen, suddenly itching to get as far from the merriment as she could. Being invisible was something she had a lot of practice in. At various times during the evening, Sara, Nick, and Eliot had tried to involve her, but she'd resisted. She appreciated the effort the boys from the Midwest had made to get to know her, how they'd quickly overcome their resistance to her moving in.

But times like this, Naomi realized she knew better: She should not even be here. She did not belong in Richie Rich's house. Naomi Foster was as far from "beautiful people" as you could be.

She knew her Beatles, though. They were tapes, not CDs, back then, that her parents used to play in the car. Her sister Annie liked to sing along, but could never remember the words. Naomi had memorized every lyric. Too bad she couldn't remember what it felt like to be happy, to feel whole, and wholly safe in that little car, just the four of them, with the four mop-tops in the tape player.

Jared's kitchen was a mess, the floor already sticky, countertops piled high with dirty dishes, stained glasses. She rolled her sleeves up and reached for a sponge when Sara suddenly appeared, hands on shapely hips. "Jared hired a caterer, remember? They'll clean up. Come sit with us."

Naomi knew she should feel grateful, but all she felt was out of place. It must have shown on her face. Sara added, "You don't have to talk to Jared and Lindsay's friends. Me, Nick, and Eliot are sitting with Wes and Candy."

Wes Czeny and Candy Dew were Sara's—and her—bosses

at *Caught in the Act*, and had been nothing but nice to Naomi. Which made her feel even less like socializing with them.

"Join us—do it for the birthday boy," Sara coaxed.

Playing the Eliot card worked. Naomi reluctantly trailed Sara into the living room, where Nick immediately scooched over to make room for her on the couch. "Have a scoop of caviar." Nick offered to spoon some of the expensive fish eggs onto a cracker. "It's salty, but hey—probably be a long time until the likes of us gets to enjoy this again."

Naomi shook her head no. In the apartment in Northridge, her mom used to try and make Fridays festive. After dinner, she'd put out a spread of crackers and cheese, a cut-up pineapple with strawberries, cookies, pie, and ice cream. The family would sit down and watch TV sitcoms together. *All for Wong* was her sister Annie's and their mom's favorite; *Home Improvement*, her dad's and hers. It was their big splurge for the week. And that was only when her dad had picked up an odd job as a handyman, or Mom had managed to score a cleaning-lady gig. The apartment, a one-bedroom in a small complex, wasn't theirs. They were subletting temporarily, and, she'd only found out later, illegally.

"The kindness of strangers," her mom had once said. "One day, we won't have to depend on that. Our family will be the kind ones."

"One day" had never come for Laura or Lonny Foster. Naomi had long given up on it ever coming for her.

"Earth to Naomi." Eliot had been trying to get her attention. She flushed. "Oh, sorry—did you need something?"

"I was asking if you did. I was taking drink orders. What's your pleasure?"

"I'm good, thanks," she replied, and turned to the exchange between Sara and Wes. "When Nick makes it as a famous model, Lionel's going to represent him, and everyone's going to want to interview him. I'd book him for *Caught in the Act* now if I were you."

Candy, already tipsy, went coy. "Nick can come in for a pre-interview any time." She rested her hand on Nick's knee—just a moment too long. Sara's face went cross for that moment.

Eliot caught it. He bolted up. "So, who else besides myself would like another drink?"

"I'll have another martooni. Make it dirty, with three olives." Candy held her empty glass up.

Wes, settled into the large armchair, seconded. "I'll go for another brewski if you've got a free hand."

Nick started to get up. "I'm ready for more beer too. I'll help carry."

Eliot looked at Sara. "How 'bout it—one tiny glass of wine or beer, anything?"

Sara didn't drink.

470

Nick nudged Sara. "Aw, come on, in honor of the E-man—just one won't hurt."

Something told Naomi that Nick was wrong.

Jared: Midnight–2:00 a.m.

Everybody's movin', everybody's groovin', at the Love Shack! Love Shack, bay-yaay-bee!

Mostly everybody *was* groovin' to the B52s, Jared noted as he surveyed the house—Uncle Rob's house, that is—everybody but him. Anxious that groovin' could turn to wildin', he policed the premises to be sure no one was getting into things they shouldn't, that nothing belonging to his uncle was touched. His crew was cool, but when you put Lindsay together with her friends, mixed in boisterous music and an open bar, destruction was a foregone conclusion.

Which had always been one of La Linz's more adorable qualities—except when *he* had to be the responsible party at the party. That wasn't fun. Her shenanigans weren't nearly as cute.

A week ago, she'd wanted, begged for, the party—supposedly for Eliot's birthday, but clearly, for herself.

A week ago, he'd told her, "What part of 'not gonna happen' don't you get?"

She'd cajoled, coaxed, kept him a very happy "prisoner" in the bedroom until he agreed.

Negotiations had begun the next morning. She'd won the round about having it in the house, 'cause, really, where else could they afford? He'd won the round about having it catered, with a clean-up crew, insisting she pay for half the expenses.

She'd countered that since Nick, Eliot, and Sara lived here too, they'd have to kick in. He'd said in that case, they got to invite their friends too. She'd make a face and gone, "Eeeww!" Until she realized, hello, how many Cali-friends did those three even have?

They were set, in agreement—everyone except Naomi chipped in. Then Lindsay came home from the second *Outsiders* audition, sick, bummed, so sure she'd lost out to Sara, that she didn't want a party, didn't want to see anyone. The drama princess wanted only to "hide in her room." She could not face the world.

So Jared had become Cajole Boy, adamant that she was wrong. She hadn't lost the part to anyone yet; she'd done a kick-ass job at the audition—yes, he had heard that through the grapevine. She should be brimming with confidence. And furthermore, he actually heard himself insisting, they were so having a party. So there!

So here.

Here he was with a house full of people, the young, restless, bold, and beautiful . . . and he, acting like a nervous parent, worried that someone was gonna break into the liquor cabinet. How'd that happen again?

In the end, he'd only asked three things of Lindsay. If anyone asked, the house was hers: She was renting for the summer. No dancing on the tables. And the biggie: no inviting anyone who might come into contact with his dad, and therefore rat him out, was allowed at the party.

She'd moaned that it wouldn't be a problem. Which cool people would want to party with a loser like her? Surely no celebrities.

So what, Jared asked himself as he patrolled the backyard, were all these bold names—the gossip and blog fodder—doing sitting in the chaise lounges and hot tub and playing video games?

Leave it to Lindsay: Her bout of self-pity had been brief, then she'd turned the house party into a tabloid's dream.

When he'd collared her, she'd waved him away dismissively. "It's Saturday night, they're only here for an appetizer. They've all got elsewhere to be. You know it as well as I do."

Heaving a sigh, Jared checked his watch, hoping the magic hour had arrived and they'd leave. So far as he could tell, no paparazzi had trailed anyone. No photogs meant no outing via any Internet sights or tabs the next day: Jared's dad would be none the wiser to his summer scam.

"Yo, Ja-*red*, wuzzup, man?" His buddy Tripp fell into stride with him as he stalked into the living room. "You're not looking too happy. Problems in paradise?" He motioned over to Lindsay, cavorting on the dance floor.

"You wish," Jared said. "Lindsay and I are good. There is no window of opportunity for you."

"Then, wazzup with the downer stares?" Tripp challenged.

"It's all good," Jared insisted.

"Well, then c'mon over. Julie can't get up, and she wants to chill with your ass."

Julie, who'd suffered a hairline fracture that night at Spider, was playing her "tragic injury" for all it was worth. "I can't dance," she complained to Jared. "I need company. Lots of it. And liquor."

"I'm here for you, Julie. What are you drinking?" Jared asked.

"A lot."

That was the theme of the night, as far as Jared and Lindsay's group was concerned. Those who couldn't, or wouldn't, dance were drinking, eating, and dishing. The talk was shop: who was up for what role, who got hired or fired, who was sleeping with the director, or wanted to; who was hooking up; who was breaking up; who was in the closet, who was about to be outed.

He'd heard it all before. Over and over. Like a loop. Jared found his attention drifting away. To Lindsay, looking hot while dancing, drinking, and giggling. He checked on Uncle Rob's belongings, the guitars on the walls, the copper bongs, the CD/record collection. No one had touched anything.

"Jared." Julie pulled him off mental surveillance. "Unknown dude flirting with your girl." She pointed across the room.

He was tall, wearing rumpled cords and a wrinkled T-shirt that read "Napster Rules." He was so not one of them. And he was all over Lindsay.

Before Jared could jump up, Lindsay led the newcomer over to their group. "Guys, this is Mark."

She was met with blank stares.

"Mark!" Lindsay squealed. "You remember, from the park." She jogged their memories. "He rescued George Clooney, and he tried out for that heinous *Heiress* movie. Neither of us got it."

Jared remembered: Mark had auditioned opposite Lindsay, and presumably Sara, for *The Outsiders*. Mark, this granola guy, was now an FOL, a Friend of Lindsay?

"Move over, guys," Lindsay urged. "Make room for us. Mark, what can Jared get you to drink?"

"Yeah, what're you having, man?" Jared grumbled, getting up to head over to the bar. He'd need another few shots of tequila if he had to hang out with this dude.

When Jared, carrying a tray full of shots, returned, Tripp was singing some old folkie song. Mark, Austin, MK, and Julie were singing along.

Jared freaked: Tripp had removed one of the guitars off the wall. Before he said anything, Lindsay leaped up. Even quasi-drunk, she realized this was a major no-no. She swiftly wrested the instrument from him and put it back on the wall.

Mark left soon after. Jared found himself relieved. A relief that lasted a microsecond:

"Body shots!" Lindsay shouted, peeling off her top—to reveal a cute cami underneath. "Let's do body shots, let's get this party movin'!"

She practically skipped into the game room, rounding up as many revelers as she could. She opened the sliding doors, summoning party-peeps inside. When she bumped straight into Sara and Eliot, she hooted, "It's your birthday! Happy—"

Eliot put his palms up. "As a birthday present, Lindsay, please don't throw up on me."

That set off a giggle-fit. Which, midway through, led to Lindsay's inept interpretation of *E.T.*—the Spielberg classic, not the TV show. She held up her finger and started chanting, "Eh . . . lee . . . yot . . . Eh . . . lee-yot . . ."

Caitlin hooted, "Wait, your finger has to glow. What's in the house that we can use to light it up?"

Lindsay, Caitlin, and Ava scouted around. Five minutes later, they returned, having glued glitter to all their fingertips. And succeeded in making Eliot turn tomato red and probably wish he really could go "Home—ET go hooomme," even as the girls were dancing around him and teasing.

The body shots had just begun: Ava was the first volunteer. Tripp had poured a tequila shot into her belly button and was first in line to lap it up. MK followed, as did Nick, then a flotilla of fellas, as Lindsay laughingly called them.

Jared felt calmer. Most of the celeb crew had split, as Lindsay predicted. No photogs had crashed the party, and so far, nothing he could see had crashed and burned.

A few body shots among friends—what was the harm in that? As long as no one was licking liquor off his girlfriend, that is. After Ava, it was Caitlin's turn to be tickled with tongues and tequila. Even Eliot had joined in by this time: no doubt because Nick had finally made sure the E-man was sloshed. Sara and Naomi remained the teetotalers in the house.

"Yap! Yap! Yap!" He heard it, even as he joined the line to do a shot off Caitlin, and whirled around. Lionel, Sara's agent, had arrived. In his arms, he carried a small rat-faced dog.

"George-fuckin'-Clooney!" Lindsay bellowed. "What's he doing at my party? And . . . who invited you?"

Lionel, who couldn't wait to rid himself of the runt, gave him over to Lindsay. "Good evening to you, too, Ms. Thing," he said. "Sara invited me, and I happened to be dog-sitting. Since you and George Clooney are already BFFs, I didn't think you'd mind if I brought him."

"Think again," Lindsay hissed, then drew Lionel into the

kitchen, where Sara immediately rushed over to them, alarmed. "I . . . I . . . ," she stuttered. "I'm sorry, Lionel, I didn't invite you. . . ." She trailed off, unsure of what to say. Lionel was a direct link to Rusty Larson, and even Sara had pledged to keep anyone away who might report to him.

Lionel beamed at her. "I know you didn't, sweetie. I called the cell phone, and Eliot said to come on over. I have delicious news for you! And I had to give it to you in person."

Jared barged in. "Come here, man, I need to talk to you." Before anyone could stop him, he'd pulled Lionel out of the kitchen, through the living room, and out to the backyard. And told the dude in no uncertain terms: He wasn't here; there was no party; Rusty Larson would know nothing about this evening. And—urgent bulletin—whatever news he had for Sara, if it was about *The Outsiders* audition, he'd better tell Jared first. No way would Jared let Lindsay be humiliated. Not tonight, and not like this.

Sara Feels the Earth Move

Sunday Morning, 2–4:00 a.m.

Sara was shaking with dread and anticipation.

"You got the part! You got the part!" Naomi repeated excitedly. "Why else would Lionel be here?"

"Is that what he said?" Sara rushed at Eliot. "Is that what he told you on the phone?"

"He said he had good news for you," Eliot explained, "and he wanted you to come to the phone."

"So why didn't you come get me?"

Nick answered for his bud. "El probably said, 'Come over and tell her yourself.' Am I right?"

Eliot offered a sloppy smile. And a hiccup.

Sara bit her nails. "But . . . how could you do that, Eliot? If he's come to say I won the audition, that would mean

Lindsay lost. And she'd know it, in front of everyone. That'd be horrible for her."

Eliot's bug eyes widened, and he happily slapped his face. "Oh. I was only thinking of you, Sara-dorable one."

She sighed. She'd been preached to her whole life about the evils of alcohol. What she hadn't understood until this summer was that liquor loosened lips, acting like truth serum. She knew Eliot was crushing on her—who in the house didn't? But she didn't think it was serious. As far as Eliot knew, she was still committed to Donald. Or had he inferred the truth, that she wasn't so sure anymore?

She adored Eliot. As a friend. A true friend, one she hoped she'd have for life. It'd never be anything more than that. And now, this thing, inviting Lionel over—in front of Lindsay—that was unlike Eliot. It was just insensitive.

Naomi read her mind. "What do you care? Lindsay's been nothing but mean to you. And besides, if Lionel is here to give you this amazing news, it just means you were the better actress, the better fit for the role."

Sara found herself saying, "But Lindsay, she'll die if she doesn't get it."

"Oh, come on, Sara." This was Nick now. "She's a drama queen. She'll get over it. And get another role, too. Lindsay's determined; she's a survivor."

Did that mean Nick thought Sara wasn't? She looked at

him. Her legs turned to jelly. Those charcoal eyes were smoldering. And those lips . . . no! She was not going to think about Nick Maharis now.

She stalked out of the kitchen, on a mission to find Lindsay. She didn't make it farther than the living room. Jared and Lionel were just coming inside. Lionel rushed up to her and threw his arms around her. He glanced over his shoulder at Jared. "So is it all right if I tell her?"

Sara had not won the role—yet. The news, Lionel insisted, was almost as good. He had just got a call from Amanda, who was having dinner with the producer of the movie. They'd narrowed the search to two actresses for Cherry, and Sara was one of them. She'd audition for the head of the studio on Monday. Wasn't that the most fabulous news ever?"

Sara stared at her agent. "I'm up against Lindsay, aren't I? She's the other person."

Lionel's silence was her answer. "Come on, Sara, you're supposed to be over the moon about this news. Why the long face?"

"Does Lindsay know?"

Lionel assured her that Jared was going to find her and give her the excellent news that she, too, was a finalist. "It's all good, Sara. Now I insist you come and talk to me. I dragged all the way out here to tell you."

Numbly, she followed him, and soon found herself in the middle of the living room, with Lionel, Naomi, Eliot, and

Nick. In a daze, she watched Nick's eyes wander the room: checking out the designer-decked dollies, as they checked him out. Yet he made no move to leave their little group.

Lionel leaned over, whispered in her ear conspiratorially, "You like him?"

She whispered back. "No! I mean . . . not in that way. It's nothing."

What Lionel said next disquieted her. "Are you sure he's straight?"

She jerked her head up. "What do you mean?"

"What's the secret, you two? Why are you whispering?" Nick nudged her.

"I asked Sara if you were straight."

Sara had never noticed Nick's vein, the one in his forehead that protruded when he was enraged, the way his lips pressed together, his eyes dulled. He bolted up without a word, headed for the bar.

Eliot was surprised. "Why would you ask a question like that? Nick's a babe-magnet."

"I heard about this thing called gaydar. . . ." Naomi hesitated. "Like radar."

Lionel shrugged. "No, nothing like that. It was an honest question, that's all. Just because girls like him doesn't mean he swings that way. Why should Sara waste lustful looks on someone who bats for the other side?"

Sara blushed and stood up. "I need to find Lindsay."

Lindsay found her first. Out in the backyard, Sara was walking toward the pool when Lindsay, completely hammered, called from behind her. "I have just one question for you, Sara. Why didn't you read the scene like I told you to?"

Lindsay had seen her audition? Sara whirled around.

The stuck-up girl was coming at her now, guns blazing. But in her eyes, those normally dancing light brown eyes, Sara saw panic. And pain. She gulped.

"You didn't believe me, did you?" Lindsay accused her. "You thought I was tryin' to trip you up?"

"I never thought that, Lindsay. Anyways, your plan worked, didn't it? We conquered the competition, me and you."

"My plan worked. Yeah, right." Lindsay laughed mirthlessly.

Sara steeled herself. "But you're right. I didn't end up reading it the way you said. I don't know what came over me, exactly, but—I know you'll think this is stupid—I've been reading the other script, the one the policeman wrote?"

"I have no idea what you're talking about," Lindsay said.

"The one you tossed into the pool that first night? And I got it out?"

A hint of recognition crossed Lindsay's face. "*That* one? How does some hack script by some random wannabe have anything to do with *The Outsiders*?"

"It doesn't. Not exactly." Sara drew a deep breath. "But there's a character in it, her name is Kate. And she sort of is like Cherry in a way. Conflicted, you know. It sort of spoke to me. And I ended up doing the reading as if I was Kate. Funny, huh?"

"Yeah, funny ha-ha," Lindsay mumbled, then turned and walked away.

Sara took a step toward her, then froze. She wanted not to care about Lindsay. She wanted to win the role of Cherry: She deserved it. Her mom deserved it—all those years of sacrifice, all that money spent on the pageants, everything the family had poured into their only daughter. This was the payoff. This was the dream come true. She saw her name up on the screen: "And Introducing Sara Calvin as Cherry." She'd be the toast of Texarkana. Best of all? It'd be because her whole family had worked for it and she'd earned it. She should win the role of Cherry, because it was right.

Lindsay. The cute, bubbly, freckled girl popped into her head, much as Sara tried to push the image away. Lindsay had worked too—she'd spent her whole childhood supporting her family. This was her moment, her destiny, too. And that was the difference between the two of them, Sara realized. She wanted the role—desperately—but she wanted it for her family, for her town, because she believed it her destiny.

Lindsay simply wanted it for herself.

Sara hung her head.

Naomi came looking for her. "What are you doing out here? Did you find Lindsay? What'd she say to you?"

"No," Sara lied, "I didn't find her yet. I'm still looking."

She stared out over the valley. The million-dollar view, Jared had called it. At night, the lights twinkled below her, around her. And this night, the air was so clear, like someone had sprinkled it with sweet jasmine, citrusy orange, and lemon.

She didn't know exactly how long she spent staring at the horizon. She was pretty sure the music had ended and several guests had left. Lionel had stuck his head out to say good-bye, to mention he was leaving the dog, since he didn't want to drive drunk with it—Amanda would have him fired if he upset George Clooney in any way—and to apologize if he'd caused a rift.

Sara strolled around the side of the house so she wouldn't have to talk to anyone. She'd gotten around to the driveway when she heard it.

The weeping: It was heartbreaking. Someone was heaving, hiccupping, sobbing like the world had ended. She looked around, but saw no one. She didn't have to. Sara knew who it was.

It was coming from the driveway, where Jared's convertible was parked. Her eyes caught a flash of copper. Lindsay was in the driver's seat, bent over the steering wheel, crying her eyes out, hiccupping.

Sara had the urge to go over and shake her! To shout, "Stop it, you haven't lost the part. It's not decided yet!"

If she did that, she might say more. She might give voice to a tiny, persistent thought, fluttering in her brain like a darn hummingbird. And she wasn't ready to swipe it away, nor to let it sing.

Shaking, Sara turned on her heel and walked back inside the house. To a shocked Nick she said, "I'd like a vodka martini. Straight up."

It wasn't the taste she took to. It was the burning feeling, stinging, punishing as it went down her throat. She asked for another.

And another. Until the truth hit her between the eyes and she let the hummingbird sing. She would not take the role from Lindsay. She'd give a horrible reading, or better, not show up for the audition. Tell Lionel she didn't want it after all. She'd kick her own dream to the curb, because giving is better than receiving, because charity, empathy, feeling for others was part of her DNA. She would let Lindsay have this role. Because it was the right thing to do. So why did it hurt so much?

"Another, please," she slurred, and held out her glass. Eliot and Naomi had wandered off. Most of the guests had left.

"Are you sure, Sara?" Nick asked, "You've had a lot . . . for your first time drinking."

"I'm so totally sure, Nick-o-lash," she slurred.

Nick's large palm cupped her chin, forcing her to look into his eyes, those smoldering charcoal eyes, now filled with concern. For her.

"Please, sir," she belched while paraphrasing *Oliver Twist.* "May I have s'more?"

He didn't get the reference; that was okay. Sara pictured him nude as he walked over to the liquor bar, watching his thigh muscles scissor, his cute, tight butt move. *I'm in lust with Nick Maharis.* There, she'd admitted it. Or was it love? Love or lust, how could she know for sure? She'd never felt this way around Donald, or anyone. Sara didn't know you could.

She'd go home to Donald, though. A couple weeks, that's all she had left of this great summer adventure. She'd retreat, defeated by Hollywood. That's how it'd look to everyone; she'd come home a failure. No one would know that she'd turned down the role of Cherry; no one would ever know that by doing what was right, what was unselfish, she'd sealed her own fate. The tears rolled down her face only when she heard Donald's voice. "I told you Hollywood wasn't for you. Now you're back where you belong." She cringed, just at the thought of his arms around her.

Nick: Sunday Morning, 4–6:00 a.m.

Nick eased Sara's arm over his shoulder, snaked his own around her slim waist, and helped her upstairs. What choice did he have? The girl was plastered, could barely stand up. Losing her liquor virginity would either be memorable or, he hoped, eminently forgettable. No little sips of wine or beer:

She'd dived into the hard stuff with a reckless thirst. Nick wasn't that good at figuring out people's feelings, but he recognized when someone was self-medicating.

Something must have happened during the party, something that'd made Sara zoom from zero tolerance to eighty-proof in the blink of an eye. Damned if he knew what it was. All he'd seen was Sara being her usual high-spirited, supergenerous self. She'd baked Eliot a cake, coaxed Naomi into joining them, and then received some amazing news from her agent.

How this became a recipe for misery was a mystery.

But, dude, girlfriend was in no shape to explain.

He led her to the loft, steadied her with one hand, and went to pull down the Murphy bed.

"No," she stopped him. "No, not here. Don't wanna be here now."

"Where do you want to be, Sara?" he asked softly.

"Your room. Let's go to your room." Her head began to loll.

She was so warm, so beautiful, so trusting and vulnerable. He wasn't blind; she'd been wanting him all summer. He stopped himself. *No, man.* He wasn't going to take advantage. Eliot was in love with her; the E-man believed he had a chance with her. He was El's best friend.

Didn't matter that Eliot had no shot with her. No way could Nick sleep with Sara either. No matter how much he wanted to.

Man, did he ever want to.

So . . . wait a minute, Nick caught himself thinking. Maybe it was her. Maybe Sara was the reason he'd ended up celibate this summer. If he'd been into her but subconsciously not allowed himself to act on it . . . maybe that's why people assumed he was gay. Was that possible? Nah. Even through a beer-buzz haze, that made no sense.

Back in Michigan, in the rare instances he'd been rejected by a girl or had put the brakes on out of loyalty to a friend, he'd gone out and found someone else. Girls had been fairly interchangeable in his life so far. He'd never fallen for one girl so hard that he had no interest in anyone else.

Sara piped up, "I want an exercise lesson! Lesh go work out, Nicky."

His stomach tightened. "Please don't call me Nicky, okay?"

"Okey dokey," she slurred happily. "But lesh . . . uh . . . I want to ball."

"What?"

"The big red ball. Show me how to do curls. You know, the ones where your tummy tightens up and I fall off and you catch me. Can we do that now?"

"No, Sara, we can't," he whispered, while leading her into his room anyway, half hoping Eliot was there, half praying his roommate was gone. "You can't work out when you've been drinking."

"Is that a rule?" She playfully kicked her shoes off and closed the door behind them. "What other rules are there?"

"You have to treat your body kindly," he said, standing unsteadily, still holding her up. He heard himself reciting some gym-insanity. "Your body is your temple. Take care of it, and it will take care of you."

The bedroom was empty, both beds were made. Which meant Eliot could show up at any moment. He hesitated. . . .

Slowly, seductively, she turned to face him. Their bodies were touching, then they were pressing against each other. His body reacted quickly. "No, Sara . . . ," he groaned. "You don't really want to do this."

Then he locked the door.

"God gives us only one body. Would you like to see mine?" she murmured.

It was exquisite, Sara's body. A guy could just stand there and worship it. Her full, round breasts were soft, just like her mouth, which was moist and sweet. And the rest of her—smooth, warm to the touch, and oh, had he mentioned soft? She was so soft, so pliable, willing, and wanting—he was on fire. Which totally meant he wasn't gay.

No one had ever touched Sara before. He knew, because she kept moaning it, over and over. No one had ever kissed her "in that way," "there," "for that long." He suckled her neck, traced her shoulders with his fingertips, caressed her breasts, stroked her all over. And over again.

Nick did not think he could slow down, but he summoned

up every ounce of self-control he could find. Making out was one thing, and a sweet thing it was, judging by her reaction. But making out was about to lead to much, much more. He had to be sure Sara wanted this, was sober enough to make a decision, and—the realization hit him hard—if her decision was yes, he wanted to make her first time special, unforgettable.

Unlike his had been.

Sometimes Nick wished he didn't remember his first time, or that he could rewrite his sex history. It happened in junior high, the time in his life when girls suddenly noticed him, and vice versa. It was after school, under the bleachers at the football field. Christy Pennington, a cute, flirty girl, had become his first "friend with benefits," at a time before that phrase had been coined. She'd given him oral, because, he'd thought, she was into him. When he found out she'd done it on a dare— some girls put her up to it, and watched!—he felt dirty, used. Neither Christy, nor her friends, thought of him as a person; he was just a boy toy, played with, then discarded. Exactly the way he felt modeling this summer.

Gently, he slid his hand to the small of Sara's back and guided her onto the bed. His bed, where he lay on top of her. Her eyes were closed, and he took in her long, lush eyelashes; her lips were open, waiting for his. Her arms held him close.

"Are you sure, Sara, this is what you want to do?" He hoped she didn't say no. Hoped he wouldn't have to stop.

"Nick. Oh God, Nick . . ." was all he could understand after that. And every time he thought she said "Don't," she added "stop."

"Don't stop, don't stop, don't stop."

He wanted her desperately. Not because he needed to prove anything to himself—right? And not because he wanted to hurt Eliot. It was because she was so damn hot. And she was in his room, on his bed, with the door locked. And she wanted him. And . . . there was no going back. He would make her first time amazing—he would pleasure her, teach her that guys could be tender and giving. That her feelings were important. It's what Eliot would do in this situation.

He pushed himself off her and took off his shirt. She ran her hands up and down his chest. He started to unbutton his trou, but she reached out. "Can I?"

Her fingers were shaking as she unzipped him. She was nervous, and it made him want her more. He thought he kept asking her if she was sure; she responded by groaning, then arching her back . . . and then, there was no going back. There was no undoing what they were doing.

It was explosive, and yet sweet; she was hungry, welcoming. They were rocking and rolling: It felt like they were on a boat, being gently tossed on wave after wave of pleasure.

"I feel it," she murmured. "Oh God, Nick—do you? Can you feel it? The earth is moving."

"EARTHQUAKE!" Eliot blasted into the room, shoulder first, busting the lock in the process, screaming at the top of his lungs. "Why was the door locked, we're having an earthquake! I can't find Sara—" And then, "Oh my God . . . Nick? Sara? What's—?"

There was something worse, Nick realized in that nanosecond, than being crushed in an earthquake: the look on Eliot's face, as if he'd been sucker punched by a thousand-ton Mack truck. He was gasping for breath, had turned ashen: Eliot, crushed by betrayal.

The floor beneath the bed suddenly swayed. It jolted Eliot into action. "Get downstairs!" he screamed. "Get the radio! Nick, turn off the gas line! Hurry!"

Panic overtook Nick. He had never bothered to locate the gas line.

Sunday Morning: 6:17 a.m.:
The Earthquake

Jared was jolted awake by a thunderous crack. Disoriented, it took him a minute to realize where he was: He and Lindsay had fallen asleep, locked in each other's arms, on the chaise lounge in the backyard. His eyes popped open to the sight of the swimming pool bursting as if a geyser had erupted beneath it, water shooting straight up.

Then the earth moved beneath them, and the pool itself seemed to come uprooted, as if something were jostling it from underneath. Water sloshed everywhere.

"Get inside!" Eliot shrieked at them from an upstairs window. "It's an earthquake! The house is going to fall on you! You'll be buried in the rubble!"

Jared shouted back, "Get away from the window!" He grabbed Lindsay's hand, to yank her up. The rumbling of the earth had started in earnest now; deck chairs and lounges toppled and slid toward the pool.

Lindsay slipped out of his grasp, bolted up, and made for the sliding doors leading into the house.

"No!" Jared screamed. "Not that way! We have to go around front; the glass could shatter!" He ran toward her, but Lindsay, in full dramatic panic, was already at the doors. She yelled back at him, "I have to get George Clooney!"

What? Was she bonkers?

"The dog, Amanda's dog! Lionel left it here. No time to go around front."

Before he could catch up, she flung the sliding doors open and dashed inside. The smashing sound that followed her was like a sonic boom, so loud, he couldn't hear himself, but he knew he was shouting. "Linz, Linz, no!"

And then, to his horror, the earth opened up and swallowed Lindsay.

Screaming, Jared raced around the shaking house, flew through the front door, telling himself she might be okay. He skidded into the living room with the vague thought of rescuing her, but it was too late—the walls were shaking, loosening Uncle Rob's guitars, which crashed onto the floor. CDs and vinyl records shaken from the shelves flew across the room like crazed Frisbees. Jared shielded his head, screaming, "Lindsay! Lindsay!" He heard a sickening noise from above: One of the giant beams across the ceiling was coming unhinged.

So was Eliot.

Their crisis-control king just lost it, completely! The dude who'd nagged them into preparation was hyperventilating, running down the steps with his head in his hands, screaming, "No, no! I can't! I can't!"

Jared shouted, "Stay upstairs!" But Eliot had panicked; he was too far out of control.

Nick, a half step behind, tackled him. "The poker table—we'll go under the poker table, just like you said. Come on! Sara—hurry!"

Eliot and Nick made it down, but the stairs buckled and imploded just as Sara, who was on Nick's heels, hit the top step. She dove down to the living room floor, landing, thankfully, on one of Uncle Rob's throw rugs, which cushioned her fall. Unhurt, she leaped up and ran toward the kitchen.

Nick tried to stop her. "Sara, no, not the kitchen, remember? Under the poker table—go in the game room!"

"Duck!" she shrieked, pointing up to the wooden railing of the loft as it came crashing down. It missed Nick and Eliot by inches. "The earthquake kit is in the kitchen, I have to get it." Sara was slipping and sliding as the floor shook. She flung open the door to the basement and shouted, "Naomi, stay down there! Stand by an inside wall!"

Sara whirled around the room. "Where's Jared? Where's Lindsay?"

"Help!" Jared yelled, kneeling by the coffee table, pointing to the mountain of glass that had been the sliding door, now joined by random pieces of furniture, sections of sofa that had torn off, shelving units that'd toppled—it'd all fallen atop the shattered glass.

"Lindsay's under there! Help—she's buried!"

Nick took charge. "El—you and Sara get under that table, now! Jared, get under—"

The unhinged beam came crashing down from the ceiling, slicing the coffee table, and the living room, in half, missing Jared's head by a fraction. It propelled Sara into action. With two long strides she was in the kitchen and instantly out again, carrying the kit with the flashlights, gloves, helmets, and radio. Struggling to keep her balance as the house rumbled and moved, she tossed them over the fallen beam to Jared and to Nick, who'd started across the rubble toward the other side. "Put the gloves on! Put the helmets on! Here's a flashlight!"

At that moment, another large quake erupted, knocking them all on their butts. Jared heard the front windows smash, and rolled away from what was left of the sofa and chairs.

Nick had fallen by the fireplace.

"Move, Nick," he bellowed, coughing from the sudden dust and smoke in the air. "The bricks . . ."

Nick took a falling brick on the shoulder, but crawled away before he got hit again. The next jolt sent more bricks and what was left of the furniture straight onto the pile of glass from the shattered sliding door. Another ripple in the ground, and the big couch, Moroccan chair, tables—every souvenir in the eclectic, cluttered living room was now atop the mountainous pile burying Lindsay even further.

Nick shielded his head from the falling debris, then managed to snatch the helmet Sara had tossed over. "Sara and Eliot, hold on to the radio and get under that table in the game room—now!" Nick commanded, and the two of them scurried toward safety.

Jared was so shaky, he fumbled snapping the helmet on, and couldn't get the gloves over his quivering hands. He felt like an impotent dunce, doing nothing while all hell broke loose around him, watching Sara and Nick take action. All he could think about was Lindsay. *Just let them get to Lindsay and let her be okay.*

"How do you know she's under there, man?" Nick called out to him.

"She ran in, through the doors—I saw them smash, and then the floor cracked open. I think she fell down." Jared struggled to keep from crying. "She was trying to find the damn dog."

Flashlight in hand, Nick carefully threaded his way over the debris toward Jared. The pile of house detritus was now easily six feet high and twice that wide. Gingerly, Nick walked around it, cupping his mouth and calling, "Lindsay! Lindsay! Can you hear me?"

Jared trembled.

All at once it was quiet. Too quiet.

"It stopped," Jared said, "The earthquake is over. I think . . . we can get her now."

"Aftershocks, man," Nick reminded him. "They could be more intense than the quake."

"Lindsay," Jared yelled into the pile, "shout if you hear me! We're gonna get you out, baby."

Nick held his hand up. "Wait . . . did you hear that?"

Jared had heard nothing.

Then, weakly, from deep beneath the rubble: "Yap."

It was no use. They'd been at it for an hour, and every time Nick and Jared thought they'd cleared away some of the mess, an aftershock rattled the walls, tossing more debris onto the pile. The bike helmets kept them from concussions, or worse. But they'd made no progress in freeing Lindsay—who'd not made a sound to let them know she was conscious.

Every few minutes, Sara shouted from the game room to assure them that she and Eliot, ensconced under the poker table, were okay. And that Naomi had wisely stayed safely in the basement. The radio was reporting a 6.1-level quake—pretty massive—that was playing havoc with the houses in the Hollywood Hills and the Los Angeles basin.

"They're saying it's gonna take rescue crews a while to get here," she yelled out. "Did you get to Lindsay yet?"

Nick responded, "Not yet. Stay where you are: We're doing good."

Then the next blast came. So loud, it rendered them momentarily deaf. It took them awhile to realize it had not come from their house. "Shit!" Nick yelled, holding his hands over his ears. "Sounds like a house blew up!"

Jared prayed no one was in it . . . but at six in the morning, that was unlikely. Then he locked eyes with Nick. Neither had to say it: They'd never looked for the gas line. No one would have shut it off.

"It's gonna be all right," Nick said, reacting to the terror in Jared's eyes.

Jared could hold it back no longer; he started to bawl. "It's my fault. I'm such an ass. We're gonna die here."

"No, you're not." A voice, steady, confident, bold, forced them to whirl around. Naomi, tiny but fierce, was standing in the doorway by the kitchen. "No one's gonna die," Naomi repeated. "I shut the gas off."

"How d-d-did you know where it was?" Jared stuttered.

"The shut-off valve is in the basement—it's next to my bed. Stay put, I'm getting a helmet and flashlight from Sara. Then I'm going to get Lindsay out."

Nick and Jared exchanged stunned glances.

Naomi returned a minute later, with a flashlight, gloves, and a surgical mask covering her mouth. "Sara and Eliot are doing okay," she reported.

"Where's your helmet?" Nick asked nervously.

She shook her head. "Won't fit. I'm going to try and crawl through the rubble to get her."

"What . . . are you . . . talking about?" Jared's teeth were chattering.

Naomi informed them calmly, "The three of us are going to clear away an opening. I'm a lot smaller than you. I'll go in."

"Are you crazy?" Nick challenged. "You can't crawl into this mound. One big aftershock and you're a goner."

"And so is Lindsay—if she's under there. That's why we can't wait."

For a moment, Jared believed—really believed—that if he blinked, he'd wake up, realize this was all a dream. A nightmare implanted in his brain by his father, to scare him into maturity. On cue, the house shook again; a broken guitar swiped his head. It was real.

Nick reached out to help Naomi climb over the mess on the floor. Gingerly, she tiptoed through the destroyed living room and over to where the guys had been trying to attack the mountain of rubble. Gloves on, she deftly and quickly started digging, shoving away shards of wood, glass, and bricks to make a tunnel through which she could crawl.

Jared babbled inanely, "If you save Lindsay, I'll give you a million dollars, I'll make sure you're never on the streets ag—"

"Shut up," Naomi said, not unkindly. "Let's focus. Keep moving these bricks out of the way. We're going to get her out. End of story."

Jared made a silent vow: If Lindsay was safe, he'd make everything up to everyone. Somehow.

A half hour had gone by, punctuated by reports from Sara, relaying info from the radio. The epicenter, she said, was in Ojai. That's where the worst damage was, and where most of the rescue teams were headed.

Another aftershock hit, sending Jared sliding on his butt toward the fireplace; if not for the helmet, the falling bricks might've killed him. Naomi and Nick scrambled right back to work.

"Okay," she determined, "there's enough room and air in here for me to burrow through and down. Give me a flashlight."

"Are you sure?" Nick asked, wiping grime and dust out of his eyes.

"It doesn't matter," she replied. "We don't have the time to make the opening bigger. Keep your light shining on me."

Thank you. You're so brave. I'm indebted to you. The words Jared wanted to stay were stuck in his throat.

"Lindsay! Lindsay! Are you okay?" Naomi's voice came from inside the cave of debris. Then, "Shit!"

"What—what is it?" Jared yelled. "Is it Lindsay?"

"I got cut," Noami shouted back. Then, "Lindsay? Are you down there?"

Then there was silence. Jared began to pace, while Nick continued to kneel by the opening through which Naomi had disappeared, his flashlight beaming.

"Why's it taking so long?" Jared felt like he was crawling out of his skin.

"Because she's gotta move slowly, man," Nick replied. "She makes a sudden move, more garbage falls on both of them."

It felt like an eternity. Suddenly, they heard music. "'Mr. Brightside'?"

"What the hell's that?" Jared demanded. "Where's it coming from?"

"Dude, it's your cell phone. Chill out."

The last thing Jared cared about was talking to anyone, about anything. Unless it was Lindsay. And what were the odds of getting cell reception buried under a pile of earthquake rubble? This must be, he thought, what hell is like. Waiting.

Then finally—it felt like an eternity—they heard Naomi. "I see her! I see her!"

"Is she all right?" Jared shouted, but Nick shushed him.

"What do you need? Can you get her out?"

Sara and Eliot appeared, she clutching the radio, he, still clutching his head. "What can we do?" Sara asked.

"Go back," Nick started to say, but Sara wasn't having it. "It's stopped. We'll be okay. We're staying out here with you. I got Eliot's cell phone; it worked, I called for an ambulance. But I don't know how long it will take."

Naomi shouted, "I've got her shoulders, but she's unconscious. I have to drag her, and pull her out backward. Nick, the minute you see the bottoms of my shoes, come in and pull."

"Is she okay? Is she okay?" was all Jared could say, on a loop.

By the time Nick had grasped Naomi and pulled both girls out from under the rubble, Jared had his answer.

Unconscious, cut up, clutching the bloody dog, Lindsay was, by far, not okay.

They hadn't been out for a half second when another aftershock rose up from the ground and a brick went flying and hit Naomi, knocking her out.

Sara, Nick, and Eliot insisted on riding in the ambulance with Naomi. Jared rode in another ambulance with Lindsay and the dog, who'd managed to survive as well. The EMT crew let him apply cool compresses to her head, which was dirty and bloodied. She'd regained consciousness soon after being freed, but was coughing from the dust and smoke. Wisely, Sara cautioned against moving her in case glass was embedded deep in her skin.

"You okay, baby?" he whispered.

Lindsay groaned, but nodded.

"You were a hero—you rescued the dog," Jared told her.

"I didn't want to lose my job—" She fell into a coughing fit.

"Let her rest," the paramedic advised Jared. "We're just about at the hospital. We'll take care of her."

Jared insisted on staying by Lindsay's side. And Lindsay insisted on trying to talk. "Naomi saved me. It was just like Johnny in *The Outsiders*—he was homeless too, and dove into a burning barn to save those children."

Good analogy, Jared thought, one a movie buff would think of.

"Is she okay?" Lindsay asked.

"I think so; she's in the ambulance in front of us. She took a brick to the head. Nick and Sara are with her."

"So they're okay?" she croaked.

"Yeah, they're good. They're fucking heroes, babe. All of them."

"Eliot. He . . . he . . . tried to tell us. Is he—?"

"He's good, he's fine. He kinda lost it, though, in the end.

He just froze. I don't get it. But if it wasn't for him . . ." Jared trailed off. He had a lot of gratitude to spread, a lot of apologies.

He hung by Lindsay's gurney as long as the paramedics would allow; when they took her to be examined, he was asked to stay in the waiting area. The place was in full triage mode. Hundreds of injured were being ferried in.

Nick, waiting with Sara and Eliot, nudged him. "Dude, answer your freakin' cell phone. It hasn't stopped ringing."

"Huh?" Jared hadn't even heard it.

"It's in your pocket, man. If you don't answer it, I will," Nick threatened.

"Hello?" Jared said unsteadily.

He'd never heard his father so discombobulated. The older man was jabbering, blubbering, sobbing, weeping. "Jared! Thank God, you're safe. I went down to the school to find you—they said no one had seen you. I was sure you were—"

"The school?" Jared, still dazed, was more confused.

Until he remembered. Sara said the epicenter of the quake was in Ojai. Where the community college was. Where he was supposed to be. Of course, his father, unable to reach him for hours, assumed the worst.

"Dad." Jared took a deep breath. "I need to tell you something."

Aftershocks: So Busted

The share house was trashed. The structure of the cozy wood-frame abode remained intact, but all the windows had blown out. Several walls had imploded, and piles of wrecked furniture and splintered wood from tables, railings, and Uncle Rob's prized guitars mixed with unhinged bricks from the fireplace. The massive detritus of what used to be CDs, posters, shelves, rugs, and knickknacks was scattered everywhere, all of it covered by a thick layer of dust and grime.

It was uninhabitable, so Jared, Lindsay, Nick, Eliot, and Sara had to relocate. In an only-in-Hollywood scenario, the scared, wounded, and terrified earthquake victims, who'd lost all the possessions left in the share house, vaulted from the depths of near tragedy to the heights of unimaginable luxury.

They moved into the Larson mansion on Stone Canyon Road in Bel Air, guests of Rusty Larson.

Naomi, having taken a concussive blow to the head and suffering other internal injuries, remained, in the week following the quake, a guest at Cedars-Sinai hospital.

"She's going to be fine," the doctors assured Sara. "We'll release her as soon as her test results come back and we're comfortable that she's fully on the mend. Are there any family members we should contact?"

Sara had looked to Naomi, asleep in her hospital bed. There were many ways to define a family, Sara thought. "We're her next of kin."

As the biological parent closest to the calamity, as well as the one with the deepest pockets, Jared's dad Rusty played father-knows-best for all of them.

He called each and every family, Lindsay's folks in Iowa, Sara's in Texas, Nick's and Eliot's folks in Michigan, offered to fly them west if they wanted, but pretty much convinced everyone that the kids were fine, and welcome to live in his house for as long as they liked.

Rusty Larson paid for all the hospital bills accrued by Naomi and by Lindsay, who'd escaped miraculously unscathed for someone who'd fallen down the rabbit hole, as she called it. Except for cuts and bruises, lacerations and abrasions, she was "good to go."

He reached his brother Rob, filming a movie half a world away, and assured him the damage was containable, and that he'd pay for the house rehab. "There's no need to interrupt shooting the movie to come home, we've got you covered," he told his younger brother, also mentioning that Jared would explain "everything" to Uncle Rob when he got home.

That was his m.o., thought Jared ruefully. Dad would go all TCB—take care of business—then the real earthquake of his father's freak-out would come. Jared wasn't sure when his dad would kill him, just that he would.

Thirty-six hours after the quake, Jared, Lindsay, Sara, Nick, and Eliot had been treated to cleansing showers, the sauna, the steam room, and the best night's sleep they'd had all summer. They'd been served a full, delicious breakfast of French toast, pancakes, eggs, bacon, sausage, and steaming-hot, buttery rolls.

For dessert, they repaired to the great room, where they dined on heaping helpings of guilt, shame, and finger-pointing.

Eliot, whose already fragile ego had taken the worst beating, laced into Nick, blaming him for taking advantage of Sara, for betraying him, rupturing their bond of trust, and ending their lifelong friendship.

Nick swallowed it all—and asked for seconds. Eliot was right, he agreed, had been right, about everything. El had confided in Nick, and Nick had been a shit, turned around and screwed him. He didn't deserve Eliot's friendship, or Sara's.

"I don't know what happened in the bedroom," Jared said, "but we should remember, Nick kept his cool throughout the whole ordeal. If not for him—"

Eliot turned all colors. "Why don't you just come out and say what everyone's thinking? I choked in the clutch. I nagged everyone to be prepared, but when it actually happened? I was helpless. I cried like a baby."

"That's bull! If not for your planning, all that stuff you bought, we might not have survived. It doesn't matter what you did or didn't do after that," Nick declared.

Lindsay added, "If we're looking for heroes, Naomi gets the gold—"

Sara burst out wailing, "It's all my fault! All of it!"

"How you figure?" Lindsay was truly puzzled.

Sara moaned, "God punished me. I broke my purity pledge, and He punished me."

Eliot's jaw dropped. "You think the earthquake was because of you? Do you have any idea how epically self-centered you sound?"

"Yeah, you finally sound like me," Lindsay quipped.

At which Sara started to weep piteously.

And Lindsay broke out in giggles.

Nick and Eliot told Lindsay to zip it. There was nothing funny about it.

Jared told them all to can it. "The earthquake wasn't anyone's fault; it's how we handled it. And in the competition for worst person on the scene, it's all me: I own that category."

Nick countered, "It's not a freakin' competition. No one knows how they're gonna react in a crisis. It's just live and learn, man. And thank God, or whoever you believe in, we all came through it okay."

"Anyway," Jared repeated, "we owe Eliot big-time. We were asses, man, to treat you the way we did. If you hadn't gotten all that stuff, the flashlights, the helmets, we'd have been royally screwed."

"I'm sorry I made fun of you," Lindsay put in, somewhat convincingly. "You were right all along, about everything. And if Sara hadn't brought that homeless girl here—I mean, Naomi—I'd be a goner. And the world would forever be denied my awesome talent." She looked around, but no one was smiling. "Oh, come on! A little levity. We are all okay."

Sara, still sniffling, said, "You're amazing, Eliot. I'm so sorry if we—no, if I—hurt you. You're the last person who deserves to be hurt."

"Oh, yeah, I'm such a great guy," Eliot snarled. "I'm smart, proactive, I'm"—he shot daggers at Nick—"a shoulder to lean on. I'm loyal."

"I am so sorry, man. There's no excuse—not the beers, not the party, not nothing." Nick put his head in his hands.

"Unless," Eliot said in a low growl, "you were trying to prove something to yourself."

"Prove what?" Lindsay asked.

Nick's jaw dropped, and he started up off the couch, ready to whale on Eliot. But he stopped in his tracks. Sat back down. "If that were true, it'd be Sara I owe the apology to."

"What are you talking—?" Lindsay started to ask, when Jared shushed her.

But Lindsay was still working out the tension between Nick and Eliot. Then a lightbulb went off. "Eliot thinks you made it with Sara just to prove you're not gay? Oh, come on, that's ridiculous!"

Nick flushed bright red.

"Nick, honey, if you were gay, you'd know it. You'd have known it long before you got to L.A."

Lindsay started to say more, but Jared jumped in. "It's not our business. Eliot saved our butts—between him, Nick, Sara, and Naomi, they're the reason we made it."

Eliot challenged the girls. "If I'm such a great guy, how come I'm not good enough for either of you?"

The color drained from both girls' faces. Awkward silence ensued.

Then Lindsay cleared her throat. "I'm just so focused on

my career, I haven't been looking for . . ." She trailed off, then closed her eyes, as if in pain. "I've been in love with one guy for a real long time. Even if I haven't always shown it."

Jared drew her closer to him, and she tucked into his chest.

Wistfully, Sara said, "I wish I knew what to say, but I don't, Eliot. I came to Hollywood this summer so sure of myself, my goal, everything. Right now, there's not one single thing I'm sure about. Least of all the shameful way I acted, toward you, toward Nick, toward myself. I'm so confused."

Lindsay piped up, "I hate to interrupt this confessional moment, but I say we get up off our guilty butts and go to the hospital to check on your stray."

It's the *way* she says things, Jared thought; that's why he couldn't help loving her. Lindsay owed her life to that stray—no one was more grateful than she. Lindsay would waste little time in proving it to Naomi.

The Larson family ride, a stretch Navigator, joined the long line of limos pulling up to the valet at Cedars Sinai, the hospital to the stars. To Sara, the scene was surreal. As were many occurrences of the past forty-eight hours. Focusing on Naomi was one way of not having to ask herself the hard questions. Questions that weren't going away. They'd be waiting for her, wherever she went. There was no hurry.

Naomi looked even scrawnier in the private suite Rusty Larson had procured for her. The waif with the huge violet eyes, dark eyelashes, and choppy black hair was watching the flat-screen TV poised above her bed.

"Nice digs," Jared quipped. "This is the floor of the hospital all the stars stay on when they're having babies, recovering from illness, plastic surgery—or just hiding from the paparazzi."

"There are smaller rooms on either side of this suite for your entourage. Not to mention your security patrol," Lindsay added.

No one laughed, but Naomi offered a weak smile.

Sara perched on the side of the bed, took Naomi's small hand. "How are you feeling, darlin'?"

"I'm okay, really. I don't know why they're keeping me here."

"But they're treating you well?" Jared asked.

"Like a star," Naomi conceded.

"What are they saying is wrong with you, exactly?" Lindsay asked. "I know you had a concussion, but there's no, like, brain damage or anything?"

"I'll never be able to figure skate again," Naomi said sadly.

Lindsay blanched.

Naomi pointed at her. "Snap! That's an old joke, Lindsay. Like I ever skated! C'mon, I'm the homeless stray, remember?"

Lindsay flushed. "A near-death experience renders me gullible."

Jared slipped his arm around Lindsay's waist and drew closer to Naomi's bedside. "There's something we all have to say—no joke. You saved my uncle's house, you saved our lives: specifically, Lindsay's. For that, well, we have a lot to apologize for and a lot to thank you for. Whatever you need, whatever you want—we're in your debt, Naomi. Forever."

"Forget it. I did what anyone would have." Naomi's eyes watered, but she didn't cry.

"No way," Nick contradicted. "You did—"

Eliot startled everyone by interrupting. "You did what someone who's been through an earthquake before would have done. Someone who had lived through it, and learned what to do." He paused. "That's what I always suspected."

"Eliot! It's like you're accusing her," Sara said, aghast.

"I meant, someone with real-life experience, who had the strength not to panic or choke," Eliot finished.

Lindsay's eyes widened. "Is that true, Naomi? Were you in that bad earthquake back then . . . but wait, how old were you then?"

Sara grew more alarmed. "Stop it, you're harassing her."

"No, we're not, we're thanking her," Jared said. "But it would make sense if what Eliot's saying is true."

"It doesn't matter!" Sara scolded them as she squeezed

Naomi's hand, "You're still pushing her, and that's not exactly a way to show gratitude."

"Time out!" Naomi coughed, raising her hand to stop them. "You're all acting like I'm not in the room. Like I'm invisible."

Chided, Sara said, "I'm sorry, we're—"

"Forget it." Naomi pointed to a button on the side of the bed. "Can you hit that, Jared? It raises the bed. I want to sit up straighter."

Would Naomi reveal herself finally, Sara wondered? There was so much she'd been wanting to ask the girl; she just didn't know how. She'd been the staunchest defender of Naomi's right to privacy, and would continue. But, of course, she wanted to know why Naomi had ended up on the streets. During the course of their nearly two months living under the same roof, the girl had said barely a word about herself.

The earthquake changed things.

The homeless girl turned out to be a hero. She'd rescued not only Lindsay and the dog but also the house itself. The questions piled up, high as the mountain of debris into which she'd selflessly tunneled to free Lindsay.

Eliot poured Naomi a glass of designer bottled water, which she gulped gratefully.

"I know you've all been wondering about me," she said calmly. "And I guess I owe you some answers."

"You owe us nothing." Sara couldn't help herself. "We owe you our lives."

Naomi waved her away. "It's okay, Sara, really. Thanks to you, I'm . . . I'm okay. You took me in—fought for me, never asked for one thing in return. You're a good person, and your parents are proud, I know it. Your God, too."

Sara began to sob quietly, but Naomi took her hand. "I did end up with a concussion, and some internal bleeding. But they've got that all under control; I'll be fine. Anyway, this is nothing compared to what happened the last time. . . ."

She drew a deep breath, then locked her eyes on Eliot. "You're right. I was nine years old in nineteen ninety-four, and we were staying at an apartment in Northridge."

Jared gasped. "No shit? Really?"

Naomi continued. "The apartment complex that got hit with the worst of it. We were in the wrong place at the wrong time."

"Your family?" Lindsay asked.

"My parents were among the fifty-five people who died," she said softly. "My sister and I survived."

"You have a sister? We'll call her!" Sara exclaimed.

Naomi shook her head. "Annie. I don't know where she is."

"You haven't been homeless since you were a kid, though?" Lindsay ventured.

"After the earthquake, Annie and I were taken in by a

neighbor. We didn't stay very long. We went into foster care, a bunch of different homes, but that didn't work out either. One thing led to another, and I ended up, you know, making do. Surviving."

"In shelters? Or just . . . the street?" Sara asked cautiously.

"Both. I usually felt safer on the street. There's a kind of community out there. But the day you asked if I needed help, that was a bad day. Things had gotten dicey and I was really scared. The last two months have been the best I've had it since the quake, the safest I've felt since that time." She laughed, and clutched her stomach. "Guess I'm living quake to quake."

"Guess we all are," Sara said. There were many ways in which the earth could shake you up.

A week and a half later, a guarded normalcy had returned to Los Angeles. Only, Lindsay mused, in her case, normal was better than ever. She felt beyond comfortable lounging poolside at the Larson mansion, pampered, protected. She felt hopeful, like she'd prosper again. Wearing a new metallic bikini, she lay back on a lushly cushioned chaise lounge, a fat new issue of *In Style* on her lap and visions of glam outfits and red-carpet appearances in her head.

It was Tuesday afternoon, and she had the pool, the entire mansion, practically to herself. Nick had returned to his modeling gig; Eliot to his classes; Sara and Naomi, healed now, back to *Caught in the Act*. Jared had surprised everyone by going for an actual study session with Adam, the kid he'd hired to take the tests for him. Boyfriend had decided to play summer school catch-up, even though Lindsay was fairly sure the big face-to-face with his father hadn't happened yet.

Everyone was still obsessed with the fallout from the quake.

Online, on TV, and in the news, there were round-the-clock updates. Financially, the damage totaled in the millions. Hundreds, like herself and Naomi, had suffered various degrees of injury. Tragically, twenty-two people had died. Most were from the Ojai area, where the quake had been centered, but a few people had perished in the shaky homes atop the Hollywood Hills.

She'd come close to being number twenty-three. She didn't remember a lot, just flinging open the sliding doors, dashing through them in search of Amanda's pooch, George Clooney, and then the sensation of dropping, falling. The earth had cracked, right under her feet, and she'd gone down. And out. Lindsay had blacked out, and so everything that happened afterward she learned about only after the fact.

The contents of the house had crashed down on top of her. She'd been buried under an eight-foot mound of glass, steel, bricks, wood, and—she giggled—knickknacks. Death by tchotchkes. She couldn't help finding that ticklish.

Here was the thing, and Lindsay faced it head-on:

Surviving a near-death experience had not changed her. Or at least, not so far. She understood that Eliot had prepared them, that Sara and Nick had acted coolly and courageously, that Jared had been sick with worry. And that Naomi, of all people, had bravely risked her own pitiful life to save hers. Lindsay was grateful, she really, really was. She would so show her gratitude; she'd buy each person an extremely trendy and expensive gift, right from the pages of *In Style*.

But . . . see, she knew it was wrong to feel this way, but still . . . it was over.

Been there, survived that, bought the T-shirt.

Earthquake. Rescue. Rehab.

Next.

Lindsay wasn't going to go all Oprah, or Angelina, or even Madonna in her red string bracelet phase. Lindsay wasn't going to dedicate herself to Kaballah, or Christianity, or any other spiritual thingie.

Except for being deeply superficial, she wasn't all that deep.

At least she was real. Life would go on and *The Outsiders* would get made. Grudgingly, she accepted that Sara probably had the role; the earthquake hadn't changed the fact that twerpy little Lionel had as much as said so. Jared was all "Keep the faith, Lindsay," insisting nothing had been determined yet.

Naturally, the final audition had been postponed due to

the quake. But movie schedules were being set: That tryout would happen before Labor Day, just a week away. Maybe there was something she could do in the screen test for the studio heads that would make them forget about Sara.

Those were the thoughts that occupied Lindsay's brain, and not for very long, either, as she rolled over on her belly for a more even tan. She wanted the role of Cherry, but if the worst happened, she'd survive to sniff out another acting part. Her time would come.

Desirée, the housekeeper, poked her head out the French doors. "Miss Lindsay, there's someone at the door to see you."

Lindsay squinted. "Who is it?"

Desirée shrugged. "Didn't say. But the lady is carrying a tiny dog."

Amanda? Lindsay leapt off the lounge and scooted inside.

Amanda was clad in a navy blue Prada power suit, and adorned with her armpit accessory, George Clooney, who snarled at Lindsay.

"Lindsay, darling, how are you?" Amanda air-kissed the vicinity of Lindsay's cheeks.

"I'm good. Great, in fact. Do you want to come sit down?" Lindsay calculated: If her boss-cum-agent had arrived just to thank her for saving George Clooney, no way would she hang out. If, however, there was news of the audition, Amanda would deign to stay a while.

The reason for the face-time turned out to be something different. Something awesomely sweet, and fabulous . . . and confusing as hell. Amanda settled onto the Armani sofa in the great room with the rat-faced runt and accepted a bottle of designer sparkling water from Desiree. She sniffed around. "I see Rusty hasn't changed decorators since Glynnis lived here," she noted.

Amanda had been a guest at Galaxy's parties, often staged here in the mansion, when Jared's parents were together and the agency was flourishing. Lindsay agreed. "Still, it all works, don't you think?"

Amanda nodded, though no way had she come to check out the décor. "So, my little client," she said, crossing her long legs. "It seems as though every good deed does not, in fact, go unpunished. You saved George Clooney's life—you get a tasty reward." She stroked the devil-dog, who promptly jumped from her arms and peed on the leg of the marble coffee table.

Amanda giggled. "Ooops, we'll need a little cleanup here. Anyway, I come bearing wonderful news: You got the part."

For a nanosecond, Lindsay had no clue what Amanda was talking about. "What part?"

Amanda looked at her weirdly. "Did your tragic earthquake experience render you dense? What part have you been auditioning for? What part will make you a superstar, the comeback story of the decade? You got Cherry."

Lindsay remained stupefied, way slow on the uptake. "But—but . . ."

"No buts," Amanda said. "Just yours up on the big screen."

"I didn't have the final audition. Neither did Sara."

Amanda smiled mysteriously, coquettishly. "And yet, here I am, in person, to inform you that no more auditions are necessary. You, Lindsay Pierce, will be playing the part of Cherry Valance. The announcement goes to the trades tomorrow.

Lindsay felt sure her mouth was wide open. And maybe there were words forming in her brain, on their way out. She remained speechless long after Amanda had bid her adieu, long after more air-kisses, long after, even, she stumbled to the kitchen for a rag and a can of Resolve to clean up after George Clooney.

Boy Confessions

Nick leaned out the driver's side window and talked into the speaker. "We'll have two double-doubles, one cheeseburger, two orders of fries, and two vanilla shakes."

"Will that be all?" came the disembodied voice from the squawk box at In-N-Out Burger.

He glanced at Eliot, in the passenger seat, looking straight ahead, lips pressed together, arms folded over his chest.

"That's it," Nick responded.

"That will be sixteen seventy-eight. Drive up to the pickup window, thank you."

Ever since the earthquake, Nick had been doing whatever he could think of to make things right with Eliot, to apologize for being such a heel. But nothing he did, or said, seemed to be enough. Nick drove El to classes each morning, picked him up at the UCLA campus each evening. He offered to buy him dinner, take him out for beers, explain what'd happened, or just shoot the breeze like they always did—anything to get their friendship back on track. But Eliot wasn't giving an inch; his shoulder was cold, turned away.

Neither had been much of a grudge-holder, but the E-man was having a really hard time letting go of his righteous anger.

Okay, Nick got it. Dude had a right to be steaming. Furious. Burned. But didn't eighteen years of friendship count for anything? Eliot's silence was killing him. Between that, his crappy job, and guilt feelings about Sara, Nick was as down as he'd ever been—lower than a pregnant ant, as his mom sometimes said.

He hadn't asked if Eliot wanted a bite to eat, just sorta kidnapped him instead of heading back to the Larson place. Nick was determined to have his say—even if he wasn't entirely sure of what that would be.

He'd driven to the In-N-Out Burger in Hollywood, remembering that Sara had gushed about it, mentioned the outdoor tables.

"C'mon, dude, let's chow down." He parked the car, hoping Eliot wouldn't be a complete jerk and refuse to move.

"Fine," Eliot answered, and followed Nick to one of the many empty tables. Most people drove up and drove away; the only other tables were occupied by kids wearing Hollywood High School jackets.

They ate in silence, Eliot picking out the onions from his burger, checking the lettuce for brown spots. Nick gazed at the clouds floating lazily across the hazy blue sky. Back in Michigan, even the cloudy skies seemed purer, more of a crystal blue. Later, when the colors in the sky turned to pumpkin orange, raspberry, and even purple at sunset, when the air was crisp, signaling the coming of fall—yeah, that's when he liked it best.

"I'm 'bout ready to head home." He had no idea he was gonna say that. Or that Eliot would finally look at him. And agree. "I'm done with classes after this week anyway."

"Just . . . just . . . ," Nick stammered. "Look, E, I don't know what else to do. I'm sorry, man." He felt his lip quiver, and bit down hard.

"The whole situation blows," Eliot agreed.

Nick opened his mouth to say something, but to his surprise, Eliot was still talking. "I feel like I've been sucker punched, Nick. Like, what a jerk I am. I never saw it coming."

"No, man, it's not like that—"

"Not like what? C'mon, Nick, you can stop apologizing for sleeping with Sara. Any guy would probably have done the same in that situation. How can I be mad at you for being who you are—a chick magnet? It's not your fault that I repel women."

Nick hadn't thought he could feel any worse; now he knew

better. But the next thing Eliot admitted helped, a little. "It's not like Sara was my girlfriend. She's not into me, and even without that Donald guy, she probably never would be. It was a nice fantasy, that's all."

Nick wished he could wave a magic wand and bring someone for Eliot, some girl who was worthy of his best friend. "You'll find someone, E. Hey! In that college, Northwestern, things will be different. The place is full of brainiacs—the gene pool of females worthy of you will be much deeper than in West Bloomfield or here in Phony-wood."

"Yeah, I'm sure my dream-geek awaits somewhere." Eliot cracked a smile. First one in many, many days.

Nick reached into his pocked and slammed a twenty-dollar bill on the table. "Bet you the girl you get? Will be a knockout. Smart, hot—and probably neurotic, if she has to put up with you."

Sheepishly, Eliot said, "Okay, Nick. I'll take your bet."

"Anyway, we could go back early, not wait for Labor Day. We could leave, like, tomorrow. There's nothing keeping us here, right?"

Eliot picked at his fries. "You and Sara. You don't love her, do you? You won't . . ." He trailed off.

"What happened between me and Sara was a mistake, Eliot. Something, I don't know what, happened at the party and she went crazy, boozing it up, and . . ." It was Nick's turn to trail off.

No need to remind Eliot that Sara had come on to him.

Eliot frowned. "That thing I said about your having to prove something. That was just stupid. I'm sorry, man. I know you're not gay—not that I'd care if you were. . . . I mean, it'd be totally okay. But it so happens, you're not."

"I know, man. I know who I am."

"It's not just Sara," Eliot said slowly. "It's what happened after. Everyone's trying to make me feel better by saying I'm such a hero. In the end, I didn't do anything. So is that who I am? Some bug-eyed geek who's all talk and no action? If a girl *was* interested in me, would I choke in the bedroom, too?"

"You think too much," Nick said, trying not to show his surprise at this revelation.

"Who thinks too much?" Nick and Eliot looked up to see Jared swinging his leg over the bench opposite them. He was carrying a tray piled with two cheeseburgers, a soda, and large fries.

"You, uh, come here often?" Eliot quipped.

"All the time. Best burgers in the West. Anyway, all that studying makes a man crave fast food." Jared admitted that he'd been on his way back from the school library, had pulled into the In-N-Out takeout line and seen Nick's car with its Michigan plates in the parking lot.

"So you're making up summer school?" Eliot asked. "Did your dad force you?"

Jared dove into his fries. "The scary thing is, I haven't even had it out with the old man yet. I know he's going to blow up at me—but so far, he hasn't. I'm trying to mitigate it by studying and taking the exams. Maybe that'll cool him off when he does erupt. Anyway, so who thinks too much? Gotta be El."

Nick gulped his shake. "We're actually thinking of heading back east. Real soon."

"Why would you want to do that?" Jared asked. "Especially now, you're finally living in the lap of Cali-luxury. Whatsa matter—being waited on, sleeping on five-hundred-ply sheets, having backyard tennis courts, lap pool, steam room, sauna, and indoor state-of-the-art fitness center isn't enough for you?"

"Maybe it's too much," Nick said, dragging a couple of fries through a swatch of ketchup. "Maybe all this stuff just gets confusing."

Jared looked knowingly from Nick to Eliot. "It's Sara, isn't it?"

"No!" they both said emphatically.

Jared laughed. "The dudes doth protest too much."

"Before I got here, I never heard that expression. I hate it," Nick groused.

Jared got serious. "Look, can I say something? I don't want to pry, and you can tell me to shut up—"

"Shut up."

"That was rhetorical. Anyway, from what I can see, Nick

is having a hard time with the whole modeling thing. It's making you question yourself, no?"

"No!" Nick said.

"That's what I thought." Jared kept on talking. "Here's the thing, dude. Maybe you hate the modeling gig not because you're uncomfortable with the people at the studio; maybe you hate it for the simple reason that it's boring. Maybe standing there in your tighty-whiteys, or whatever they make you pose in, maybe it makes you feel like some brainless hunk, some subhuman. Maybe it makes you feel like you have nothing else besides perfect pecs and six-pack abs. Maybe the reason you're ready to ditch it has nothing to do with which way you swing the bat. In other words, maybe the whole time, you questioned the wrong thing."

Nick stared at Jared, openmouthed.

Jared shrugged and bit into his second burger. "I'm just sayin'."

"That kind of makes sense, Nick," Eliot said slowly.

Jared pointed to Eliot. "And you—what can my psycho-babble help you with?"

Nick piped up, "He thinks he's a failure, because, you know, in the earthquake, he kind of . . ."

"Froze? Oh, you mean, just like I did?" Jared inquired. "I've given that a lot of thought. Not to rationalize the way I stood there like a spoiled do-nothing rich kid, in way over his head . . ." He paused to see if they were smiling. In spite of themselves, they were.

"Here's how I'm looking at it. It was teamwork. Eliot got us started, then passed the bat to Nick and Sara. And Naomi came in for the save. Lindsay, of course, nabbed the most dramatic part, the damsel in distress—that's who she is. And me? Well, we did end up at my house, and my dad is making reparations to everyone. So I guess I contributed my family money and clout. We all did our part, the best we could."

Eliot looked surprised. "That is the most sense you've made all summer."

Nick flashed back to their first day in L.A.: Jared's reaction to having been caught with his pants down. The guy had been so smooth, Nick had totally worshipped him. Three months later, he still did.

"I have an idea," said Jared. "Let's go catch a movie—some guy thing where a lot of shit blows up."

Nick waved his arms up and down, a worshipful motion.

True Confessions: Go, Girls

Lindsay embraced her superficiality, but she wasn't stupid. Something had gone down behind the scenes, something that eliminated the need for a final audition and took Sara out of the running.

Amanda insisted that Lindsay was more talented, that

she'd given the better reading. Jared agreed with Amanda, and further speculated that maybe no one wanted to risk a big-budget movie on someone as inexperienced as Sara. Rusty claimed blissful ignorance; he was just thrilled that a client from his agency had landed a role. It meant money in his pocket.

Lindsay was left to figure it out for herself. There was something no one was telling her, something no one was whispering about: She'd checked with Caitlin, Julie, Ava, MK, Austin, and Tripp, anyone with connections and an ear to the Hollywood ground.

Lindsay's portrayal of Cherry wasn't better than Sara's: It was different. It *was* possible the powers-that-be had decided on her take. But no way would they do it without a tryout in front of the studio bosses. The director and producers were notoriously risk-averse, and their bosses dined out on the power to make the final selection. So what was up this time?

She was forced to do something totally counterintuitive: observe Sara's behavior. The tall Texan had briefly congratulated Lindsay on hearing the news, but didn't blather on about how the best person had won, destiny, all her usual perky upbeat nonsense.

Of course, Sara was still freaked out about the earthquake, giving up her precious virginity, hurting Eliot, breaking up with Donald, yada yada. Losing the part in the movie was probably far down on her misery list. Maybe Sara even believed she deserved to lose the part—who knew what went on in that blond head?

Still, something gnawed at her, told her Sara knew the truth. Finally, when she could stand it no longer—she'd wasted an entire day shopping and obsessing—she pounced on an unsuspecting Sara, just home from the day's work and hauling grocery bags, as if they still lived in the Hills house, as if the staff here didn't do the shopping and cooking.

"What do you want, Lindsay?" Sara tried to brush by her, but Lindsay stood blocking her way past the foyer.

"I want to know what you know." Lindsay stared into Sara's sky-blue peepers. "What Lionel told you, or what you told him."

Sara stepped to the side, attempting to walk around Lindsay. "I don't know what you're talking about. Anyway, why do you care? You won the role. I congratulated you, didn't I?"

Lindsay only caught a brief glimpse, but there was a look in Sara's eye. Of what? Regret? And suddenly, it hit her. Like a sledgehammer. "You . . . you pulled out? You freakin' took yourself out of the running! You told them you didn't want the part, didn't you?" Lindsay was incredulous. And sure she was right.

Sara tossed her hair back—a very Lindsay-like motion, it

occurred to her—and stood firm. She didn't deny it, though. "What makes you think I backed out?"

"Because it's the only way I'd have gotten it without that last audition."

If she thought Sara was going to reach out to her, take her hand the way she did Naomi's so often, or say something soothing and insipid, Lindsay was wrong. Sara said nothing, just tried again to walk away from her.

"You have to tell me why you did it!" Lindsay insisted, frustrated at Sara's silence. The girl had been so open, so easy to read all summer long. Lindsay was having none of her silence now.

Sara managed to brush by her finally and head toward the kitchen. Lindsay found herself trailing the statuesque girl, feeling ever so much like a kid pulling at the back of her mom's coat, begging to be paid attention to. She didn't care, though. She had to know. "Please, Sara," she whined. "I'd really like to understand what happened."

Finally, Sara whirled around, set the grocery bags down, and crossed her arms. "I called Lionel and told him I didn't want the part."

"Why would you do that?"

"Because you wanted it more than I did."

Lindsay's mouth fell open. "Well, yeah, but what's that got to do with anything?" she finally managed. "You . . . you . . .

rehearsed! You told your people back in Texas—won't they be disappointed?"

"No doubt." Sara sighed.

"And you kicked ass at the audition. You really did. I snooped."

Sara smiled ruefully. Which made Lindsay feel even worse. "I did want it, Lindsay. But you needed it. That's the difference."

Sara always did what was needed. Naomi needed shelter, needed help and a friend. The house needed cleaning, the lawn needed seeding, the rent needed to be paid. Sara, ever so righteous, did the right thing. Always.

Standing there in the massive hallway between the foyer and the kitchen, Lindsay didn't try to stop her lip from quivering, or swallow the lump in her throat, or tell herself she wasn't acting. "I've been a bitch to you all summer long," she blubbered.

It was then that Sara finally touched her, cupped Lindsay's chin in her palm. "This is your dream, Lindsay. You go for it."

"But . . . don't you have a dream too?" Lindsay asked, wiping away her tears with the back of her hand.

Sara's eyes clouded over. "I'm sure I do. I thought I knew what it was, but everything went topsy-turvy this summer. I'm waiting to figure it out."

• • •

Sara had told Lindsay more truth than she'd meant to. More than she owed the selfish girl. In her heart, Sara was still the righteous girl she'd always been—and she knew she'd done the right thing. So why did it hurt so much? Her skin felt sore, every molecule ached.

"Ouch! Is it always this hot?" Naomi, trying out the hot tub for the first time, yanked her foot out of the bubbling Jacuzzi.

"Take it slowly," Sara advised. "You'll get used to it."

In a bid to cheer Sara up, Naomi had suggested an after-dinner soak in the Larsons' magnificent marble tub, which made the one at the share house look scrawny. This was "the Gucci of Jacuzzis," as Rusty Larson had proudly bragged, state-of-the-art, featuring several tiers to sit on, two carved-in lounges, and jets shooting pulsating water at you from every which way.

"It's supposed to relax your tense muscles," Sara said.

"Or fry my skin," the dark-haired waif muttered.

Sara chuckled. "You weren't afraid to dive under the wreckage in an earthquake; you're going squeamish now?"

"*That* was all adrenaline," Naomi pointed out. "*This* is bizarre."

Sara had thought so too, back when she'd first come to Los Angeles. All these big, shiny, material things: profligate, extravagant, decadent, toys for people with so much money they don't know what to do with it.

That was then. Now? Her core values hadn't changed. But this, she kinda liked: If you allowed yourself to sink into it, to feel—and not think—it felt real, real good.

Naomi carefully slid in, pressed her back against the side. "Wow!" She giggled. One of the power jets had hit the small of her back. "This is definitely . . . weird."

"It's supposed to pound your muscles, take out the knots," Sara explained, as she sank neck-deep into the bubbles.

Sara wondered if the girl from the streets would find herself liking her first Jacuzzi experience. It was so easy to succumb (the word came to her unbidden) to all kinds of temptation, to things that made you feel good, feel important, to people who made you feel special.

No. She didn't want to go back there. She closed her eyes. What she'd done the night before the earthquake had set off a chain-of-pain reaction. Nick was wracked with guilt, Eliot was devastated, poor unsuspecting Donald got dumped—for what could she do now but break up with him? She felt responsible for all of it.

When she opened her eyes, she realized Naomi was staring at her. "We all do things out of anger," Naomi said, "no matter how hard you try not to."

The words popped out of Sara before she could censor herself. "So, what, you're a mind reader, too? Is that one of the skills you learned on the streets?" Horrified at her outburst, she slapped her hand over her mouth. "Naomi, I am so sorry. I didn't mean that—but you seemed to know what I was thinking."

"I don't have to be a mind reader to know what you've been obsessing about; it's written all over your face. And don't worry, no offense taken."

Sara considered. "So you're saying I got drunk, broke my purity pledge, had sex with Nick, all out of anger?"

"Pretty much."

"Who am I supposedly so angry at?"

"Yourself, Sara. That's who."

She wanted to say, "I have nothing to be angry at myself for." She wanted to say, "I live—or lived—a righteous life. I did the right thing." But the words got stuck in her throat, never made it out.

Naomi continued. "Backing out of the audition so Lindsay could win the role was off-the-chart unselfish. Lindsay isn't even worthy! You knew it. So you wanted something in return, something for you: something to make you feel good. On a visceral level—the most basic human level."

"Nick," Sara mumbled, starting to tear up again.

"You've been wanting him all summer."

"Something else written all over my face?" Sara asked sarcastically.

"Not just your face, sistah."

Sara swallowed hard. So she had been that obvious, much as

she'd tried to kick those feelings away, to not name them. It'd never occurred to her, not in a million years, that she'd act on them. She turned to Naomi. "It's actually not good to stay in the tub longer than fifteen minutes at a time. You'll get dizzy."

"Let's not risk it." Naomi hoisted herself out of the water and brought over a couple of soft, oversize beach towels.

They sat on the edge of the Jacuzzi, wrapped in terry cloth, legs dangling in the hot water. "Nick's not the right guy for me," Sara heard herself saying. "Neither is Donald. There's no future with either of them."

"Agreed."

Sara was a little surprised Naomi said that so quickly.

"Look, Sara, just because you did something once doesn't change who you are, cancel out your beliefs. You're still you, and Nick's a great guy, but on no planet are the two of you remotely right for each other. At heart, he's a simple, good-time frat-guy, more brawn than brains. You're deeper. You're always going to be searching, questioning, looking for answers. And helping other people—that's such a huge part of who you are. You're not going to stop, even if there are times, like this one, you got hurt doing it."

"Who died and made you Yoda?"

Ah, leave it to Lindsay. As if proof were needed that people, in fact, never do change. Neither Sara nor Naomi had heard her pad outside in her spa slippers. But what shocked them was not her intrusion, nor her itsy-bitsy bikini. It was the sight of Lindsay Pierce, diva divine . . . carrying a tray? With *three* fancy salt-rimmed margarita glasses and a pitcher full of the pale green drink.

Lindsay said, "Sounds like I walked in on the juicy stuff— girl-talk confessions. I am *so* all about that. Mind if I join? I come bearing gifts."

"Yes, we do mind," Naomi started to say, but Sara overruled her. "Oh, what the heck. We hardly have any secrets anymore. What's in the pitcher?"

"Margaritas: my own private recipe," the freckled girl replied, setting the tray down and pretzeling her legs. "Most excellent." She narrowed her eyes at Sara. "I assume we are still drinking?"

Sara hesitated, then shrugged. "Maybe I'll stick with only one."

Lindsay poured the glasses full and handed them out. "So, what's our topic, besides self-flagellation? I'm not a big fan of self-criticism."

"Yeah, we noticed," Naomi quipped.

"But I am an expert on matters of the heart. And flesh."

"No kidding." Naomi again.

"And who'd guess my little savior had a sarcastic streak?" Lindsay shot Naomi a smile, grateful and genuine. "We have something in common after all."

Naomi sipped her drink. "Not so much."

"So, Nick." Lindsay grinned at Sara. "So yummy!"

Sara and Naomi shot her a look.

"Not from personal experience, girls," Lindsay assured them. "The guy is scorching! Who wouldn't want to get into his pants?"

Sara looked stricken. But she had no answer for Lindsay, who was, as advertised, spot-on.

Lindsay finished her drink and poured another. "I don't get you, Sara—and in truth, I never cared that much before."

Bracing, brutal honesty: That's Lindsay. Sara wasn't the least bit pissed.

"You're like 'bass-ackwards,' if you catch my drift. I'm shitty to you, so you go all overly kind to me. You sacrifice the part in the movie for me. You go to Nick for comfort—you feel great, 'cause who wouldn't, being with him? And then you feel bad about feeling good. I mean, if you really think sex is bad, why did God make it feel so good?"

"Lindsay, don't take this the wrong way, but you know nothing." Sara was beginning to feel the tequila.

"I know about wanting. You wanted something for you. Something . . . oooh . . . *forbidden*!" she taunted. "I don't understand what you don't understand. We all want forbidden fruit— I don't have to tell you the story of Adam and Eve, do I?"

Sara felt her jaw drop.

"You're only human, Sara. You only think you're better than the rest of us. I might not be religious, but back when I starred on *All for Wong*, we did a special Christmas episode one year. The lesson was, most people believe in a higher power who forgives your sins. Don't you?"

"I can't believe I'm saying this, but she has a point, Sara." Naomi looked shocked.

Sara slipped back into the hot tub, leaned her head against its smooth lip, and stared at the sky. "So, what do you do with those feelings? You can't give in to them every time you're attracted to someone."

"Yeah, that'd just be slutty." Lindsay giggled. She joined Sara in the Jacuzzi. "But if you're asking me personally, we'll need at least one other round of drinks."

"I'll go." Naomi started to get up, but Lindsay stopped her. "There's an intercom by the door. Hit the button and tell Desiree we need munchies and 'mas 'ritas'—that's Spanish for 'more.'"

When the housekeeper appeared a few minutes later with a tray of salsa and chips, guacamole, and another huge pitcher, Lindsay tried to answer Sara's question. "First, you admit your feelings. They are kind of natural, by the way. You don't have to act on them. I'm all about live and let live. But since you found this out already, sex is pleasurable. I would think it has to be that way, so people would want to procreate. I mean, I don't know that much . . . I'm just sayin'."

Damn—that is, *darn*—Lindsay. When she was right, she was insufferable. Sara didn't want to debate the Bible, or her belief in waiting for marriage. She'd always look to the Bible for guidance. But maybe, just maybe, she'd also learn to listen to her own voice. Maybe that's what this summer had taught her.

She turned to Naomi. "What about you, little one? Ever fallen for the wrong boy?"

"Me? It's more like I've put my trust in too many of the wrong people," Naomi confessed, draining her glass. "I'm in a different situation. I did what I had to, to survive. I never had the luxury of a boyfriend or thinking about who I wanted to be with." She said it without bitterness.

"You've been very sheltered, Sara," Lindsay pointed out. "You were bound to have some eye-opening experiences this summer. I hope at least some of them were good."

Sara reflected. A lot of them were not just good, but great.

The tequila seemed to open Naomi up more too. "So now that we've dissected Sara and me, what about you, Lindsay? I mean, *really*? I know when someone's fronting. You pretend to be so worldly, like you've slept around so much. Something tells me that's bull."

Lindsay rolled her eyes. "Okay, okay, we get your point, Yoda. You know, you even look like a little troll."

Sara splashed her, hard. "That's a terrible thing to say!" But all three were laughing.

Lindsay added, "So much knowledge, spouting from the fountain of one tiny human. I do sort of, you know, love Jared."

"Why?" Sara and Naomi had to high-five since they said it at the same time.

Lindsay licked the salty rim of her glass. "Habit?"

Naomi laughed. "Like you're getting away with that! Spill."

"You can't tell us you've never thought about it before," Sara added.

Lindsay drew a deep, dramatic breath. "I know he's not the hottest guy around, not like Nick. Looks-wise, I could probably do better. And he's not the smartest guy on the planet. He's no Eliot Kupferberg."

"Stop saying what he's not—and tell us what he is," Naomi demanded.

"Jared's kind of the best of both, straddling the fence between brains and brawn, never coming down fully on one side or the other. So, no lust-magnet, but he's sexy and smart enough, if that makes sense. He always knows the right thing to say and make it sound sincere. He's chameleon-like, snaky and shrewd, wrapped in a very nice glittery package."

Sara listened to Lindsay, and it was like a klieg light going off in her brain. Lindsay loved Jared because he was handsome, vapid, and cagey in a hollow kind of way. Just like the town he lived in. Jared embodied Hollywood, and that's ultimately what Lindsay saw in him. Jared can make magic happen; he's a walking all-access pass.

Sara had never met anyone like Lindsay or Jared before. She'd held her private thoughts about them, but hearing Lindsay say it out loud, admit to believing it, set off another klieg light.

"I have an idea," Sara said.

Jared's Big Idea

When Jared, Nick, and Eliot returned from the movies, they found Lindsay, Sara, and Naomi sloshing around the hot tub, happily sloshed, deep in the heart of "Margaritaville." To Jared's amusement, it was Sara who immediately jumped up, wrapped herself in a towel, and collared him. "Can I speak to you privately?" she asked.

Jared didn't have long to wonder what was on Sara's mind. The minute they got inside the house, out of earshot of the others, she blurted, "You said you wanted to make amends, right? After the earthquake, you said you'd do anything for us?"

"Yeah, absolutely." Only . . . Sara was pretty hammered—not quite slurring her words yet, but on the verge. "What'd you have in mind, Sara?"

"I need you to read something."

• • •

Late the next afternoon, Jared jumped into his car and drove to Galaxy's offices in Beverly Hills to see his father. He didn't have an appointment, so he waited, pacing the anteroom for close to an hour while Rusty Larson finished with his meetings and then ran a teleconference.

The whole time, Jared gripped the screenplay tightly, as if someone walking by might rip it away from him, trick him into dropping it, giving it up. This treasure was titled *Hide in Plain Sight*; he'd read it only because he'd promised Sara. He'd totally planned to scan about ten pages, make short shrift of it, let Sara down gently. But . . . in the "who'da thunk it" department, *he* couldn't put it down!

He flipped through the 149 pages again nervously: He'd read the thing three times. Each time, he came to the same conclusion: Here was a great story, with equal parts intrigue, edge-of-your-seat action, sweet romance, laughs, and poignancy—the elements that make a movie a blockbuster. Or, expressed another way: This was *the shit*! And, the earthquake notwithstanding, the single most unexpected event of the summer.

All the stars were aligned, Jared was sure of it: The script could be had for cheap, since the screenwriter was a nobody, just a cop he'd happened across. It'd be a Galaxy exclusive, which meant his dad's company would make boatloads of money on it.

547

The wheels in Jared's head had not stopped spinning since he'd finished reading it the first time. Now, as he paced, he ran through a mental list of Galaxy clients for the lead role, not unlike a list of *People* magazine's sexiest: Matthew McConaughey, Jake Gyllenhaal. Ewan McGregor could do it, potentially Bradley Cooper—no, he's too pretty to play the cop. Pitt was possible, or you could go older, Denzel even.

For the lead female, there was no list. One person was born to play that role.

Rusty flung open the door to his executive office. "What are you doing here?" On the "I'm-so-happy-to-see-you" meter, his dad's tone was subzero.

"I was hoping we could talk." It dawned on Jared that maybe this wasn't, in fact, the best time to bust in on his old man. The scowl on his dad's face hinted that Rusty had had a crap day.

"You came here to talk?" Rusty said. "About what? What a little liar you've been all summer?" His dad wearily dropped into his enormous boss-worthy leather throne and impatiently hit delete on his keyboard.

Okaaaay, so Jared had been a little hasty just dropping by. And so excited about the screenplay, a lot forgetful that a certain volcano had not yet erupted. He tried not to flinch. He'd not prepared a speech, an explanation, rationalization, or even a bald-faced lie. "Uh, yeah, that was part of the reason I came. I want to apologize."

"Bull," Rusty muttered. "You came here because you want something. I'm so sick of your lies, Jared. Do you ever tell the truth?"

"Only the parts that matter."

The quip was cribbed from the TV show *Entourage*: He and his father had laughed hard when the wily agent had said the line. Now? Not so funny.

"How could you be so disrespectful?" Rusty demanded. "I'm your father. I sent you to summer school to make up your lousy grades and you just blow me off, do whatever you want. Where do you get the balls?"

Jared lowered his head. He knew from rhetorical questions.

"And don't give me any crap about me and your mother being divorced, and some other 'poor misunderstood rich kid' garbage. I've read all those scripts. They all stink."

Jared hadn't planned on going there. Nor would he interrupt his father's soliloquy. He knew when to "hold 'em."

"Besides," Rusty growled, "if you think you ditched school to screw me, you're not as smart as I give you credit for, 'cause you only screwed yourself. And then squatting in your uncle's house and charging those people rent—what were you thinking?"

Not that he'd be outed to his father by Mother Nature, that's for sure.

Rusty echoed his thoughts. "Obviously, you didn't count on an earthquake." Suddenly, his dad went emo, teared up. "If you had been at that school, and if something had happened, I'd never have been able to forgive myself for forcing you to go there."

Yeah, Jared thought. Now you're off the hook, you can go on blaming me. Thoughts unmuttered were often best.

"I want the raw truth, Jared. This is your moment. Don't blow it. What possessed you to do this?"

Jared deliberated. There was too much at stake here. He went with full confessional: "I've been trying to tell you, Dad, for a long time."

"I'm listening now." Rusty put his feet up on the desk, crossed his arms behind his head, and leaned back. Jared talked. And talked, babbling on like some James Cameron movie desperately in need of editing.

"It's not that I don't respect you, I just don't agree with you, Dad. I don't belong in school. I belong here, at Galaxy, with you. I thought if I made you believe I'd pulled it together this summer, got good grades, and at the same time did something to help the company—"

Rusty's hand went up in a stop motion. "You think Galaxy needs help?"

Jared swallowed. "Well, doesn't it?"

"We've had better times," his dad conceded. "What has Lindsay been telling you?"

"Nothing." The one lie he told, he told for her. He rushed

on. "I know you think I'm a slacker, I'm lazy. How many times have you said I'm just like Uncle Rob? Take the easy way out, never live up to my potential?"

It was his father's turn to remain silent.

"And I am"—Jared's lip trembled unexpectedly—"I am lacking in a lot of ways. I messed up this summer, but not in the way you think. I was stuck up, I misjudged people big-time. I belittled Eliot when he tried to prepare us, I made fun of Sara, and I tried to kick Naomi out. Naomi! If not for her . . ."

He couldn't continue.

Rusty offered him a tissue but remained silent, listening.

Jared wiped his leaky eyes. "Lindsay might not have made it. 'Cause she was buried, and I was no help. Everything I have—money, access, style, everything that made me so self-important, me, the ultimate cool Hollywood insider—it all turned out to be worth nothing. I wasn't brave or smart. I was a sorry-assed wimp whose main contribution was whining."

Truly, truly, truly, he told himself, opening up like this to his father had not been premeditated. In no way had he meant to butter up the old guy so Rusty would forgive him, so he'd . . . oh God . . . be in a prime position to make his pitch. To get Rusty excited about *Hide in Plain Sight*. It was his moment; he had the floor, and his dad's full attention, and empathy. Jared blew his nose, wiped his eyes.

"I didn't go to school this summer, but I learned a pretty big life lesson. And I hope that counts for something. I'm no hero, and I suck at school—but I do have talent, and I know this business, show business. I live and breathe it. And I . . . Dad, I found a screenplay. . . ."

Finding Naomi

"This is a joke, right?"

Five heads shook in unison. Jared, Lindsay, Sara, Eliot, and Nick were serious as a heart attack. Naomi had been in the bedroom, sitting in the window seat (imagine!) reading a book, minding her own business, when they ambushed her, just flung open the door, brandishing a dozen long-stemmed red roses, a bottle of champagne, and a proposition—one at which they assumed she'd jump.

She stood still. "Guys, this is so sweet. But there are other ways to say thanks. You don't have to offer me a part in a movie. It's overcompensating."

"Asking you to star in *Hide in Plain Sight* has nothing to do with gratitude," Jared assured her. "It's—"

"Bra*sheet*," Lindsay interrupted. "That's Jewish for 'It's meant to be.'"

"It's Yiddish," Jared corrected, "and it's pronounced *beshert*."

"It's ber*serk*," Naomi told them with finality.

Had it only been Jared or Lindsay pushing this insane idea, it would've been easy to dismiss them. But they had allies—Eliot, Nick, and Sara—and she was feeling seriously ganged up on, under pressure to explain herself. 'Cause no way, no how, not ever would she consider their beyond-ridiculous proposal.

Nick put a friendly arm around her. "This is a big movie, Naomi. Most people would think they've died and gone to heaven, to be asked to star in it."

Most people—did she really need to point it out?—were not her.

"A month ago, Lindsay and I would've fought you for it!" Sara exclaimed.

"And so would Naomi Watts, and Reese Witherspoon, and any of the Kates—Bosworth, Beckinsale, Blanchett, Winslet, Hudson—you name 'em," Lindsay put in.

Naomi rolled her eyes. Had they all gone bonkers? Was she the only sane one in the room? And how had everything suddenly moved into warp speed? Listening to them made Naomi dizzy.

Just a few days ago, Sara had asked Jared to read *Hide in Plain Sight*. In the span of seventy-two hours, he'd read it and taken it to his father, who'd agreed that the screenplay was pretty wonderful. Galaxy quickly secured the rights from an overjoyed Officer Ortega—now, officially, a screenwriter! Because there are no secrets in Hollywood, word got out quickly, and the whole showbiz community sniffed out the new "buzz-worthy" screenplay. In swift succession, a producer and director signed up. Paramount Pictures snapped it up, and *Hide in Plain Sight* got "greenlit"—Hollywood-speak for happening. The casting process was about to begin.

Jared refused to allow any actresses to audition for the starring role until Naomi took a shot at it. Which she stubbornly refused to do.

"You read the script," Sara reminded her. "And somewhere deep inside, you know you're perfect for the part of Moxie."

"Why don't you want to even try out?" Eliot asked.

"Hello? Not an actress—remember? Or did the earthquake give you all amnesia? Girl from the streets. Sara's stray. A homeless ho," Naomi fired back.

"Ooops." Lindsay genuinely blushed. "You heard that, huh?"

Naomi narrowed her eyes at Jared. "Just two months ago you thought I was a crackhead killer. Now you think I'm a movie star. Make up your mind."

"Who said you couldn't be both? They're not mutually exclusive."

It was Lindsay's quip, but Jared elbowed her in the ribs. "A lot can happen in two months," he said. "A lot did happen. I was exposed as the jerk, the asshole, any horrible thing you can think of: Fill in the blank. But I'm still an opportunist, and if it helps you to see it that way, go for it."

"What he's saying—" Lindsay started, but Sara stopped her.

"He doesn't need you to interpret. What Jared means is, if you agree to read for the role and things work out, Jared wins too. It makes him look good to his father and raises his stock in the biz. It's win-win, Naomi."

Naomi arched her eyebrows. Sara on Jared's side? What had the summer come to?

"It's totally quid pro quo," Lindsay put in. "You saved our lives. We give you a part in a movie where you'll earn millions. The movie makes billions, we save Jared's dad's company. We're all heroes. It's so Hollywood! See?"

Naomi did not see. Their idea was harebrained, insane. And impossible. What were they thinking? This wasn't some fantasy, and she wasn't their own Eliza Dolittle, or Julia Roberts in *Pretty Woman*. The homeless waif from the streets becomes a rich movie star? That only happens in the movies. Not in real life, and certainly not in *her* real life.

After the quake, when Eliot had guessed she was a survivor, she'd told them about her past. The version she gave them was abridged. If she went along with the crazy idea to read for the role in the movie, and if she actually got it? Too much info would surface. She couldn't take that chance.

For the first time since Sara had taken her in, Naomi felt caged. She pressed her back against the window-seat wall. "As much as I want to help you look good, Jared, I can't do this."

"Can't? Or won't?" Eliot said it gently.

"I can't! I can't be famous. I'm an under-the-radar person."

"That's in the past. Everything's changed now," Sara said soothingly.

"How do you even know I'd be good?" Naomi challenged. "Just because the role calls for a kid who runs away and ends up on the streets? If that's the criteria, why not go to Hollywood Boulevard, pick up any homeless girl, and offer her the part?

"Eeeww!" Lindsay couldn't help herself.

"Only you can play this part," Sara said. "You have so much soul. You look like you've seen so much sadness, like you're wise beyond your years. It comes across in your eyes. That, and your fierce determination—we saw that during the earthquake. It's like you were someone else. You were born to play Moxie."

"And," Lindsay noted, "you'd come cheap."

Jared shot darts at her.

"Well, she wouldn't cost what a Cami Diaz would, or Reese, or Charlize. Even a TV star—God forbid!—would charge more. That's meaningful to the studio."

"How 'bout you don't say any more," Nick suggested.

Lindsay furrowed her brow, then turned to Naomi. "Wait a minute. I get it. You don't want to do the role because you think people will find out you were really homeless? And look down on you?"

"Gee, Lindsay, I wonder why she'd think that?" Eliot said sarcastically.

"You're so not seeing the big picture, Naomi. Rags-to-riches stories are classic—they never go out of style, they're totally on trend. It's the cover of *People*. You'll be America's sweetheart."

Naomi shuddered.

A light went on in Jared's head. "Oh, crap, there's more, isn't there? You haven't told us the whole story."

"She doesn't have to tell us any more than she wants to." Sara fell right into default mode, defending Naomi.

Thoughtfully, Jared said, "Not to sound like more of a jerk than you already think I am, but, Naomi, whatever it is, whatever you're hiding that you think is so terrible it would keep you from this—I bet I can fix it. Spin it so it's a good thing, not a bad thing."

"That's what's so sick. You really believe that." Naomi's laugh was bitter.

Jared took no offense. "I'm not Superman. But there are things I can do, places where I have influence. Let me—"

"Save me? Let you save me like I saved Lindsay? Did it ever occur to you that maybe I don't need saving? Maybe I've been saved one time too many."

A plunging sadness gripped her as she packed her few belongings. She finally got them off her back by agreeing to think about trying out for the role.

She'd lied. Naomi didn't need to think. None of them would ever, ever understand what her life had been like, that to have people know her name—to be in the spotlight, to be exposed? It was unthinkable.

The days after the 1994 earthquake were a blur. She'd gone in and out of consciousness; all she remembered was waking in a strange place, asking her sister Annie where Mom and Dad were. She'd come to understand she was in a motel with Annie, saved by Mr. Knepper, the tall, kindly man who lived in the apartment above theirs. Annie was eleven; she was nine.

Over the next several weeks, Mr. Knepper explained what'd happened. The earthquake had demolished most of the apartment complex, and many of the people who lived there, including their parents, had perished. For a long time, Naomi was incapable of comprehending more. She'd never see her parents again. That was too big; it blotted out everything else.

The story Mr. Knepper told the girls got worse. The apartment, he alleged, wasn't even theirs legally. "Your folks weren't paying rent; they were squatting. Their name was never on any bills. So it's not like you gals can make a claim or anything." He told them if they tried to contact the police, everything would be exposed. Their parents would have died criminals, and they themselves would go to jail, to juvie.

Annie and Naomi believed him. They were kids, just dumb, terrified kids who, in the blink of an eye, were orphaned. They didn't have other relatives they knew of—they'd spent most of their lives on the road with their parents. They didn't know how to search for potential kin. Mr. Knepper saved their lives, dragged them out of the rubble, he said, fed and sheltered them. They thought they were safe with him; that's what he told them.

When he asked about school, they told him the truth: They'd been home-schooled. He vowed to continue their training, right there in the motel.

They rarely left the motel. They didn't know they could. When he told them he'd always wanted daughters and he felt like a father to them—that's when the sisters began to be uneasy in his presence.

They knew it was wrong when he began to act more than

paternally toward them. Annie hatched a plan. Naomi never knew exactly what her sister had done to immobilize Mr. Knepper, how she'd gathered food, some clothes, stolen some money—planned their escape.

They made up different names, different birthdays. They'd stayed in Griffith Park for a while but were soon picked up by the LAPD. Having no identification, no one to claim them, no one who had filed a missing persons report, they were turned over to child services.

It wasn't until they landed in foster homes that they were separated. "Never tell," Annie had tearfully warned her. "Never tell what happened. We'll get in bad trouble."

"Why?" Naomi had asked. "We didn't do anything wrong."

"I did," Annie said. "I had to. Swear you won't tell. If anyone finds out what I did, I'll go to jail. Or worse."

Naomi swore. She believed that, one day, after they were out of foster care, they'd live together, be a family again. But that's not how it worked out. Naomi ended up in a string of foster homes, and eventually she ran away for good, never finding Annie. A part of her believed that if she stayed on the streets, Annie would find her. It'd been years now. Still, she clung to that belief.

And now here comes Jared Superstar. A rich kid with resources, money. Giving her this hooey about making her a star—and maybe he could. Maybe Annie would find her. But if she went public, Annie's secret—Naomi now believed Annie may have done something bad to Knepper—it would come out. She'd go to jail.

"She's gone!" Sara scurried down the elaborate staircase of the Larson mansion, calling out to the others. "Naomi bolted."

"What do you mean, she's gone? Gone where?" Jared appeared at the bottom of the steps, Lindsay, Nick, and Eliot on his heels.

"Her room's empty, bed's made—like no one ever used it," Sara reported.

"Did she leave a note?" Nick asked

"She's not suicidal, you dunce. Jared just scared her away," Eliot declared. "You moved too fast, you overwhelmed her. Of course she ran."

"Who made you the expert on all things Naomi?" Jared demanded. "When's the last time someone got offered a movie role and reacted by running away? Get real, Eliot."

"You shouldn't have come on so strong, man." Eliot looked at Lindsay and Sara. "You either."

"Enough, all of you. We have to find her," Sara decided.

"Hopefully, she didn't get too far—if she's on foot, we should be able to catch her. If she took a taxi, that's another story," Jared calculated. "I'll get the car. We'll go after her."

"No!" Lindsay crossed her arms.

"No what? We don't try to find her?" Nick asked.

"Not you guys. Sara and I will go. We'll have a better chance of finding her, 'cause we're smarter than you, and when we do, she'll open up to Sara."

Jared handed Lindsay the keys to the Lexus. The girls made a left out of the long, winding driveway, keeping their eyes peeled for a small, thin girl with choppy black hair and huge violet eyes.

"I think she'd probably head for the main road," Sara opined after they'd circled the area a few times. "She's more likely to find a taxi there."

Lindsay turned right, toward Sunset Boulevard. "I hope she isn't trying to hitch a ride. You never know what kind of jerks are on the road."

Sara pressed her lips together, her eyes darting left and right as Lindsay drove—remembering her first day in Los Angeles, when those sleazy guys tried to lure her into their car. If *she* had enough sense not to go with them, Naomi surely would resist, no matter how desperate she was.

"I don't get it, exactly," Lindsay mused. "Why would she run away? Why not just say thanks but no thanks, I'm not interested in your movie?"

"I'm guessing she figured we wouldn't let up on her, we'd pressure her. And I'm also guessing that running from scary situations has kept her alive all these years."

"How can you compare our offer to make her a movie star with scary street situations? That's ridiculous."

"To you, maybe. Who knows what goes on in her head," Sara pointed out.

They had no luck finding any pedestrians at all along the winding, palm-tree-lined Sunset Boulevard, so they headed east toward the shopping district. They wound up and down the side streets, checking coffee shops, bookstores, any place Naomi might've gone into. No luck.

"What about turning onto Hollywood Boulevard," Lindsay suggested, "where you first found her?"

They rode in silence for a while. Every so often, Lindsay's cell phone rang: Jared asking for an update.

Hollywood Boulevard was crowded, commuters coming home from work, shoppers out and about—tourists, skinheads, the usual carnival of weirdos, beggars. No Naomi.

Out of nowhere, Lindsay blurted, "I'm not going to try and force her to do this movie. I owe her, Sara. I owe her everything. If she wants to stay underground, I owe her that, too. But I'd like to give her money, at the very least, so she can do what she wants. And I want to her to know that she always . . ."

Silently, Sara finished the sentence: *that Naomi always has friends. People to turn to. Always.* Sara reached over and squeezed Lindsay's shoulder. "I know. Me, too."

They passed Big Al's Tattoo Parlor, Bondage Babes

Leather 'N' Thongs, Off-Track Betting, take-out places. "Where would she go?" Lindsay said for the eighteenth time.

"She'd go where she feels safe," Sara said.

"Oh, my God!" Lindsay exclaimed. "We're such duh-heads. We should have thought of it right away!"

In the middle of traffic, in a completely illegal move, accompanied by the outraged horns and curses of dozens of cars, Lindsay slammed on the brakes and made a U-turn.

Naomi was sitting at the property's edge, several feet from where the pool had once been.

Lindsay had managed to squeeze the car between the huge yellow-and-black CAT construction trucks, which took up half the winding street in front of 5905 Chula Vista Lane. It was nearing sunset and the workers had gone for the day, but the big cleanup trucks had remained.

Without exchanging a word, the girls threaded their way around back. The quake had caused an upheaval in the yard, Uncle Rob's property now ended in a minicliff. Naomi was on it, her legs pretzeled under her; she leaned back on her arms for support. She stared out into the valley.

Naomi didn't seem the least bit surprised to see Sara and Lindsay, who settled on either side of her.

For a few peaceful moments, no one spoke. The valley spread out below them, the hills all around, and the sun, a big red rubber ball floating in the sky, brushed the top of the mountains.

Lindsay murmured, "Awesome view."

Naomi nodded in agreement.

"It's so great that Rusty is getting the house rehabbed," Lindsay noted, "so when Rob gets back, he won't have to deal with the mess."

Sara gazed at the sky. "Nature caused the earthquake, but look what nature gives us. Nothing can take away the glory of this landscape."

"These past two weeks," Naomi said quietly, "at Jared's house? It's the first time in my entire life I ever had my own room. But I was happiest in this place, in the basement. Funny, huh?"

"No, not at all," Sara said. "I feel completely out of place at the Larson mansion."

Lindsay whipped around. "Really? Not me. I feel right at home there."

"Will you live there some day?" Naomi asked Lindsay.

"Oh, I don't know. I'm not thinking that far ahead."

"But you'll end up with Jared, right?" Sara asked. "You love him."

"You two are made for each other," Naomi put in.

Lindsay had no quip. She seemed to mull whether she should say anything. Finally, she said, "Remember that night in the hot tub, you guys asked what I saw in Jared? I didn't tell you everything. I love him because, at the end of the day, he'd do anything for me. He's crazy about me. He accepts me even when I'm selfish, and snobby, and—"

"You? Selfish? Come on!" Sara jabbed her, and they all laughed.

"Jared has seen me at my worst. And he loves me anyway."

"Then why do you sound so mournful?" Naomi asked.

"Because . . ." She took a breath, "Because I hurt him once before. And I could hurt him again. At least I think I could. If something came up and, say, Jared wasn't in a position to help me, career-wise? I could leave him. I could do that."

Sara glared at her. "You're full of shit, Lindsay."

Naomi and Lindsay gasped.

"You . . . you . . . cursed!" Naomi stammered.

"Well, I'm tired of hearing Lindsay talk trash about herself. You do, you know! You make jokes out of everything, pretend to be heartless and selfish, and, okay, I'll grant that in some ways you are. But when it matters, you've got a heart of gold, girl. You really do."

A tear streaked down Lindsay's cheek. "If you ever tell, I'll kill you."

"Your secret's safe with me. Now, go on and tell Naomi what you came to say." Sara smiled knowingly.

Lindsay sniffed. "I'm sorry we freaked you out, Naomi.

You don't have to read for the movie; you can forget about it, if that's what you want. You don't have to tell us why. But—"

"No buts," Sara scolded mildly.

"Just let me finish, okay?"

Lindsay looked into Naomi's eyes. "Here's the thing. Whatever's going on in your head, whatever you need—for whatever reason—we can help you."

Sara said, "We became like a family this summer, Naomi. All of us. And family help one another. If you need money, if you need to stay under the radar—whatever you need, we're there for you."

"You don't have to be alone again. Ever." Lindsay and Sara leaned in and hugged her.

You'd expect huge, gloppy tears to fall from those ginormous anime eyes. When Naomi cried, they did.

October: *Beshert*—
What's Meant to Be

"What's the word from our guys in the Midwest?" Jared asked Lindsay, who'd just shut her cell phone. The pair were lazing in Jared's backyard on a balmy Saturday afternoon, with Linz looking exceptionally luscious in her metallic bikini—so "in," as she advised him, and so perfect with her copper hair, golden brown eyes, and faded rusty freckles.

A stab of pain shot through him. Lindsay would be leaving soon for the location shoot in Oklahoma for *The Outsiders*. After much haggling, the movie studio decided to remain faithful to the original, in setting at least. She'd be gone for three months, and though Jared would visit as often as possible, he missed her already. He'd be busy, doing double-duty. As part of the big Larson compromise, Jared had agreed to really go back to school, to take classes, and to work part-time at Galaxy.

From her lounge chair, Lindsay leaned over and gave him a peck on the cheek. "Nick's at college. He joined a fraternity—and big surprise, he's already got a girlfriend. He thinks he's gonna be a business major. I think we convinced him he could open a chain of fitness centers one day. I'd invest in him."

Jared laughed. "I bet you would, cutie-pie. And with all the money you're gonna make on *The Outsiders* and the plans I have for your career, you'll have lots of money to invest."

"Bet on it," she said dreamily.

"And Eliot, our neurotic-genius friend?"

"Emergency El is doing fantastic," she reported. "I got an e-mail. That school in Chicago is like his dream environment. He's even got—are ya sitting down?—a girlfriend!"

Jared punched his fist in the air. "Yessss! Awesome!"

"I texted him; he's gonna send a picture. I told him we could probably all get together over Christmas. I mean, I'll be in Oklahoma—how far could that be from Chicago and Michigan?"

Jared chortled. "That's my Linz. Don't ever change, baby, okay?"

She narrowed her eyes. "I think you just made fun of me."

He reached over and cupped her chin. "Never. I'd never make fun of you." The kiss was tender, and sweet, and lingering.

"Mr. Jared, a delivery came for you." Desiree's voice wafted from the French doors. She held up a large manila envelope.

Jared knew what it was—he'd asked Amanda to please send it over on Saturday so he could surprise Lindsay before the rest of the showbiz community saw it on Monday. He opened it in front of her.

Lindsay's hand flew to her mouth, her eyes went wide. "Oh, my God, Jared! That's . . . that's . . . where did you? When will this come out?"

They were staring at a poster, the first draft of what would eventually be used on billboards, magazines, and in TV ads to advertise *The Outsiders*. The final version wouldn't be released for many months, but Jared and Amanda had fought for the wording on it, and Jared wanted Lindsay to see it.

The poster pictured the seven male stars standing shoulder to shoulder—including Mark Oliver, the young actor Lindsay'd met in the park—their names listed beneath the photograph. On the side, in her own spotlight, was a profile of Lindsay's sparkling face, with the words, "And starring Lindsay Pierce as Cherry."

She gulped. "You did this for me."

"Well . . ." Jared tried to hide his grin. "It was really your agent, Amanda, who did the heavy lifting. But, yeah—as the son of the owner of Galaxy, I put my two cents in. C'mere, you." He held his arms out.

Lindsay joined him on the chaise lounge, tucked herself under his arm.

"And you know, Ms. Pierce," Jared said, "this is only the beginning. Galaxy and I have big plans for the likes of you."

Through her tears, she giggled. "Tell me again."

"We're gonna pitch *Leave It to Lindsay*, a half-hour TV series, and it's all you. It's you being single and funny and free in L.A. It's you being clueless and brilliant at the same time, it's you being self-centered and intensely generous. It's you and your coterie of friends—it's *I Love Lucy* meets *Sex and the City*. You should be planning that Lindsay Pierce doll now."

"And the perfume," she sniffed. "Everyone has a scent."

"Okay, you two, get a room!" Sara sashayed into the back-yard, wearing capris and a snazzy V-neck top accessorized with a golden cross necklace.

Lindsay bolted upright and gave Sara a huge smile. "Wuz-zup, Saint Sara?"

Jared looked from his girlfriend to Sara. A strange feeling overtook him. He had the distinct feeling Lindsay knew why Sara was there. Which intensified when Lindsay, who never could contain her excitement, suddenly shot off the lounge chair and started prancing about, circling him.

Sara laughed and pulled something out of the Hermès Birkin bag that Lindsay had pressed on her. She'd only agreed because in her new job—while still auditioning for acting roles—she was always toting around scripts and papers.

Sara had not gone back to Texarcana, not gone back to Donald. She'd decided, after much deliberation, to stay in L.A., to continue trying to find acting gigs and to work with Naomi. Once the formerly homeless girl accepted them as true friends, as family, she'd opened up. Told them about her missing sister, her fears of finding Annie, or of not finding Annie.

Lindsay had offered to help. Jared's family had the resources to be discreet, to be sure no harm came to anyone, no unwanted publicity. They hadn't found Annie Foster yet, but they had earned Naomi's trust. In short order, that trust had led her to audition, finally, for the role of Moxie in *Hide in Plain Sight*.

The newbie actress needed a manager, someone to protect her, look out for her interests. They created that job for Sara at Galaxy.

"Well, come on!" Jared was getting antsy. "What are you and Lindsay up to?"

Slowly, just to mess with him, Sara extracted a rolled-up poster from her bag and gave it to Jared. "Unroll it."

Jared did not enjoy being stealthed. Warily, he slipped off the rubber band and unfurled the poster.

"It's a first draft," Sara warned. "It's not final."

"But the wording is!" Lindsay squealed.

It was Jared's turn to tear up. McSmoothy became McMush. The poster was for *Hide in Plain Sight*. And it wasn't the billing, "Introducing Naomi Foster as Moxie," that moved him to tears. It was the top billing:

"A Rusty and Jared Larson Production."

Epilogue:
One Last Laugh

Later that night, Lindsay and Jared were still outdoors; hadn't moved from the chaise lounge. They had one more surprise visitor.

"Uncle Rob!" Jared exclaimed. "You're back! You're . . . here!"

Indeed he was. The tall, craggy, forever-hippie Robert Larson, Jared's favorite family member, loped into the backyard. He'd be bunking here at the mansion, he told them, until his own house at 5905 Chula Vista Lane was fully operational again. He stretched out on the chaise next to the couple and turned to Jared.

"So, nephew, how was your summer?"

Jared shrugged. "Oh, you know, nothing exciting. Same old, same old . . ."

Lindsay began to giggle. The giggle became a guffaw, which morphed into peals and peals of staccato laughter, bouncing off the canyon walls and through the valleys, around the hills, drifting into the perfect California night.

About the Author

Randi Reisfeld is the author of numerous original series and novels for teens, including three *New York Times* bestsellers. Her series with HB Gilmour, T*Witches, is the basis for two popular Disney Channel TV movies. Her trilogy Starlet also reflects her lifelong obsession with all things Hollywood. Randi lives in Washington Township, New Jersey. Visit her on the web at www.randireisfeld.com.

Like what you read?

Turn the page for a look at
two other beach reads!

The Shore

Shirt and Shoes Not Required

Todd Strasser

One

"School's out for . . . ever!"

Okay, so maybe it was one of the lamest songs ever to come out of the 1980s, but Avery James had to admit that thumping out of the radio in her pickup, it sounded dead-on. Driving with the windows down and the warm June breeze whipping her light brown hair, she turned the music up a little louder.

Summer, there was nothing like it. And this year, she was going to make the most of it. It was June 23, and the rest of her life stretched before her, beginning with two months of sun, sand, all-night parties—and no one checking IDs too close—to celebrate her release from the minimum-security prison known as high school.

Cruising down the road toward Wildwood, New Jersey, the salty smell of the ocean filled her nostrils and a thrill ran up her spine. *This is it!* Ever since she was a kid she had heard about the beachside community that was the summer hangout for thousands of high school and college students. Now she was finally going to see for herself.

She drove over the causeway—the breeze adding a ripple to the green water below—and into town, passing the blocks of rental houses and condos, motels, gas stations, and liquor stores that serviced vacationers. Her first impression was that every other car was a brand-new convertible or a tricked-out import complete with spoiler and rims. Compared with them, her rusty, dented red truck was almost an eyesore. But that was okay; she liked being different. A girl driving an old pickup stood out in the crowd. It didn't matter that the real reason she drove the pickup was that it was free. The truck was a hand-me-down from her uncle.

The sky was blue and cloudless, the sun big and yellow. Its rays warmed her arm in the open window. Avery tucked a strand of hair behind her ear and double-checked the addresses for the house she would be sharing. She was looking for number 15. As she drove toward the beach the numbers got lower. 93 . . . 87 . . . 81. The houses were mostly two stories and larger than she had expected. Some were freshly painted with neatly trimmed green lawns. Others were victims of the salt air and harsh winter weather—paint flaking, battered shutters hanging askew. Houses like that anywhere else might have been considered dilapidated, but here they seemed charming and rustic.

She passed number 19 and slowed the pickup, but her heart

sped up in anticipation. Seven people would be sharing the house, including her boyfriend, Curt. No parents, no rules, nothing to hold them back from having a great time. Daytime, nighttime, all the time. That was, *if* they could stand one another. She wondered what her housemates would be like. Maybe it wouldn't be important. Her cousin had once shared a house at Wildwood with three other girls and swore she never saw two of them more than five times the entire summer.

A brisk ocean breeze swept in the open window, and Avery tasted the salt in the air. She couldn't wait to get into her bathing suit. The scent of suntan lotion and ocean water mixed with the aroma of funnel cake and popcorn. *Ah, bliss!*

Her thoughts turned to Curt. He should have arrived two days ago with his band. Almost instantly the muscles in the back of her neck began to tighten with nervous tension. They'd had a fight the last time they'd seen each other because she didn't want to live in the house the other band members had rented for the summer. Curt hadn't called her cell to let her know he'd arrived, so she was pretty sure he was still annoyed. But she knew she'd made the right decision. He was so involved with that band, it was hard to get him alone. She wanted time with him this summer. It wasn't that she didn't enjoy hanging out with the other musicians; she just wanted something different, something special. As she pulled up to number 15, her new summer home, she hoped that she had found it.

Avery parked the pickup on the street outside the house.

Like most of the other houses on the street, it was two stories tall. The dull gray paint and black trim were weather-beaten but not yet flaking. What lawn there was had been recently cut, but already a few gnarly looking weeds poked up through the grass.

She pulled her cell phone out of her pocket, pressed the 2 on the speed dial, and got Curt's voice mail. His clipped message, "You know what to do," was followed by the requisite beep. "I'm here and it looks great," Avery said. She hung up and breathed in the warm air for a moment, had another thought, and hit redial. "I can't wait for you to see our place if you haven't already. . . ." She paused and found herself unwilling to hang up. The memory of their argument was fresh in her thoughts, and she didn't want their summer together to begin on a bad note. "I really think you're going to love it. We'll get to have time together and it'll be fun. I can't wait."

She got out of the truck and looked around. The street ended two houses down, and beyond that was the beach and then the vast blue green ocean stretching out to the horizon. White-tipped waves crashed on the velvety golden sand, and sprays of water looked like millions of diamonds glittering in the sunlight.

"What a dump," someone behind her muttered. Startled, Avery turned to see a girl with expertly highlighted honey blond hair, tan skin, and stormy blue eyes climbing out of a cab. She was wearing a tight pink baby doll tee with a light blue terry cloth miniskirt. While neither was see-through, they might just as well have been, given what they revealed about her drop-dead figure. She was carrying a brown Louis Vuitton overnight bag. The cabdriver opened the trunk and placed two large matching suitcases on the curb.

"Ahem." He cleared his throat and held out his hand.

The blonde gave him a perplexed look.

"I don't drive for free, sweetcakes," said the cabbie.

Where Avery would have apologized like mad for the oversight, the blonde merely looked annoyed as she opened her bag and paid him.

"Ahem." The driver cleared his throat again.

The blonde gave him an exasperated "Now what?" look.

"You ever heard of a tip?" he asked.

Rolling her eyes dramatically and acting as if he'd just asked her for one of her kidneys, she opened her purse and pulled out a hundred-dollar bill. "Got change?"

The driver frowned. "That's all you got?"

"Sorry." The blonde stuck the bill back in her purse.

Muttering to himself, the cabbie got into the cab. Avery couldn't help but feel a bit shocked that the blonde had stiffed the guy. From the looks of things, she could have easily afforded the tip.

"Excuse me." Leaving the matching luggage on the sidewalk, the blonde pushed past Avery. *Pretentious blue blood*, Avery thought. *The kind who spends a thousand dollars on designer clothes tailor-made to give the wearer a casual, just-thrown-together look. What is she doing renting a room in this place? Mommy and Daddy can probably afford to buy her a beach house of her own.*

The blonde rang the doorbell. Almost instantly it was opened by a guy who looked about twenty years old. It seemed to Avery that he must have been waiting for the knock. His straight brown hair fell down his forehead, almost into his eyes, and he was wearing a white T-shirt, and green plaid shorts that revealed pale, bony arms and legs. The black socks and shoes did little to enhance the look. Behind his thick, black-rimmed glasses his eyes sparkled with excitement.

The blonde wrinkled her nose. "You're . . . not one of my new roommates, are you?"

"No, I'm Fred, your landlord," he said, extending his hand.

"Oh! The landlord! So nice to meet you!" The blonde's frown turned into a smile, and her voice became sweet. "Sabrina Morganthal," she said, taking his hand in hers instead of shaking it. "Would you be a dear and help me with my bags? They're too heavy for me, but I'm sure they'd be no problem for you."

It was Avery's turn to roll her eyes. *She has to be kidding. Fred may look a little dense, but he has to see that she's playing him!*

All Fred seemed to see was Sabrina's hand holding his, and the bare arm, and amazing body behind it. He smiled wide. "My pleasure."

Sabrina batted her eyes. "Oh, thank you. I really appreciate it." She sailed past him and into the house.

It was hard to believe how quickly Sabrina had gone from being rude to the cabdriver to sugary sweet with Fred. The poor guy practically tripped over himself in his rush to get her bags. He didn't even notice Avery on the walk as he dashed past her and tried to pick up both bags at once.

"Uhhh!" He grunted and struggled to drag them up the walk. Meanwhile, Avery went inside the house. Sabrina was standing in the middle of the living room with her back toward her and her hands on her hips, surveying the place. Avery immediately liked the way the light streamed through the windows. The walls were painted a pale seafoam green, and the carpet was the color of sand. The living room had two sofas, three comfortable chairs, and a television set.

"Decorated it myself," Fred announced proudly once he made it inside and let go of the bags. "Well, with a little help from my mom. The entertainment center has a wide-screen TV, DVD/VCR with Surround Sound. The CD player holds twelve disks. *And* we've got Wi-Fi. Nice, huh?"

"Fabulous," Sabrina said with feigned enthusiasm. Avery wasn't particularly interested in the entertainment center. Instead, she focused on the staircase that led up to a second-floor landing. She could see several doors, no doubt bedrooms.

"And over here is the kitchen." Fred was still giving Sabrina the guided tour.

"You don't say," Sabrina replied. "I never would have guessed."

Avery bit her lip to keep from laughing. Fred couldn't be more than a year or two older than her. This must have been his first venture into real estate, and he was too eager to please.

Sabrina flipped her hair in that way that seemed to come naturally to beautiful girls. People had told Avery she was beautiful, but she'd never quite believed it. Maybe that was why she wasn't blessed with awesome hair flippage.

Meanwhile, Sabrina was getting impatient with Fred's house tour. "Can we get to the bedroom already?"

An astonished look spread over Fred's face. It suddenly occurred to Avery that he might have misunderstood the statement, especially if one believed all those stories about how wild "summer girls" could be. She clapped a hand over her mouth to keep from laughing while Fred moved toward Sabrina, almost as if he was going to embrace her, clearly misreading her intentions.

Before he could get too close, Sabrina raised a hand to stop him. "Isn't there something you should take care of first?"

Fred scowled, raising one eyebrow, then the other, clearly wracking his brain to figure out what she meant. Meanwhile, Sabrina laid a hand gently on Fred's arm. "I meant, my bags, Freddy. Someone has to get them upstairs."

"Oh . . . uh, right. Right!" Fred hurried for the bags while Sabrina, with the air of a queen, went up the stairs.

Avery's cell phone rang. "Hello?"

"Hey, baby." It was Curt, and he sounded like he was in a

good mood. She felt a tingle of relief. "Got your message. You seen our room yet?"

"Not yet. The landlord's got his hands full with one of the other renters," she said ruefully.

"Okay, I'll be there in ten."

"I love you," she said.

He'd already hung up. Well, at least he'd sounded happy. She closed her phone and slid it back into her pocket. Fred came past with Sabrina's bags.

"Excuse me," Avery said. "I'm Avery James."

"Be right with you." Fred lugged one bag up to the second-floor landing, then turned and hurried back down for the second.

"I'm also renting here this summer," Avery said.

"In a minute," Fred gasped under the strain of the heavy bag, his forehead beginning to glisten with sweat as he headed back up the stairs.

Annoyed, Avery seated herself on the couch and listened to the sound of footsteps and doors opening and closing as Sabrina inspected the upstairs bedrooms and Fred tagged along. It was only when she heard footsteps coming back down the stairs that she looked up.

"—and that's why I need the big bedroom, sugar," Sabrina purred to him as he followed Sabrina down the steps.

The big bedroom? Avery felt a jolt, then stood up and cleared her throat. "Excuse me? Fred? I thought my boyfriend and I are supposed to have the large bedroom."

Fred stopped and looked flustered and confused. "Oh, gee. I'm sorry, she . . ." He gestured toward Sabrina but then trailed off, like he wasn't sure what to say.

"We paid for that room in advance," Avery stated, trying to sound forceful but fearing that she sounded wimpy.

Fred bit his lip and glanced over at Sabrina, who gave him a coy smile and batted her eyes. He turned back to Avery. "I'm really sorry, but she was here first. If it's the money you're worried about, I'll refund the difference."

Now Avery was pissed. "Actually, I was here first. But she pushed past me. And my boyfriend has been in town for two days, but you told us we couldn't check in until today, so he waited."

Again Fred's eyes slid to Sabrina. Avery realized that he was under her spell and there was probably nothing she could say that would make a difference. She took a deep breath and calmed herself. She was here to have a good time this summer, not make enemies on the very first day. Besides there had to be another decent bedroom. If Curt didn't like it, she'd let him work it out with Fred.

"I get to pick the next bedroom," Avery said. "No matter who shows up next."

"I promise," Fred replied. Having put out that fire, he sidled over to Sabrina. "So, uh, I was wondering if you had any plans. . . ."

Sabrina gave him puppy dog eyes. "Oh, Freddy, I just

remembered I promised a friend that I'd meet her on the beach."

Disappointment spread over Fred's face, but he quickly caught himself. "Yeah, okay, maybe later?"

"You're a sweetheart." Sabrina gave him a peck on the cheek and ran back upstairs to her room. *Which had been my room,* Avery reminded herself bitterly, then sighed. *Oh, come on, get over it. It's not worth ruining your first day for.* She went outside to get her bags out of the truck. The sun was strong, and she liked the feeling of heat on her head and arms. *This is going to be a great summer.*

Then she heard the voice that she hoped was going to make it so great. "Hey, baby." It was Curt, strolling toward her on the sidewalk. Tall and lanky, he took his time, with that slightly disheveled look that made it seem like he'd just woken up. His black hair was tousled, and he wore baggy jeans and a black long-sleeved Metalhead T-shirt that was so wrinkled, it looked slept in. He had a bag slung over his shoulder and a couple day's growth of dark stubble on his jaw. Comparisons to Colin Farrell were not out of the question.

She threw her arms around him, and he dropped his eyes down to hers. They were dark like his hair and smoldered with an inner fire. "Miss me?" he half asked, half growled in the voice that always made her heart pound. He wrapped his arms around her and kissed her. In the heat in his kiss she tasted something unexpected and pulled back. "Drinking already?"

Here we go, Curt thought, annoyed. They'd hardly been together a minute and Avery was already upset about something. What was the big deal, anyway? He'd only had a beer. So what if it was the middle of the day? She probably thought he was just goofing off, and didn't understand how hard he'd been working to get his band, Stranger Than Fiction, or STF, ready for a summer of shoreline gigs. The afternoon beer was just a way to relax a little, cut through the tension and stress of trying to get the guys in STF to rehearse. Especially when they were so close to the beach, beautiful water, and lots of babes in bikinis. Avery would understand soon enough. In the meantime, he wanted to check out the house where she'd insisted they stay this summer instead of with the band. He had to admit that from the outside, at least, the place looked nice, nicer than the dump his bandmates were renting.

"They're a corrupting influence," Avery said, referring to the other members of STF. She was only half teasing.

"That's what they say about you," he replied, also only half teasing. He slid his fingers through her soft brown hair. He liked the way her eyes sparkled when she gazed up at him. *Like I'm the only guy in the world.*

She let go of him and moved to the back of the pickup and began unhooking the tarp. He got on the other side to help her. "You bring the rest of my stuff?" he asked.

"Of course." She paused. "Where's Lucille?"

Lucille was not a person, it was a cherry red 1975 Fender

Stratocaster guitar and, Avery sometimes suspected, the closest "woman" to Curt's heart.

"I'm going to keep her at the other house," Curt answered. "It's easier than hauling her back and forth."

"Oh." Avery averted her eyes and busied herself with the bags, but Curt knew she was disappointed. It was some dumb symbolic thing to her, like if he left his guitar with the band, then he wasn't entirely there with her.

A nerdy-looking guy with brown hair and black-framed glasses came out of the rental house. He was wearing plaid shorts with black socks and shoes. "You two moving in?"

"Fred, this is my boyfriend, Curt," Avery said. "Curt, this is Fred. He's our landlord."

Curt was surprised. While nerds often had an ageless quality, this Fred guy didn't look much older than he was. Kind of young to own properties.

"How did you know my name?" Fred asked Avery.

She looked stunned. "I'm Avery, remember? We just met. You know, inside, when that other girl stole our room?"

"Someone else got our room?" Curt asked with a frown.

"Oh, uh, I'm really sorry about that," Fred said sheepishly. "Like I said, I'll refund the difference in rent to you, and I'll be glad to show you the other rooms right now."

Curt bristled. Half the reason he'd agreed to stay here instead of with the band was that Avery had told him she'd found a really nice room for them. "You mean someone else snagged our room and you didn't do anything about it?"

"I tried," Avery mumbled.

Curt knew Avery wasn't real big about asserting herself, but given what a wimp this Fred nerd was, he thought he could take advantage of the situation. Curt narrowed his eyes menacingly at the landlord. "We paid for that room in advance. You had no right to give it away."

"Look, I said I'm sorry and I'll refund the difference," Fred answered uncomfortably. "I'll let you have the next best room."

"I think you'll have to do better than that," Curt said with just a hint of a threat in his voice.

"I . . . I don't understand what you mean . . . ," Fred stammered.

"Think about it," Curt said.

"Oh, well, I guess I could give you a discount on the other room," Fred said.

Curt smiled. "There you go."

"Let me show you what I've got." Fred turned and led them into the house. Curt grabbed a couple of bags from the back of the pickup, and he and Avery followed.

"I still think we should bag this whole thing and stay with the band," Curt muttered to Avery as they entered the house.

"I want us to have more privacy," Avery replied.

"Privacy?" Curt scoffed. "In a house full of strangers, that's a good one."

The Shore

LB (Laguna Beach)

Nola Thacker

One

"Headbanging sex," said Linley Cattrel, thrusting open the door of the dorm room.

Without looking up, Claire Plimouth used the old standard: "Not tonight, I have a headache."

"Again?" said Linley.

"Always," said Claire. "It's how I've maintained my purity." She turned the page of her Intro Psych notes.

Leaning over the desk where Claire was working, Linley splayed her hand across the page. Her golden hair swept forward in a perfect curve across her sun-golden cheeks. Somehow she managed to smell like a good day at the beach, Claire noticed not for the first time, even though they were a continent away from Linley's California home.

I probably smell like libraries and books and long, cold New England winters, thought Claire. *Not sexy.*

Not that she knew what sexy smelled like. Or sex, for that matter. Aloud, she said, "Philosophy exam tomorrow?"

"I act, therefore I am," said Linley. "Descartes."

"I'm not quite sure that's how it goes."

"Can't study anymore. Besides, our first year of college is *over*. We should be partying. Hooking up. Sucking . . ."

"Suck off," said Claire. "I'm studying. It's not over until the final bell rings."

"Suck-up. That's what you are!" said Linley.

"I fail to see how studying for my last final of my last class of my first year of college is sucking up," said Claire. "I like to think of it as the intelligent choice. The way you think of, say, condoms. Or tequila as opposed to gin . . . although I don't entirely agree with that. . . ."

"That's because you're from New England," retorted Linley. "Home of the WASP drink by which you are embalmed alive."

"Don't have martini envy on me *now*," said Claire. "Go away and play."

"These are extremely worthy parties! One's been going on for at least two days. They need reinforcements."

"Well, may the reinforcements be with you, Luke Skywalker. But I'm not one of them. Now Go. Away." Claire held her notebook up to block Linley from her sight. She'd been seduced into acts of reckless abandon by Linley too often. Not tonight.

"You know, you will die of stubbornness if you're not careful. Stubbornness killed the cat." Linley flopped down on her bed and flung her arms wide.

"Curiosity killed the cat, I'm not a cat, and no one has ever died of stubbornness." Claire was trying not to laugh now.

"Headbanging sex," said Linley again.

"Where? The party?" asked Claire.

"No. The house. The summer . . . the beach . . . *this* summer . . ." Linley's voice trailed away dreamily.

Was she imagining having headbanging sex on the beach? Claire wondered. *Could* a person have headbanging sex on the beach?

Linley cut across the room to her. "The head-banging sex is contemplated for both of us, on another coast, for the summer. Said summer to also include parties; jobs that are not internships, career builders, or network opportunities; and, oh yes, a house on the beach. Laguna Beach, to be exact."

"Beach house? What beach house?" Claire said. She snapped her notebook shut.

Linley grinned. "Uncle Martin came through. He got a stunt gig last minute on a shoot in New Zealand. And when his favorite niece called all sad about her summer plans—i.e., none—he told her—me—that I could have his beach house for the summer."

"*Merde*," said Claire.

"*Merde non*," said Linley. "It's big, it's old, it's funky, and it's free, except we have to pay the utilities and make sure it's all nice and tidy when he gets back." She thought for a moment and added, "That's why I'm appointing you house manager."

The Pacific Ocean. Claire had never seen the Pacific. She'd spent her whole life in New England boarding schools, and now a small New England college, making her grades good and her parents proud. Well, making good grades, anyway. Parental pride might be stretching it. When Claire brought home perfect marks, her parents took it in stride. Good grades was just part of what a Plimouth did, like living in Lexington, Mass.

A summer job in her father's Boston bank was also what a Plimouth did. Her sister, Melanie, the investment banker had started that way. So had her brother, Jim, the corporate lawyer. And that was where her mother had met her father, her mother also being "in banking." Claire sometimes wondered if they had a marriage or a corporate merger.

"I can't," said Claire.

Linley jumped to her feet. She put her hands on her hips and somehow made herself look taller.

Towering and glowering now, Linley said, "I'm actually considering murder at this moment." Then she leaned forward and swatted Claire on the back of her head with the palm of her hand.

"OW! What was that for? Did your mother teach you nothing? Hitting is wrong. Bad Linley." Claire leaned back in case Linley decided on a repeat.

"It's a dope slap," said Linley. "I learned about it from listening to public radio."

"You? Public radio? I doubt that," Claire scoffed, still keeping a safe distance.

"*Car Talk*," said Linley. "It's good for bonding with my dad. But that's beside the point. The point is, what *are* you, a Woman or a WASP? After I go to all this trouble to set up a perfect summer, this is what you say?" Linley pitched her voice into whine key. "I can't. Oooh, I'm afraid. Oh no, no, no, no."

Amused and annoyed, Claire said, "Linley, you don't under—"

"No," said Linley. "No words unless they start with 'yes.'"

"But—"

"No. . ."

"My father has—"

"No."

"The bank—"

"No. . ."

"Linley!"

"NO!"

They glared at each other. Claire looked away first. She thought of the cold, respectable corridors of the bank. One day, she would go into one of those vaults just as her sister and brother had, and never come out. But did she have to start now? Right this minute?

This summer?

Did people in banks have headbanging sex?

Not her father. Not her mother. She shuddered at the thought. Best not to think of that at all.

"California," said Claire, almost dreamily.

Linley smiled triumphantly.

Then Claire remembered where California was.

She looked up at Linley, her eyes tragic.

"What?" said Linley. "Claire, what's wrong?"

"I hate flying," said Claire. "I did it once. That was enough."

The two girls stared at each other.

"Some suggest," Linley said slowly, "that fear of flying is actually fear of sexual pleasure."

"It's not *all* about sex. In this case, it's about being in a silver tube with stupid wings that don't even have feathers being driven by someone who maybe is having a bad day and might not see that mountain or, say, the other plane headed—"

"Stop," said Linley. She considered a moment, then brightened. "Okay, drugs. No problem."

"I don't do—"

"One little pill. Trust me. Now, what word are we looking for here?"

Claire looked at Linley. Linley the beautiful, Linley the spoiled, Linley the most fun person Claire had ever known. Life was never dull when Linley was around—dull, as in a summer spent in a bank under her father's eyes.

Claire looked at Linley, into eyes she thought might actually be the color of the Pacific Ocean. She took a deep breath.

What could it hurt, to spend a summer in California? She'd find a way to convince the 'rents.

"One word," Linley prompted.

"Yes," Claire answered.

"You'll like Jodi." Linley had been talking ever since the plane had taxied into takeoff.

So far, Claire had neither shared the contents of her mostly empty stomach with the rest of the passengers nor passed out. In fact, she was pretty sure she'd loosened her grip on the seat arms. Fractionally.

"I've told you about Jodi, remember? We were the Two all through high school." Linley held up two fingers and waggled them to demonstrate.

The plane leveled out. The FASTEN SEAT BELT sign blinked off.

A flight attendant appeared and looked at Linley. Linley looked at her two fingers and grinned. "Vodka and cranberry, rocks," she said.

Suddenly, absurdly, Claire felt like giggling. She raised one hand and fluttered her fingers. "Me, too," she sang. It seemed like a very good idea. The ground was leaving the plane so very, very fast. No, wait—it was the plane leaving the ground.

"I'll need to see some I.D.," said the flight attendant.

"I'm twenty-two," said Linley, smiling her gazillionwatt

smile. "And no one ever believes me." She flipped open her wallet, and the attendant glanced at the fake I.D. and nodded.

"But my friend isn't," Linley went on. "She's only twenty. She'll have cranberry juice and soda."

"What?" said Claire, trying to feel indignant. "I have I.D. I . . ."

Ignoring Claire, the attendant smiled and handed the wallet back to Linley. "Coming right up," the attendant said.

The guy in the aisle seat said to the attendant, "Scotch, rocks, and let me take care of their drinks."

"Thanks," said Linley.

"I want a real drink, too," said Claire.

"No, you don't," said Linley. She lowered her voice. "Not with what you're flying on, you don't. That little pill is plenty all by itself."

Claire giggled again. She couldn't help it.

"First time you've ever flown?" the guy said to Claire. But he only glanced at her. He was really talking to Linley.

"No," said Claire.

"She had a terrible experience as a child," Linley said.

"What?" Claire sputtered.

"Are you from California?" Linley asked him.

He laughed. He had those white square teeth that Claire had always thought weren't real outside of photo ops. "I wish," he said.

The flight attendant returned. He was good-looking, Claire

noticed. Maybe it was the uniform. She wondered if Linley had noticed too.

"Massachusetts," said Claire. "I'm from. . . ."

The guy said to Linley, "I'm a graduate student. Headed for a summer internship in San Diego."

"Nice," said Linley. She leaned closer, sliding a finger down his arm, her voice dropping.

To be a part of this conversation, Claire thought crossly, *I'd have to sit in Linley's lap.*

But then suddenly, she didn't mind. Peering out the window, she discovered that the earth had gone missing. Below were only clouds. Ahead, the sun was setting. Pretty. *Look at me, I'm flying into a postcard,* she thought.

She yawned.

Beside her the voices dropped to a murmur.

She was on her way to California. She, Claire Plimouth. All because of Linley.

Linley was a pain. Linley was insane. Linley was the kind of roommate Claire had avoided all her years in the best boarding schools of New England.

It hadn't been hard, avoiding those girls. They'd barely even known she'd existed.

But she was good with that. She figured someday she'd own the company that they—or their husbands—would work for.

When Linley had burst into her dorm room that first day of

college the previous fall, Claire had winced. Black clothes and pink shoes—what was *that*?

It was, as it turned out, two of Linley's favorite colors. She'd looked at Claire in her khaki and navy and said, "Wow, your eyes are the most amazing color. They're, like, golden!"

"Brown," Claire had corrected. "Light brown."

"No, golden," Linley had corrected back.

And somehow, they'd become friends. Not all at once. Claire had tried to keep her distance. But Linley didn't seem to notice. She'd made Claire join her on what Linley called her "party rounds." She'd dragged Claire shopping and talked her into "colors, for god's sake."

And then made Claire wear the fuzzy cropped sweater Linley said was "Caribbean blue" to a party. Had included Claire in nighttime pizza attacks.

She had a sudden memory of a weekend in Vermont. The snow had been perfect powder. Linley, in electric pink and several other colors unknown in nature, had stared down at the snowboard strapped to her feet. She'd looked up at Claire. "What the hell," she'd said, and taken off.

She hadn't made it. But she almost had. Claire had boarded down to check on her and found her laughing at the bottom of the hill.

"You okay?"

"Oh, better," Linley said. "That was amazing. Awesome. The absolute second best thing in the universe."

"The second best?" said Claire. "And the first?"

She'd expected Linley to say "sex," but Linley had surprised her. "Surfing," she'd said. "And I can tell by the way you board that you're going to love surfing too."

"Right," said Claire, thinking, *Like I'm ever going to get anywhere near a surfboard.*

"You'll see," Linley had promised, scrambling to her feet. "Now, teach me how to get down that hill."

She'd asked Claire to show her—not some cute guy, not some instructor. That, Claire thought, was the day they'd become real friends, because she'd realized she had something to offer Linley in exchange for the excitement and color—literally—that Linley brought to life.

That night, hanging out in the ski lodge, they'd swapped snow and surf wipeout stories. Claire described learning to ski from her mother, who had, as far as Claire could tell, never fallen off her skis.

"Didn't you just want to push her?" Linley had said, and Claire, shocked, had said, "No!" and then, bursting out into laughter, "Yes!"

Linley had talked, a little bit, about growing up in San Francisco and going with friends to the beach and then discovering surfing. Had laughed at how her parents had tried to make her "respectable" and then finally given in and let her buy her first surfboard.

Many nights of many drinks and talks and pizzas and old

movies had cemented their friendship, but that had been the beginning, the real beginning.

And now Claire was on her way to California, where, Linley had promised, she was going to learn to surf.

Friends, thought Claire. *That's a good thing.*

First friends, then a boyfriend. How hard could that be? And then she'd no longer be . . .

Nope. She wouldn't think about that now.

From somewhere, she'd acquired a blanket. She hitched it up over her shoulders and settled back in her seat. *Sleep,* she thought. *That's a good thing, too. And when I wake up, I'll be in California.*

As she fell asleep, she vaguely heard the guy asking for another round of drinks.

When Claire woke up, she wasn't in California. She was in the dark.

Not total darkness, but the hushed darkness of a plane where people were sleeping.

Claire squinted at her watch. Two hours had passed. She felt peculiar.

Her drink was gone, her drink tray folded away. But next to her, Linley's drink sat half-full on the tray. Linley had disappeared.

Claire reached out and took a sip of watery, slightly warm cranberry and vodka.

Her whole stomach did a flip.

Barf bag or bathroom, Claire thought frantically, and staggered to her feet. Barely noticing the startled faces peering up from books held in tiny pools of light, or eyes turned toward her from the personal movie screens, Claire lurched down the aisle, one hand over her mouth, the other grabbing at anything she passed for balance.

A woman emerging from a row of seats took one look and jumped back.

Claire grabbed the bathroom door and fumbled it open. She barely got it closed behind her before she lost it.

She didn't know how long she was sick, but when she was finally able to bathe her face and rinse her mouth, the face she met in the mirror had gone all-American hag. The French braid had started to unravel, and wisps of dark hair stuck damply to her forehead and neck. Sleep marks hashed one cheek.

The only solution was to go back to her seat and pull the blanket over her head. Lurking in the toilet was not helping, anyway. Resolutely, Claire opened the bathroom door and stepped out.

She came face-to-face with Linley.

"Claire?" said Linley. Her face was as flushed as Claire's was pale. And she had what Claire would have called bed head hair at any other time.

"Hi, Linley," Claire said, trying to sound normal.

Glancing back over her shoulder, Linley hastily pulled shut the bathroom door.

She frowned and peered at Claire. "Did you just get sick?"

"No," said Claire. "I'm fine."

"Right," said Linley. She clamped her hand on Claire's arm. "If that's fine, I don't want to see you on a bad day. I'm walking you to your seat."

"I'm fine," Claire insisted, but she was too whipped to argue and she let Linley steer her back down the aisle. She kept her eyes lowered, trying not to look like I-just-barfed girl to the whole plane.

They reached their seats, and Claire half-fell into hers.

"I'll be right back," said Linley. A moment later she sat down by Claire and pulled the blanket around Claire's shoulders. Then the guy in the seat next to Linley was there, handing Linley a plastic glass.

"Thanks," Linley said to him, then to Claire, "Drink this."

"Not thirsty," Claire croaked.

"Seltzer," said Linley soothingly. "That's all. It'll settle your stomach. And take this with it."

"But—"

"Claire," said Linley. "Do it. Or else."

Or else what? thought Claire. "Drug pimp," she said to Linley.

"Whatever," said Linley, and practically shoved the pill down Claire's throat. "Now, count to a hundred," she ordered Claire.

"Bossy drug pimp," muttered Claire.

"One hundred, ninety nine . . . ," Linley said.

"Ninety eight, ninety-seven . . . ," said Claire.

"How bad is she?" the guy whispered.

"Shhh!" ordered Linley. To Claire, she said, "Keep counting."

Claire kept counting. But she was losing track. Whatever Linley had given her was pulling her under. Fast.

She saw the guy reach down and pull something out of his pocket. He leaned into Linley and said softly into her ear, "You forgot something."

Seventy-three, seventy-two . . . Even in the semidarkness of the cabin, Claire recognized the scrap of silk underwear. *California pink,* she thought. Linley's.

Seventy-one, seventy . . . Claire saw Linley glance at her watch, then smile up at her new friend. "Keep them," Linley said. "Maybe I'll get them back later."

He laughed. She laughed.

Sixty-nine, Claire thought, and passed out.

Did you love this book?

Want to get access to
the hottest books for free?

Log on to simonandschuster.com/pulseit

to find out how to join,

get access to cool sweepstakes,

and hear about your favorite authors!

Become part of Pulse IT and tell us what you think!

  SIMON & SCHUSTER BFYR

simonTeen

Simon & Schuster's **Simon Teen**
e-newsletter delivers current updates on
the hottest titles, exciting sweepstakes, and
exclusive content from your favorite authors.

Visit **TEEN.SimonandSchuster.com** to
sign up, post your thoughts, and find out what
every avid reader is talking about!

  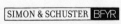

LOOKING FOR THE PERFECT BEACH READ?

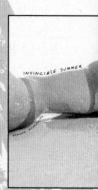

Need a distraction?

Lauren Strasnick

Arlaina Tibensky

Amy Reed

Christine Johnson

Deb Caletti

Lisa Schroeder

Eileen Cook

Charity Tahmaseb & Darcy Vance

Go Ahead, Ask Me.
Nico Medina & Billy Merrell

Sweet and Sassy Reads

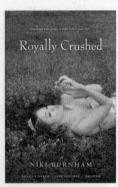

One book. More than one story.